About Tania]

Tania Joyce is an author of contemporary and new adult romance novels. Her stories thread romance, drama and passion into beautiful locations ranging from the dazzling lights and glitter of New York, to the rural countryside of the Hunter Valley.

She's widely traveled, has a diverse background in the corporate world and has a love for sparkles, shoes and shiraz.

Tania draws on her real-life experiences and combines them with her *very* vivid imagination to form the foundation of her novels. She likes to write about strong-minded, career-oriented heroes and heroines that go through drama-filled hell, have steamy encounters and risk everything as they endeavor to find their happily-ever-after.

Tania shuffles the hours in her day between work, family life and writing. One day she hopes to find balance!

Visit www.taniajoyce.com

RUINED - The Price of Play

Everhide Rockstar Romance Series – Book 2

by

Tania Joyce

RUINED – The Price of Play by Tania Joyce

Published by Gatwick Enterprises 2019

Brisbane, Australia.

RUINED – The Price of Play

Everhide Rockstar Romance – Book 2

EPUB format: ISBN: 978-0-6482543-4-8

Mobi format: ISBN: 978-0-6482543-5-5

Paperback: ISBN: 978-0-6482543-6-2

Cover design by DesignRans

Edited by Lauren Clarke

For more information on the author or to report any typographical error, please visit:

www.taniajoyce.com

Keywords and Subjects

New adult romance, young adult romance, contemporary romance, rockstar romance, rock star romance, enemies to lovers romance, accidental baby, secret baby, celebrity romance, music romance, angst romance, music genre, lyrics, bands, touring, artists.

This is a work of fiction. Names, characters, businesses, places, events and incidents are either the products of the author's imagination or used in a fictitious manner. Any resemblance to actual persons, living or dead, or actual events is purely coincidental.

For lovers of truth and kindness.

Chapter 1

Kara Knight wanted to be anywhere, anywhere other than in Hunter Collins's opulent five-bedroom penthouse in New York, celebrating the engagement of her rock star royalty friends, Gemma Lonsdale and Kyle McIntyre. Getting a Brazilian wax, having teeth pulled, or being hung upside down from the top of the Empire State Building sounded like better options. Anywhere was better than here.

While it thrilled her that Gemma and Kyle were getting married, it was hard to keep her cheery face in place. Being dumped two months ago had seen her own dreams become unzipped.

She snatched another champagne from the dining table, knocked it back, and let the bubbles glide down her throat. It didn't deaden the pain.

In the crowded living room, forty of the happy couple's friends, work colleagues, and entourage jostled each other. Music blared through the sound system. There was laughter. Dancing. Cheer. None of it lightened her mood.

Dodging the flailing arms, Kara weaved her way through

the dancers and headed for the balcony. Drawn to the table overflowing with gifts tied with colorful satin ribbons, she stopped in her tracks. The ache inside her heart flared. *Damn it.* How did she get love so wrong?

Dreams of a family didn't matter anymore. Today's doctor visit proved it. The prognosis was worse than she'd thought. Children would never be an option.

A party popper exploded, raining confetti into the air, and the hoots and hollers from the crowd jarred her from her thoughts. She rolled her shoulders back and took a deep breath. *I'm done. I will not feel like crap anymore.*

She'd cried enough tears over her ex, been angry long enough about the fate she'd been dealt, cursed enough to make the devil blush. Instead of a sparkling diamond ring, she got a broken heart. Instead of a healthy body, she got bits that didn't work.

So be it.

For the rest of the night, she wouldn't think about her troubles. Time to have fun.

Taking a step back from the gift table, she collided against someone's chest. Male. Tall. Smelled of citrus and spice. Rather than moving away, he nudged closer. He held out a bottle of Bollinger to one side of her, a champagne flute to the other. She was trapped in his pungent embrace.

"Whatcha doing Kaaara?" Hunter's voice hovered too close to her ear.

"Ergh!" she groaned. "Get off me."

Of course, he didn't. He wrapped his arms around her, and placed his chin on her shoulder, his wavy brown hair tickling her skin. "What's got you down in the dumps? It's my solemn duty as host to ensure everyone is having a good time."

Shrugging out of his hold, she turned to face him and stared square into his azure eyes. Eyes that belonged to a wolf on the prowl. "I'm fine . . . It's just been a rough day."

"Here. Have a refill." He poured champagne into her flute, spilling some onto the floor.

"Thanks . . . for that." Sarcasm rolled in her tone as she rushed forward to gulp mouthfuls from her overflowing glass.

Hunter downed his champagne, then a deep furrow formed between his long, straight brows. "You're not still upset over Conrad, are you?"

"Upset?" She jerked her head back. If only it was that simple. After four years with Conrad, she'd thought he was about to propose, not toss her aside like last year's must-have coat. But Hunter didn't need to know how much she'd been hurt, or how today's doctor visit had gone. "What makes you think something's wrong?"

"Hmm . . . let me see." He tossed his hair, sending confetti strands onto the floor. "You're staring vacantly at the gifts. Drinking alone. Being unsociable. And . . . you're usually having a sling-fest with me about something—drinking, girls, being an asshole. Need I go on?"

Since Kara had started supplying clothes for Everhide—Gemma, Kyle and Hunter's rock band—cutting down Hunter's ego had become a specialized sport. But she wasn't in the mood for games tonight. "I can't be bothered to waste my breath on you this evening."

"Ha! That's the spirit." He hooked his arm around her shoulders. "You know"—he nudged his hip into hers—"the best way to get over your ex is to sleep with someone else."

She laughed at the ridiculous notion. Who had time to go on dates and meet someone new? The mass of orders from the September fashion week had her working overtime at Conrad's Fashion House. Her family had her tied up with must-be-seen-at social events for Halloween, Thanksgiving, and Christmas. "Why? Are you offering your services?"

"God no. Don't be stupid." Underneath the soft glow from the fairy lights, his expression changed from a hell-no grimace to one of smoldering sexiness that should have been illegal. "Unless . . . you want me to? I'd make you forget about Conrad in a second."

She blushed at the twinkle in his gaze. The way Hunter's voice rumbled deep in his throat, like a purring wild cat, had her believing he could make her forget her own name.

With a reputation that made Justin Bieber look like a saint, Hunter was so wrong in so many ways. She didn't have enough fingers to count them. Rock star god-like sex symbols did not sleep with someone like her. At twenty-four years old, she was a nobody. Not his type.

Shaking her finger at him, she took a step back and her backside hit the table. "Just because I'm single doesn't mean I'd sleep with you. Regardless of how good looking you are." She winced, her fluster getting the better of her.

An irresistible smile spread across his mouth. "You think I'm good-looking."

Kara groaned. She'd been flippant, not blind. "I shouldn't have opened my big mouth. You know you are. But I don't like you as a person. You're arrogant, egotistical, and an asshole."

"True. And you're nothing but a privileged, daddy's little princess. Drag you away from some gala event, did we?"

Her mouth gaped and her hand shot to clutch her strand of pearls. While she *was* missing a gala night at the MET, she'd rather be here. And just because she was born and bred on the Upper East Side, into one of New York's most well-respected families, didn't mean she was a daddy's girl. Her older sister Naomi wore that crown, and her overbearing, control freak of a father continually told her so. "Is that how you see me?"

"Pretty much," Hunter said matter-of-factly. "Doesn't mean I wouldn't fuck you."

Heat flooded her cheeks. *He'd what? Since when?* Him wanting to sleep with her was absurd. "No, you wouldn't. If you're offering, thanks, but no thanks."

She went to step around him, but he blocked her path. "Are you sure about that?" His playful tone caught her off guard. *Oh shit!* He was serious. He scanned her up and down, paused at her double D-sized cleavage, before his gaze returned to her face. "You're attractive enough, in an above-average sort of way."

Greaaat. She didn't think she'd rank that high on his scale.

"And you're tall," he said. "I like tall. I would do things to you I bet Conrad never did."

Butterflies flitted in her belly. What was wrong with her? His sexually-fueled banter never affected her. She shouldn't play his game, but when it came to Hunter, she couldn't resist ribbing him. Tilting her chin a fraction, she threw him a challenging glare. "Like what?"

He placed his bottle and glass down onto the table beside her. Slid his hands around her waist and drew his body flush with hers. Against all her instincts, she let him. His champagne breath made her head spin. His voice lowered to a gravelly whisper. "It would involve my tongue. Between your legs. And that's just for starters."

Her eyes fluttered closed and her thighs clenched. With her mind hammering like a needle on an industrial sewing machine, she swayed. "What makes you think I'd like that?"

A sly smirk slid across his mouth. "All girls like that."

She wasn't all girls, but he had a point. This conversation was getting out of hand. Reining in the jump in her pulse, she pushed against his chest. "Keep dreaming, Hunt. It's. Not. Going. To. Happen."

She shoved past him. With her head reeling, she mingled with the crowd.

"Hey." Gemma caught her on the arm. Kyle was glued to her

side. "Are you okay?"

"Absolutely." The lie curdled in Kara's stomach as she bent to give her best friend a hug. Gemma, even in her heels, barely reached above Kara's shoulders. "Hunt's just being his usual charming self."

"Oh no. That bad, huh?" Gemma grimaced, slipping out of Kara's hold and back into Kyle's clutch.

"I find it's best to ignore him." Kara flicked her long ponytail over her shoulder and glanced past Kyle. Hunter stood by his new grand piano a few feet away, talking to the members of their backup band. His eyes pierced through the soft lighting like bright blue LEDs. Warmth flooded her cheeks, and when he winked at her, it took all her strength to look away. Giving herself a mental slap, she turned back to Gemma.

"It's your night. We're here to celebrate." Kara knocked back the last few mouthfuls of champagne and thumbed toward the kitchen. "I'm going to get another drink and some water. Can I get you guys anything?"

"No-pe. Thanks." Concern filled Gemma's eyes and she rubbed Kara's arm. "Is there something else bothering you? You haven't been yourself tonight."

There was no way Kara would dump the news she got today onto Gemma and turn tonight into a tear-fest. She wiggled her finger in front of Gemma's face. "Don't go all motherly on me just because you're getting married."

"Never." Gemma gave a there's-no-chance-of-that-ever-happening laugh and pointed toward the kitchen. "Go get that drink and promise me you'll have some fun."

"Well . . . " Kara arched her eyebrow, sneaking a glimpse of Hunter watching her. "Who knows? The night is young. I'll see what I can do."

Turning on her pumps, Kara headed into the kitchen. The tangy spice of buffalo wings filled the air. Plates of their remains lay on the counter next to empty mini noddle boxes, used glassware, and bottles of alcohol. She put her flute down and grabbed a water from the fridge. When she closed the door, her heart slammed against her ribs.

Hunter stood in front of her with the Bollinger held toward her. "Another top-up?"

"Sure." She waved to her glass on the counter, cracked her water open and took a sip. "Are you following me?"

"Maybe." Deep dimples highlighted his chiseled cheekbones. He placed the bottle on the counter beside her and stepped in close, leaving only a foot between them.

"Why?" Narrowing her eyes into button-hole slits, she held his gaze.

He let out a long, slow breath and brushed his hands down her arms. "Well . . . it's a party. I've had a few drinks. I'm in the mood for fun. So before we head back on tour tomorrow, and before some new swanky uptown country-club douchebag snaps you up, I think we should take advantage of this opportunity."

The reminder she was single was like a punch to the gut. And a reminder he was nothing but trouble.

"With opportunity comes risk, Hunt. And with you"—she patted the side of his face—"the risk is too high. I don't feel like catching an STD today."

"FYI, I have no STDs." He tugged on the cuffs of his navy dress jacket. "But if you're content to continue pining and masturbating over Conrad, that's fine by me."

She jabbed her finger against his chest. "You know nothing about me or my problems."

"Don't want to either." He captured her hand and kissed her palm. She flinched when the touch of his lips sent warmth charging across her skin. His eyes glimmered and a mischievous smile played across his mouth. "But I could make you forget them for a while."

She twisted her hand free. "Maybe you have too many issues of your own. Are you upset that Kyle and Gem are engaged?" Did he have lingering feelings for Gemma, even though it had been over eighteen months since they broke up? "You're the one who broke her heart, sleeping with Amie, and now she's marrying your best friend."

Hurt flashed in his eyes, but within a blink it disappeared. "Let's not dwell on my fuck-ups. I have no unresolved feelings for Gem. You know that. Gem and Kyle deserve to be together. We've all moved on."

"Good." She was only teasing him but maybe she'd hit a sore spot.

With him standing so close, her body temperature simmered. She fanned her face and rolled her water bottle over her cheek and neck. "Do you think you can turn the heat down?" It was mid-fall outside but felt like summer inside.

Hunter stared straight at her.

"What?" She drew her head back.

"I'm trying hard not to be envious of those droplets slipping toward your chest."

"Envious, hey?" She skimmed one of her long, manicured nails slowly down her neck, then squeezed her arms together.

His eyes darkened as he glanced over her, like he wanted to rip every thread of clothing from her body with his teeth. Her nipples hardened so much she thought they'd burst from her bra. "Hmm. Kara. If you tease, you'll end up in trouble." He grabbed the champagne and knocked back a mouthful.

His long throat, smoothly shaven, and his chiseled jawline moved with every swallow. Thick veins pulsed rhythmically in his neck. Visions of running her tongue over his hot skin and tasting the champagne on his lips flashed through her mind.

Oh god, I'm in trouble.

Metal tinged against a glass, bringing the room to attention.

"Time for speeches. Later, Kars." Hunter winked, poured her a fresh champagne, and they shuffled out into the crowd.

In the center of the gathered guests, Hunter stood behind her, too close. Every time he brushed against her, or whenever he laughed and it reverberated through her system, her heart beat erratically. Had the lack of sex made her lust-crazy? The first show of interest from a man had her body sparking. But Hunter? She wasn't stupid or naïve. She knew what he was after. Could she do it?

After Kyle and Gemma spoke, and Hunter's well-wishes and comical tales embarrassed them, Kara thought she had escaped Hunter's advances. But after using the bathroom, her steps slowed when she saw him lingering at the hall's entrance to the living room. Standing with Lexi and Hayden, he drank straight from a bottle of champagne. The moment he saw her, he excused himself and slinked down the darkened passageway toward her. She sighed and rolled her eyes, unable to stop herself from smiling. She had to give him credit. He was persistent, if nothing else.

She met him halfway and leaned back against the wall. His hand appeared beside her head, trapping her.

"Are you still fighting this?" He swayed closer.

Shuffling back, her heels hitting the wall. "There's nothing to fight." Except her body had a mind of its own. Her chest arched toward him and an ache stirred between her legs.

"Come on, seriously. Haven't you ever thought about sleeping with me?"

She'd never thought about sleeping with Hunter. Until now. With his face looming eight inches away, she had to keep his Manhattan-sized ego from swelling. "No. I have better things to do."

"You're thinking about it now. Aren't you?" Hunter's wicked

smile heated her from the inside out. "I can tell. Your cheeks are flushed."

"I told you, it's hot in here. That's all." Her voice came out nice and steady, but her stomach quivered and quaked. "Hunt, what you're suggesting is weird. We're friends. You're Gem's ex."

"We tolerate each other, and Gem won't give a shit."

The more Kara played with the idea, the crazier her heart beat. Soon she'd need a cold shower. To have his hands on her skin, his husky voice whispering in her ear, those lips against hers . . . *sweet Jesus!* She grabbed the bottle of champagne from him and downed a few mouthfuls. "This is the most bizarre conversation I've ever had with you."

"I've got a semi if that's any consolation." He snaked his hands around her waist, clutched her ass and drew his hips against hers. *Oh God! Was that a . . . ?* "When was the last time you did something exciting? A little dangerous? Spontaneous? The rules are set. Just one time. No strings attached."

This was nothing but a game to Hunter. For some unknown reason she was his target tonight. She'd be nothing but a conquest, a statistic, another notch in his bed head. A meaningless fuck. She'd never done anything like that before.

His eyes burned into hers. "No one will know we're gone. Give me half an hour . . . max. That's it."

"Why do you need that long?"

"Well . . . how many orgasms do you want? Two? Three?"

Her core clenched. She'd never even had two orgasms during sex. Ever. "Don't be ridiculous." She searched his face for evidence of his joke. But there was no waiver in his determined expression. "Three? Really?"

"Let's just say, I know what I'm doing."

God, he was so full of himself. But was he that good? No man was that talented in the bedroom. Were they?

Guess she could find out.

Hunter groaned, and his head fell back. "This is taking way too much effort. You're killing my buzz, Kar. Are you up for it or not?"

She placed her hand on his chest between the two open buttons of his red shirt and played with the cross on his chain.

Damn you, Hunter. Was this how he got all the girls? A little bit of charm and a touch of flirting, all mixed with a bucket-load of bullshit? She hated to admit that it was working.

Could she sleep with someone she didn't have feelings for? Could she sleep with Hunter? Someone who used women for nothing but sex, and didn't care about anyone or anything other than himself? He was everything she didn't want in a man.

Except he was drop-dead gorgeous.

And triggered her curiosity.

He circled his thumb over her hip, heating her flesh beneath her vintage-style dress. "Stop over-thinking this."

What Hunter wanted to do pushed her beyond her boundaries and took her miles out of her comfort zone. That terrified her, thrilled her, and excited her. Knowing she had captured his wandering eye gave her low self-esteem a boost. This wasn't about love or dating or romance. Hell. No. This was about forgetting her problems. Having some fun. A sharp breath caught in her lungs and her heart rate jumped. A naughty smile inched across her lips. Oh yeah . . . and Hunter was the type of man her father would despise.

She liked that very much. That clinched it.

Laughter and cheer drifted down the hallway. A glass shattered out in the living room and another champagne cork popped. Surely the partygoers wouldn't miss her and Hunter for thirty minutes. Glancing over his tailored jacket, her heartbeat's tempo jumped. She'd seen him in his underwear at fitting, but what would he look like completely naked? Those toned arms? That ripped stomach? That fine backside?

Sleeping with him was crazy. Her insides screamed, *yes, just do it.* This may be her last chance to have sex as a whole woman.

She promised Gemma she'd have fun.

Screw it. Here goes nothing.

Her eyes met his. She caught her bottom lip between her teeth and held up three fingers. "Okay ... Three ... Let's go."

Shock flashed across Hunter's face before his gorgeous grin widened. His eyes smoldered and glimmered in the darkness. He picked up the Bollinger, grabbed her hand, and led her down the hallway.

There was no backing out now. For half an hour she wanted to forget Conrad, forget about her work, and forget about her pending medical procedure. This was what she needed. Her hands shook, and her veins burned with doubt, panic and feverish anticipation. But she didn't hesitate once on the way to his bedroom.

Chapter 2

The moment Kara walked through the door into Hunter's darkened bedroom, he turned to face her. Their eyes met. He closed the door behind her and flicked the latch to lock. *Click.* Her heart skipped a beat, then pounded harder and faster with each breath.

Heat from his body sent shivers up her spine. His intense gaze weakened her knees. This was madness. She could do this. She'd left her want for a relationship, the need for love, and her issues on the other side of the door.

If only the butterfly disco dancing in her belly would settle, she'd be fine.

Taking her hand, Hunter drew her into the center of the room that smelled of his intoxicating cologne. "Wait here."

She fumbled with her necklace as he placed the champagne on the drawers next to his bottle of Dior Sauvage cologne and framed photos of Everhide at award shows—the Grammys, MTV, and the AMAs. Hitting a button on the wall by his room-sized walk-in wardrobe, the black block-out blinds lowered to hide the view south over Tribeca. Soft light from the master bathroom trickled into the bedroom and gleamed golden on the collectible guitars mounted above his headboard.

He ripped off his jacket, shoes and socks, then with a whoosh, he tore the bed coverings back as if it were a sacrificial altar.

Her mouth ran dry. "So . . . how do you want to go about this?" She kicked off her stiletto pumps and smoothed her clammy palms over the skirt of her dress. "Do you just want to strip naked and jump under the covers, or what?"

Hunter stood in front of her and ran his thumb over his lower lip. That infuriating, sexy smile curled across his mouth. "How about you let me do what I'm good at?"

Knots cinched inside her tummy. "And what are you good at exactly?"

"I'm gonna show you."

He ran his hand over her head, sending tingles shooting across her scalp. With a gentle tug, he pulled her hairband free, and slipped it over her wrist. Warm fingers threaded through her long, thick hair that fell loose half way down her back.

Hunter massaged the base of her neck. "Kara, relax."

She sucked in a sharp breath. "I'm trying." Having Hunter touching her was weird. Rolling her shoulders, she fought the urge to slap his hand away.

Inching closer, he glided his hands down her side and encircled her hips. "Let's have some fun."

She couldn't think of anything when he stood this close.

"Are you going to kiss me?" She placed her shaky hand on his chest, twisted the fabric of his shirt between her fingers, and felt the gentle strum of his heartbeat.

Please kiss me.

He half-smiled. "All in good time."

Placing the slightest pressure on her waist, he turned her around. He drew her hair aside, pressed his lips against her neck and trailed a line of kisses up to her ear. Goose bumps skittered across her skin. His rock-hard chest molded against her back, the buckle on his belt pressed hard into her lower spine, and his erection nudged against her ass.

"I thought this was supposed to be a quickie." She ran her hand down his thigh. Taut muscles flexed underneath her fingertips. *Hot.*

"It will be." He nibbled on her ear lobe. "After three orgasms, you'll have to be nice to me."

"This is sex, not magic." It would take more than a couple of orgasms to change her opinion of him.

His hands skirted up her sides and cupped her breasts. Fingers circled the silky fabric of her dress, hardening her nipples against her bra. Her heart hammered, and she arched into his touch.

"I wanna touch you all over, Kar." His voice was so low and deep, her panties nearly slid down to join it. His hand ventured down her stomach, over her hip to the top of her thigh. "Wanna set you on fire." He toyed with the hemline of her frock. She gasped when he dug his calloused fingertips into her flesh and dragged her skirt up. At the apex of her legs, he slipped his hand under her dress and rubbed his palm over her silky panties. "Wanna make you wet."

Shit!

She already was. She winced, and she spun around to face him.

His hand fell away. "You want to stop?"

To hell with the jitters. It was time to play. "No. I'm good."

"Okay." His eyes shimmered with sinful sexiness. "You know you can touch me. I won't bite. Not yet anyway."

Her hands quivered as she slid them down his solid arms and squeezed his biceps through the fine cotton of his shirt. "You have nice arms. Not big like a body builder. Just right."

Hunter chuckled. "Did you compliment me on something?" Creases crinkled the edge of his eyes. "Well, holy shit. Because you know, I'm nothing but an asshole."

"Whatever. I'm just saying—"

"You really know how to talk dirty. Keep that up and I'll cum in my pants."

She socked him in the arm.

"Ow. Guess I deserved that." He grabbed her hands and hooked them around his neck before slipping his around her waist. "So, where were we?"

"I've forgotten," Kara whispered, mesmerized by the perfect shape of his lips—thin, curved, and kissable. *Let's do this.*

Clasping the back of his head, she pulled his mouth to hers. Fire sizzled across her lips like a scorching summer heat. Her heart thudded with profound fervor. Shivers charged across her skin, and her equilibrium tilted.

He moaned against her mouth. Strong hands curled around her back and crushed her body against his.

Flicking and rolling his tongue against hers, the taste of champagne was like a sweet elixir. The fine hairs of his stubble tickled her upper lip, tempting and teasing. With a tug on his hair, she deepened her kiss. Harder. Hotter. Heavier.

It was like an itch being scratched—a craving being met. It was totally addictive. Every cell in her body screamed. More. More. *More.*

Panting, she drew back and stared at him. She didn't know what to make of the buzz that surged through her veins. Licking her lips, she savored the taste of him. "Wow . . . not bad."

"Not bad? That was hot. Very hot."

Cupping her cheek, he kissed her again, sucking on her top lip, her bottom lip, and diving into her mouth with his tongue.

She clutched at his shirt, fumbling for his buttons. With frantic fingers, she peeled the Gucci from his skin. Tossing the shirt onto the ground, her hungry eyes skimmed over his toned physique. Smooth chest, snail trail, man-groomed perfection. Her hands twitched, desperate to touch him all over.

With a trembling fingertip, she traced over the intricate swirling tattoo on his upper left arm, held captive by the way his muscles tensed and flexed beneath her touch. "I like the tattoos."

There weren't too many. Nothing overdone. All were pure, sexy, wickedness—the pattern on his arm; the letters GKH on his inner left forearm, the initials of Gemma, Kyle and Hunter; and there was a snake around a guitar on his left shoulder blade she'd seen many times at his fittings at work.

"I'm glad you approve. Now, shh." Hunter guided her backward across the room until she hit the wall with a thud. His lips found hers again. His breath seared her skin as he worked his way lower until he nipped and kissed her nipples through her dress. Why did that send the most delectable pulses through her system? Even her toes tingled.

Slipping his hands behind her, he lowered her zipper and eased her dress away. It pooled at her feet like a sheet of chiffon. "You looked nice in that dress, even better now it's on my bedroom floor."

Heat flushed her cheeks and she lowered her gaze. There she stood in her plain, full-coverage, pink bra and panties. Nothing slinky. Nothing sexy.

He lifted her chin with the tip of a finger. "Kar, you have a rockin' body."

She didn't think shapeless pillars with boobs were his thing . . . but whatever.

Reaching around her, he released her bra's clasp, and slipped the straps from her shoulders. It joined her dress on the floor.

He ook her breasts in his hands and rolled his fingertips

across each peaked nipple. "Hmm . . . fabulous." Dipping his head, he closed his lips over one of her aroused buds. Gentle yet firm, he licked, and sucked, and swirled his tongue. Goose bumps shot across her skin. His mouth. Hot. Wet. Divine. With a rush of warm air over her breast, he grazed his teeth over the tender tip and tugged on it.

Her knees buckled. *Holy shit.* What he was doing had her close to coming already.

Knotting her fingers through his hair, she drew his mouth up to hers. Adrenaline charged through her veins faster than crowds rushing through the doors at Macy's on Black Friday. Not even Conrad had made her insides tick like this.

Boldness took charge. The champagne she'd drunk boosted her confidence. She reached between their bodies and ran her hand over the length of his hardened cock straining beneath his trousers.

He broke their kiss and a saucy smile played across his lips. "You like what you're feeling there?"

"It'll do."

If he fucked like he kissed, she was in for some mind-blowing sex. *Bring it on.*

She flicked his belt undone and unzipped his pants. Grabbing his shaft firmly through his boxer-briefs, she rubbed him—he was hard, hot, and solid. Her core clenched, begging for attention, while she tried to ward off the knots tightening in the pit of her belly. The memory of the stinging, the pain, and the discomfort she often experienced when having sex jumped to the forefront of her mind. But then Hunter deepened their kiss.

He thrust his hips, forcing her back against the cool wall, and drove his throbbing cock into her hand. "Shit, that feels good. Rub harder."

She tightened her grip, sliding her hand up and down

his long length. He hissed in her ear, wild and possessive. He slapped the wall beside her and took half a step back. *Did she do something wrong?* But he fell to his knees and whisked her panties off. Vulnerable and naked before him, her hands shot out to cover herself. She winced. She hadn't waxed in weeks. Or shaved her legs.

"Don't." He drew her hands away. "You're actually kinda beautiful."

If she recalled correctly, he'd said she was above-average, not beautiful. He could say what he wanted, she wouldn't take it to heart. "You're only saying that because you wanna fuck me."

He circled his hand around her calf and kissed his way up the inside of her leg. "You have sensational legs."

Her insides clenched with each tease, stroke, and tickle. The breath rushed from her lungs when he slipped his finger through the folds of her skin and circled her clit. Round. Up. Down. Repeat. Want for him burned deep inside her, like a fire about to break containment lines.

His mouth claimed her. Her knees weakened, and she slipped an inch down the wall. His tongue traced along the length of her seam, flicked her swollen bud. Driving his finger into her arousal, he probed her slow, tender. She closed her eyes, her head falling back against the wall. *Oh yes.* She'd died and gone to heaven.

This was surreal. Hunter . . . on his knees, between her legs. She giggled. He'd said he'd wanted to do this to her earlier in the evening. In a daze, she lifted her leg and hooked her ankle across his back. Gave him more access. He licked her harder, slipped his tongue inside her. *Holy shit!* Her eyes rolled back into her head. Conrad had never done that. Her thighs shook. Her pulse whooshed in her ears. She clutched a fistful of Hunter's hair and rocked her hips against his mouth. "Oh . . . yeah. There."

With a swirl of his tongue, he took her over the edge.

Electricity shot up her spine, and every muscle in her body quaked and convulsed. Her mind circled like a spinning wheel. Hunter's tongue was pure magic.

He kissed his way up her body. A smile of satisfaction glistened on his lips. "That was orgasm number one." He reached over and took a few sips from the bottle of champagne. "How many orgasms did you say you wanted? Three, right?"

"I'm good with one." She pressed her palm against the side of her face to cool down.

"We're nowhere near done."

Her eyes feasted on him as he stripped off his trousers and boxer-briefs and tossed them to the side. *Wow!* His entire body was manscaped—waxed chest, trimmed, manicured, and refined nether region. His erection, long and hard, stood gleaming before her. The tip shined with a droplet of pre-cum. *Hmm.* She'd love to taste him. Take him in her mouth and swirl her tongue around him.

"Kara?"

"Hmm?" She blinked and drew her gaze away.

A huge grin beamed across Hunter's face. "You up for number two?"

She nodded. *Hell yeah.* She wanted that inside her.

He dug and searched around in the drawers beside him, cursed a few times, then pulled out a condom, and ripped it open. After rolling it onto his shaft, he snapped the rubber into place. Her pulse hadn't had time to return to normal when he kissed her once again.

He pushed his knee between hers. With gentle nudges, he worked his erection toward her opening. *Oh yeah.* This was happening. Desperate to have him inside her, she slipped her hand between their bodies and guided him into place.

She couldn't believe she was doing this. But to hell with consequences. She needed this to happen for herself—not anyone else.

He clutched onto her hips and slowly entered her. Just the tip. Just a fraction. The head of his throbbing cock burned hot against her arousal. Her heart couldn't beat any faster. With her eyes locked onto his, their breaths panted in time. A muscle in his jaw ticked and he drew his brows together. With a deep thrust he penetrated her, hard, burying his full length inside her. She gasped and dug her fingernails into his back.

"Now that . . . being inside you . . . feels incredible," Hunter growled, snaking his hand around her leg.

She wriggled her hips and allowed her body to adjust to his size. There was no pain—just a little bit of discomfort. All was good. "Just hurry up."

"My pleasure." Hunter's broad smile curled into a wicked grin. He lowered his mouth to hers and moaned, gravelly and needy. He was really into this. *Hot.*

He drove into her, slamming her lower back against the wall. Sparks shot through her and hit every nerve ending. Ogling her jiggling boobs, the cutest smirk lit his face. With a tilt of his hips, he thrust hard and stayed buried deep inside her.

Her eyes widened. *Oh wow.* She drew up onto her tippy-toes. She clenched around him. Tighter and tighter and tighter. Rubbing and pulsing. Then snap. Her body exploded, shuddering against him.

"Holy shit!" She burst out laughing and wrapped her arms around his neck, entwining her fingers with his hair.

"Two." He curled his arms around her waist, withdrew from her and guided her toward the bed.

She lay down on the mattress, her arms falling wide. "I'm done. I can't possibly have another orgasm. I've never had more than one at a time in my life."

He hovered over her body, licking and kissing one breast then the other. "You've been missing out." He peered up, flicking his tongue over her hardened nipple. Where did he get his stamina from? *Oh . . . fit rock star. That's right.* "And besides . . . I haven't come yet. And I promised three."

"You're a machine." How did he have such control? Didn't she turn him on enough?

"That I am." His eyes glistened. "I don't think I can hold out much longer." He nestled between her legs, drew one of her knees up towards his hips, and entered her.

Ow! The pressure of his penis against her uterus stung. She winced and clamped her teeth.

He stopped moving. "Kar? What's wrong?"

Attentive, concerned, controlled. She wasn't expecting that from him. She shook her head. "Nothing." It was all right. Like always, nothing she couldn't handle.

"My big cock too much for you?"

"Don't flatter yourself. Your dick is decent. Not that big." She wriggled around to find a comfortable position. Nothing was working. "Roll over." She pushed against his chest.

He flipped down on to the mattress, and a hell-yeah grin lit his face. She giggled, mounted his hips and guided his shaft inside her.

This was better. Didn't hurt as much.

Taking her weight onto her hands, she arched over him and kissed him. She pulsed and rocked her hips, rubbing hard, up and down, against him. Delectable pulses shot over her skin, and heat radiated toward her core.

He cupped her face and stroked her hair, flicked his tongue against hers. "God, you feel amazing." Slipping his fingers between her legs, he strummed and stroked her clit. He knew exactly how to play her. From now on, she'd be jealous of any instrument ever held in his hands.

The veins on his neck bulged and his jaw tensed. "Keep fucking me like this, Kar, and I'm gonna blow real quick."

Seeing him bite his lip, close his eyes and strain his muscles, lost in pleasure created by her, had a profound effect on her heart. It did her self-esteem wonders. "Like this?" She lowered onto him, taking him deep inside her.

"Uh-huh." He cupped her breast, took the nipple into his mouth, and flexed his hips up to meet hers.

Her head fell back. His breath rushed like a desert wind over her skin. Digging his fingers into her hips, he tugged her against him. Drove into her. With one huge thrust, his head collapsed back into the pillow, and he stilled.

"Oh yeah," he moaned. His whole body shuddered beneath her.

Seeing him orgasm was the most beautiful thing she'd ever witnessed. The grin quivering on his lips, eyes blazing blue, heat flushing his cheeks.

"Don't stop." Her legs shook beneath her. "I'm close."

"I've no intention of stopping." His fingers slipped back between her legs. She rubbed against him, and her every muscle screamed for release.

He drew her lips to his. Kissed her so hard her head spun. "Come for me," he whispered, low and husky, nipping on her earlobe, nuzzling into her neck. That was all it took to send her over the edge.

"Number three." He chuckled, running his warm hands over her back, her breasts, her thighs. Everywhere he touched tingled with electricity.

She struggled to catch her breath. "Show off." She slapped him on the arm. "I didn't think that was possible."

"I can usually hold out longer." He brushed the loose strands of her hair back from her face. "I lose control in this position. Or . . . you turned me on too much."

"I doubt the latter." She trailed her fingernails across his chest, circling his nipples, enjoying the way they hardened beneath her touch. But hell yeah . . . she'd taken him over the edge.

He patted her on the butt. "While I'd love to stay buried inside you all night, we have to move."

She rolled her hips, savoring the feel of him inside her for one more second, before she slipped off his body and lay beside him. He discarded the condom in a tissue from his nightstand, and she grabbed the bedsheet and drew it over them. She needed a moment for her heartbeat to return to normal.

He shuffled around on the mattress to face her. His hair was a shaggy mess, his lips curled with the most adorable smile. With a glint in his eye, he traced his fingertips across her collarbone and drew the sheet lower and lower. "Wanna go for four?"

She smacked his hand away and realigned the sheet. Her cheeks burned with fire. Between her legs throbbed. She stung a little. And time was ticking. They had to get back to the party. Best to end on a high, not in a painful mess or be busted by their friends. "I don't think I can handle another. We're not here for an all-night marathon." She glanced at her watch. 11:03p.m. "On that note, we better go."

She went to get up, but Hunter caught her on the shoulder. He leaned in and kissed her, languid, slow, belly-coiling. "Mission accomplished."

Her legs wobbled as she crawled out of bed and redressed. Hunter lay there, watching her. His eyes, blazing with shards of blue fire, tempted her to go back for more.

"We're done, Hunter."

"Come on. One more."

"No. Thank you." *Four?* She wouldn't be able to walk.

Hunter flopped against the pillow. "Spoilsport."

Kara fixed her hair, straightened her dress, and slipped on her shoes. After using his bathroom, and the pulse between her legs had subsided, she headed across the room.

"Kara. Wait."

But before her head and heart did something even more stupid, she opened the door. "Bye, Hunter. Thanks. That was fun."

She stepped out and closed the door behind her. Resting her head back against the smooth surface, she let the coolness seep into her skin.

Wow.

That was, without a doubt, the best sex she'd ever had in her life. Ever.

They were the best orgasms. The best kisses. The hottest, craziest thing she'd ever done.

With Hunter . . . *Fucking* . . . Collins.

She giggled. She'd got what she wanted. To have sex before her operation. To have a few moments to forget about her problems. To have her curiosity well and truly sated. *Damn* . . . he was good. And best of all, no one would ever know they'd been together.

Chapter 3

Nineteen thousand screaming fans filled the Wells Fargo Center in Philadelphia. Blinding flashes from the bright stage lights and huge digital screens flickered in Hunter's eyes. He was on show. And he loved it. Craved it. Flipping the mic in his hand and pumping his fist, he strutted and strode across the stage with Kyle and Gemma. Song after song, adrenaline coursed through his bloodstream like high-octane fuel.

But thoughts of Kara bombarded his mind. Gemma had said she was coming tonight. Kara never came to their concerts outside of New York. Why was she coming to this one? Was it to see him?

Crap.

He didn't want her here. *God no.*

Shading his eyes from the spotlights, he glanced toward the crew area at the side of the stage. He still couldn't see her.

Thank Christ.

What happened two weeks ago at Gemma and Kyle's engagement party was nothing but alcohol-induced fun and games. It was one night and one night only with Kara. She was too smart, sophisticated, and intelligent to assume otherwise. *Wasn't she?*

He rubbed at the unfamiliar tightness in his chest. Had he read Kara wrong? He hoped not. There would be no second round. Not ever.

Kyle shoved him on the shoulder and gave him a what-the-fuck glare. "Move it."

Shit.

"Sorry, bud." Hunter flicked his sweaty hair from his eyes and covered his mistake of missing his choreographed cue. With a quick skip and shuffle, he rushed to the other side of the stage. It was hard enough concentrating on lyrics and moves and singing without having distracting thoughts of Kara added into the mix.

As their backup band played the overture to their next song, Hunter grabbed his guitar from their technician, Hugh. They played, Gemma on lead guitar, Kyle on bass, and Hunter on rhythm. Stepping toward his mic, a shudder shot up his spine. He whipped his head around toward the crew area.

She's here. Kara's here. But . . . wow.

His breath hitched. There she stood, leaning up against the wall, with her long golden–brown hair hanging forward over her shoulder. His hand flinched, remembering how it felt to entwine his fingers through it. Her knit-dress that barely made it to mid-thigh showed off her gorgeous long legs. Legs he'd kissed every inch of. And those boots. Blood rushed to his groin at the sight of her black knee-high boots that screamed 'come fuck me.'

Oh yeah!

How he'd love to strip her naked and nail her while she only wore those boots.

No. No. No. No. *No.*

If he wasn't careful, he'd end up with a boner onstage.

He struck hard at his steel strings. The reverberations from the amps coursed through his body. Falling in sync with Gemma and Kyle, they churned out their number-one hit, "Come Back".

Kyle flicked his long bangs off his face and cupped his mic to sing the first verse. His voice swung low and deep.

> *Do you think of me when you go to sleep at night?*
> *Does your heart hurt knowing I'm not by your side?*
> *I miss you in my arms and holding you so tight.*
> *Hate not making love to you in the morning light.*
> *Come back baby, please don't make me beg.*
> *I'm sorry if I was wrong or if it was something that I said.*

Gemma took to the mic and the crowd screamed.

> *You used to call me baby when you kissed my lips.*
> *You'd touch me all over, said I was yours for keeps.*
> *You used to hold me close and we'd lose track of time.*
> *Where did we go wrong? Because I didn't see the signs.*
> *Come back to me, baby, please don't make me beg.*
> *I'm sorry if I was wrong or if it was something that I said.*

The audience waved their banners over their heads and cheered. Glancing around the auditorium Hunter absorbed the energy. He pressed his lips to the mic to sing the chorus. Just for fun, he threw Kara a wink.

> *So if you want me I'm right here waiting for you.*
> *Don't have to ask I'll get down on my knees for you.*
> *When I'm with you everything seems all so right.*
> *You are the one I want for the rest of my life.*
> *Without you near me I can barely breathe.*
> *You belong here, by my side, right next me.*
> *Come back to me, baby, please don't make me beg.*

He got nothing. No reaction. Not even a smile. It was like a stab to the chest. What was wrong with her? While he didn't want her to throw herself at his feet, some small acknowledgment he'd rocked her world with three orgasms would have been nice. Where was the gratitude? The lasting impact?

Wow . . . maybe he wasn't as good in bed as he thought.

Nah.

He was good. He was great at fucking. She couldn't deny that.

Ripping out a riff, he let the roar from the fans repair the dent Kara made to his ego. No girl was worth losing his head over. He'd learned that the hard way. And would never make the same mistakes again.

After half a dozen more songs and an encore, pyrotechnics exploded.

Boom. Bang. Pop.

Another show done.

Glitter settled on the crowd, and Hunter sprinted offstage behind Gemma and Kyle. Past the crew, down the corridor and around the corner.

With the fan's chanting and hollering still echoing in the auditorium, the rush from performing was like a heroin high. Sweeping past Kara, who was waiting at the door, they dashed inside their dressing room. She followed and stood too close to him for his liking. The scent of her floral perfume hit him like he'd been struck in the back of the head with a guitar. It sent him into a daze. So what if she smelled divine, like something he wanted to devour. He had to keep his dick in his pants.

But he had to know why she was here. Find out in his usual charming way by slathering on a coat of cheek and suaveness. He ripped off his T-shirt and wiped the sweat from his body with a towel. "Did you come all this way to see me, Kar? I'm flattered, but you shouldn't have."

She folded her arms and lifted her chin. "I didn't. I came

to see Gem, catch up with suppliers, and go to the ballet with my cousin for her birthday." She scanned his sweaty chest, his abs and arms. Her cheeks flushed a rosy pink that matched the color of her lip gloss. "Would you like me to add something else to my plans?"

Shit. His gut clenched and he rushed to grab a fresh T-shirt from his backpack and pulled it on. Was she throwing him some usual banter or was she hinting at a rendezvous? He hoped not the latter, for her sake. She'd only end up disappointed.

Kyle threw him his jacket. "Hunt, here." Hunter caught it just before it hit his face. "Hurry up."

"Quick. Let's go." Gemma grabbed her duffle bag and Kara's hand, and dragged her out the door. "Run."

Hunter picked up his backpack and fled down the passageway, following Kyle and the girls. Security ushered them into the waiting Mercedes van and slammed the door behind them. The car sped off into the night.

"This is crazy." Kara's eyes glistened, the city lights flickering across her face. "Why the rush to leave?"

Sitting next to Kara, Hunter rested his head back on the seat and tried to catch his breath. "We've gotta get back to the hotel before we're mobbed."

There would be no backstage parties tonight. Not when they had another show tomorrow.

Gemma sat next to Kyle on the seat opposite, her face still fiery red from the exertion of the show. "So Kar, is the plan to hang or go out tonight?"

Kara shuffled around on the seat. "If it's all right, can we just hang? I've already checked into the hotel. Can we order room service and have a drink or two?"

Hunter grunted and rolled his head against the headrest. That figured. Stay in and be boring. Kara never went out much. She didn't come to many of their parties, and if she did, she never stayed late. He'd known her for four years. All that time she'd been with Conrad. He could hardly recall a moment when he hadn't seen her latched onto him.

Maybe that was why they broke up. She'd suffocated and smothered him. *Screw that shit.*

"I'm down with that." Gemma wiped her hands on her skinny jeans. "Let me shower, then come to my room."

The van veered sharply around a street corner. The tires screeched. On the slippery leather seats, Hunter slid against Kara. *Shit. Should have my seatbelt on.* With his thigh pressing into hers, heat flared across his skin. *What the hell?*

His gaze fell to the swell of her breasts. He could still feel them bare against his chest. His teeth nipping her flesh. Her hardened nipples in his mouth. The way her body shuddered underneath the flick of his tongue. *Hmm . . .*

Kara punched him in the arm and shoved against his chest—her hit was so light he didn't even move. "Ew. Get off me. You're all sweaty, and you stink."

"I'm just admiring the view."

"Why? See something you like?" Challenge flickered in her eyes.

He gave her a 'been there, done that' smirk. "Like? Yes. Want? No."

"Then get off me." She pushed hard against his shoulder.

"As you wish." He mustered a chuckle, sat upright, and peeled away the sweaty strands of hair that had stuck to his face.

It didn't matter how freaking sexy she looked when her dark blue eyes shimmered at him, or how much he'd love to have her long, gorgeous legs wrapped around his waist—he couldn't lead her on. Couldn't sleep with her again.

Gemma stabbed her finger at him. "Leave Kara alone. She doesn't need to be corrupted by you."

Too late. He smiled and placed his hand on his chest. "Me? Corrupt someone? Never."

He needed a distraction. He had to do something, anything, to get Kara out of his head. A few stiff drinks and heading to the hotel's club to hook up with some other hot chick would do the trick. Someone quick and easy. There would be no up-until-dawn escapade, not with tomorrow's agenda. He knocked his knee against Kyle's. "Whatever we do tonight, remember we're going to the autism center before tomorrow's show."

"I haven't forgotten." Kyle ruffled his hands through his damp hair. "Midday, right?"

"Yep. Bright and early." Hunter nodded.

"What are you doing there?" Kara asked.

He grabbed the handle above the window and met her inquisitive eyes. He never liked talking about private matters. Too many people had abused and taken advantage of Everhide's celebrity status over the years. Used them as a money-making machine—like their old record label, SureHaven—rather than acknowledging their talent, their skill, or caring about the causes that affected them. But Kara was Gemma's friend; he guessed she could know. "They want to become involved with my autism foundation. After a meeting, the three of us will hang out with the kids in the center. Do some singalongs. Play games. It's fun." Hunter shrugged as if it were no big deal.

"You? Run a foundation?" She folded her arms. One manicured eyebrow arched high. "How did I not know this?"

He smirked. "You never cared to ask."

She wrinkled her nose. "Of all the organizations you could support, why autism?"

Hunter clutched his hands together in his lap. "My sister's autistic." He stroked the scar on the back of his right hand that Jenny had given him when she'd hit him with a toy guitar. He'd been twelve years old; Jenny had been six.

"Oh. I'm sorry." Kara tugged on her gold hoop earring. "I knew you had a sister. I didn't know she was autistic."

"Jenny's cool, but she's on the severe spectrum and needs full-time care." The harsh truth pressed against his skin. His sister may have bruised and battered his body, and filled his head with nightmares, but he set his heart on helping families like his—he didn't want them to suffer like he had. "Our foundation provides homes for young adults with autism. We have carers, programs, and support in place that enables families to have a break."

Kara's hand splayed across her chest, and her face lit up. "That's amazing."

The softness in her eyes sent a warmth spreading across his chest. He didn't think this part of his life would impress someone like her. He angled his head toward her and threw her a charming smile. "I am amazing. And adorable."

"Don't push it," she said, pursing her lips.

It was a constant battle for him to keep his family life separate from his public one. Privacy and their safety were everything. Jenny hated the media; the cameras freaked her out. While his foundation was important, he wanted to be known for his music, not his home life.

The van slowed to a crawl and eased past the mass of fans gathered on the hotel's pavement, waiting to catch a glimpse of Everhide. When the driver pulled to a stop, and they stepped out of the van, ear-piercing shrills filled the air. After a few waves and air kisses, security ushered them inside.

"Are you on this level too?" Hunter asked Kara, following her out of the elevator, Kyle, Gemma, and security tailing close behind.

"Yes." She pointed along the hallway. "Gem said Bec booked me the room next to yours."

Next door? *Crap!* Knowing she'd be sprawled out in the bed

on the other side of the wall from him made his palms sweat.

Stopping outside Kyle and Gemma's room, Hunter high-fived them. "Great show tonight, guys."

"Hell yeah," Gemma said. "But what was up with you?"

Her emerald eyes flashed, sharp and watchful. He'd stab a fork into his hand before lying to her again. The last time he wasn't honest with her, it nearly tore them apart. That was something he never wanted to live through again.

He ruffled the top of her head. "It was a momentary lapse in concentration." That's all Kara was. "It won't happen again. I promise."

"Good," Kyle said, opening the door. Gemma slipped into his arms and he talked back over his shoulder. "We'll see you soon. Don't rush . . . if you know what I mean." Kyle kissed Gemma on the neck, and the two of them fell, laughing, into their suite and shut the door.

Hunter slapped his hand against the closed door. "So we'll see you two in about five minutes?"

"Make it half an hour." Came Kyle's muffled voice.

Hmm . . . he glanced at Kara. He could do a lot in half an hour.

He loved that rush of picking up a girl after a show, bringing her back to his hotel room, and bonking her senseless. It was as exhilarating as a line of cocaine. Cocaine he hadn't touched in years. But girls . . . well . . . the couple since Kara had been as thrilling as listening to soul music on slow. *Shit!* Was there something wrong with his libido?

Scanning Kara's body, heat simmered through his veins. Those boots. That short dress. Those tits. Yep. Nothing wrong with his libido. Not at all.

Before he did something stupid, he needed a cold shower. *Hmm . . . Kara. In the shower.* His pulse jumped, and his balls ached. So. Not. Good. He had to get away from her, now. He clutched onto the strap of his backpack and walked backward, thumbing toward his room. "Okay, Kar . . . I'll leave you to it. I stink, so I better go freshen up. I'll meet you in Kyle and Gemma's room soon."

At his door, Hunter waved to Mick, his bodyguard, who was on duty at the end of the hallway, swiped his access card, and strode into his room. He let out the breath he didn't realize he'd being holding. *Damn.* Kara was doing his head in.

He dumped his backpack on the ground by his suitcase, his jeans, hoodies, socks, and T-shirts falling over the edge. The king-size bed, made without a wrinkle in the crisp white cover, took up nearly every inch of the tiny space. Beat the hell out of sleeping on their tour bus. He grabbed a fresh pair of boxer-briefs, popped the chocolate left on the nightstand into his mouth, and headed into the bathroom.

Under the warm water, he grimaced, unable to stop pictures of Kara flooding his mind. *Slender body. Sexy legs. Sensational tits.* His pulse jumped from *moderato* to *vivace*. Blood charged to his groin. *God damn it.* Lathering himself, he stroked his cock. Long, languid, hard rubs. *His tongue between her legs.* He tightened his grip. Pumped his fist. Quicker and quicker. *His dick pounding into her. Over and over again.* His breath hissed through his teeth. He squeezed his eyes shut. Thrusting his hips, he found release. He sighed and shook his head. *What was wrong with him?* He just jerked off to Kara.

Stepping out of the shower, he jumped when the doorbell rang.

"Hotel management."

What? He hoped it wasn't some crazed fan who'd got onto their floor. But security wouldn't let anyone near his room. Maybe it was a mix-up.

"Just a minute." He half dried himself, wrapped his towel around his waist, and peered through the spyhole.

His breath caught in his throat. *Shit.* He stretched his neck side to side, trying to rein in his pulse. He opened the door.

There stood Kara. Gone was the sexy dress, replaced with pale pink, silky pajamas. She scanned him up and down, and his body hummed.

He smirked and propped his arm against the door. Best to act cool, calm, and collected. "Can I help you?"

"You're infuriating. You know that?" Kara said, her lips tight. He smelled whiskey on her breath. Had she drunk half the minibar?

"I try my best." He grinned. "But could you be specific?"

"You. Onstage and in the car. Looking good, all hot and sweaty. Flirting. And teasing. Being suggestive."

What was she going on about? He'd been well-behaved. "I'm always like that. What's wrong with it?"

"You're driving me crazy. We had a deal. One night and one night only. Never again." She dragged her long nails down her cheeks.

His back flinched remembering her digging those claws into his flesh. "Yep. That was the deal."

"So why are you tormenting me?"

"I always do."

"I know. But since sleeping with you, things have changed. I still don't like you . . . but the sex was soooo good." An awkward smile quivered across her lips. "I was wondering if we could . . . renegotiate. Can we do it again? Just once more. And that will be it. I swear."

Oh shit.

His heart jolted against his ribs. This was what he wanted to avoid. He had a mantra to never sleep with the same girl twice. He didn't want to get involved, or hurt anyone, ever again. "You? Want to have sex? Again?"

She twisted the bottom of her pajama top around in her

fingers. Tiny wrinkles formed at the corners of her eyes. "Yes."

Fresh blood flooded toward his groin. So much for his release in the shower.

No. Stop. Sleeping with her again would lead to problems. He didn't want that. There had been a point in time, eighteen months ago, when he'd thought he wanted a girlfriend. He'd given it his best shot. With Gemma. Then Amie. But everything had ended in disaster. He wasn't about to fall into some friends-with-benefits fiasco that would only end up with her getting hurt.

But . . . damn, he wanted to fuck her.

It was *just* sex.

Shit. No. No, he couldn't.

Could he?

He rubbed his forehead. His dick ached. He closed his eyes. Flashes of Gemma broken with tears streaming down her face, and Amie with her cold, callous laugh flickered behind his eyelids. He'd caused too much pain to people he'd cared about. Hurt people he loved. Got trampled by those who he'd fallen for. The permanent scars on his heart were too brutal.

"I'm sorry, Kar. I can't."

A you've-gotta-be-kidding-me look flared in her eyes. It stung him like a slap to the face. But before she had time to say another word, he let the heavy room door fall shut.

When the latch clicked, he sat on his bed and buried his face in his hands. What normal guy turned down an offer like hers?

He'd left normal behind years ago. He was such a prick. But what else could he have done?

The hurt in her eyes when he said no cut deep into the marrow of his bones.

Fuck.

This was for the best.

He should have known better than to screw around with

Gemma's friend. *His* friend. It was better to let her down now rather than later. This was the price he had to pay for playing around. Because anything was better than letting anyone get close to him ever again.

Chapter 4

Kara placed her hand on her queasy stomach and stepped out of the cab into the alley in West Hollywood. The cool wind snapped at her trench coat and tangled her hair. She adjusted her Dior sunglasses to stop the dust stinging her eyes. After finishing her training course yesterday, dinner and drinks with friends had gone on well into the night. Now she was paying the price. Her head ached, and she felt sick.

After dashing through the gust, she went through the security check point. Her eyes strained at the gaudy street art illuminating the walls of the otherwise dull industrial buildings. With a free day before heading home, she'd come on set to watch Everhide film their new music video. She was here for Gemma. Not Hunter. She wouldn't let him get to her. Not after his rejection in Philadelphia a week ago.

It had taken three drinks from the minibar and every thread of her confidence to knock on Hunter's bedroom door, and with one snip, he'd sent it tumbling to the floor. Another round of mind-numbing sex would've been a great antidote to stressful news. She'd found out earlier that day her operation had been brought forward. When Hunter had said no to sleeping with her again, she'd never been so humiliated and embarrassed in her life. *Asshole.* He didn't hang out with her, Gemma, and Kyle that night either. *Jerk.* Today, if he resorted to his usual suggestive banter, she'd ignore him. She'd count knitting stitches in her head. And she hated knitting.

With deft footwork in her stiletto ankle boots, she ducked under the sound booms, around the rigging and lighting, and skipped over the thick cords and cables that snaked across the ground. Drawing closer to the trailer, her chest tightened. She climbed the metal-grid stairs and hesitated. Her stomach swirled like an unsettled ocean. Taking a deep breath, she straightened her coat, fixed her hair.

I got this.

She gave her hands a quick shake to get rid of the nerves, rapped on the trailer door, opened it, and stepped into utter chaos.

Pacing the length of the forty-foot trailer, Bec, the band's personal assistant, cursed profanities to someone on her cell phone. Sophie, the band's manager, threw heated words at three guys wearing shiny puffer jackets emblazoned with 'All-Hyped Productions' on the back. The band's publicist, Kate, sat at the table, typing like a demon on her laptop. Kyle, Gemma, and Hunter sat on the luxurious white leather sofa like they were on the set of *Friends*.

Gemma caught sight of her and her face lit up. "You made it." She rushed to Kara and gave her a warm hug.

"Yeah. Traffic was good for LA standards."

When Gemma pulled away, her face morphed from happy to worried. "You don't look so good. Are you okay?"

Kara brushed her fingertips across her feverish forehead. "Not really. I went out last night. Had too much to drink. I've been sick, and I never throw up from alcohol."

"Can I get you anything?"

"No, thank you. I'll be fine." She peered over Gemma's head. The second she met Hunter's gaze, she gritted her teeth. Her nostrils flared.

Knit one. Purl one. Knit one. Purl one.

So what if he made an old sweatshirt and jeans look like he'd stepped off the Prada runway. If she had real knitting needles, she could stab them through his eyes.

She sucked in oxygen and stuffed all her hurt into the spandex around her heart. Nothing would burst her seamlines today. Especially not him.

Hunter ripped his eyes away, his wavy hair curtaining his face.

That would be right. Hide. You sack of shit.

Peeling off her coat, she flicked Hunter from her mind and surveyed the mayhem. "So . . . what's going on, Gem?"

"The plan for today's shoot has turned into a nightmare." Gemma stepped out of Bec's way. "No outfits."

"What? Where are Margo and Carla?" Kara looked around for their stylist and make-up artist.

Kyle leaned forward and rested on his elbows. "Margo's sick. She fainted at dinner last night. Carla's taken her to the hospital."

She could relate to not feeling well. Her belly still bubbled with nausea. "I hope she's okay."

"Crap." Bec threw her cell phone onto the table and jammed her hands on her hips. "That was Emily, Margo's assistant. Emily forgot to send the outfits. They're still in New York."

Kara drew her shoulders back, towering over Gemma. "Bec, do you need clothes for the shoot?"

"Ah . . . yes." Bec's biting tone made it clear she was not in the mood to be messed with.

"I can help." Kara placed her coat and Luis Vuitton purse

onto the kitchenette counter. "We're close to Conrad's store on Rodeo Drive. I'll call Adrian, the manager. We'll pull items off the shop floor. Whatever we use, we'll add to Everhide's account."

Bec rushed forward and grasped Kara's arms. "That would be incredible. I don't have time to go shopping."

"Sure. No worries." Kara's stomach flipped a gazillion times. She'd done nothing like this before, but she knew she could pull it off. "Tell me what you need?"

Bec scanned her cell phone. "Margo's brief is here somewhere . . . Here . . . *Nothing torn or faded. Plain-colored outfits. We don't want them blending into the graffiti on the walls.* Do you think you can have them within the hour?"

Doubt flickered through Kara's mind. That seemed tight. She was a designer, not a stylist, but she knew clothes, her friends, and their style. "Yes."

Sixty minutes to make it happen. *Holy shit!*

"You're a lifesaver," Sophie said, then wiggled her finger at Everhide. "You guys . . . be ready the minute Kara gets your outfits. The rest of us will take Brandon for a coffee down the street. Let's hope there are no more delays because he is pure asshole."

Kara smirked and jutted her chin at Hunter. "One of your mates, is he?"

"Ha ha ha ha ha. No . . . he's the videographer." The deep timbre of his voice sent a strange wave of vibrations coursing through her body. What the hell was wrong with her? She really was sick.

Sophie grabbed her purse. "We'll leave you to get organized. Call me if you need anything."

Kara stepped clear of the doorway and Sophie led the management team and production crew out of the trailer, leaving Kara with her friends. Without a second to waste, Kara dived into her purse for her notebook and cell phone and called

Adrian.

Ten minutes later, she stood at the counter and scribbled some notes to make sure she'd ordered all the items they'd need.

"Hey."

She jumped, sending a pen mark skidding across her page. *Hunter.* Where had he come from?

Leaning his hip against the counter, he crossed his arms. "Can I help?"

She skimmed over his long legs, broad chest, and solid . . . rock-solid . . . toned arms. Her pulse quickened, remembering how his naked body had felt against hers. That night, three weeks ago, was still too vivid in her head. But so was his rejection.

Rib stitch. Knit two. Purl two. Knit two. Purl two.

"Yes, you can help." Her whole body went rigid. "Stay out of my way."

"Just offering." He held up his hands and returned to the sofa.

Breathing space was what she needed.

After straightening Gemma's hair and a much-needed cup of coffee, Kara carried the garment bags Adrian's shop assistant had delivered to hang them on the clothes racks by the rear bedroom of the trailer. Before she made it to the short hallway, Hunter blocked her path.

Her shoulders slumped. "Are you just going to stand there or move? Why do you have to be so irritating all the time?"

He held out his arms. "I'll help you."

"I don't need your help."

"Kar, what's wrong?" He pinched his brows together. "Is this about last week?"

"Shh. Gemma and Kyle will hear." She flicked her gaze toward the other end of the trailer. Gemma sat at the makeup counter putting on eyeliner, and Kyle stood behind her styling his hair. They were lost in their own private conversation. She spun back to Hunter. "Have you told them we slept together?"

"No."

"Good. Don't." The guilt gnawed at her as much as his rejection. There were unspoken rules between girlfriends, and she'd broken a big one. He was Gemma's ex.

She rammed the bags against his chest, forcing him to take a step back. Her whole body shook. "Yes, I'm upset with you. Isn't it obvious?" She seethed through her teeth. "You slammed the door in my face."

He sighed and rubbed the back of his neck. "I'll admit I should've used more tact. I'm sorry. But you knew the rules when we slept together. We had a deal. One night. One night only."

She clutched onto the garment bags until her fingers hurt. "I didn't think you were serious. I wanted sex, not a fucking marriage proposal."

The muscle in his jaw ticked. "This is an *'it's not you, it's me'* thing. Our night together was great . . . really great. But that's it."

She pushed past him and hung up the bags. "Why? Did you think I'd do something stupid and fall for you?" Distaste dripped from her tongue like she'd eaten an over-ripe banana. "I like my men mature and cultured, so there's no chance of that happening. Ever." She poked him in the chest. "And if being with someone only once is your approach to everyone you're with, you'll end up a very lonely old man."

Hunter's eyes clouded over, but within a blink the hurt was gone. "I'm not lonely. I love my life. I don't do relationships or need any complications."

She drew herself tall with as much regal elegance as her designer jacket. "Fine. I got it."

How could anyone block themselves from the prospect

of finding someone to love? What a sad existence. But being rejected still hurt like a bitch.

"Kar?" Gemma called out. She was still doing her makeup, applying smoky eyeshadow. "Everything okay?"

"I'm fine. Hunter's helping me with the clothes."

"Okay," Gemma said. "I won't be long."

Hunter folded his arms and leaned against the wall. "Kar, I don't want anything to change between us. I like tormenting you. It's our thing. I'll make it up to you somehow. Just no sex."

Standing this close to him was having all kinds of effects on her pulse, her breath, and her heart. On the one hand, she wanted to curse and scream and hate him even more for making her feel so crappy. On the other hand, she wanted to tear his clothes off, throw him down onto the bed, and ride him until she saw shooting stars. *Well, that's not going to happen.*

If he liked tormenting her, she better strap on her battle armor, because two could play this game. "Are you sure about that? There's a bed right there."

He drew in a long breath and held it. His Adam's apple lurched. "Yes . . . I'm sure."

"Good." She sensed a crack in his resolve, and could have pushed it, but she backed off. She didn't want him to think she was into him. Because she wasn't. Absolutely not. No way. "Now strip. Time to get dressed."

With quick hands, she unzipped the bags. Running her fingers over the beautiful coats, trousers, and shirts from Conrad's latest ready-to-wear collection, the knots in her neck dissipated. The majority of the clothes were black. Soft cashmere, leather, twill, and denim slid beneath her fingertips.

"I love these coats." She sighed, rubbing a woolen sleeve, the smooth leather of the handmade toggles, and the little ridges of the contrast stitching. She always wanted to influence what people wore, create new trends. But that would never happen when she had to work within the constraints of Conrad's creative directive.

Hunter snatched it out of her hand. "Kara. Stop. It looks like you're about to come in your panties." He lowered his voice to just above a whisper. "And I know, because I've seen that look on your face. Three times."

She closed her eyes. *Naked flesh. Hot kisses. Bodies entwined.*

Heat flooded her cheeks. She straightened her shoulders and looked him square in the eye. "Please don't make me regret sleeping with you."

"You won't."

Her head fell back and she groaned. Every word Hunter whispered frayed at the edges of her control. He'd never learn. Never change. This was Hunter being Hunter. "You're impossible. You know that?" She selected a pair of trousers and a long-sleeved top and threw them at him. "Here. Put these on."

His eyes locked onto hers and dimples dented his cheeks. He slipped past her into the bedroom without closing the door behind him, reached over his head, and ripped his T-shirt off.

Damn. He made that simple move so sexy. Her gaze ran over his six-pack abs, his broad chest, the arch of his collarbone, and his wicked tattoos.

"Kara?" He unzipped his jeans and pulled them off.

"Mmm?"

"Stop."

"Stop what?" Her voice sounded distant, not her own.

"Stop looking at me like that."

She drew herself up. "There was no look."

"Liar." The corner of his mouth hinted at a smile. "You want what you can't have."

"No. I don't. Been there. Done that. Moved on." She was getting better at this. She could handle Hunter.

When he finished dressing, she grabbed a thin cashmere

scarf and wrapped it around his neck. His soft stubble tickled her fingertips and sent tingles shooting up her arm. Her equilibrium wobbled.

Shit. She really wasn't well.

He leaned in. "I prefer you taking clothes off me rather than putting them on."

She cinched the knot tight to his neck. Why did he always have to resort to jokes? "You had a second chance; you blew it. So tough. Now it's my job to dress you, not undress you." Her voice remained steady and firm, unlike her stomach that flipped. "Somehow, after everything that has happened between us, I have to go back to tolerating your existence. So for the rest of today, be professional."

"If I must." He winked.

The trailer floor creaked and Gemma shuffled toward them. She stopped in front of Kara and Hunter, her eyes ping-ponging back and forth. "What's with all the whispering?" She slapped the back of her hand onto Hunter's chest. "I don't know what's got into you two lately, but it has to stop. Hunt, be nice to Kar. She's helping us out."

Hunter hooked his arm around Gemma's neck, and drew her into a headlock. "I'm always nice."

Gemma tackled Hunter around the legs and tried to trip him up, but Hunter just laughed. She pushed and pushed, unable to budge him an inch. Kara giggled. These two were the biggest kids at heart. It made Kara miss having fun at her own job.

"Okay. Stop. You'll muck up my hair." Gemma punched him in the ribs. Breaking out of his hold, she flicked her hair back and smoothed it into place.

"Are you two done?" Kyle jumped up from the sofa, clapped his hands and grapevine-stepped down the trailer. "What have you scraped together for us, Kar? Let's get this shoot over with."

Yes. The sooner Kara got away from Hunter the better.

***

Kara eased onto the stool at a high table in the hotel's bar surrounded by Everhide and their entourage. Today's video shoot had been long and tiring. She sipped on her iced water and rolled her aching feet. Her stomach muscles hurt from laughing so much. Everhide had filmed take after take, sang, and zipped through their choreographed moves. When they messed up, Hunter goofed off, danced around and made everyone laugh. When Kara changed his outfit, he posed and strutted his half-naked hot body around in the trailer, making her concentration lapse more than once.

After a great afternoon, she could put having sex and being rejected by Hunter behind her.

She glanced over Gemma's shoulder. There Hunter stood at the bar surrounded by three gorgeous Kendall Jenner lookalikes. Her chest tightened. Her skin crawled with ants. She'd seen him pick up girls before. Why should she be bothered?

He had his mischievous smile on, the one that drew his perfect lips into a broad curve and dimples highlighted his cheeks. His eyes glistened, looking at each girl vying for his attention. What was ticking through his mind? Was he assessing which one he would take back to his room?

Kara's eyes darted to the barman, to Sophie and Bec, to Gemma and Kyle, to her drink, but she always found herself drawn back to Hunter. He leaned in and talked in one of the girl's ears. Laughed at another one's jokes. Brushed his hand down someone else's back. Kara's skin itched, and she closed her eyes. Why did she want him to do that to her when she wanted nothing to do with him?

If this was jealousy, she wanted to distance herself. She shuddered and turned back to Gemma and Kyle sitting opposite her. "I'm gonna go. It's nearly ten o'clock, and I have to get up early for my flight back to New York."

"No. Staaay." Gem had knocked back a few JD's and swayed in her seat. "Have one more drink with me."

"No, thank you." She had to get out. Away from Hunter. *Fast.* "I'm exhausted and need to go to bed. You stay and have fun." She waggled her finger at Gemma. "But behave. You have a show tomorrow."

"Always." Gemma sat straight, a defiant, blissed out grin on her face. "I'll be fine."

"We'll see about that." Kyle scooped Gemma's long brown hair back over her shoulder and rubbed her back. He was the sweetest.

After hugs with Kyle and Gemma, Kara threw Hunter a quick wave goodbye and headed into the lobby.

"Kar, wait," Hunter called. His footsteps grew louder on the tiles. He caught her on the arm before she could hit the elevator button.

She held up her finger and pointed it straight into his chest. "No. I'm done. Good night."

"What's wrong?" He took a step back, splaying his palms toward her.

"What's wrong?" Her blood pressure shot skyward. "I'm tired and I don't want to sit in the bar and watch you pick up girls."

"What?" Confusion rippled through his eyes. "I was just talking to them . . . well . . . okay . . . I was putting in some groundwork. What's wrong with that? You've seen me hook up before."

"Yes. I have." She glanced around the lobby. Other than a sole person at the check-in counter and Mick, the place was empty. She leaned in, so Mick couldn't hear. "But that was *me* three weeks ago. Seeing you all over those girls reminds me of how I lowered my standards for one night of sex. I don't want to watch you play your games and pursue your next victim."

His hands clenched at his sides. His eyes turned a frosty blue. "What are you going on about? We've talked about what happened in Philly. I apologized. Don't tell me you're hung up on me?"

Hung up? She'd had a punch to the guts, not a knife through her heart. "Get over yourself." She folded her arms. "I'm not hung up on you. You're the last person on the planet I'd want to be involved with. I'll be fine. To quote your words back at you, this is about me, not you. I want to put you behind me. Go back to the bar, your girls." She waved toward the bar's entrance. "Go and get laid."

Hunter lowered his chin and stuffed his hands into the back pockets of his skinny jeans. When he lifted his gaze, his eyes were hard like ice. "You're nuts. You know that? I'm sorry if I upset you. Wasn't my intention. But I'm not going to change. For you. Or anyone."

She shook her head. "I'm not asking you to."

"Good." He blew at a strand of loose hair.

"Some regard and consideration wouldn't go astray though."

He wiped his hand across his face, erasing the tension. "That's why I came after you." His tone softened. "I wanted to say thank you for helping today. People who go out of their way for us mean a lot. When you come from nothing, you never take anything for granted. I wanted to let you know I appreciate what you did for us on short notice."

Wow. Where did nice Hunter come from? "Hunt, I had a good day. I loved seeing you work with Gem and Kyle. It was the first time I saw you could be a decent guy."

His grin broadened, and he tucked his long hair behind his ear. "What can I say? I'm irresistibly charming."

"More like crazy."

"I'm all kinds of crazy."

A smile quivered on her lips. *He's so infuriating.* "We had fun today. Let's not ruin it."

His gaze bordered on being innocent and he grazed his teeth across his lower lip. Her nipples hardened. Those same teeth nipped and bit her flesh. *Damn it.* Why did her body react like that?

"Good night, Hunt. Enjoy tour." She pressed the elevator button. Once. Twice. Three times. *Hurry up.*

"See ya, Kar. Have a safe trip home." He stepped forward and kissed her on the cheek.

Her breath hitched, and her hand shot to her face. The elevator doors pinged and opened. Dashing inside, her knees wobbled. She shut her eyes until the doors closed.

In her room, she fell onto the bed and stared at the ceiling. Touching her forehead, her fingers trembled. The ache in her chest threatened to escape. Turning on her side, she punched her pillow. All day she'd been adamant about not letting Hunter get to her. Then he went out of his way to thank her and give her a kiss. Why? Why did he have to kiss her? It was only a friendly gesture, but it did her head in.

He was hot, then cold. Flirtatious, then a jerk. Arrogant, then modest.

Why did he rile her?

Grr. She missed having a boyfriend. She wanted a new guy, but who'd want her after her operation? She had to get her mind and body under control because someone like Hunter was not the man for her. He was a rock star from the gutters of New Jersey; she'd been born into one of New York's elite families where tradition and bloodline mattered. Like polka dots and stripes, Hunter and Kara would never mix.

Placing her fingers over her lips, she closed her eyes and fought back the urge to vomit. Her nausea had lingered most of the day. Unable to stomach food or face alcohol, she must have a bug. When she got home, the first thing she had to do was see the doctor. Being sick had gone on for long enough. She didn't need illness to delay her operation.

After the rollercoaster day, there was one thing she was adamant about. She had to get Hunter out of her head. Put their night together behind her. It meant nothing to him. It was time for her to see it the same way. Thank God he was on tour. She didn't have to see him, talk to him, or work with him. The longer he was away, the better. With him absent, temptation was gone.

Chapter 5

"Kara. You're pregnant."

"I'm what?" Kara's heart dared not take another beat. She blinked a hundred times in the span of a second. "What did you say?"

"Pregnant," her doctor repeated.

"It's not possible. I can't be. There's no way—"

Oh shit! The color drained from Kara's face and her heart barreled up her throat. The wall clock's soft tick clanged like church bells in her ears. Her breath seesawed in and out of her lungs. *Crap.* She was hyperventilating.

"Well . . ." Dr Lloyd handed her a sheet of paper detailing her test results. "Your blood and urine samples say otherwise. That's why we called you back in."

Kara clutched at her belly. Tears stung her eyes. "No. No. No. No. *NO*. They can't be right. There must be a mistake." She'd visited the doctor two days ago after arriving back from LA, thinking she had a stomach bug. Not this. Her period was late, but not that late.

Dr Lloyd swiveled on her chair and furrowed her brow.

"Kara, what's wrong? Isn't this exciting news? This is what you and Conrad wanted, right?"

Kara closed her eyes and swallowed the dry lump in her throat. "Conrad and I broke up about three months ago. It's . . . not Conrad's."

"Oh . . . has this happened too soon with your new partner?"

Bile swirled in Kara's stomach. Her whole body shuddered and ached. She wanted to curl into the fetal position and cry. "I don't have a new partner. It was one night. But the guy I was with . . . we used a condom."

Her doctor took on a lecturing tone. "Although condoms have a very high success rate, they can fail. Age, storage conditions, improper usage . . ."

Flashes of Hunter digging around for a condom in his drawers and slipping it on flicked behind her eyelids. He of all people should know how to use a condom.

Kara wrapped her arms around herself. "Even if it failed, how did I fall pregnant? I have endo."

"Many women with endometriosis, like yourself, have trouble falling pregnant naturally. If you used contraception, I would say this is nothing short of a miracle. Since breaking up with Conrad, your body may not have been under so much stress. Along with the right timing, it is technically possible."

Kara's head spun. She'd tried for months to fall pregnant with Conrad. They'd wanted a baby desperately, and it had never happened. All the ovulation checks and monitoring had gotten out of control. One night with a man she could barely tolerate had achieved what Conrad never did. *Shit.*

Dr Lloyd bowed her head. "Do you know who the father is?"

Kara squeezed her eyes shut, tight. Bitterness swamped her mouth. "Yes," she whispered.

"When was your last period, or do you remember the day you had intercourse, so we can work out your due date?"

"Um . . ." Kara shivered in her chair. One amazing night with Hunter at Gemma's engagement party had turned into her worst nightmare. She wanted to scream and shout and tear his God damn hair out. "My period was during the second week of October. I was with the guy three and a half weeks ago. October 21st."

Kara's doctor typed away on her laptop. "So that was your date of fertilization. This explains why your breasts are tender, and you've been feeling sick. You have morning sickness, my dear." Dr Lloyd kept her eyes on her computer screen. "The due date of your baby is calculated from the time of your last period. That puts you at just over five weeks on the chart. You'll be due around July 13th." Dr Lloyd gave her a sympathetic smile. "Kara, this has obviously come as a shock. Take some time to think things over. If this is an unwanted pregnancy, you have options available. We can talk about them if you wish."

"No. Not now. I don't know what I want to do."

Three and a half weeks ago, she'd been given the news she had to have a hysterectomy to put an end to her severe endometriosis. Having her own child was not an option. Now she was pregnant. Was this her only chance to ever have a baby?

"Okay." Dr Lloyd nodded. "You have a big decision to make but one that needs to be made quickly." The doctor stood and opened the door. "Let's leave it there for today. Come and see me in a couple weeks."

"Thank you." In a fog, Kara picked up her purse and headed out of the doctor's office.

She was pregnant? PREGNANT!

With Hunter's baby.

Oh God. What the hell was she supposed to do?

Chapter 6

"I'M PREGNANT, YOU ASSHOLE!"

Hunter's heart jerked like a tow strap. Searing pain crippled his ability to breathe. His eardrums rang from Kara's shrill voice screeching down the phone. All the blood drained from his face, and his brow broke out in a sweat. "What are you talking about? It's not possible."

"Oh, you're right. It shouldn't have happened." Raging anger and pure animosity boiled in Kara's voice. "Did I miss something? We used condoms. Did it break, and you didn't tell me? Take it off for some cheap thrill? I don't want one of your God-knows-how-many sexually transmitted diseases."

He grabbed a fistful of hair and he paced the length of his hotel room in Houston. "I told you, I don't have any STDs." He hissed through his teeth, trying to keep his voice in check so Gemma and Kyle wouldn't hear from the suite's living room. "Second, no, it didn't break. And third, I didn't take it off. Are you crazy? As if I'd take a condom off. I've never had unprotected sex. Ever. I'm not stupid."

"Well . . . somehow I'm pregnant. It's yours." Her sharp tone stabbed him like an arrow to his chest. "After feeling sick in LA, I went to the doctor and had blood tests done. It's all confirmed. That's why I was ill onset. It wasn't from food poisoning or alcohol. It was morning sickness."

"Whoa. Whoa. Whoa. Slow down. Is this some psycho joke? You've gone too far." His jaw cramped. "It can't be mine."

"Well, it is. This is no joke. Somehow those little suckers of yours got inside me."

Hunter's knees buckled, and he collapsed onto the edge of his bed. That night with Kara at the engagement party replayed at high speed through his mind. He went down on her, nailed her up against the wall, and then did it again on his bed. It had been the best sex he'd had in months.

But pregnant? How could this have happened? Had that moment after orgasming, when he stayed inside her until his cock softened, resulted in this epic failure? Didn't he pull out in time? Had some of his cum leaked from the condom? *Shit . . .* no, wait. The condom from his drawers had been in there for a long time. *Fuck!* He should have used the new ones in his nightstand.

Fuck. Fuck. *Fuck.*

He didn't need this crap at eleven a.m. He had a show tonight. "This is bullshit."

"I know. But it's your baby. I haven't slept with anybody else."

He rubbed his stomach, wanting to throw up. Staring out over the Houston skyline, his vision blurred. This couldn't be happening. After growing up with an autistic sister, he was adamant about not having children. He'd had scares before. Two girls had falsely accused him of fathering their children. Neither had been true. He never had unprotected sex. When he was with someone, he always pulled out in time. He never took a girl to his room when he was too drunk. He always, always, always, used condoms. Even if the girl said she was on the pill or used other forms of birth control.

He was not a father. And didn't want to be. Ever.

But this . . . coming from Kara. It was a nightmare. She had no reason to lie. Did she? Was she after his money? Surely not. She had enough of her own.

He squeezed his eyes shut and grit his teeth. He wasn't one to get angry, or mad, or fly off the handle. He hated confrontation of any kind. Growing up with Jenny, he'd learned to hide and control his emotions. His outlet was his music. But Kara had him at breaking point. "I don't believe you. But if it is mine . . ." His stomach lurched. He swallowed hard to keep his nausea at bay, " . . . you need to get rid of it."

Silence.

More silence.

Even more silence.

Not a sound.

Not a breath.

Tension mounted in his temples with each passing second.

"Kar?" Her name caught in his throat.

She sniffled and snuffled.

"Kara?" He pummeled his fist against his forehead, praying that this was a bad dream. "Please tell me you're going to get rid of it."

"I only found out about this two days ago. I'm here, sitting in Bryant Park on my lunch break, numb. With you having shows on at night, I didn't know when else I could call you." Kara blubbered. "I'm so scared. I don't know what to do, Hunt."

"There's only one option. There's too much risk involved. My genes could be defective. It could turn out autistic like my sister." His shoulders hunched at the pain erupting in his chest. Was he being selfish? But what else could he say? He had to be honest. He loved his sister—but it terrified him that his own children could suffer the same fate.

"There's risk in any pregnancy, Hunt. But you don't understand. This is not an easy decision for me."

"It should be."

"No . . . it's not." Her voice quivered.

"Then please explain, because I don't understand," he seethed, trying to keep calm and handle the situation. "Why would you want to keep it when we don't even like each other?"

"Trust me," she snapped, "you're the last person in the universe I'd want to have a child with. But a baby *is* what I've always wanted. It's my body. My say."

"Bullshit." He ripped his fingers through his hair. What was it going to take to get through to her? She couldn't have this baby. "I do have a say when it involves me."

"No. You don't. The universe and Mother Nature have pulled a hell-of-a-job on both of us."

His heart constricted. His head ached. This wasn't a game anymore. "Kara, I'm begging you. Do the right thing for both of us. Please, put an end to this before it goes any further."

"I don't know if I can do that." Her voice rasped above a whisper. "I need more time to think. We'll talk later. I gotta go back to work."

"Kara? Wait."

But she hung up.

Now what the hell was he supposed to do?

He shot to his feet, stepped over to the window, and stared out at the gloomy Houston sky. Autumn colors had sucked the life out of the leaves in the park below. Like the cold mid-November temperature outside, numbness consumed him. Anger, frustration, panic, and fear festered inside him, but he couldn't move. He wanted to take the nightstand lamp and smash it on the desk. He wanted to tear the flat-screen off the wall and hurl it out the window. He wanted to pick up the chair and break it into a thousand pieces.

A baby would ruin his life.

He banged his head against the glass window. Why was this happening to him? Kara was supposed to be nothing but a bit of fun, not a life sentence. There was no way they could have a child together.

He should've known there would've been consequences after sleeping with her. But he'd never expected anything like this.

They'd slept together once. *Once!*

Shit.

His brain rattled. He had to come up with something, anything, to make sure she made the right decision.

In three weeks' time when he had a few days' break from tour, he would visit his parents in Chicago to celebrate Jenny's twentieth birthday. He had to convince Kara to come and meet his sister. See the harsh reality of why she had to terminate. It wouldn't be too late by then, would it? When could you legally put an end to this sort of thing? He'd have to google and find out.

A knock on his bedroom door made him jump. "Hunt, you ready?" Gemma's voice came through muffled. "We have to go soon. I've made you a coffee."

"Coming. I'll be out in a sec."

Shit. He had to clear his head. He had promotional duties and a show today.

For the briefest of moments, he mulled over not telling Kyle and Gemma. But they were his best friends—Kyle since elementary school and Gemma since high school. He needed their strength to get through this mess. No more secrets. This was one conversation he was not looking forward to.

He finished dressing, grabbed his coat, and stumbled out into the suite's living room. Gemma and Kyle sat together on the sofa with cups in hand. His drink sat on the coffee table, curls of steam rising into the air. Just the smell made Hunter's belly lurch. He wasn't sure if he could stomach it.

"Hunt? What's wrong?" Gemma watched him flop into the single sofa seat. "You look like you've seen a ghost."

"This is much worse." He leaned forward and rested his elbows on his knees. His gaze jumped from Kyle to Gemma as he tried to gather his composure.

"What's happened? Who were you talking to on the phone?" Gemma blew on her hot drink.

Hunter clasped his hands together, cutting off the circulation to his fingers. "Kara."

Kyle chuckled. "Did Conrad screw up one of your suit orders or something?"

Hunter squeezed his eyes shut and let out a slow breath. "No . . . she's pregnant."

"What?" Gemma sat straight. "She called you before me?"

He gulped, his throat burned with acid. His heart ached with every beat. "Yes . . . because it's mine."

Gemma choked on her coffee and Kyle slammed his cup down on the table.

"What the hell?" Kyle's pitch soared. "You? Slept with Kara? You can't stand each other."

Gemma thwacked her cup down. She grabbed the damask cushion from behind her, and bashed Hunter over the head. He covered his face, but he let Gemma beat him. He deserved every thump.

"No. No. No. Not Kara," she wailed. "Why do you always have to sleep with my friends? Why Kara?"

"Enough, babe." Kyle stood and dragged Gemma away. Exasperation hovered in his voice. "I want to hear this."

Kyle sat back down with Gemma on the sofa. He wiped his hand over his chin, scratching his stubble. The shock and disappointment on Kyle's face was another low blow to Hunter.

His stomach twisted and turned like it was trying to swap places with his intestines.

"It just happened." Hunter winced, hating his pathetic explanation.

"Oh, right," Kyle groaned. "Your cock just accidentally slipped into her pussy."

"It happened the night of your engagement party," Hunter blurted.

"Our engagement?" Hurt rippled through Gemma's eyes.

"We had a few champagnes. We were flirting. I was horny." Hunter flopped back in the sofa chair, rubbed his eyes, and gave Kyle and Gemma a blow-by-blow account of the party and the conversation he'd had with Kara on the phone.

"Surely there's some kind of mistake." Concern flooded Kyle's eyes.

"She says she hasn't been with anyone else since we slept together." He stared at the ceiling. "I told her to get rid of it."

"Yeah, I'm sure that's what every girl who's knocked up wants to hear." Kyle looked at him like he was the biggest idiot.

Maybe he was. But he didn't want this baby.

Gemma twirled the tassels on the cushion in her fingers. Deep etches formed in her brow. "What if she decides to keep it?"

Hunter sat upright, vertigo spinning his head. "She can't. She just can't."

"I'm so mad at you right now." Tears pooled in Gemma's eyes. "I can't believe you knocked up my best friend."

"I'm sorry. I wanted to tell you we'd been together, but Kara got all thingy about you being my ex."

"What?" Gemma grimaced. "I don't care about that. That was a lifetime ago."

"That's what I said." Hunter dug his fingers into his knees. "But now this. This is just fucked. I'm always careful. Guys, what am I going to do?"

Gemma came over and sat on the armrest next to him. Sliding into his side, she kissed the top of his head. "You know not to keep secrets from me because I always find out. I love you, and I'm here for you. But I know Kara a lot better than you do. You're going to have to face the fact that she may want to keep the baby. Whether you like it or not."

A chill swept over him, and he shivered. He wrapped his arms around Gemma's waist and gave her a hug. "I have to make sure that doesn't happen. Help me convince her to meet me in Chicago. Spending a weekend with my family should be enough to make her see that getting rid of the baby is the only option."

"I'll help you get her to Chicago," she said. "The rest is between the two of you."

He rested his forehead against hers. "Thank you."

The doorbell rang.

Kyle stood, smoothed out his jeans and headed for the door. He called out over his shoulder. "Hunt, whatever you need to do, we're here for you. Always will be. This is going to be one major mess to sort out."

Kyle opened the door and in charged Bec, Kate, and Sophie, followed by security—Sam, Chester, and Mick.

"Sort out what?" Kate's curious eyes jumped from Kyle, to Gemma, to him.

"Nothing." Gemma stood.

"Not yet, anyway." Hunter feigned a smile. His head still spun, and his palms sweated. How was he going to get through this?

"Good. I like to hear that." Kate adjusted her sunglasses on top of her head.

"Let's move." Sophie slapped Kyle on the back. "We have promo at River Oaks Shopping Center, then we'll head out to the concert arena. Show number thirty-seven. But who's counting?"

"Me." Bec waved them toward the door. "Three months down, six to go until the end of tour. Woohoo!"

It sounded like a lifetime, but Hunter loved touring. He got to be onstage every night in front of thousands of adoring fans. That was where he belonged. Not at home, with screaming babies and tantrums and diapers and toddler toys. *Dear God, please, please, please, make this baby disappear. Make it all go away.*

Leaving his untouched coffee behind, he picked up his backpack and led Kyle and Gemma out the door, down the elevator, and into their waiting car. As they headed out to the concert arena, Hunter closed his eyes to avoid the worry embedded on Kyle's and Gemma's faces.

He'd screwed up with Kara. Big time. But he didn't need to wallow. He would do anything and everything to stop Kara having the baby. She had to come to Chicago and meet Jenny. He'd load on the charm and fly her first-class. She had to see that there was only one course of action, so he could put this mess behind him and get on with his life.

Chapter 7

Kara touched down in chilly Chicago early Friday evening. Her blood pressure was still high after bad weather delayed her flight. Hunter had flown in earlier that day, so he picked her up in the passenger zone, driving his mom's silver Audi. After he tossed her luggage in the trunk, she slipped into the luxurious leather seat beside him and let out a long breath.

"Made it." She stuffed her purse onto the floor beside her feet.

"Good. Let's go." Hunter pulled out into the heavy traffic.

On the clogged highway, horns beeped. Slush made the going slow. As they headed toward his parents' house in North Shore, Kara's brain hurt trying to make conversation.

"How's tour?" she asked.

"Fine."

"How are Kyle and Gem?"

"Fine."

Knots twisted like twine in her gut every time he tapped his fingers against the steering wheel, shot her an anxious glance, or wiped his palms on his jeans over and over until she thought he'd wear holes in them.

Kara was under no illusions. She knew why he'd flown her here. He wanted to change her mind about having the baby. But she had her own agenda. She wanted to change his.

Whatever the cost, whatever his ultimatum, there was one thing she was sure of. She would have this baby.

Hunter turned into the driveway of his parents' home. Early December snowfall covered the gardens, making it a magical wonderland she yearned to explore. She hugged her arms around her belly and daydreams swirled around her head. Snowmen. Sled-riding. *Her* baby. But would Hunter be involved?

"You ready for this?" Hunter drove into the garage, parked next to his dad's red Ford Ranger emblazoned with a blue and yellow *Morton Home Constructions* logo, and killed the engine. "I've warned you, my old man's football crazy, Mom will smother you, and Jenny . . . well . . . she's either going to love you or hate you."

Kara stared at the door that led into the house. She'd never been around an autistic person before. But how bad could Jenny be? "I'm as ready as I'll ever be."

She went to open the car door, but Hunter caught her arm. "Um . . . my parents don't know you're pregnant. I'd like to keep it that way."

The fear in his eyes snagged her heart. This weekend wasn't going to be easy for either of them. "Okay. And remember, just because I've agreed to pretend to be your girlfriend, there's no PDA whatsoever."

His eyes flashed with shards of ice. "There has to be some or my parents will get suspicious. The odd touch. No kissing. Deal?"

She met his cold glare. Her teeth clenched. "Fine. Keep it to a minimum."

"Thank you. I hate lying to my parents, but I had to tell them we were dating, otherwise inviting you here would seem weird." He tied his hair back into a man-bun. "And sorry about the sleeping arrangements. It's only a three-bedroom house, so I'll sleep on the floor in our room or on the sofa. All right?"

Butterflies swarmed in her belly. With him in the same room as her, she'd be up all night watching him sleep—in turmoil over being pregnant with his child, being frustrated by her overactive hormones, and wanting to be anywhere but under the same roof as him.

She forced herself to nod. She could do this. Meet his family. Convince him about the baby. Pretend to be his girlfriend. Easy, right?

Hunter grabbed her carry-on case from the trunk. Taking a deep breath, she followed him into the house. Mouthwatering smells of roast beef wafted down the hall. A football game blared from somewhere deep within the home.

Galloping footsteps charged toward them. Kara jolted up straight. Shielded behind Hunter, she couldn't see what was happening. Seconds later, he was wrapped in a hug from his sister.

"Hunter." Jenny's chubby hands patted his back. "What took you so long?"

"Kara's plane was delayed." He kissed the top of her head.

Jenny stepped back. Kara smiled at the charming young lady before her. She had rosy round cheeks, bobbed dark brown hair, and a full figure, and was a good half-foot shorter than Hunter. Her piercing blue eyes never left his face.

"How was the drive to the airport?" Jenny swayed from side to side, not letting go of his forearms. "Did you take the I-294 or the I-94? It's Friday, so the I-294 should've been good. Should have taken you thirty minutes. Right?"

"Yep. I took the 294." He ruffled her hair into a shaggy mop.

Jenny giggled and slapped his hands away. She peered around his shoulders. "Are you my brother's girlfriend? I didn't invite you to my party."

"Oh." Kara glanced at Hunter. Should she hug Jenny? Shake her hand? Or what? But of course, he gave her nothing. She took a steady breath and drew on her sweetest smile. "Hunter said it would be okay for me to come."

Jenny's inquisitive eyes scanned Kara up and down, as if she was trying to work out whether she was friend or foe. Then a grin lit her face and she clapped her hands. "Okay. You can stay. Mom's about to serve dinner." Jenny pulled on Hunter's arm for him to follow, but he tugged it free.

"Just a sec," he said.

Hunter zoomed in to hover a few inches from Kara's face. Unease swam in his eyes. "We'll talk after dinner. I promise."

"Okay." She whispered and removed her scarf but stopped when Hunter's eyes drilled deeper into hers. "What?"

He stuffed his hands into the back pockets of his jeans. "Did you bring a turtleneck?"

"No. Why?" She peered down, and then it clicked. She splayed her hand across her cleavage. "Shit, is this top too low for your parents? Or is it you who can't keep your eyes off my chest?"

"Both."

The mischievous glint in his eyes sent heat rushing to her cheeks. His gaze hardened her nipples. They ached for some action, like they had on their night together where he nearly made her orgasm from tantalizing them with his hands, his mouth, and his tongue. Just thinking about it made her core clench.

"Fine," she groaned. "I'll keep my scarf on." She wrapped it around her neck and tied it into a loose knot. "Better?"

"No. But yes." He nudged her arm. "Come on. Let's get this

over with."

With tentative steps, she followed Hunter and Jenny down the hallway, past an office, a restroom, and out into the open living and kitchen area. It was huge. Modern country charm met chic urban living. His mom dashed around the kitchen, opening the white cabinets, laying plates out on the black granite countertop, and stirring pots on the stovetop. Jenny joined her dad on the floral sofa in front of the television. Kara glanced over the upright piano standing by the window. She wondered if she'd hear Hunter play during her stay. With the small Christmas tree covered in twinkling lights standing by the gas fireplace and flower arrangements adorning almost every surface, the room was filled with warmth and coziness, unlike her parents' place, which resembled a don't-touch-anything art gallery.

His mom looked up. "Oh, Hunter. You're back. I didn't hear you drive in. Stupid football is always too loud." Hunter's mom, tall and slender with azure eyes and wavy brown hair like Hunter's, wiped her hands on her apron and came around the kitchen island to greet her. "Hi, Kara. I'm Lillian. Have we met in New York?"

"Nice to meet you. And no, we've never met." Kara wiped her clammy palm on her jeans before she shook Lillian's hand.

"Have you been to Chicago before?" Lillian asked.

"No. First time." Kara fidgeted with the fringe on her scarf, sensing Hunter's eyes on her. Was she doing okay at pretending?

"I look forward to getting to know you. "Lillian smiled warmly. "You're the first girl Hunter's ever brought home. It's very exciting." Her eyes sparkled at Hunter.

What? Hunter had never brought a girlfriend home? Kara rubbed her arm. Her skin prickled. She wasn't his girlfriend either.

Catching sight of a steaming pot, Lillian's eyes widened.

"Please excuse me." She dashed over to stir the gravy. "Dinner's ready. Is it okay to serve, or Kara, would you like a few minutes to settle in?"

Kara's belly grumbled, eager for food. It had been hours since she'd eaten. "No, I'm good."

Hunter placed his hand on the small of her back, and her pulse jumped. Warmth simmered on her skin beneath his touch as he guided her over to the living room. "Dad, I'd like you to meet Kara."

"What? Oh, yes. Righto." Hunter's dad, with the build of a football tackler, shuffling forward to the edge of the seat. He propped his hand on the arm of the sofa, groaned as if every muscle in his body ached, and stood. He ran his fingers through his thick graying hair and wiped them on his Rutgers football jersey.

"Kar, this is my dad, Arthur." Hunter gave a lackluster jerk of his thumb in his dad's direction.

"Call me Art." He winked at her and thrust his huge bear-like hand out to shake. "You like football?"

"Ahh . . . no." She grimaced at the thought of having to watch a game. With her country club upbringing, her sports of choice were tennis and golf. They didn't interest her either. "I like ice hockey and ballet. I don't get to go to either anymore. Work is too busy."

"Don't lie, Kar. You went to the ballet a few weeks ago in Philly." Hunter smirked.

He remembered?

Hunter scratched his stubble. "You won't ever get me to the ballet. Couldn't think of anything more boring. Didn't know you liked men in tights, Kar?"

She plastered on a teasing smile and ran her hand up his hoodie-covered arm. "What's not to like? They're so fit, flexible, strong." His muscles, toned, taut, and terrific, tensed beneath her touch. She squeezed his bicep and her heartbeat quickened. *Hmm.* On second thought, maybe she'd like pretending to be his girlfriend. "I'm not sure you compare."

He jerked his arm free. "You've never complained about my body before."

Nope. No, she hadn't. She pursed her lips to suppress her smile.

Art chuckled and patted his belly. "I like you already, Kara. Hunter needs someone to keep his ego in check." He stepped around her and headed into the kitchen. "Lillian, would you like help with the roast?"

After taking their plates from the kitchen to the table, Kara sat next to Hunter across from Lillian and Jenny, with Art at the end. Kara's head spun with the quantity of facts and figures Jenny kept blurting. If the conversation didn't focus on football statistics and players, it centered around Hunter and his music.

"Hunter, your latest single 'Stay' had over thirty-five million views on YouTube in the first four days. That's the same as Taylor Swift's 'End Game.'" Jenny's voice boomed with pride. "Your video for 'Horizon' is still your most popular with over two billion views. Aaaand you now have over twenty-seven million subscribers to your Vevo channel."

"Really?" Hunter tilted his head. "I thought 'Escape' was our top video."

"Nah-ah." Jenny shook her head. "I think you should release 'Better' next. It's my favorite song. Isn't it, Dad?"

"Unfortunately." Art grunted over a mouth full of peas.

Lillian took a sip of her wine. "What do you do for work, Kara?"

"I'm a junior designer at Conrad's Fashion House . . . I was in couture . . ." Kara hesitated when Jenny covered her ears with her hands and rocked back and forth, "but now I work on the ready-to-wear retail lines . . ." Kara glanced at Hunter who was staring at Jenny. What was going on? "We provide Everhide . . . with . . . evening . . . and casualwear."

"La la la la la. Hmm hmm hmm hmm hmm hmm." Jenny's chants grew louder and louder.

"Jenny, put your hands down, dear," Lillian said calmly and placed her hand on Jenny's arm.

Jenny pointed a rigid finger at Kara's face. "She talks too much. Make her stop. Make her stop."

Kara's heart hammered against her ribs. She didn't know if she should say something or not. Lillian's eyes clouded with weariness, Art slouched, and Hunter's neck flushed red. Had she talked too much? She didn't think so. She'd been anxious about having dinner with Hunter and his family but hadn't rattled off her tongue.

Hunter slapped his hand on the table, making the cutlery jump. "Kara is our guest. Stop. Now."

Jenny huffed at Hunter and crossed her arms. "I don't like your girlfriend. She talks too much. She's not invited to my party anymore."

"Yes. She. Is." Hunter snatched up his glass of JD. "Apologize now or there's no present from me tomorrow."

Jenny gasped. Kara didn't think it was possible for Jenny to pout any further, but her bottom lip puffed out like a plump pillow. "Sorry Kaaa-ra."

This was what Hunter wanted Kara to see. Jenny. Her behavior. Did he think it would change her mind? He was wrong. She fumbled with the napkin in her lap. "It's okay, Jenny. I didn't mean to upset you."

Jenny lowered her chin and stared at the table.

Lillian sighed, holding her wine to her lips. "Jenny's normally not like this. She's very protective of Hunter. I think she's jealous of you."

Jenny? Jealous? All Kara had to do was allow time for Jenny

to get to know her, and Jenny would quickly realize that she was no threat.

***

After dinner, Kara and Hunter finished cleaning up, Lillian excused herself, said good night, and dragged a reluctant and sulky Jenny upstairs to bed. Art shuffled off to the den downstairs to watch more football with a six-pack of beer, shutting the door behind him. Left on edge by Jenny's outburst, Kara now had to deal with Hunter. Her nerves jittered like a jackrabbit. They were alone. Time to talk.

"Can I get you a drink?" Hunter asked, pouring himself another JD on ice.

"I'd love a glass of wine, but I'll have to settle for a cup of tea."

He gave her a that's-not-funny grunt and he filled the stove-top kettle with water.

"Would your mom have anything herbal? I'd like to avoid caffeine." The list of foods and drinks to avoid while pregnant boggled her mind. "I brought some if she doesn't."

He opened and peered into a tin on the counter and drew out a satchel. "Mint tea okay?" She nodded. He waved toward the living room. "Want to go and sit by the fire? I'll bring it over."

"Sure."

She sat on the sofa that was too soft for her liking and curled her feet beside her. She took off her scarf and placed it on the coffee table.

Carrying the drinks and the bottle of JD under his arm, Hunter flicked the kitchen lights off with his elbow, shrouding the living room in a soft glow from the two lamps on corner tables and the golden blaze from the gas fire. "You warm enough?" He held out the cup of tea. "You want me to turn up the heat? Get you a blanket?"

"No. I'm fine, thank you." She took the cup from him and inhaled the steam's sweet scent.

He stepped past her, and she caught a fine view of his ass. Tight. Grabbable. *Mmm.* Her fingers twitched. He placed his drink onto the coffee table and sat beside her, shuffling around until he faced her.

"What?" he asked.

"Nothing." She smiled and blew into her tea to cool it. If only she could do the same to her body temperature.

He pulled out his hair-tie and ruffled his fingers through his hair, sending soft waves down to the top of his shoulders. Kara ogled, gripping her cup tighter. More crazy thoughts. She'd love to thread her fingers through his hair. Comb her nails through the silky strands. Clench handfuls of it during wild, hot sex. Loads and loads of hot, *hot* sex. But that was what got her into trouble in the first place.

Hunter grabbed his JD and took a gulp. He swallowed so hard she heard it. She sensed his unease; it matched the somersaulting knots in her stomach.

"Can we talk now or are we likely to be interrupted?" Her voice came out soft, shaky.

"No, we're fine." He twisted his glass in his hands. "Mom will be lost in some book, and Dad will have a few beers and fall asleep in front of the football. He usually goes to bed about one."

"Am I imposing on your time with your parents? You don't get to see them very often."

"Nope. I wouldn't have asked you here otherwise."

"You seem to get along with your mom. What about with your dad?" She rested her elbow on the back of the sofa and propped her head against her hand.

Hunter smirked. "Not exactly. He's not a fan of my career choice. He wanted me to be a pro footballer, not a fucking rock star. When I was a kid, he tried to teach me to play ball, but I was too uncoordinated. He begged me to try out for the high school team, but instead of going to training I snuck off to play music with Kyle and Gem."

"You rebel." Sounded like herself. She'd done everything to learn her craft: art, graphics, and technical design.

He shrugged. "I didn't see it that way. I knew from about the age of six what I wanted to do. My parents were too preoccupied with Jenny most of the time to even care."

"But you've become so successful."

"They only see the late nights, the partying, drugs, and alcohol—the gossip, the women, the craze." He swayed his glass at her. The soft light from the fire refracted on the cut crystal before he downed its contents. "They don't see the hard work."

"Your parents sound like mine." She traced a flower on the sofa's printed fabric. "Mine were mortified when I wanted to go into fashion. My father wanted me to follow in his footsteps and become a trader on Wall Street, like my sister, Naomi. She's their star favorite. But I couldn't do it. He reluctantly let me go and got me into the best design college, hoping it was a passing fad. When he realized it wasn't, we continued to clash."

A quiver rippled deep in her chest, and she dropped her gaze. Maybe coming to Chicago wasn't a good idea. Because she didn't know how to handle this. The more time she spent with Hunter, talked to him on the phone, the more she realized all they had in common—they loved fashion and treasured their careers, and their family lives were not all sequins and sparkles. Was that why they got on each other's nerves? They were too much alike?

She cleared her throat. "My father knew Conrad's family and got me my internship. I had my career, and I thought I'd found my man." Old heartache threatened to escape as she stared at the faded photo from Hunter's parents' wedding on top of the piano. Lillian and Art gazed at each other, love in their eyes. Hunter's mother's long white dress was classic elegance. His father, handsome. *I want that. Will I ever find someone to marry if I'm a single mom?* "I thought Conrad and I would get married. Have a baby. Nothing has gone to plan."

Hunter puffed through his nose. "That's the biggest understatement of the year. My plans involve Gem, Kyle, and music. Nothing else. We're twenty-four years' old. At our age it's about our careers, making money, traveling, and partying, not having babies."

Kara placed her hand on her heart. "I like those things, but they don't fulfill me like I know having a baby will."

He drained the last drop from his glass and refilled it. His hand shook so much he spilled some on to the table. "You're supposed to have kids with someone you're in a relationship with. With someone who wants kids. I'm not that guy. We're not a couple. I'm certainly not marrying you. So before this goes any further, we need to put an end to this mistake."

The cold bluntness in his tone stabbed her heart. How could he hold no regard for the life growing inside her? Maybe she'd think differently if she had her health. She slid her cup onto the table and with all her inner strength, she steadied her breath. "I know your goal was to bring me here to meet Jenny and plead your case. But you're wasting your time. I talked to my doctor. The risk of our baby being autistic is low. So, with or without you, I've decided to have it."

His whole body went rigid. Fear flashed in his eyes. "You can't. Can't you see what you could be in for? Jenny was well behaved tonight. She's not always like this. My parents have suffered for twenty years raising her. There's no end in sight. I lived under the same roof as Jenny for twelve years. I still have nightmares about the violence, the screaming, the uncontrollable fits. I love Jenny, but it doesn't change the fact that she needs constant care. Our baby could be like that."

Kara closed her eyes, fighting back tears. "I understand your concerns. I really do. But this *is* my only chance to have my own baby. I'm terrified, but I'll go through this alone if I must. For me, there is no other choice."

"You *do* have a choice." His voice shook.

The knots in her neck were so tight it took effort to move her head and nod. "I'm an educated woman; I know there are options. I can't go down that path." She swallowed the dry lump in her throat. "And you need to know the reason why."

She fumbled her hands on her lap. Wrung her wrists. Tugged on the edge of her sleeves. "I've got severe endometriosis."

Hunter's face drew blank. A tick twitched in his jaw. He wriggled backward, deeper into the sofa. He closed his eyes, and a deep furrow formed between his brows. "What's that?"

"It's a condition that affects my uterus and ovaries. During my monthly cycle, tissue grows on the outside of my uterus as well as inside. It's very painful and uncomfortable. The likelihood of me falling pregnant naturally was near impossible. I tried for twelve months with Conrad and it never happened. My endo is so bad, I was booked in to have a hysterectomy after fashion week in February."

"Shit." The color blanched from his face, and he dragged his hand across his five o'clock shadow. "One night with me, using protection, was all it took to fall pregnant?" A smirk twitched at the corner of his mouth, but no humor touched his eyes. He swiveled his glass around on his knee. "I'm sorry. What you have sounds awful, but it doesn't change anything. You can't go through with this."

She turned to the heavens. "Yes. I. Can." Her calm control cracked. "This was an accident. We have to deal with it." She stabbed a finger against her leg over and over. "I know my body, my mind, and my heart. I'm going to have this baby."

"For fuck's sake." His whiskey breath crashed into her face. "Do you hear what you're saying? This will stuff up our lives."

"Why?" Fiery blood surged through her system. She threw him a daggered glare. "You don't have to be involved."

"I am involved." He slammed his glass down on the coffee table. Veins bulged like strangling vines in the side of his neck. "Why don't I get a say in the matter?"

The agony, desperation, and pain in his voice shattered her heart, but she had to stay strong. She'd hadn't done many or made many of her own decisions by herself before, but for her baby she would fight until her last breath. She grabbed a cushion from behind her and clutched it to her chest to stop herself from trembling. "You just don't. Your involvement, and how much you want to be part of our child's life, is up to you. That's the only decision you get to make."

"Gee, thanks." His tone was bitter. "You know the life I lead." He flicked his hand through the air. "I travel all the time. I live and breathe music. And . . . shit . . . when I'm home, we may operate in different social circles, but we have common friends. You can't raise our child and it not know I'm its father."

"I know." Her chin trembled. If he decided to have nothing to do with their baby it could affect her in more ways than one. Her heart squeezed, sending a shudder down her spine. "If you want nothing to do with our baby, if I have to sever ties with you and Gemma, stop dealing with you as a client at work, and even if I have to move to a different part of Manhattan so we never cross paths, I'll do it. This is how serious I am."

Hunter leaned forward, resting his elbows on his knees. His fingers sliced into his hair.

All the things she rattled off terrified her. But if she had to act on them it would be a small price to pay. "I know you were hoping for a different outcome, but this is going to happen. You're going to be a father. I need to know what you want to do so we can come to some sort of an agreement."

"What?" He looked up. Hate flared in his eyes. "You want money?"

"God, no." She gasped, splaying her hand across her chest. "I don't want your money. I'm happy to sign anything to free you of that burden if money is all you care about." Money was the furthest thing from her mind. Thanks to her father, she had more than enough of her own. "It's my baby, but I'd like it to know its daddy."

His eyes bore into her. His jaw locked. "Kar . . . I beg you. Please don't do this."

"I have to." She blinked tears from her lashes. The clock on the mantel ticked over to 11:27p.m. She couldn't go around in circles with Hunter anymore. If he kept arguing with her, she'd end up scratching his eyeballs out. Nothing would change her mind. "It's my baby. Our baby. A part of you is growing inside me. Let's work out our differences for our child's sake. Please?"

"You're asking too much of me, Kar."

She took a few shaky breaths. "I know it's a lot to take on, but we'll get there. I promise."

"I doubt it." He scoffed.

Stretching her neck from side to side, a headache loomed behind her right eye. Exhaustion seeped into every bone. It'd been a long nine hours since she left New York. "I'm tired. Can we please continue this conversation tomorrow?"

The stress hadn't left his face, but he nodded. "Yeah, okay," he whispered. "You need anything?"

"No. I'm fine."

"I'll show you to our room."

Hunter carried her luggage upstairs and grabbed her a towel for the shower. After a quick good night, he disappeared downstairs. With every step she took around the bedroom, the hollowness in her chest grew heavier. She had to face the real possibility he'd want nothing to do with the baby. While she was determined to face the challenge of being a single mom head on, was she prepared to uproot her whole life?

Her heart palpitated. Her head spun. Every day presented new obstacles. Some would be bigger than others. Some potentially drastic. But nothing and no one, not even Hunter, would stop her from having this baby. Her decision was final.

Chapter 8

Hunter didn't want to feel anymore. Since Kara went to bed, he'd only moved from the living room sofa to fetch his guitar and use the restroom. He refilled his glass with a splash of JD and gulped a mouthful. Sinking back into the sofa, he stretched out his legs on top of the coffee table, let his head fall back, and stared at the wrought-iron chandelier.

He embraced his guitar and quietly strummed at the strings, wishing the music would ease his mind. But it didn't. The reality of having a baby terrified him. After talking to Kara, he was at a loss. He'd exhausted all his options. What else could he do to change her decision? He'd tried to be reasonable and understanding. He'd hoped she'd see that getting rid of the baby was the right decision for them both. But nothing had worked.

Damn stubborn woman.

And then she threw in the whammy. Her health complications. An unexpected ace to play.

Crap.

The alcohol burned through his veins. The clock on the mantel chimed one a.m. As if on cue, the door to the den banged open and his father staggered along the hall.

Rubbing his bleary eyes, his dad yawned. "What are you still doing up?"

"You forget," Hunter grumbled. "These are my normal hours. On tour, we rarely get to bed before three or four in the morning."

"Is that why you don't get your ass out of bed until lunchtime?"

"Yep." Hunter slipped his fingers along his strings, playing low chords.

"Why the damage to the whiskey?" His father pointed to the half-empty bottle on the coffee table beside his feet. "Before you drink it all, can I join you for a nightcap?"

"I'm not in the mood for company." He wanted to be left alone. And pray for a miracle.

"Tough." His dad grabbed a crystal tumbler from the sideboard, poured a drink, and sat in the armchair opposite.

Hunter closed his eyes, concentrating on the quiet sounds of the night—the soft music from his guitar, the clock ticking, the fridge thermostat clicking on and off, the fireplace flickering. Anything to stop thinking of the baby. But thoughts hammered his head like heavy metal music. Panic gurgled up his throat and squeezed it tighter and tighter.

His dad cleared his throat. "Are you going to tell me what's bothering you?"

Hunter tipped his head forward. Why would his dad care? He hadn't any interest in his problems for the first twenty-four years of his life.

"I can't talk about it."

"You taking drugs again?"

"What?" Hunter's jaw dropped. "No. I haven't taken drugs since our first tour. That shit fucks me up. I drink; that's it. And I don't even do that on tour very often now. It screws with my vocals."

But tonight had called for it. And with two more days before he went back on the road, he intended to do even more damage to the bottle in front of him.

He reached for his whiskey, knocked it back, savored the burn in his throat, and poured another.

"What's got you in this state?" His dad's salt-and-pepper hair shone silver in the night light, making him look older than his fifty-two years. "Has it got anything to do with your girlfriend?"

Girlfriend? What a joke. "Kara? No. Yes. I mean . . . no. Yes. Fuck. I said I don't want to talk about it." He clamped his hand around the neck of his guitar. Pressure mounted in his temples.

His father chuckled. "She's got you by the short and curlies, hasn't she?"

"It's not what you think. It's complicated." *Zzzzzpt.* His fingers slipped down the strings.

"Try me."

"Dad, I can't. I don't need you telling me off again about how disappointed you are in me, or how stupid I am, or immature, or whatever else it is you hate about my life."

"Hunter . . . I'm not disappointed in you. Not at all."

Since when? His dad had always been on his case when he was younger. *Play football. Go to college. Get your head out of the clouds.* After a while, Hunter had learned to switch off.

"You chose a very different path in life to what I expected," his dad said. "You defied my advice and fought me at every turn. I may not be the best father in the world, but I never . . . never stopped you from following your dreams. I may have tried to influence you to take a different road every now and then, but you were so adamant about music. I couldn't comprehend it. But I am proud of you. Even prouder of how successful you've become."

Hunter's gut lurched as if he'd been socked in the abdomen. That was the first time he'd ever heard his dad say something like that. Was his father finally noticing that he had talent and what it took to make it in the music industry? Maybe his old man was softening in his old age.

If his dad could change, anyone could. Had his father learned to accept and deal with things that were out of his control?

Shit. Was that what Hunter had to do with Kara?

Pushing her out of his mind, Hunter shot back his whiskey. The vapors made his head spin. His dad was only sucking up because he liked his money to pay for this house they lived in, and for Jenny's care. Nothing else. "Dad, you hate my music."

"Jenny plays it aaalll the freaking time. Give me Metallica any day over the pop-rock shit you sing. If I hear 'Better' one more time, I swear I'm gonna lose my shit."

Hunter laughed. Irking his father might help him forget his troubles for a while. Striking the notes on his guitar, he softly sang.

> *I knew my life would get better, the minute you walked away,*
> *So pack your bags, get out of here, I've got nothing left to say.*
> *My friends all never liked you, I should have taken note,*
> *But now I see their point of view, guess they get my vote.*

His father shook his head and covered one ear with his hand. Hunter kept going, drawing from deeper down in his diaphragm.

> *Oh, now I know it took me way too long to see,*
> *That you're an evil spirit, trying to live inside of me.*
> *I've found someone who's better, in every possible way,*
> *So good riddance to you and your shit, I've seen the light of day.*

Tapping his foot, and with a huge grin, his dad joined in the song.

> *Took me a while to find my strength and pick myself back up,*
> *Wasn't giving up on love even though I'd lost my luck,*
> *But the good thing is I don't care for you, no, I do not give a fuck.*

His dad's voice was flat, off-key, and sore to the ear, but Hunter kept on singing.

> *Now I've found someone new, who put me back together,*
> *Taken away the heartache, and I couldn't feel much better.*
> *Life is great without you, stop calling me on the phone,*
> *We're well and truly over, babe, my heart's found a new home.*

> *Oh, now I see who you really are,*
> *Wasted too much time with you,*
> *Now I've raised the bar.*

"Why do you have to write such God damn catchy tunes?" His dad downed his whiskey and poured another shot.

Hunter glanced at a photo on the piano of him, Kyle, and Gemma at the Grammys. "It might be catchy but the lyrics are therapeutic. I wrote that song with Kyle and Gem after being dumped by Amie. Bitch from hell." It always reminded him not to get involved with someone ever again. That way he could never be hurt. People thought he was shallow, but Amie was worse. All she'd ever wanted was a career, money, and men. He'd been blind to it all and had fallen for her hard. He'd never make the same mistakes again.

"You shouldn't have screwed your manager. You haven't slept with the new one, have you?" His dad's eyes filled with concern. "What's her name? Sophie?"

"No . . . I've got the wrong genitalia for Sophie. I've enough women throwing themselves at me without having to waste my time and effort on those that are gay."

"So, I'll ask again." His dad swirled his whiskey around in the glass. "What's the story with the one upstairs?"

Kara wasn't a story; she was his worst fucking nightmare.

Hunter put his guitar down, leaned forward, and rested his elbows on his thighs. "She's a friend of Gem's."

"And?" His dad rolled his hand through the air.

"I've fucked up." His voice snagged low in his throat. His heart pummeled against his ribs. "I mean it. I screwed up, big time, and I don't know what to do."

He'd searched his brain over and over again for another valid reason for Kara to see his way was right. Nothing came to light. He was doomed.

"It can't be that bad?"

Hunter ignored the arrogance in his father's tone. "Worse. First, she's just a friend, *not* my girlfriend. Second, she's pregnant . . . and it's mine."

His father choked and spluttered on a mouthful of drink. He sucked in a huge breath and thumped his fist on his chest.

Hunter braced himself, prepared for the worst ear-bashing of his life. He deserved every bit of it and more. But his dad just sat there, not saying anything. It made Hunter's stomach curdle and unnerved him, because his dad always had an opinion.

He couldn't take his father's vacant gaze any longer. "It happened at Kyle and Gem's engagement party. Before you go off at me for being reckless"—Hunter threw up his hand—"we used protection. But it failed."

"Didn't you learn from your last accusations?" The disdain that was so often present in his father's tone returned. "If you've slept with half the number of women I hear about, I'm amazed it hasn't happened sooner."

"Not. Helping. Dad."

"Is she after your money?"

"No. She's loaded. Her dad is some guru on Wall Street. He gave her and her sister portfolios worth a gazillion dollars each on their eighteenth birthdays."

"Lucky her." His father rolled his eyes and wiped his hand over his mouth. "But pregnant, hey?"

"I don't want it. I told her to get rid of it. But . . . she wants to have the baby. Dad?" He never asked his dad for advice, but now he felt like getting down on his knees and begging. "What am I going to do? I'm scared. Scared because it could turn out like Jenny. I brought Kara here hoping that meeting Jenny would make the decision a no-brainer. I know it's selfish and wrong to think this way, but I can't help it. It's hard after what I grew up with. I've seen how much you and Mom have suffered over the years."

"I'm not going to lie to you. It hasn't been easy." The sorrow in his dad's voice struck Hunter hard. "Some days, it felt like we took two steps forward and twenty back. But Jenny's grown so much. She goes to school. She's got a job at the nursery. And she has time at the group home."

Hunter wished he could do more to relieve the burden and hellish days for the families who had to live with autism. With two homes established here in Chicago, and more homes opening soon, his Collins Foundation was only one note trying to make a difference to a symphony of songs. He knew his efforts made a small difference to people's lives.

"It's got better," his dad continued. "Life has changed for Jenny since moving from New Jersey. The school here has been the best thing for her. But, like in all families, there are good and bad days."

Hunter closed his eyes, trying to erase the nightmares from

his memory. "I remember I used to lock myself in my room when Jenny had one of her turns, or to get away from you and Mom fighting." He'd huddle under his bed with his pillow over his head, trying to block the screams and shouts. "Music saved me."

"I know it did. Hearing you play and sing tested my patience to a whole new level." His dad's grin was more of a pained smirk. "But please understand, we've never regretted having Jenny or you. Ever."

"I didn't exist." The hollowness in his chest ached. "You gave up everything for her."

"Like what?"

"You always talked about the school here. The moment I offered to pay, you moved halfway across the country for her. Your life revolves around her. She'll always be your responsibility. There's no end in sight."

Pain flickered through his dad's eyes. "No, no, there's not. We're fortunate to have help and support. But surely even you can see Jenny's changed. She kicks my ass in football tips— knows every statistic under the sun. She's memorized every lyric and detail of your music, from your first gig, to your biggest concerts, to every date and venue of your tour schedule. She's like my own personal Wikipedia. Stop seeing the terrible things about Jenny and look at the good."

Hunter recalled talking to her on the phone. Jenny would rattle off the highlights for him to see in the cities he'd visit on tour. Unfortunately, with their busy schedule and stalking fans, he hadn't see any of them. "I do see those things. But she's a constant handful."

"So were you. Just in a different way. I know we weren't always there for you. Doesn't mean we didn't love you. You always craved our attention—you'd perform in the living room, sing, and play for us. When Jenny got worse, you found what you needed in music and we supported you. There were the constant singing, guitar, and piano lessons. School musicals and performances. Your mother and I had to find extra work to pay for it all."

Hunter's lips twitched. "That was for Jenny's care. You did everything possible to keep me out of your way." *Great way of showing love.*

His dad humphed. "Your version of the truth is incorrect. Not everything was about your sister. We tried to give you what you wanted and more."

Had that been the case? Were his memories skewed?

Maybe.

Maybe things weren't as he remembered.

"Somedays you worried me more than Jenny ever did." His father lowered his chin. "Especially when you started playing gigs and signed that record deal with SureHaven. The touring, the girls, the drinking, the drugs . . ."

"I told you. I don't do drugs. Not since I cut my arm crashing through that glass door in London on our first tour." He rubbed the zigzag silver scar that ran down his left forearm. "It scared the living crap out of me that I'd never play again. Music is my life. Kyle and Gem—we live and breathe it together. There's no room for anything or anyone else."

Shit. Was that how strongly Kara felt about having a baby?

"It sounds like that will have to change." His dad tugged on his ear. "I can't say I'm excited at becoming a grandfather. But wow . . . a grandbaby. If Kara's adamant about having it and it's yours, you need to take responsibility. Time to be a man, son."

"I can't have a child." Hunter ripped one hand through his hair. "I'm not in love with her, and she's not in love with me."

"Didn't say you had to be." His father shrugged. "It's about being responsible for your actions. You help that girl out in whatever way you can. I know you had a rough time growing up with Jenny, but it gave you strength and a heart of gold, which you don't let people see often enough. You hide behind your ego too much. But don't miss out on something wonderful because you're too scared to take a risk. You have some tough decisions ahead of you. Welcome to the world of being a grown-up." His dad placed his empty glass on the table and stood. "It's late. I gotta go to bed. Party day tomorrow. Oh . . . and I don't want to be around when you tell your mother. Remember, I like my roof where it is."

Guilt crawled beneath his skin. *Crap.* Now he had to tell his mom. Just when he'd said to Kara he didn't want to say anything. But if she was going to have the baby, they'd find out sooner or later.

Hunter shrank back into the sofa. Telling his mom would be tough. She'd be over-the-top excited or filled with utter disappointment because he and Kara weren't together.

His dad scuffed his slippers against the floorboards and headed up the stairs, humming the tune to "Better." Hunter couldn't help but grin.

The moment his father disappeared down the upstairs hallway, Hunter's reality crashed into him—the nightmare he'd tried to deny, ignore, and drown with booze. There was no escape. Numbness only lasted so long. Now, he felt everything.

He clutched at the pain in his chest. The night's darkness pressed heavily into him. Dizziness swam through his head. He leaned forward and grinded his palms against his eyes. *Damn it!* This weekend hadn't gone to plan.

He had no other options. No other card to play. He'd lost the battle.

He was going to be a daddy. A fucking daddy.

His heart jolted as if he'd been zapped with high-voltage electricity.

There was no way out of this. How was he going to deal

with this impossible situation?

Kara was going to have the baby. *His* baby.

Fuck.

Shit.

Fuck.

Chapter 9

Kara couldn't get out of the bedroom fast enough. Distance and clarity were needed. Having Hunter sprawled out on the floor beside the queen-sized bed had her hormones overheating. She'd come to Chicago wanting him to be involved in their child's life, but maybe it was better he wasn't. Seeing him lying there wrapped in a quilt, with the stress from last night's conversation no longer evident on his face, listening to him breathe . . . The last thing she needed to do was develop feelings for him. She put on her slippers and shrugged her fuchsia hoodie over her pajamas in record speed. Grabbing a chamomile teabag from her suitcase, she made her way to the kitchen.

The smell of pancakes hit her. Her hand shot to her tummy. Morning sickness rolled in her belly like a boat on restless waves. There was no way she could let Hunter's mom know she was suffering.

"Morning, Kara. Sleep well?" Lillian, bright and cheery, stood in front of the cooktop with a spatula in her hand. A dusting of flour smeared her cheek. "Would you like some pancakes?"

Kara slid onto a stool at the kitchen counter. She rubbed her belly and burped under her breath. "No, thank you. But I'd love a cup of tea."

"Sure." Lillian grabbed the kettle and filled it. "What did you two get up to last night? Have a late one?"

"Yeah. We sat up talking. It was nice." *Liar.* It had been a long, emotional night with no closure. What could she do to make his no become a yes?

"Art's taken Jenny out to pick up the cake for the party. Jenny insisted on pancakes when she gets home. Are you sure you don't want any?"

"No. Thank you." The sweet smell of the fresh batter assaulted Kara. She closed her eyes and fought down the nausea swirling in her belly. *Oh no.* She leapt off the stool, dashed down the hallway to the restroom, and vomited.

Shit.

A cold sweat broke out on her brow. Kara looked in the mirror; her skin held a greenish tinge. *Crap.* With shaking hands, she splashed water on her face and tried to de-redden her eyes. *What a mess. How embarrassing.*

On wobbly legs, she dragged herself back to the kitchen where her cup of tea sat waiting.

"You okay?" Lillian's sympathetic smile did nothing to ease Kara's shame.

"I'm sorry. I must've drunk too much last night."

Lillian made a disconcerting *hmm-hmm* sound in her throat—the one that someone made when they knew you were lying. "I don't recall seeing you have any alcohol." Lillian flipped a pancake and placed it on the cooling rack.

Kara suspended her cup of tea halfway to her mouth. *Did Lillian suspect something?* Please no. Kara needed to talk to Hunter, not sit here and skirt around the truth with his mom. Her blood pressure had not come down since landing in Chicago.

Loud footsteps trudged down the staircase, and Hunter strolled into the kitchen dressed in long navy pajama pants and his faded red hoodie. He headed straight for his mom and gave her a kiss on the cheek.

"You're up early." Lillian's tone was full of playful sarcasm. "It's only ten thirty."

"Funny as always, Mom." Hunter grunted and scooted over toward Kara. He placed his hands on the countertop and leaned forward. His sexy bed hair fell forward across his face. "How are you this morning?"

Since his broad shoulders were blocking the view from his mother's watchful gaze, she whispered, "I'm sick."

Lillian peered around Hunter. "Do you want any pancakes, Hunter?"

When he stood straight, Lillian's curious gaze jumped back and forth between the two of them. Kara slouched in her chair under the weight of her suspicions.

"Nah. I'll have a Pop-Tart," he said. "I never get to eat them on tour. Nutritionists controlling what we eat sucks. I need a total sugar blow-out."

Kara's stomach curdled at the thought of a Pop-Tart. She swallowed hard, resisting the urge to be sick again.

Lillian grabbed a Pop-Tart from the pantry and slipped it into the toaster. "You want one, Kara?"

"No. I'm not much of a breakfast eater." She usually ate a feast every morning, but since falling pregnant she couldn't tolerate anything. "I'll just have tea."

"Okay. But you might want to try some ginger and lemon tea. It can help to settle your tummy." Her gaze was full of compassion. "You know . . . in your condition . . . of being hungover and all."

Hunter's face paled. His eyes flared wide at Kara, and he mouthed, *"Did you tell her?"*

"No," Kara whispered.

"Kara looks like she could use some fresh air." Lillian patted Hunter on the shoulder. "Why don't the two of you go out somewhere and be back after lunch for the party?"

"Mom, I can't just *go out*." Hunter waved his hand toward the front door.

"I'm sure you can think of somewhere to go where you don't need an army of security with you." She handed him his toasted Pop-Tart on a plate. "There are no photographers lurking at the front gate like last time."

A shiver shot up Kara's spine. She hadn't considered the paparazzi. But right now, she was more worried about throwing up. The aroma from the toasted berry-flavored Pop-Tart flipped her stomach. She jumped up from the chair. "I think I'll go get changed."

Hunter stuffed the rest of the Pop-Tart in his mouth and licked the crumbs from his fingers. "Me too. Let's go for a walk. There's a park down the end of the road."

Kara rushed for the stairs. "Excellent. Just hurry."

***

The overcast sky offered no warmth. Rugged up in her new red, thigh-length Conrad Designs puffer jacket, beanie, scarf, and fleece-lined leather gloves, Kara strolled along the tree-lined street and inhaled the cold, fresh air. The chill on her cheeks was like an icepack to a fevered forehead.

Alone with Hunter again.

He strode alongside her, his shoulders rounded. He'd tucked his hands deep into the pockets of his navy anorak. If he wasn't giving her concerned looks, he was searching the road—forward, back, and down any side street they crossed. On the lookout for the paparazzi. His caution set her paranoia into overdrive.

"Is it okay for us to go out?" On constant guard, she scanned every hedge, every car, and every fat tree trunk.

"There was no one lurking at the house. We'll be fine. Trust me." His posture relaxed, and his gait hit cruise speed. "I'm an expert at hiding when I have to. I just prefer not to. I'll do my best today to avoid attention if you like."

"Yes, thanks. I don't want to be your next gossip-fueled headline." Kara skipped over a muddy puddle. Gossip would only be another drama to add to her excessively long list.

"We can agree on something. No press." Snarkiness clipped his tone, but then it softened. "Are you feeling any better yet?"

"I'm getting there." Kara ducked to avoid a bare branch covered in snow. "I think your mom suspected something."

"Yeah. I got that vibe, too." Hunter's breath misted in the air. His nose glowed red in the cold. "I slipped up and told Dad last night. He wouldn't have said anything to Mom yet. But now I'll have to tell her before we leave."

"What? It's too early. I'm only eight weeks." She swore under her breath. And he was the one who hadn't wanted to tell anyone. *Grr.* "I haven't told my parents yet. They're so not going to be happy."

She could picture the mortified looks on her parents' faces. Her mom would pop a Valium or two. Her dad would be beyond furious, possibly even disown her. So be it.

"Although I share that sentiment . . ." Hunter kicked at a mound of snow on the edge of a driveway, sending snow spraying through the air. " . . . why not?"

"You're everything my parents despise. You're a long-haired rock star with a wild reputation. You haven't gone to college. You come from the wrong side of the river. And you drink too much. Oh . . . and you have tattoos. My mother loathes tattoos."

"If I recall correctly . . ." Hunter flashed her a smoldering grin, holding out his hand to help her across the icy road,

" . . . you said you liked 'em."

Even through gloves, his touch sent warmth shooting up her arm. She held on because she didn't want to fall. "What I like and what my parents like are extreme opposites."

She bit her bottom lip hard to prevent a smile from creeping across her face. She loved his tattoos. Especially the one on the back of his shoulder of the serpent wrapped around a guitar. Totally wicked.

Stepping onto the sidewalk, her foot slipped. *Ice!* She lost her balance. *Argh!* Her hands flailed.

Hunter caught her arms and held her until she regained her footing. Her pulse quickened when his face hovered inches from hers. Her breath misted with his.

His gaze intensified. "You wouldn't have to tell your parents about the baby if you changed your mind."

"No chance of that happening." She tugged free of his hold and headed toward the coffee shop.

To avoid Hunter attracting attention, she grabbed two hot chocolates and met him at the park's entrance.

He stood under a snow-covered conifer and winked at her. "Told you I can go unnoticed."

Damn his smile. It warmed her from the inside out. But enough with niceties. It was time to talk. Again.

With a shaky hand she handed him the hot chocolate, and they headed into the park along the wide path. Snow crunched under each footstep. The chilly air held a musty, damp-earthy smell that tickled her nostrils.

Kara peeked a sideways glance at Hunter. "Are you still upset after our talk last night?"

He sighed, his gaze turned to the cloudy sky. "I'm trying to process everything. Can we have time-out and not talk about babies?"

"What? Our baby is why I'm here. It's not going to go away."

"I know. But I'm on a rare day off from tour, not stuck in a hotel or on a tour bus, and I don't have people chasing me. Can we just enjoy our walk?" He took a sip of his drink and pointed into the distance. "There's a lake up ahead over the ridge that only the locals know about. Let's go check it out."

She inhaled the cold air to clear her head. "Fine." She couldn't deny that a break from stressing might do her and her baby some good. "Lead the way."

Over the rise, the small lake stretched out before them, frozen solid. A few parents and children darted over its surface, their skates scratching loudly on the ice.

"Wow. Ice skating. I haven't skated in years." Kara leaned her elbows on the wooden railing and watched the people glide in a semi-coordinated circle. Kids zipped in and around their parents. "I was on the girl's ice hockey team in high school."

"You were what?" His eyebrows shot skyward. His cup hovered an inch from his lips.

His perfect lips. And mouth. And tongue. Oh, that tongue that made her insides coil.

"Yep." She pulled off the lid from her chocolate and drained the last mouthful from the cup. "I loved ballet, but I was too tall. My parents assured me I'd never have a career in dance. They insisted I do a sport. They tried to push me into tennis and golf, but the moment I saw the ice hockey team at our local rink, I wanted to play. I begged and pleaded, and eventually they let me try out."

"I did *not* pick you to be a brutal hockey player." Hunter shook his head. His eyes glistened with intrigue. "You're quite the rebel. You keep on surprising me, Kar. I thought you were more of the day-spa, don't-break-a-nail, stay-at-home type."

"I stopped doing many things I loved when I was with Conrad. He was the hermit, not me. Remember when Gem, Lexi, and I went on holidays after your last tour? It was me who suggested the snow. I love snowboarding. Poor Gemma was stuck in the cabin the whole time with her broken leg."

"Thanks for the painful reminder." Hunter scuffed his boot against the ground. "I still feel bad about that."

"You should." She play-punched him in the arm. "You crashed an equipment truck into her."

"Yes. I'm beginning to realize I'm accident prone." He took her empty cup and threw it in the trash can with his.

"Come on, let's keep going." He caught her by the arm. "No, wait. You have chocolate on your lip." He pointed to the side of her mouth.

Her hand shot up to wipe it off.

He shook his head and chuckled. "You're missing it by a mile. Here, let me."

He stepped in close and wiped his gloved fingertip over her skin, half an inch from her lips. But rather than a quick it's-gone stroke, he kept brushing his thumb against her cheek. The blue in his eyes darkened and a half-smile formed on his lips. "What am I going to do with you, Kar?"

Her skin ignited beneath his touch, and her knees weakened. Her body was like a disobedient dog. It never did what it was supposed to. Every cell inside her begged for him to kiss her, hard, hot, and heated.

There was no chance of that happening. Not when he despised her for wanting their baby.

She needed to put distance between her and him. Yes, distance. A lot of distance. "Walk." She lowered her gaze and drew his hand away. "We need to walk."

"Mmm." He cleared his throat and turned along the path. "Good idea."

With her mind swirling, Kara strode along. Her puffer jacket swooshed against her thighs. A hundred yards from the edge of the lake, she reached a wide section of the park lined with trees and gentle slopes. She stopped when she realized Hunter was no longer beside her.

She turned to see where he was. Before she had time to think, a snowball hit her, square in the face. *What the hell?*

"Woohoo. Gotcha!" Hunter cheered, his hands pumping the air.

Oh no, he doesn't. Two could play this game. There was no way she was going down without a fight. "Why . . . you . . ." Scurrying onto the snow, she scooped up a handful. Mushing the snow into a ball, she threw it at him with force. It splattered against his shoulder. Another ball hit her in the back, and a shriek burst from her lungs. Her next ball hit him fair in the neck.

"Argh, that's freezing," Hunter cried out, loosening his scarf and shaking away the snow.

She pelted him with two more balls.

He charged at her with a battle cry, throwing snow, and chasing her over the slope.

Her heart pounded with each sidestep and dodging dash. She laughed—she hadn't had so much fun in months. She jumped to a stop and made another ball.

"Oh no you don't." He ducked to avoid her next assault. But he tripped, tumbled over, and slid backward down the hillside before coming to a halt.

He pulled his scarf down and winced in pain. "Ow, my butt."

When he didn't get up, Kara rushed over. Was he really hurt? She dropped to her knees, resting them on the edge of her coat. "Are you okay? Is your butt insured?"

"No." Agony strained his voice. "Only my face."

Kara thumped him in the shoulder. "You and your million-dollar face." He wasn't joking about being insured, but it made her laugh. *He* made her laugh.

Covered in snow, he rolled onto his side and rubbed his ass.

"I'll be fine. Just give me a sec."

The next thing Kara knew, Hunter's arm flung around her waist and pushed her down onto the hill. Her squeal echoed across the park.

"That's for making me fall." He pinned her hands beside her head.

"What? Me? You started it." She twisted and tried to tug her arms free, but he was too strong. After several attempts, she gave up and just lay there, giggling.

But then she stopped.

His face loomed a few inches from hers. His eyes glimmered with victory. Snowflakes dotted the loose strands of hair that had strayed from underneath his beanie. His smile was as wide as Lake Michigan. His cheeks blazed red.

Her heartbeat rose, so did her body temperature. *Oh no.*

The muscles in his arms slackened. Her breath hitched and misted against his. The delicious aroma of chocolate filled the air.

Her gaze fell to his mouth. His lips, dark pink, mesmerized her. She wanted them, sweet and delicious, against her mouth. She wanted him to consume her and taste the chocolate on his tongue. She wanted to do many things that involved chocolate and him. Drinking it wasn't one of them.

The cutest of smiles inched across his mouth. "Do you concede?"

Oh, I want to concede my whole body to you. But she couldn't. She'd had enough of her hormones, lust, and frustration playing havoc. Her mind was clear. Enough games. And games were all Hunter ever played.

"Never." In a move she'd learned in high school self-defense classes, she tore her hands free of his hold, grabbed him by the front of his anorak, hoisted him forward, and body rolled him over the top of her. His back hit the ground with a thud and she straddled his hips. Grabbing a fist full of his coat in one hand, she pointed at him with the other. "Are we going to keep playing this game, or do *you* concede and *I* win?"

His eyes widened. "How the hell did you do that?" He held up his hands in surrender. "That was fucking incredible. My god, woman, who are you?"

"Your worst nightmare." She flicked her ponytail back over her shoulder.

"You got that right." He slapped her on the thigh. "Now get off me and help me up. We're getting wet. It's time to head home."

She slid off his hips and stood. Her mind filled with images of him underneath her. She could feel his body between her thighs. The want for him ached deep within her core. *Stupid hormones.* She brushed the snow off her jacket and pressed her cold gloves to her face, hoping the walk home, the darkening cloud cover, and the dropping temperature and falling snowflakes would put an end to her overzealous thoughts.

He'd made her laugh. He always did. But this time, it wasn't from his smartass banter or stupid ego taking over; it was from hanging out with him, being spontaneous, and having some crazy fun.

He was different. Kind. Civil. Why couldn't he be like this all the time? She'd known egotistical Hunter for so long, she struggled to comprehend this new side. It gave her hope that behind his guarded wall he did have a heart, and he'd support the baby. Or was that wishful thinking?

With each step closer to his home, her pace slowed. The tightness in her chest returned. With Jenny's party on this afternoon, she only had tonight to talk to Hunter about the baby and find out what he wanted to do.

She hated having to do it, but to avoid stress and drawn-out complications, she had to give him an ultimatum.

Yes or no?

Are you involved, or not?

Timeout was over.

She needed to know. And she needed to know tonight.

Chapter 10

Kara, conscious of the time, followed Hunter into the back of the house and hung her wet jacket next to his in the mudroom. In less than twenty-four hours she'd be heading back to New York, with or without Hunter's support.

Delicious smells of home-baking filled the air. Was that apple pie? Kara's belly rumbled. This time it wasn't from morning sickness. This time it was from hunger.

Jenny screamed from the kitchen. It vaporized all Kara's thoughts.

"No. I won't take it."

"Jenny. Stop. Take your medicine." Lillian's firm voice held a hint of exasperation.

Kara followed Hunter inside. She froze in the doorway and gaped. Jenny stood by the counter, swinging her fists wildly and pounding into Lillian's arm.

Hunter dashed over. "Jenny. No." He grabbed her, dragged her back and shoved her onto one of the kitchen stools. He held her steady until she stopped fighting.

"It's okay, Hunter." Lillian rubbed her red arm. "She doesn't like the taste of this tablet." She placed the white pill in a medicine cup and put it down in front of Jenny. "Take it. Now."

Kara eased forward, eying the bruises on Lillian's arm. Horror rippled through her bones. Was this a regular occurrence? Was Jenny violent at times?

"Jenny, I'll get you some water." Hunter dove into the fridge to grab a bottle and placed it in front of her. "Take your medicine. Hurry up. No party until you do."

Jenny reluctantly swallowed the pill and pulled a sour face. Hunter came over to Kara and placed his hands on her arms. "Medicine time can be a drama. You okay?"

Fear, anguish, naivety and sympathy barreled together and wrapped around Kara's spine. Shaken and stirred, she managed to nod. "Yes."

"Oh no. The pie." Lillian reached for the potholders and dived toward the oven. She reefed open the door and a plume of smoke billowed up to the ceiling. After fanning it away, she ripped out an overcooked pie.

"Yuck. What's that?" Jenny pointed to the dish on the countertop.

"It's a pumpkin pie. Hunter loves it. I thought I'd make one since he missed Thanksgiving."

"Aw, Mom. Thanks. You didn't have to." He swept over to her and gave her a hug. "It's only the crust that's burnt. Cut that off and I'll still eat it." A huge grin slid across his face, and he winked in Kara's direction.

Humph. Kara crossed her arms. *Always full of charm. Even for his mom.*

Jenny wailed. "I hate pumpkin pie. It's yucky." With a brush of her arm, she sent the hot dish tumbling to the floor. *Smash!* Lillian, Kara, and Hunter jumped back to avoid being sprayed with scalding orange goo. Jenny screeched, "*Ow*," clutching her burnt fingers.

Kara didn't move, worried that Jenny would send something else flying off the counter if she as much batted an eyelid.

"JENNY." Lillian's cheeks flared red. Kara didn't know if it was embarrassment or rage. "Go to your room. Now."

"No," Jenny blurted. But the minute Lillian took a step forward, she jumped off the stool and stormed off.

"Mom, I'll clean it up." Hunter fetched the roll of paper towels from beside the cooktop. "You go deal with Jenny. Check her hand."

Lillian nodded, her face pale. Untying her apron, she rushed out of the kitchen.

Hunter fell to his knees and scooped up the pie. "Another fine day in the house of Collins."

Kara grabbed the dishcloth with shaky hands and helped. "It's okay."

"No. It's not." His anguish tugged at her heart. "This is what you could be in for. Are you sure you still want to have my child?" He didn't look up, just kept scrubbing the floor.

Seeing Jenny's outbursts had certainly unnerved Kara. How would she cope if she had to face something like this? A child with special needs? A disability?

Like Lillian. Lillian had been strong but caring. Firm, but stoic. Loving, no matter what. The kind of mother Kara wanted to be.

Hunter had done Kara a favor by bringing her here. It had brought her out of her sheltered world and helped her mentally prepare for the fact something drastic might go wrong.

She placed her hand on his. An ache swelled in her chest. She understood his pain and fears, but it didn't shift her mindset. "Yes. I am."

***

By two o'clock in the afternoon, the party was underway. Jenny was a changed woman. She hugged and kissed everyone when they arrived and ripped into presents the second one was placed in her hand. Lillian had changed, too. After knocking back a few of Hunter's JDs, gone was the Martha Stewart wannabe, and in her place was a hollering, screeching Courtney Love. Kara giggled each time Lillian's voice grew louder and louder.

Twenty-five people filled the open-plan living area and space outside on the heated pergola. Jenny blasted Everhide's latest album through the speakers and danced in the middle of the living room with two of her friends.

After birthday cake, Hunter held everyone entranced by playing the piano. He sang "Happy Birthday," and churned out several of Jenny's favorite songs. Kara had seen Hunter sing many times, but in this intimate environment he was more captivating than ever. With every note he sang, butterflies took flight in her belly and weakened her knees. She steadied herself against the dining table chair and took a sweeping look around the room—at Hunter, his family, and their friends. An emptiness flared inside her chest. She wanted a family and friends like this.

One day she'd find a man who felt the same way. Would that dream ever become a reality as a single mom?

Being alone scared her, but she had to embrace her future. She had to push her swinging emotions for Hunter aside and prepare herself for the worst. For the sake of her child, she was ready. Ready to be a mom, no matter what.

***

At the end of the party, Kara helped Hunter put the last of the leftovers away. His nervous gaze jumped from hers to the clock on the wall. 8.10pm. With Jenny curled up asleep on the sofa, Art and two of his mates in the den watching football, and Lillian at the table polishing off a bottle of wine with one of her friends, now seemed the perfect time to talk to Hunter.

She placed her hand on her belly and took a deep breath. "It's getting late. We need to talk."

He lowered his chin and nodded. "I know. Can I get you anything to eat or drink?"

"No, but I need to sit." Her feet ached from standing for most of the afternoon.

"Sure. I'll grab a refill."

He poured a half glass of JD into a fresh crystal tumbler, and she followed him down the hallway and sat next to him on the bottom step of the staircase.

He looked as tired as she felt. She wanted to brush her fingers across his brow and erase his worry lines. Run her hand over his tensed jaw to smooth away his fears about the baby. Curl her arm around his and rest her weary head against his shoulder. But that would be too intimate. Too friendly. Too much.

He sipped his drink, and the ice clinked against the side of the glass. "Thanks for today. You survived?"

"Yeah. I've actually had a good time." Kara rested her elbow on the step behind her. "I wasn't expecting that this weekend."

"Neither was I." His grin flickered, then disappeared. He gulped a mouthful of JD and stared into his glass. "I haven't been able to stop thinking about you . . . I mean . . . the baby, all day. It's like this constant drumming in the back of my head."

She tugged the long sleeves of her gold-knit top over her hands and wrapped her arms around herself. No more games and distractions. It was decision time. To hell with the consequences. "Same. This is not how I planned to have a baby. But it's my one and only shot. I don't want to stress anymore. So, if you want no part in this, I need to know now so I can get on with my life."

Hunter stared at the wall opposite the stairs. Faded family

holiday photos in mismatched frames adorned its length. A gangling teenage Hunter with a mass of unruly curls and stick-thin frame on the beach brought a smile to her face. That awkward kid had been voted "Sexiest Man Alive." Twice.

With a hardened face, Hunter's eyes glassed over. "I could never ask you to move or stop hanging out with Gem. She'd kill me. I'm not that much of an asshole." He closed his eyes. "I can't comprehend why you want to do this. I hate that there's no way out." He turned to face her and sucked air hard into his lungs. "I don't want to fight anymore. If I can't change your mind, and you're going to have this baby, I have to do what's right. I have to support you."

Her heart leaped and his words rang in her ears. She stared into the depths of his blue eyes for what seemed like a minute but in reality, it was only a few seconds. She lunged forward and threw her arms around his neck. "Thank you."

Their baby would know its daddy. She couldn't ask for anything more.

But her relief was short-lived. When she slid back and saw Hunter's face, her stomach fell through the floor.

Gone was Hunter's ego, the playful glint that resided in his eyes. Instead, he sat there, broken. His eyes were swollen with tears. His brow was furrowed, and his shoulders slumped.

Her heart cinched, like it was laced too tightly into a corset. She'd done this to him. She wanted to reach out and comfort him, and tell him everything between them would be all right, but how could she when she didn't know that for sure?

He shuffled back on the step. He rested his arms on his bent knees, and his head drooped forward. His glass looked as if it would slip from his fingertips at any moment. "I'll have to discuss things with my lawyers." His voice was so low and deep it was hard to hear. "But as for actual involvement when it's born . . . I don't have an answer yet. I don't know what you expect of me."

She wanted the fairytale ending, but he was no knight in shining armor. And no doubt they would have to make compromises to find common ground. But this was a start down the right path. "I'll be near due when you finish tour. Do you want any updates and scan details before then? Do you want to be at the birth?"

The color drained from his face. "Shit . . . I don't know. We have a couple of weeks off after tour, then promo. Our calendar for the next two years is chaotic. I have no consistent schedule. I can't see how we're going to make this work."

She curled her arms around her legs and placed her cheek on her knee. She knew he led a hectic life. When he was around, she'd ensure that their child was available to him. He wanted to be involved; that was what mattered. "We've got seven and a half months to work everything out."

He downed his JD in one gulp, screwed up his eyes, and gasped. "Ahh. I needed that."

He licked his lips, leaving a sheen of moisture glistening in the dim light.

Her core flared hot and needy. *Oh God. Not again.* Damn her body. She wanted his hands on her skin and to taste the whiskey on his lips. To entwine her fingers in his hair and crush his chest against hers. Preferably naked. She tightened her grip on her legs and dug her fingers into her flesh—anything to help distract her from having these crazy thoughts in the middle of a serious conversation.

Concern flashed in his eyes. "You okay?"

Drawing air deep into her lungs, she ignored her raging hormones. She nodded and slid closer to him, curled her arm under his, and rested her head against his shoulder. To hell with not showing she cared. "Yeah. I'm just happy. Happy for our baby. Hunt, after seeing you with Jenny, I know you will be a good father."

She rubbed his arm with languid strokes. His long-sleeved T-shirt slipped and glided beneath her fingertips. Muscles, hard as rock, tensed beneath the fabric.

She squeezed his biceps. *Mmm . . .*

Shit! Did that sound come out of her mouth?

"What are you doing?" He looked at her hand.

"Sorry." Heat burned her cheeks and ears. She pulled away and fiddled with her ponytail. "I can't help it. My hormones are out of control. I keep getting . . . horny. Being around you is not helping the situation."

"You're what?" His eyes widened and he lurched away from her. His shoulder thumped the railing.

Kara winced, wishing for a rug to crawl under. But she was being honest. "I know it's different for you. You're on tour. You probably sleep with someone new every other day, night, whatever. But I haven't been with anyone since you."

Closing his eyes, he rested his head back against the bars. "I haven't been with anyone since I found out you were pregnant." He brushed his hand down his face and revealed haunted eyes. "I'm petrified this will happen again." He drained the last drop of JD from his glass and placed it on the step beside him. "You've totally fucked me up."

"I didn't think this would affect your sex drive." Knowing Hunter, he'd get over it. Some attractive girl would resolve his situation soon enough. With Kara's raging hormones, she'd gladly help him out. "I have a solution. I'm already pregnant. We could have sex," she said, half joking, half not. She leaned back on the stairs, resting on her elbows, and stretched out her legs.

Hunter's foot slipped off the stair. His eyes flared with arctic fire. "What?" Redness crept up his neck and blotched his cheeks. "That's what got us into this mess. There's no chance in hell—"

"Calm down. I'm kidding." She wasn't, but she hadn't expected him to lose his cool.

Rejection this time didn't leave a scratch. She'd known his answer before he'd said anything. It was stupid of her to ask, but she wouldn't have hesitated in the off chance he'd said yes. She play-punched him in the arm. "Don't be so dramatic."

"Not. Funny," he growled.

"Yeah, it was."

But this was a firm reminder he wasn't into her. All his glances, his smiles, his touches—that moment in the park when she'd thought he would kiss her—they were nothing. Just her hormones wishing for something that wasn't there. She had to get control of her yo-yo emotions.

Hunter took several shaky breaths. Normal color crept back into his face. He even managed a chuckle. "Don't do that again."

"Whatever. I was trying to lighten things up." She brushed her hands over her jeans. "It's getting late, and I'd love a cup of tea before bed. But before we move, can I ask for one small favor? It's been an emotional weekend. After everything we've been through, I need one. I mean . . . I really need one."

With him agreeing to support their child, the only thing she had to do now was work on their friendship. For the sake of their baby.

"One what?" He pinned her with his gaze.

"I need a hug."

His shoulders relaxed. He puffed out a breath and a subtle smile touched his lips. "Yeah, I can do that."

He slid toward her and curled his arms around her waist; she slipped hers over his back. Sighing, he buried his face into her neck. His breath warmed her skin and sent a shiver down her spine. She inhaled his citrusy scent and rested her cheek against him. *Mmm.* Rubbing her hands over his soft shirt, she clutched him tighter. "Hunt, I know it's not going to be easy. But having our baby will be worth it. It will be the best thing that happens to us. You'll see."

Chapter 11

Grey snow-filled clouds darkened the morning sky. In the kitchen, the smell of burnt toast lingered in the air. Hunter grabbed a mug to make Kara her tea. But the whole time, his heart beat an erratic rhythm. Late last night, after the last partygoers had long gone, he'd sat next to her on his bed talking about Christmas, about fashion week, and about tour. Pickled with too much JD, he must have drifted off to sleep somewhere near 12:30a.m. He'd fallen asleep beside her. When he woke, he shot out of bed as fast as the flicker from a strobe light and stumbled down the stairs. It took him a moment to collect his thoughts and make sure he hadn't done anything stupid . . . like kiss her . . . or worse. Going by how much his balls hurt, he was sure nothing had happened.

Every time he looked at her, his heart screamed. She was a constant reminder that he was trapped in hell. He would be paying for his mistake for the rest of his life.

This weekend hadn't gone to plan.

He'd lost the fight.

Major. Epic. Fail.

He was going to be a father.

His palms turned clammy, and his stomach swirled. *Shit!* Surely he wasn't experiencing sympathy pains? He didn't feel any sympathy, only contempt.

He grabbed a glass of water and gulped it down. After rubbing his belly, he wiped his mouth on his shirtsleeve. *Ergh!* He was never queasy. Not after drinking. What was wrong with him?

Snow falling outside the kitchen window caught his eye. Pictures of Kara ran through his mind. Her smile and the sound of her intoxicating laugh rang in his ears. He'd learned more about her in the past two days than he had in the few years of knowing her. It had taken grit for her to defy her parents and follow her passion into design. He wouldn't have guessed that she loved the outdoors. She'd dripped off Conrad for so long, he'd never seen this side to her. Not that he'd ever taken the time to get to know her either.

He ripped open the tea packet and placed the bag into the cup. Shaking his head, he couldn't believe he was standing here, making her a stupid cup of tea, while she slept in bed.

Was he in more trouble than he'd thought? Because last night, when she'd joked about sex, his head, heart, and body had been so twisted with anger, hurt and turmoil, stress, anxiety, and dismay over the baby, he'd come so close . . . so close . . . to taking her by the hand and dragging her up to the bedroom. He wanted to fuck her because he hated what was happening to his life. Fuck her because he needed to vent his frustrations. Fuck her because he was horny. Then there were those reasons that made him question his sanity—the ones he had to get out of his system quick. What had his bloodstream burning was the fact that he wanted to fuck her because he felt a pinch of attraction, he'd liked sleeping with her the first time and he wanted to do it again.

But reality was a cold spoon to his dick and put an abrupt halt to his stupidity. Kara being pregnant changed everything. He didn't want to hurt her any more than he already had. He had no room in his life for love, for commitment or a relationship. In a few hours, he'd be on a plane and heading back to tour. That was his life.

Just because she was nice, didn't mean she could cut the chains that protected his heart. He wasn't sure anyone ever would.

He snatched the kettle off the stove and poured the boiled water into the cup. The door to the basement flung open and his mom crashed through with a basket of laundry.

"Here, let me help you with that." He dashed over to relieve her load.

"Thanks. Please leave it at the bottom of the stairs. I'll deal with it later." She plopped down on one of the breakfast bar stools and massaged her temples.

"Bit seedy this morning?" Hunter patted her on the back. "Want a coffee? I've made a fresh brew."

"I've already had three and some Advil, so no, thank you. I'll be fine." She glanced at the time on the microwave. "It's nearly lunchtime anyway."

"True." Hunter shrugged a shoulder. "Kara and I head off at one o'clock. I've confirmed the driver and security to take us to the airport."

Crap. He still had to tell his mom about Kara.

His mom continued to rub the sides of her head, her eyes closed. "Where are you heading to?"

"Seattle." He scratched his chest. "We have a few more cities before we're back in New York for Christmas, two shows at Madison Square, and the New Year's Eve concert. Then it's off overseas."

His mom smiled, but it held no festive cheer. "Another

Christmas without you."

The sorrow in her voice tugged deep in his chest. Last year he'd been in LA doing Christmas concerts. The year before that he was in London. And even though he was with Kyle and Gemma, he always missed his mom's cooking, his dad's pathetic jokes, and Jenny's carol singing. Maybe next year he'd make it home.

Shit! He'd have a kid.

"Hopefully next year," he said, despite his arid throat. He jiggled the teabag around in Kara's cup. Out of the corner of his eye, he saw his mother watching his every move. He stopped, folded his arms, and leaned against the counter. "What, Mom?"

"Nothing." Her tone may have sounded aloof, but he knew better than that.

"Mom?"

"It's just that . . . well . . . Kara seems lovely. Is everything okay?"

He placed his hands on the counter and closed his eyes. His throat tightened like an overstrung guitar. "You know. Don't you?"

His mom entwined her fingers and placed them on the counter. "The fact that she's not been well . . . or the fact that she's pregnant?"

"Both." The anguish in his mother's eyes tore his chest in two.

"I was wondering when you were going to tell me. I had a strong suspicion yesterday when she was sick. Your father must know, because he's avoided me every time I've tried to talk about you. I gather it's yours."

Hunter moved his chin a fraction of an inch in his best effort to nod. While he made a coffee for himself—anything to keep his mind numb—he relayed the whole story to his mom. The engagement party. The baby. Why he didn't want it. Kara's health and her decision to have it. His mother sat there in silence and listened, occasionally playing with her earrings or nodding.

His mother drew herself up three inches taller, her eyes glassy with sympathy, sorrow, and sadness. "I can't tell you what to do, or how much you should be involved. I wish I could. You're the only one who can answer that. The thing I will say to you is . . . be careful. Be careful and conscious of Kara's heart. You're both emotional and vulnerable right now. If you want to be friends and not hurt each other, make sure you don't sleep with her again."

"I haven't. I won't." A knot tightened at the base of his neck. Because when he'd woken up next to her, he'd wanted to reach out and touch her and kiss her perfect lips. Like he'd wanted to do yesterday in the park on more than one occasion. What the hell was wrong with him? He hated her for what she was doing to him. "She's not even my girlfriend."

"I worked that one out, too. But I've seen the way she looks at you." His mom's tone cautioned. "And I think you're conflicted about how you feel as well. It may be just about the baby, or it may be something more. So, if you don't want any more complications, make sure you keep it in your pants."

"Noted." Hunter threw his teaspoon and it clanged in the sink. Tinny and empty. Like his heart.

His mom was wrong on one count. He felt nothing for Kara. Nothing more than a thin friendship, and now, obligation. If his mom sensed an area of concern, it was time to rein it in. He had to make sure Kara understood they'd never be a couple.

He could do that.

Yes. Yes, he could. He had to. Keep his distance. Keep communications formal, through his lawyer.

"When is she due?" Lillian asked.

"Um . . . mid July." His heart seized. Suddenly, that date seven months into the future didn't seem far away. "Tour finishes end of May."

"Are you okay?"

"Nope. Not at all." He was a fucking mess. As well as dealing with baby crap, he had to get his head straight and focus on the shows. "But I have to be."

His mom hopped off the stool and walked around the counter. She wrapped her arms around him and gave him a big hug. Resting her head against his shoulder, she squeezed him tight. "I love you. I pray your baby is born happy and healthy. But on the off chance it isn't . . . I know you will do anything for it. Like you've done for Jenny."

"Thanks, Mom."

"I can't believe I'm going to be a grandma." She brushed the side of his cheek.

"Please, don't get your hopes up about seeing the baby," he begged. "I don't know how involved I can be."

His mom nodded and returned to her seat. The sadness in her eyes made him feel like he was kicking a dead dog over and over again. How many people were affected by this? Kara? His family? Her family? Him? On top of every other worry, guilt riddled him. And he hated that. He liked to ignore issues, not face them. For the first time in his life, he couldn't escape. Whichever way he turned, he was trapped.

He picked up his coffee and Kara's tea. "I gotta go and get someone out of bed."

As he put one foot in front of the other, an icy grip took hold of his heart. It was time to put up an extra barricade to protect himself. He could handle pressure from the record label, and deal with fans and face the media daily, but this new responsibility scared him senseless. Facing fatherhood and finding an amicable ground with Kara was a colossal chasm of unknown. Hearts had to be left out of the equation. He didn't want Kara falling for him. Not ever.

With his steely resolve in place, he slid into his room—and froze. There she lay, asleep. Her long hair was a mass of waves on the pillow. The sheet, tucked under her arms, covered breasts he'd licked and sucked and fondled all those weeks ago. Daylight from the window shimmered on fair skin he'd kissed every inch of. His breath lodged in his chest. She looked like an angel.

An angel who was screwing with his life.

Chapter 12

Hunter dashed out of the car and through the large glass doors into the medical center on Lexington, right behind Kara. This was not where he wanted to be. Since landing in New York a few days ago, Kara and Gemma had ganged up against him and he'd reluctantly agreed to come to the baby's first scan. He couldn't understand what the big deal was.

His breath eased when he and Kara made it into the elevators unnoticed. Watching over his shoulder, he trailed behind her, down the bright white corridor toward the obstetrician's suite. He bumped into her when she halted halfway along the hallway and turned to face him.

"Can we not do this, please?" Her eyes flashed with anger. "It's hard enough dealing with the baby without adding you ignoring me to the list."

He tilted his head back and groaned. "I'm not ignoring you."

That was only partly true. He'd stuck to his plan and kept conversations and messages to a minimum over the past few weeks. What had him breaking out in a cold sweat on the drive here was her twelve-week-old baby bump bulging underneath her knit top. She'd grown since he'd seen her four weeks ago.

Kara folded her arms, accentuating her rounded tummy. "You've hardly said anything since you picked me up from work."

While most of the population enjoyed the Christmas–New Year's break, Kara seemed as flat out at work preparing for fashion week as he was with his music and tour. He'd flown into New York on Christmas Day. Wrote himself off the next day with a bottle of JD to celebrate his birthday. Performed two shows at The Garden. Today was Friday. Tomorrow he had rehearsals. Sunday was New Year's Eve. Monday he was off overseas. His brain hurt trying to keep up with his schedule.

"I'm sorry," he snapped. "I've got a zillion things on my mind. On top of shows, I'm talking to lawyers. I've got a huge meeting at Sony this afternoon. And being here is stressing me out."

"I know." She folded her arms. "Just talk to me about the baby. Whenever you need to. It's the only way we will work through this."

His jaw tensed and he drew his shoulder blades back. He was still torn between doing the right thing and wanting to walk away. "We have talked. It's got me nowhere. I don't have a solution. How can you possibly want me to be a father when I'm only going to be around on a casual basis?"

"Because *you* are the daddy." Her tone softened. "Whatever level of involvement you decide upon, our child will know you're a hard-working man and will respect you and what you do. Our baby will treasure the time it gets to see and spend with you."

Was that what she thought of him? *Wow.* He sighed, and rubbed at the warmth exploding in his chest. Kara had knocked him out of the park. She saw him for his good points, his talent, his strengths—not just his partying bad-boy ways, the gossip and the slander. She saw a different side to him—and he liked it. But he wasn't ready to give up his wild ways.

Kara stabbed her finger against his chest. "Don't make me hate you by ignoring me and being rude."

He closed his eyes and took a deep breath. When he met her gaze, his stomach bottomed out. Her beautiful blue eyes had faded to dull gray. He wished he could wash her worries away. "Shit, Kara, you constantly do my head in."

She ran her hand down his arm. Her touch sent his pulse into a frenzy. "Hunter, I've seen glimpses of the good in you. That's what I hold onto. That's what I want our child to see."

Was he going to be a disappointment? Would his child feel unwanted, unloved and unsupported like he had? He didn't want that. It churned his blood and filled him with grit and determination to ensure that wouldn't happen. He swallowed hard and stuffed his hands into his jacket pockets. He wasn't going to be anything like his own father.

"Have you broken the news to your parents yet?" he asked.

"Yes." Her voice was deadpan. "That storm on Christmas Day was my father unleashing his disappointment. My mom hasn't stopped downing scotch. It shocked Naomi but she's supportive because she knows how much I wanted a baby." She waved her hand down the hall. "And this is a fine example of my father controlling my life. He made some phone calls and got me booked into this obstetrician. Supposedly she's one of the best in New York."

"Why do you let him do things for you if you don't like it?"

"It didn't bother me when I was younger. I didn't know any better. But since breaking up with Conrad and falling pregnant, I see things differently. Having this baby is the first decision I've made on my own. I have to choose which battles to fight; this isn't one of them."

He could relate to picking his battles. Luckily, he never had too many with Kyle and Gemma. But with Kara . . . he'd lost every one.

He stared at her. Clenched and released his fists. She'd changed the course of his life. But the longer he looked at her, the pent-up tension in his jaw disappeared. She radiated. He wanted to trace the freckles that had become more prominent across the bridge of her nose. Stroke her rosy cheeks. Thread and comb his fingers through her long hair and rub the base of her neck. "You look good, by the way. You've got that glow about you."

"Glow?" The pink in her cheeks deepened. "I'd say *the glow* is caused by the continual wave of nausea."

"You still get morning sickness?"

"Yeah. Most days, it's all day. After today, I'll have to tell work I'm pregnant. I can't hide my baby bump anymore. The excuse of gaining a few pounds and wearing loose-fitting clothes has reached its expiration date." She glanced at her watch and pointed down the hallway. "Come on. Let's go."

Hunter walked ahead, then opened the door to the medical suite for Kara. As he did so, a bald man stepped out. Hunter's knees buckled.

Son of a bitch.

The man's beady eyes bore into him. "Well, well, well. Now . . . this *is* a surprise. I would *never* have expected to see *you* here, Mr. Collins." His eyes lit up like fireworks on the Fourth of July.

"*Gerard.*" The name dripped like rancid acid off Hunter's tongue.

"What a pleasure to see you." Arrogance swung in Gerard's tone.

"Can't say the same thing about you." Hunter's stomach flipped. Of all people, why did he have to run into one of the biggest jerks in journalism?

"My wife's doctor is running late, so I was on my way to grab a decent coffee from the café downstairs."

"What are you doing here?" Hunter spoke through tight lips. "Don't you live in LA?"

"I got a promotion." Gerard straightened his necktie. "I'm now on TV for *Entertainment On-Show* and moved to New York two months ago." Gerard eyed Kara, who was standing with her arm brushing against Hunter's.

Stress throbbed in Hunter's temples. "Shouldn't you be on vacation like most people?"

"Oh no. This is the busiest time of the year for us. All the New Year's parties. The concerts. The shows. There is always something of interest to report." An evil smile drew across Gerard's weaselly face. "So . . . who's this lovely young lady?"

"Just a friend." Hunter gripped harder onto the door to stop himself from shaking.

"I seeee." Gerard's sleazy drawl and cocked eyebrow were clear evidence he didn't believe what he was hearing. "I'm Gerard." He thrust his hand out at Kara. "And you are?"

"I'm Kara. Nice to meet you."

Hunter's skin crawled as Kara shook Gerard's hand. This was not good.

Gerard eyes shot to Kara's belly then back to her face. "Are you pregnant?" Kara stiffened beside Hunter. But her lack of response gave Gerard his answer. "Congratulations. How nice of Hunter to bring you to your appointment during his hectic schedule. You must be *very* good friends."

Kara gaped. "We're . . . um—"

"Gerard, we're done. This is none of your business." Hunter's voice sliced through his clasped teeth.

"It is now." Gerard's voice rose higher and higher. "Are you the father?"

"You can burn in hell." Bitterness rolled off his tongue. "Kara needs to get to her appointment."

Hunter wanted to wipe the smug look off Gerard's face, but he had more pressing matters. He placed his hand on the small of Kara's back and ushered her in to the clinic.

His whole body trembled. Of all the doctors in New York, Kara had to end up in the same place as Gerard and his wife. *Just. Fucking. Great.*

While Kara checked in at reception, Hunter sat with his back to everyone in the waiting room. Panic gurgled in the pit of his stomach. His and Kara's situation was about to blow out in epic proportions. The world would know he was here by the time morning broke, thanks to Gerard.

"Hey?" Kara took a seat next to him. "Who was that guy?"

Hunter scraped his hand over his face. "That was Gerard Rivers. Remember the drama Gem, Kyle and I had in Hawaii, and there was a heap of gossip printed about our relationships? Gerard was the guy who had interviewed us." He sucked in a jagged breath and tried to clear his head. "Kar, I know we wanted to keep this quiet, but it's about to explode. We'll be in the headlines by tomorrow."

"What are we going to do?" Fear flashed in her eyes. If she twisted the scarf in her lap into a tighter knot, he was sure it would tear. She had enough to worry about without having to deal with the paparazzi. But they'd be after her within a matter of hours.

"We better meet with Kate, Bec, and Sophie as soon as possible. Maybe after the meeting at Sony, if you're up for it." A cold chill seeped into his bones. "And here I was hoping that no one would ever find out about this. So much for wishful thinking."

He loved the cameras, the attention, and the spotlight. But this was different. This wasn't about him. Kara had never wished for a life in the limelight. She'd always hung back from the mania that followed Everhide everywhere. "Kar, I'll organize security for you straight away. Might be best until this blows over."

"I don't need a bodyguard."

"You will once this gets out. Trust me."

Hunter cursed under his breath as he texted Mick, his bodyguard, Sam, their head of security, and Kate. His shaky fingers wouldn't co-operate. Predictive text kept replacing his misspelled words with utter nonsense. Finally, he managed to send the messages.

He could understand what Gemma and Kyle had gone through. Protecting those close to you was all that mattered. *Shit!* Was he falling into the realm of caring about Kara and what happened to her?

He had to make sure she was safe. Kate needed to prep Kara on how to deal with the media, how to respond and handle their onslaught of questions. He'd thought he had months to get these elements in place, but now he had a matter of hours and days. Whether she liked it or not, Kara's life was about to change.

"Miss Knight?" The doctor peered over the rim of her glasses, standing in the hallway that lead to the medical suites.

"That's me." Kara stood, hooking her purse over her shoulder.

Flicking his jacket collar up high to avoid recognition, Hunter followed Kara into the doctor's room.

A huge mahogany desk inset with dark green leather sat to one side of the office, and an examination table lay to the other. The sickly vanilla smell from the diffuser on the desk churned his stomach, and the gynecological lamp seemed to stare at him, mocking him wherever he looked within the room. His heart pounded. Sweat broke out on his brow. Maybe he was the one who needed to lie down.

The doctor closed the door behind them. Hunter pulled on the neckline of his shirt that suddenly seemed tight around his throat. There was no way out. Nowhere to run.

Shit!

"Please sit down." Dr. Blakley pointed to their chairs in front of her desk and took her seat. Her wide frame squeezed between the arms of her office chair. "Nice to meet you, Kara. And who's this?"

Hunter and Kara glanced at each other, and he wondered if the doctor was joking.

"Um . . ." Kara turned back to the doctor. "If you don't know who this is, can you assure me that what goes on in this room, stays in this room? There *is* strict doctor–patient confidentiality, right?"

"Yes, of course." Dr. Blakley looked down the bridge of her nose.

"Good. I can't believe you haven't recognized him by now, but this is Hunter Collins. He's the father of my child."

Hearing those words made his heart batter his ribs.

"Mr. Collins. Nice to meet you. Should I know who you are?"

A short, sharp laugh burst from his mouth. "Are you serious? I'm sorry, but I don't meet too many people who don't know me. I'm in Everhide."

"Who or what is Everhide?" Dr. Blakley looked from him to Kara and back again.

"Aaaaa . . . rock band." Hunter sat back in his chair and gave the doctor a disbelieving look. Where had this woman been to not know who he was? "We're performing tomorrow night at the ball drop."

"The name sounds familiar, but I don't listen to much music by the young generation." She typed on her keyboard, scrolled and clicked through some computer screens. "While you'll be singing and partying, I'll be delivering babies, which is much more fun and reason to celebrate." She smiled at Kara and placed her hands together on the desk. "Kara, your GP has sent me a report on your history. Because of your endo, we need to monitor the baby's progress closely. We'll do a scan today, then one at twenty weeks. Let's start, shall we?"

Hunter swapped chairs with Kara to keep out of the way. His mind blurred as the doctor checked Kara's weight, and blood pressure, and sent her to the bathroom to pee in a cup for testing. For what he didn't know. This whole baby thing was like a foreign language to him. He had absolutely no idea what was going on. When Kara returned with the cup in a brown paper bag, the doctor snapped on a pair of rubber gloves.

The color drained from Hunter's face.

"Right, Kara. Up on the table for the ultrasound. I'll take some measurements, check the heartbeat, and be able to confirm how far along you are."

"Okay." Kara slipped off her shoes, lay down on the table, shimmied her skirt lower and rolled her shirt up to her bra-line.

Oh wow . . . her boobs were even bigger than before. Now where was he supposed to look? He dug his fingernails into the palms of his hands and his stupid leg wouldn't stop jiggling.

"Mr. Collins." Dr. Blakley waved at a chair. "If you'd like to go around the other side of the table, you'll be able to see the monitor as well."

Hunter shuffled around next to Kara. As excitement lit her face, something tugged deep inside his chest. After all their arguments, differences, and fights, she still wanted to have this baby. It was something he couldn't understand.

"You ready, Hunt?" She realigned the pillow underneath her head.

"No. Not at all." He pulled the chair in closer to the bed. He wasn't ready for babies. Or for Kara to get inside his head. Or for her to look so radiant and happy.

The doctor squished clear gel onto Kara's tummy.

"Ew . . . that's warm and disgusting." Kara's hand shot out and clutched onto his arm. Her fingernails dug into his flesh, and his muscles tensed. The heat from her touch and the sharp scratch of her nails matched his crazy thoughts. Pleasure and pain. Turmoil and a lack of logic. Every moment he spent with her, talked to her, read an email from her, the more his confusion grew. She was so stubborn, pigheaded, and determined. She never wavered; she knew what she wanted and pursued it with her all. And he hated to admit it, didn't want to admit it, but he liked that about her. Baby stress had messed with his head.

He took her hand and gently placed it on the bed. "You'll be fine. I'm sure."

The doctor ran the probe over Kara's belly. The softest and tiniest grunts and groans rumbled in Kara's throat as the doctor pressed against her skin.

"Let's find your little one." The doctor watched the monitor.

"How big is it supposed to be?" Hunter squinted to make sense of the blur on screen.

The doctor steadied her hand and an image formed. Hunter's breath snagged his chest when the kidney bean shape came into view.

"If Kara is twelve weeks, it should be about two-and-a-half inches long. About the size of a plum."

Hunter leaned in closer, resting his elbows on the side of the bed, mesmerized by the image before him.

The white outline of the skull came into focus. The curve of the baby's face and button nose. "This is the head. I'll take the measurements." The doctor clicked some keys and typed on the keypad.

"I don't see it." Kara twisted her head this way and that, peering at the monitor. "I can't see my baby."

The doctor ran the cursor across the screen and pointed to the fine little ridges that formed the spine. "This is the back, the tummy, and the legs."

Hunter's hand shot over his mouth. Every little curve and wriggly line hit him right in the chest. What was happening to him?

The doctor continued to scan over the fetus. "Do you want to know the sex of your baby?"

Hunter's mouth ran dry. He looked at Kara, not sure if he could speak. It wouldn't make any difference to him. The choice was hers. He cleared his throat. "It's up to you."

Kara nodded to the doctor. "Yes, please."

The doctor scanned across her tummy and focused on the baby's legs. "Ah, there we go."

"I still can't make anything out. It's just blurry lines. I can't see my baby." A tear fell from Kara's eye and ran toward her temple.

"Hey. Come on. Here. See." Hunter leaned over and pointed at the screen. "Here's its head, its back, and . . . oh . . . something big between its legs." Okay . . . it was a nub. "Is that what I think it is?" Hunter's pulse rose like the crescendo in a song.

"It's too early to be one hundred percent sure." Dr. Blakley peered closer. "But at this stage it looks like it's a boy."

Hunter clutched his chest. His eyes watered, and the hairs on his arms stood on end.

Holy shit! A son!

"A boy?" Kara's voice wailed. Her head sunk deeper into the pillow. "Oh God please help us. Another Hunter Collins in the world? Are you sure it's a boy?"

"Look at him." Hunter beamed. The baby on screen rolled and spread his legs. "He's like me already. Proud of his package."

"Your package got me into this predicament in the first place," Kara moaned.

The doctor continued. "Let's check out his heart."

Hunter's eyes fixed on the monitor. Little pulses shimmied across the screen. Red and blue squiggles shot this way and that.

"Would you like to hear the heartbeat?" the doctor asked.

Hunter stared at the screen and nodded. He didn't care what Kara wanted. He wanted to hear it. This was mind-blowing, absolutely insane, crazy shit.

The doctor turned a dial on the panel before her and a swooshing noise filled the room. Hunter's heart raced as fast as the heartbeat on the monitor. Some invisible force wrapped itself around him and tightened with a hard tug.

That was his baby. His son.

There.

On the screen.

In Kara's belly. Just inches away.

This was not how he expected to feel. Like landing their first record deal, like their first number-one single, like winning award after award—*this* was one of those life-changing moments he'd never forget.

"Ryan." The name shot into his mind and whispered across his lips. "His name. Can we call him Ryan?"

"What?" Kara asked. "Where and how on earth did you come up with that?"

"It just came to me. With my good looks and talent, and your smarts and creativity, he's going to be one handsome, popular man. He'll be hotter and more skilled than Ryan Reynolds and Ryan Gosling combined."

"I haven't even thought about names." Kara's hand shook as she brushed her hair from her forehead.

"Don't bullshit me, Kar." He gave her a lopsided smile. "You've probably had names picked out for years."

She closed her eyes. "You're so irritating. Sometimes, I hate you so much. You know that, right? Because Ryan was one of the names at the top of my list."

It was? How freaky was that?

"So . . .?" He rubbed her arm. "How about it?"

She smiled. It was like sunshine. Warmth glowed in his chest.

"Yeah. I love it. Ryan. Our baby boy is going to be called Ryan."

Hunter fought his watery eyes. He gazed at Kara. Tears trickled down the side of her face. Hunter grabbed her hand and kissed the back of it. "Hey. You okay?" He turned back to the monitor. "See that? That's our baby. We're going to have a baby, Kar. We're going to have a fucking baby."

***

Folding the printout of the baby scan picture into his wallet, Hunter followed Kara out of the doctor's office. Mick met them in the building's lobby.

"Bud, two photographers are outside." Mick jerked his head toward the door. "The car is waiting. Let's get you out of here."

Shit! Gerard!

"You protect Kara." Hunter jammed on his beanie and knotted his scarf. "I'll follow."

Mick shielded Kara, and they dashed out the door. Cameras went off as the three of them raced for the car. The commotion attracted curious gazes from several pedestrians. Hunter slipped into the back seat after Mick and Kara, and slammed the door shut.

He turned away from the cameras flashing outside the window. "Go. Go. Go," he called out to the driver.

The car took off down Lexington. Hunter rested his head back against the seat and stared at the roof. Until now, the baby had been nothing. It wasn't tangible to him. Seeing that heartbeat on the monitor made it a reality. There was no turning back. Kara was carrying *his* child. *His.* That little munchkin inside her belly had somehow cast a spell on him.

After the scan, his heart beat to a new rhythm. One for Ryan. "Hey, Kar?" He turned to face her. "Thank you for persisting and making me go with you. That was amazing."

"You mean that?" Her voice was soft and wary.

"Absolutely."

She touched his cheek. "Thank you for coming. I'm glad you got to see one scan. You won't see him again for five months. I'll be super fat and ready to pop when you get back."

An ache lodged in his chest. He was going to miss seeing Ryan grow.

"Subject to time zones, can you call me after your appointments? Will you send me updates? Because, Kar, that little guy in there is all that matters."

"You're serious, aren't you?" A tear fell on to her cheek.

He placed his hand on her knee and squeezed. "Yeah. I am."

His cell buzzed in his coat pocket. He grabbed it and read the screen.

"Who is it?" Kara asked.

"It's Kate." He fumbled with the phone in his hands, knowing that life for Kara was about to change. "She'll meet with us after our meeting with Sony. Are you ready to be the fox being chased by a pack of hungry wolves?"

Chapter 13

Kara held her breath. Her heart raced as she gripped onto Giles's shoulder. Her bodyguard, courtesy of Hunter and Everhide's management, had become her latest accessory. The only positive was he looked like Channing Tatum. She kept her head down to avoid the onslaught of cameras flashing in her face. In the span of forty-eight hours, her world had become manic.

Giles guided her into the lobby and up to the ballroom of the Times Square Intercontinental Hotel for Conrad's Silver New Year's Eve Ball. She wanted to put the madness of the past couple days behind her and enjoy the evening's festivities. Put Hunter out of her mind.

Stepping into the crowded function room, Kara inhaled the fragrant air. White long-stemmed roses with silver glittered edges stood in tall glass vases on the banquet tables. Silver baubles, the size of large beach balls, hung from the ceiling. Crystal chandeliers, twinkle lights, and blue LEDs turned the room into a metallic palace. Huge TVs were mounted on the walls streaming the events happening out in Times Square.

Although the DJ here was pumping out the tunes, Hunter and her friends would be visible on the screens later in the evening, right up until the countdown and ball drop at midnight.

"Kara. You're here." Lexi, her best friend next to Gemma, appeared out of the crowd. "You look gorgeous. I love the dress."

Kara put her clutch and coat down at their banquet table and smoothed her hands down her flowing silver liquid lamé dress. "Thank you."

"You don't look pregnant." Lexi splayed her hands toward Kara's stomach. "I can't believe you kept this from me."

"I didn't. It was too early to say anything." It felt like the millionth time Kara had said that since friends and family had inundated her with calls and messages. "The media has been crazy, hasn't it?"

The world knew she was pregnant, thanks to the paparazzi. Gerard's article had hit the Internet within hours of her scan. Other gossip sites were quick to follow. Hunter warned her not to read any of them, but she hadn't been able to resist. The stories ranged from outrageous and hurtful, to the cold, hard truth, to hilarious.

Hunter's mystery girlfriend is pregnant. We have proof.

Hunter Collins is going to be a daddy.

Hunter sews his seeds in the fashion world.

Lexi flicked a curl of her updo off her forehead. "What a nightmare. I saw a bunch of reporters outside your building this afternoon when I drove past."

"They still there?" Kara rubbed her arm. "After having this huge meeting with Hunt and his team, I was so frightened. They suggested I stay at his place until the security at my apartment is upgraded. Gem and Kyle have been staying at Hunt's too, which is nice. Makes it less stressful and awkward."

"Tough gig having to stay at his penthouse," Lexi teased as

she stole a champagne from a waiter walking past. "Just so you can avoid a few paparazzi?"

"A few?" Kara had to laugh, otherwise she'd break down in tears. "The ones outside his place are tame compared to the ones that were at work. Thank God Hunter insisted on me having a bodyguard. Giles has proved to be more than useful." She should remember to say thank you, send Hunter an email if she didn't see him before he left. "Yesterday I had to go into work to finish the decorations for this evening, and there were fifty reporters outside the building. They kept shouting, screaming and shoving cameras and phones in my face. They kept asking awful and stupid questions like, '*Is it true you're carrying Hunter's baby? Is this a scam? Are you after his money? Is he really the father?*'"

"That's dreadful." Lexi sipped her champagne. Sidling closer, meekness slid into her tone. "So . . . how are you two handling the situation? I didn't think you got along."

"Hunter's turned into Dr. Jekyll and Mr. Hyde. One minute he's tolerable, the next, he's an utter control freak."

He'd turned into her father. *Ergh. Men!*

"How's he controlling?" Lexi asked, eying the waiters and their platters of hors d'oeuvres, and grabbed a cranberry and feta bite.

Kara put on her best Hunter impersonation. "'*She will have security. Twenty-four/seven. She will have a new phone and private cell number. She will have surveillance cameras installed at her home.*' That's what he insisted on at our meeting with his management team." Kara hated how he made her baby feel like a business transaction. It was all lawyers, security and procedures.

"Those things don't sound too bad." Lexi stuffed her food into her mouth, chewed and licked her fingertips. "What else has he done?"

"He's being . . . nice." Her voice came out breathy and full of exasperation. "He had lunch delivered when I couldn't get out of the office because of the reporters. And he even sent me flowers."

While she had said to him to be kind and not ignore her, the sweet gestures were not what she had expected. Not what she'd wanted.

"So he's controlling you . . . by being nice." Lexi raised a cynical eyebrow. "What a prick."

"Yes, he is and no, he's not. I just want to make my own choices. I don't want to be an item on his check list. I feel like I've become just one of the many moving parts in the Everhide empire."

And she didn't want him to make her think he cared.

Because he didn't.

And that meant she couldn't.

"Sorry to say it, babe, you have." Lexi stepped in closer to let a group of people pass behind her. "But Hunter sending flowers and food? That's new. When did that change?"

"At the baby's scan." Kara's taste buds happy-danced when she plucked a crumbed cheese ball from a waiter's tray and popped it into her mouth. After finishing her mouthful, she continued. "He was so against the baby until seeing the ultrasound. Now he's gone googoo gaagaa and become overprotective."

Lexi laughed. "Hunter? Googoo? I can't wait to see that." She took a sip of her champagne and seriousness transformed her face. "Is there any chance of something developing between the two of you?"

"God no." Kara's heart wavered. She wanted a man who would be around, not jet-setting and sleeping his way across the globe. Tomorrow, he'd be gone for months. That would give her time to get her spiraling feelings for him under control. She was counting down the hours until he left.

"All right then. Put him out of your head. It's time to have fun. Let's go grab a drink." Lexi took her by the hand and led her across the floor. At the edge of the four-people deep line-up, she stopped. "Stay here. I'll get our drinks. You don't need to be jostled and bumped by this mob. Gotta protect your little bub."

"Thanks. I'll have a Sprite."

Kara hung back and felt dozens of eyes upon her. Conrad's clients, suppliers, and celebrity guests turned in her direction. Fingers were pointed. Loud whispers rustled.

"That's Kara. The one who's pregnant. To Hunter Collins."

Kara groaned. She shouldn't have come tonight. She didn't need to hear more gossip.

A disturbance across the ballroom caught her eye. Conrad, dressed in a tailored silver brocade tuxedo, dashed toward her. With his blond hair sleeked into a Gatsby style, his hazel eyes glimmered as he came toward her with an exaggerated confidence. This was another conversation she wasn't looking forward to.

"Kara, my darling. You look absolutely stunning." He kissed her cheek, one side then the other. "Love this color on you. It's simply divine. And those stilettos are spectacular. Jimmy Choo Violas. Nice."

"Good evening, Conrad." She clutched her hands in front of her.

Conrad stepped closer, leaning into her ear. "Why didn't you tell me about the baby? And of all people . . . Hunter . . . is the father?"

"It's none of your concern," she snapped.

"It is. I care about you. We need to talk." He drew her over to a bar table in a small clearing at the edge of the dance floor. When he turned to face her, tension ticked in his jaw. "I could say so many things, one—how unprofessional of you to sleep

with our client; two—I thought you hated each other; and three
. . ." Kara followed his gaze to see Jasmine, the intern Conrad
had dumped her for, standing at the bar. "I want to know what's
going on between you and Hunter. Is it serious? Are you in a
relationship with that egotistical jerk?"

Kara gaped. She'd never heard Conrad talk about Hunter
like this. He was always polite about his clientele. Especially
Everhide. They were so easy to deal with compared to some of
their other customers. "Not that it's any of your business, but
no, we're not in a relationship."

"Did you sleep with him to get back at me?"

Her eyes widened. She couldn't believe what she was
hearing. "Oh yes, Conrad. I went out and got knocked up by
some asshole rock star who's never going to be around for his
child just to piss you off."

Conrad stiffened. "Don't get upset." He stroked his hands
down his vest. "We tried to make a baby for months. We broke
up and you fell pregnant straight away. How do you think that
makes me feel?"

She choked on her own breath. "Um . . . relieved? Don't go
feeling inadequate. You left. Remember? You weren't in love
with me."

"Oh Kara." He placed his hand on her arm, but she flinched
away from his touch. "I did love you. It just got too hard."

His words stung like a wasp bite. The hurt in her heart
blistered. "Yeah well, I don't need someone who walks away
when things get tough. Hunter may be a lot of things, but he's
not a quitter. He fights me at every turn, questions my sanity
with every breath, but he's being as supportive as he can be."
Everything about Hunter rubbed her the wrong way . . . and the
right. Got her pulse racing and her tearing her hair out. What
was with that? "One thing I've learned out of all this mess is
there's only one person I can count on . . . and that's me."

It scared her. But it was the truth. Each day she was getting stronger and better at being on her own. She didn't care what people thought anymore.

"Kar, you've changed. What happened to my little lamb?" Conrad looked at her as if she was a stranger.

"I've grown up. That's what happened. I've had to change." She lifted her chin. "I'm raising this child by myself. I don't need you, or Hunter, or anyone else. Now go back to your girlfriend." Kara twinkled her fingers and gave a cold smile to Jasmine who watched them like a hawk from the bar. Kara spun back to Conrad. "You now know the news, like everyone else."

Conrad flicked the lapels of his jacket. "I wish you could have come and told me sooner. That's what hurt, Kar. Why couldn't you trust me?"

"It wasn't a matter of trust, Conrad." She rested her elbow on the bar table, resisting the urge to roll her eyes. "I was waiting until after my scan. But all hell with the media broke loose."

Conrad's expression softened. "I do care about you. Always have. Always will. If you need anything, all you have to do is ask." He gave her a quick kiss on the cheek. "I have to go mingle, my darling. Promise me you'll have fun tonight."

"I'll try."

"Enjoy." He turned and scooted over to Jasmine's side.

Kara wiped the remains of his kiss off her cheek and collapsed onto the bar stool. What a messed up few days.

"Here." Lexi placed her Sprite on the table and slid her arm around Kara's shoulders. "Whatever Conrad said, ignore him. I know he's your boss, and your ex, but he's a dick. I can say that now you're not together. He's too up himself. Don't you think?"

Lexi might have been on to something. "I think he's jealous that I'm getting more attention in the media than his fashion."

"Of course he is." Lexi flicked her hand through the air. "He's an egotistical shithead. You're so much better off without him. He makes Hunter look normal." Kara laughed. Hunter and normal did not go together. Lexi took a sip of her vodka and cranberry cocktail. "Let's go sit for dinner. After we eat, we'll hit the dance floor."

At the end of the three-course meal, Kara danced with Lexi and some girls from work. Her eyes kept darting toward the TV screens filled with Everhide singing. Although they were on mute, Hunter's voice resonated in her ears, like he was right beside her. His onstage presence, wild and captivating, snared her heart. He'd be gone tomorrow for months. Why did it feel like she would miss him?

As midnight approached, the TV volumes were turned up.

The countdown began.

The ball dropped.

Ten. Nine. Eight. Seven. Six. Five. Four. Three. Two. One.

Happy new year.

All around Kara, everyone cheered, and party poppers popped. Champagne disappeared down people's throats and couples kissed.

Kara twirled around in the center of the floor and caressed her belly. She had so much to look forward to this year. She would have her baby. Nothing could go wrong.

By 2:00a.m., Kara's feet ached. It was time to go home. But when she went to say goodbye to the girls, a shiver ran up her spine. It froze her to the spot. Lexi's eyes widened, and she pointed over Kara's shoulder. Kara had no time to turn. The air around her filled with his citrusy scent, interlaced with a whole lot of whiskey. It nearly knocked her out cold.

Her heart wanted to clamber out of her chest.

Strong fingers encircled her hips. His hard body pressed against hers, his chest against her back. His breath like fire on her neck.

"Happy new year," he whispered in her ear, and her knees

buckled.

"Hunter?" Butterflies turned to birds in her belly. "What are you doing here?"

"Shh." He nuzzled her hair. "Dance with me."

She closed her eyes. He should not be touching her like this. Every bone in her body screamed for him to stop, but somehow, he'd possessed her.

Unable to resist, she swayed with him to the beat of the music. She reached up and cupped the side of his face. The whiskers on his cheek. His soft long hair. His warm skin. Oh God, he felt so good. Every cell in her body sparked with electricity.

One dance. Just one.

His hands brushed down her arms and left goose bumps in their wake. He slid them over the silky fabric of her dress, across the curve of her hips. Down. Lower. Slower. Swirling on the top of her thighs.

Heat skittered beneath his touch. His strong fingers dug into her leg, dragging the skirt of her dress up just an inch or two, nothing more. Her knees weakened. *Oh wow.* He was turning her on. Being in his arms made her dizzy. Intoxicated. She leaned back against his chest to steady herself. Gliding his hands upward, he shimmied up her sides, and settled them on her belly.

On *Ryan.*

It was the first time he'd touched her tummy. He splayed his fingers wide. With slow circles, he caressed their baby. Tears welled in her eyes as she placed her hands over his and entwined their fingers together.

"I'm gonna miss him." Hunter's voice snagged in his throat.

Oh crap! He left her lost for words.

Her eyes fluttered shut as the warmth from his body enclosed around her. He kissed beneath her earlobe, her neck, her shoulder. She forgot how to breathe. How long had she wanted him to kiss her again? Have his hands on her?

But not like this. Not when he was drunk.

He shouldn't be here. Everything was so fucked up. Her heart couldn't handle Hunter anymore.

His arms wrapped tighter around her, and every muscle in her body seized. Pain erupted in her heart. This had to stop.

Now.

She stepped out of his hold, turned, and met his bloodshot eyes. Even with his hair a disheveled mess, he looked like he'd walked out of the pages of *Vogue*. "What are you doing?"

Hunter shrugged. Swayed on his feet.

She glanced around. A dozen sets of eyes were on them. She lowered her voice. "Why aren't you with Kyle and Gemma? I thought you had a party to go to?"

"We did. But I left. I came here."

Lexi and the girls danced near her and Hunter, but they weren't really dancing, they were more intent on the scene unfolding before them. Necks craned past other people's heads. Others whispered into ears, their eyes on her and Hunter. Kara groaned. She didn't need more gossip about her and Hunter in the headlines tomorrow.

She stormed past him and made her way to her table. As she stepped off the dance floor, he caught her on the arm and spun her around. "Kar, wait."

"How did you get in here anyway?" Her mind blazed with confusion, with things she shouldn't be thinking and feeling.

He brushed his finger over the tip of her nose. "You forget who I am. I think I was on the list anyway." He studied her face and zoomed in closer. "What the hell?" He cupped the side of her cheek. "You've been crying. What's happened?"

She pulled her chin away and brushed a tear from her cheek. "Everything. You. Conrad. The baby. It's been a long day. I'm going home."

"But I just got here." Disappointment clouded his eyes. "It's time to party."

"Do it without me. I'm done." She went to charge past him, but he stepped in front of her, blocking her escape.

"No. I came here to see you."

"Why?" She looked him square in the eye. Her heart was crying. "Why, Hunter? Please tell me, because I'm not a mind reader."

He sashayed forward and placed his hands on her hips. "Because . . . I thought we could have some fun together. It's New Year's Eve. Let's party."

"You're drunk."

"That's never stopped me before." He waggled his eyebrows and grinned.

"I can't do this, Hunt." Another tear slipped to her cheek. "Stay away from me. Please?"

His arms fell to his sides. "I can't do that."

"Why not?"

"Because you're having my baby. *Our* baby."

She tilted her head back and stared at the crystal chandelier. Why couldn't life be all glitter and sparkles? Exhaustion weighed on her shoulders. "I know. But we have to keep everything between us black and white. All the mixed signals you've been sending me over the past few days have to stop." Her head spun like a carousel. "Has something changed? Do you like me? Do you want to be with me?" The notion was so ludicrous she wanted to laugh. But her heart hammered. What if he said yes? What would she do? Because she doubted every one of her beliefs and dreams about what she wanted in a man when she stood in front of him.

The color drained from his face. He raked his fingers through his hair. "*Fuck.* No. No, I don't."

Just what she thought. The hint that he might have been

leading her toward a relationship had him reeling backward faster than a tape set to rewind.

"Good. Because I'm not into you either." She pointed her finger at his chest. "Don't send me flowers. Don't buy me lunch. Don't dance with me like you just did. And please . . . don't ever kiss me ever again."

Her heart plummeted to the floor. It took all her strength to remain upright. Confused by her own growing feelings for him, she had to reset the boundaries. She had to protect herself from falling.

"I'm sorry, Kar. I sent those things to you because you said you wanted me to be considerate. I came here because I needed to know you were going to be okay when I left." He slumped and swayed. "It's been a fucked up few days. The scan. Ryan. Doing shows. The wolves after us. Worrying about you. Your safety. Everything is doing my head in. Guess I haven't been handling it well. In fact, not at all."

Seeing Hunter crack under the stress tore at her soul. She had to take some of the blame. She hadn't been exactly nice to him. She wanted to hold him and comfort him and at the same time, keep herself emotionally detached. How could she find the balance between tough love and kindness? How could they be good parents to their child without hurting each other? She remembered the way Hunter's face had transformed, lit up and shone when he saw Ryan. In that moment, everything had been perfect. She wanted that Hunter without the drama.

"I'll be okay," she said. "And so will you. We'll get through this. I know we will. But as friends. Okay?"

He nodded, lowering his gaze to the floor.

"I'm going to go home." Before she ended up a blubbering mess.

He wriggled his finger at her. "Now that . . . I can do. I'll take you."

While he made a call to security, she gathered her belongings. When she was ready, he grabbed her by the hand and led her through the crowded ballroom. The guests parted for him like the sea did for Moses. She tried to pull free of his hold, but he gripped onto her tighter. "Don't let go." He drew her closer, held her hand against the small of his back. "Let me get you to the car. Safely. Please?"

"Okay."

He didn't break stride as he led her out of the room, past the stunned glares of the partygoers and the bewildered look on Conrad's face.

With her coat on, her clutch under her arm, and her shoes hooked over her fingertips, she tucked in behind Hunter's broad shoulders, followed him across the hotel lobby, and met their security guards. He shielded her from the camera flashes and helped her out into the waiting car. Once they settled on the plush leather seats, he wrapped his arm around her shoulder. Did he not listen to her? Ever?

Too weak with tiredness, she couldn't be bothered to fight him anymore. Instead, she savored the warmth of his body heat. His protective and comforting hold. His constant, steady heartbeat.

She closed her eyes and rested her head against his shoulder for the entire journey home. She nuzzled against his jacket. It smelled of whiskey . . . and him. Her neck still tingled from his kiss.

Chapter 14

Hunter had been gone for seven weeks. Life had returned to normal. Kara wasn't sure how long normal would last. Grabbing her tote and a swag bag left over from Conrad's fashion week showing yesterday, Kara stepped out of the car in front of her apartment building. She avoided planting her foot into a pile of snow and turned to Giles. "Is it still necessary for you to be my bodyguard now the paparazzi aren't hanging around?"

No one staked Kara out anymore. After New Year's Eve, the gossip and reporters following her had been crazy for a few days. Online news sites overflowed with headlines like, *"Hottest couple in town", "Hunter spotted with baby's mom,"* and *"Did Hunter propose on New Year's Eve?"* She'd learned to take on board Hunter's, Kyle's, and Gemma's advice, and not read online news. Now she seldom checked the internet.

Giles closed the car door behind her. "Miss, protecting you may not be necessary, but it's what I get paid to do."

"You're a sweetie, Giles." Kara shivered in the cold. "But it must be boring."

"It's a good thing I like people watching. It helps to pass

the time. You have a good evening." He swished his fingers in a casual salute goodbye. "I'll see you in the morning. Oh . . . and happy Valentine's Day."

Boom!

The emptiness in her heart erupted. The first Valentine's Day in years when she'd be alone. And the way things were going, it wouldn't be her last. At eighteen weeks pregnant, no guy would want her. Dating was not an option, on hold indefinitely.

"Thanks. You have a nice night with your wife." Kara tried to inject enthusiasm into her voice.

She dragged her feet toward her building. After New Year's, it had been refitted with a new high-tech key-code access door, and renovated foyer. There was a new full-time doorman, and CCTV cameras had been mounted inside and outside of the building as well as on every floor.

Taking the elevator, she went up to her apartment on the second story, dumped her belongings on her sofa, and made her way into her tiny kitchen. As she went to unclip the Chinese takeaway menu off the fridge she hesitated. Glancing at the printout of Hunter's tour schedule next to it, she scanned down the long list of dates. She found February 14. Today, they were in Paris.

How romantic.

She ripped the menu off the fridge and ordered takeaway for one. Maybe she should get a cat. A hamster. A dog. Anything for company. But not to worry. In four and a half months, she'd have her baby.

Since Everhide had left to continue their overseas tour, she'd hardly heard from them. Different time zones didn't help. Gemma snapchatted when she could. Hunter sent the odd text. Often, his messages only detailed the name of the city he was in.

In Auckland. In Sydney. In Melbourne.

Now that fashion week was over, and she didn't have to put in such long hours at the office, she didn't need Hunter back in the forefront of her mind. She had to find a new project to occupy her brain.

With the delicious smell of the honey chicken she had for dinner lingering throughout her apartment, Kara crawled into bed at ten o'clock. She performed her nightly ritual of placing her headphones over her belly and switched her iPod on to play Everhide's music to Ryan. She leaned over to turn her light off and her tummy fluttered.

She gasped. Her hand shot to her belly. She'd never felt anything like it.

Then it happened again.

A smile charged across her face. She ripped the headphones off and placed her hands onto her skin. A little flicker, soft and gentle like the wings of a baby bird, pulsed inside her tummy.

"Oh wow." Kara spoke to her bulging baby bump. "I can feel you. Is that you kicking?"

She grabbed her cell phone off the nightstand and sent a text to Hunter. He'd said he wanted to be informed with any baby updates. This was epic.

Felt Ryan kick for the first time tonight.

Coolest thing ever.

She hit send and nestled back against her pillows. The little ripples from the baby's kicks thrummed low in her abdomen. She sucked on her lip, unable to stop the water pooling in her eyes. This was the most amazing thing ever.

With her hands splayed across her tummy she snuggled down, deeper into her bed, warming up underneath her quilt. She jumped when her cell phone rang.

Hunter?

She glanced at the time. 10:18 p.m. Doing a quick calculation in her head, she worked out it was after four a.m. in Europe. *What the hell?*

She swiped the screen. "Hello?"

"Hey, Kar. You felt him move?" His voice was so quiet she could hardly hear him.

"Yeah. It's so awesome," she gushed. "I wish you were here to feel it. It's so weird."

"Weird? How so?"

"Why are you whispering?" She realized she was talking at the same level.

"Um . . ." She heard a door close. "We've just got back to the hotel. We went out after the show and had a few drinks. We're traveling tomorrow, so I'll be able to catch up on sleep."

"Are you sharing a room with Kyle and Gem?"

"Ah . . . no." He hesitated. "I've got my own room."

"Then why are you being so quiet?" Then it hit her. "Oh . . . shit. You've got someone with you. Haven't you?" Her heart fell from her chest and rolled across the floor, slipped through a crack in the boards, and disappeared.

"No. Yes." Stress rippled through his voice. "It's not what you think."

Her cell phone shook in her hand. "What am I supposed to *not* think, Hunter?" Even she could hear the bite in her tone. She had no claim over him. She wasn't stupid. So why did it hurt so much? "You're on tour. You have girls. I get it."

"Kara," he snapped. "It's not like that. Every time I've come close, *you* pop into my head. It's a real mood-killer."

She'd been called many things before. But mood-killer? That was new. She was fat, pregnant, and single. A total mood-killer. But like he'd said, he'd been *close* to doing something. At least he was getting *some* kind of attention. Did *close* mean he was making out with girls, or were they just getting down on their knees for him? Her stomach churned at the thought. Why was she so jealous?

"I'm sure you'll get over it." A bitter taste burned her tongue. "Like now. Considering you have someone with you. Who is it? Some hot French girl? A groupie?"

Silence. She looked at her phone thinking the connection had dropped out. But then she heard him breathe.

"It's Amie."

"Amie? Who the hell is—" Kara's hand shot to her chest. "Oh shit. You're kidding me? Your ex is in your room? Even after she screwed you over?" The baby rolled from one side of her tummy to the other. "Ow! Ryan doesn't like that either. You should've felt what he did."

"What did he do?"

"He kicked the crap out of me. What the hell are you doing with her?"

He wouldn't sleep with her again, but Amie was fine? Oh! This made her feel so much better. Not!

Something thumped. Sounded like he hit a wall. "She was at the same bar. She's in town on tour with one of her bands. We had a drink."

"And you brought her back to your room." Kara winced at the cattiness in her tone.

"I haven't slept with her." His voice grew harsher, louder. "We're just talking. Catching up."

"Yes, I remember Gemma telling me how you and Amie *just talked.* If I recall, it involved a ripped shirt, lipstick stains, and scratch marks on your chest." She clutched and twisted a handful of her quilt around in her fist, tighter and tighter and tighter.

He sighed, his breath heavy through the cell phone speaker. "Come on. That was a long time ago."

"Hunter, there is no you and me. You can screw whoever you want. It's Valentine's Day. Go for it." A tear slid down her cheek.

She didn't want to get upset, but since falling pregnant with his child, she'd hated the thought of him being with anybody else. Hated it. "She's your type, isn't she? Drop-dead gorgeous, and dresses like a slut. Something I'll never be or do."

Thud. Thud. Thud.

Was he hitting his head against the wall?

"I wasn't with Amie for her looks, if that's what you're insinuating,"

"Bullshit." Kara wasn't blind. Amie was model tall, skinny as a rake, and cosmetically enhanced to perfection. She was a man magnet. "Don't kid yourself."

"I'm not. We were friends for a long time. It grew into something more. Something I thought was real. Something . . . too short-lived." Then he paused. His voice lowered and came out slow and pained. "Because I wasn't good enough for her. I was never enough for her."

What? Hunter not good at something? That was a first. But the vulnerability in his voice hit her deep inside her chest. He made her head spin and her heart wish for something that was unfathomable. Since New Year's, she'd been holding out for a miracle. That he'd change. She'd change. That they'd put their differences aside, fall in love, and raise their child together. But she'd been duping herself for far too long. She wanted a man who was loyal, faithful, and adored her. One who'd be around. Hunter would never be that guy. A chill swept over her and her heart hardened. "Hunt, you have Amie in your room. What you do with her is none of my business."

"Stop. Please?" He pleaded. "Amie and I were talking about you. The baby. How things were going."

Shit!. Kara jabbed her palm against her forehead. Why did he always get her so worked up? Why did she always think the worst of him? "I'm sorry. I didn't mean to flip out. I'm tired. Fashion week was exhausting."

"How was the showing?"

She closed her eyes and filled her lungs. Having this baby and building their friendship was a team effort. She had to be more tactful, caring and considerate, not jump when he did something she didn't like. Massaging her temple, she found her inner calm and fell into conversation with him. Talking about her week and his tour took her mind off wanting to rip his head off and eat it like a praying mantis. The gentle tone in his voice had a soothing effect on her. Made her miss him. And that was something she shouldn't be feeling.

She covered her mouth and yawned. "Hunt, it's late. I gotta get some sleep. Thanks for calling and the catch up."

"Wait," he said. "I want to see how big he's grown. Put video on."

"What?" Had she heard him correctly?

"Please?"

"You're sick."

"I think we well and truly established that fact a long time ago."

"You want to see my belly?"

"Yeah. I know I'm not there, but I want to see him growing. See every little change."

See? There was the nice Hunter. He could be so adorable. *Sometimes.*

Going off at him tonight like some psycho jealous ex was wrong. She didn't want to be like that. Ever. He had his life. She had hers. She had to focus on being his friend.

She hit the video button and pulled up her pajama top. As she positioned her cell phone camera to focus on her baby bump, Hunter's face filled the screen.

"Are you in the bathroom?" Kara could make out the shower in the background.

"Yeah." Her cell phone shone with his gorgeous smile. "Cute

snowflake winter jammies, Kar . . . Oh wow, look at the size of your tummy . . . he's grown so much. Oh . . . mega wow. Look at the size of your boobs. They're fantastic."

Even though her breasts were covered, she lowered her shirt an inch and glared at him. "And they hurt like hell. Nothing good about them."

His eyes glinted. "Oh . . . yes there is."

She blushed. *Just ignore him.* Then, Ryan moved. "There . . . I feel him." She placed her hand on her abdomen. "It's like little flutters and bubbles." Kara wriggled lower on the mattress and angled her cell phone for Hunter to see her whole tummy. Ryan kicked again. "You can't see anything move yet. Won't be long until you can."

"Can't wait." Hunter's eyes twinkled, then darkened. "Thanks, Kar. I hate not being there to see him. But knowing you're doing okay makes me feel better." He glanced at his watch. "I better go and send Amie on her way. I'm off to Spain in a few hours. Only fourteen weeks of tour left, and then I'll be home."

She was counting down the days. "I'll be super fat by then."

"And super sexy and beautiful."

Her heart swelled. It shouldn't have, but it did.

He waved at her. "Look after our bubby. Stay in touch. Chat soon. Bye."

The screen went blank. She put her cell phone on her nightstand and her heart deflated. She tugged the pillow under her head and turned the light out. Drawing the quilt up, she cuddled it tightly under her chin. Tears dampened her cheeks as she stared at the streetlight filtering into her room through the gap in her curtains. The heating element on her wall crackled and creaked as the outside night temperature plummeted.

Damn hormones made her cry at the slightest of things. Kleenex tissue ads. Pampers ads. Life insurance ads.

And . . . Hunter.

If she wasn't more careful when she spoke to him, she'd push him away. And she didn't want that. Whether it was Amie or not, he would be with someone else soon enough. And in the future, so would she. It was just going to take her longer than she'd originally planned.

Hunter was going to be a great dad. He gloated like a proud daddy already. What was he going to be like when Ryan was born? Kara smiled and wiped her runny nose. He was going to be there for the baby. Just like she wanted. She could never ask for anything more.

Valentine's Day hadn't been too bad after all.

Maybe it was time to plan the nursery for Ryan. That would be her new project. She could do this single mother thing. She'd had enough of dramas, outbursts, and emotional swings. Surely, nothing else could go wrong. The rest of this pregnancy was going to be a breeze.

Chapter 15

Weary from lack of sleep, Hunter slipped into the leather seat of the private jet bound from Paris to Barcelona. Kyle took the seat opposite. After partying all night, his eyes were bloodshot and puffy, and he nursed his head. Hunter's head spun, too. But it wasn't from too much alcohol. It was from talking to Kara about Ryan's first kick.

Ryan kicked. Epic.

As their backup band shuffled down the aisle to the seats at the rear, Gemma stood in a huddle at the front, chatting with Sophie, Bec, and Kate. Her eyes glistened as she giggled and carried on about something.

"What's got Gem in such a good mood this morning?" Hunter asked Kyle.

A lazy smile slid across Kyle's face. "We confirmed a date for our wedding. October. Belize, here we come."

"All right, bud." He high-fived Kyle. "That's awesome."

Hunter did a quick calculation in his head. That was three months after his baby was due. Kara should be able to make it.

"Excuse me, Mr. Collins, Mr. McIntyre." Juliette, their flight attendant, rested her hand on the back of Kyle's chair. "The snowfall has caused some minor delays. We have about thirty minutes to wait before takeoff. Can I get you anything in the meantime?"

Hunter shook his head and looked out at the tarmac of the Charles de Gaulle airport. Airplanes taxied toward the takeoff runway, wind gusts swirled clouds of snow, and vehicles with flashing lights zipped past.

"Um . . . yes," Kyle said. "Two coffees, please?"

"Sure." Juliette took off toward the galley at the back.

Hunter strummed his fingers on the mahogany table between them. "If we're celebrating wedding dates, shouldn't you have ordered champagne?"

Kyle dragged his hands down his face. "Ergh, I can't face alcohol right now. And besides, we need to talk."

What did Kyle want to talk about? The wedding? Hunter inhaled a sharp breath. "Sure. What is it? I've already agreed to be your best man."

"Ah, no. Not about weddings." Kyle looked over his shoulder in the direction of the flight attendant, then back at him. "That. You ignored a smoking hot attendant again. Normally you'd be all over her in an instant."

Hunter leaned out into the aisle and checked out Juliette. With her blond hair knotted into a bun, she had a nice smile, curvy hips, and long legs. She had that sexy, sweet, come-and-do-me look about her. Yeah. Normally, she was someone he'd bang in an instant. But nothing about him was normal. Not anymore. "She's all right. But I'll pass." He shrugged it off like it was no big deal.

"This is more serious than I thought." Kyle leaned forward, eyes narrowed. "Sam said you left last night with Amie. Like . . . what the hell? She's the devil."

Hunter winced. Amie was the devil. Seductive. Alluring.

Hot. And someone he should stay away from.

Carla and Margo shuffled past them. Carla play-punched him in the arm as she passed. They joined Gemma's conversation at the front.

Kyle straightened his legs. "Who let Amie into our private bar area?"

"I did." Hunter's leg jiggled at speed.

"You what?" Kyle's sharp tone hit him like an uppercut to the chin. "Why?"

"When I saw her by the main bar, I had to see her. See how she was doing." He needed to find out if she'd suffered like he had, regretted hurting him, held any remorse for screwing up Everhide's contract with SureHaven Records. She didn't. It had hardened his heart even more. "I wanted to find out why she was there. I thought . . . that we could talk."

But he was kidding himself. When he was with Amie, they'd rarely talked. All they'd done was fuck. Fuck like rabbits. That was all he was good for. Sex. Nothing else. He'd meant nothing to her.

Juliette returned with their coffees and placed them on the table between them.

"Thanks." Kyle dismissed her and grabbed his cup. "Please tell me you did nothing stupid, Hunt?"

"It depends on what you define as stupid." Hunter smirked, picked up his coffee, and took a sip. "I didn't know she was high on coke until we got back to my room."

Kyle slammed his cup down. "Why did you take her to your room?"

"To get away from everyone—the cameras, the gossipers, the fans."

"Please tell me you didn't fuck her? Or do drugs?"

The temptation to do both had been there. For less than a second. He wasn't going to end up a screwed-up mess again—

over her, or drugs. He had a baby due in a few months. That was all that mattered.

"She can be *very* persuasive." Hunter sighed. "You know Amie." The moment the door to his room closed, she'd tried to tear his clothes off. Her lips had been hot on his. She'd torn his shirt open. Her frantic hands had been through his hair, on his ass, all over his body.

He closed his eyes and tried to block the memory from his mind. She'd felt so good, her flesh pressing against his. He'd been so hard. Turned on. But when she'd reached for his belt, he'd stopped her. He'd stopped her because all he could think about was Kara. About Ryan.

"Amie's an addictive drug." He gripped his coffee cup tighter. "One I no longer need. I didn't sleep with her. We talked about Ryan." Before she passed out on his bed on a drugged-up high.

"Are you sure about that?" Kyle interrogated him like he was a criminal on trial.

"Yes."

"Thank Christ for that. I don't know what's going on in your head, Hunt. You haven't been yourself this tour. I understand Kara falling pregnant hasn't been easy on you, or her. The past few weeks, you're up and down all the time. You gotta stop bottling up whatever is eating you inside. You know you can talk to me, Gem, or both of us about anything."

"That's just it." Hunter gulped down a mouthful of coffee as the jets on the engine roared to life. "I can't think straight anymore. Kara's fucked with my head, my life—my very existence." *Changed the path of my future.*

The phone conversation with her flickered through his mind. Hearing her voice. Seeing Ryan. No matter how hard he tried, he couldn't stop the grin spreading across his face. "Kara texted last night. She felt the baby move for the first time. I called her. I couldn't see him move, but I saw how much her tummy has grown. Ryan's getting bigger every day. It's so wicked."

"A-ha." Kyle scratched at the stubble on his cheek.

Hunter grabbed his cell phone from his jacket pocket and opened the photo Kara had sent him. He stroked his thumb over the picture of her smiling and showing off her baby bulge. *So awesome.* With a flick of his wrist, he flashed the picture to Kyle. "He's eighteen weeks."

"Look at you." Kyle shook his head. "You're gloating, and it isn't even born yet. I never thought I'd see the day."

Hunter stared at the image of Kara. She was sexy, lying on her bed, with a rosy glow in her cheeks. He swiped the screen to off.

"Can you be honest with me?" Kyle dropped his head back against the seat.

"Always."

"Are you into Kara in any way? At all?"

"What?" That was one of the questions he asked himself every day. How could he reply to that when he couldn't give a straight answer? Kara was a melody of mayhem. Funny. Irritating. Annoying. Sexy. Sassy. Frustrating. Stubborn. Smart. She drove him freaking crazy. One minute he wanted to kiss her, fuck her, and the next minute he couldn't run in the opposite direction fast enough.

She'd altered his life. Trapped him. She'd taken him down a path he never knew he wanted. Ryan had changed everything, and not all for the better. "I think about her and the baby every day. How can I not? In a few months, my life is going to change forever. I've had to deal with it, accept it, and take responsibility. Seeing Amie last night made me realize I've changed. I've had to change."

"I know. But you didn't answer the question. Hunt, you should see the way your face lights up when you talk about Kara. And seeing that photo." Kyle pointed to the cell phone in

Hunter's hand. "Is that buzz for the baby, her, or both?"

Kyle's observation sent a chill through his veins. Made his head ache.

What Hunter had been feeling since New Year's terrified him. He was so protective of his own family, and he couldn't believe it now included his son. He'd do anything for Ryan. There'd been one crazy nanosecond when he danced with Kara, when her body had felt so perfect next to his, that he thought he wanted to let his guard down and take a chance on her. But it was just the JD talking. His dick wanting some action. There was no way he was into her. She'd made it perfectly clear they were only ever going to be friends. And she was right. He didn't want a relationship. He wasn't ready to settle down. So that *buzz* for her had to be eradicated. He had to focus on his son. "It's for Ryan."

"And you're sure about that?" Kyle swiveled his cup around on the table. "Because this is exactly what happened during our last tour. My head was so screwed up over Gem, and so was yours. The way you're acting now is how you were back then when you struggled with your feelings for her. You question every look, every touch, and every moment. Is that what's going on with you and Kara?"

Being with Gemma had been different. He'd had strong feelings for her. He'd taken a chance on seeing if it was something more. But there wasn't. He loved her like a sister. Nothing else. But Kara? This was deeper. Harder. More intense. "I've questioned everything I feel about her. From hating her to thinking there might be something. But there's not. It's been hard coming to terms with having a baby. That's all."

The PA bell dinged. "This is your captain speaking. We have been given clearance for departure. Cabin crew, please prepare our guests for takeoff."

Kyle cupped the nape of his neck and stretched it back.

"Hunt, you're not picking up girls. You've got this vacant look about you half the time. You're here physically, not mentally. You switch on for the shows, then off the minute we're offstage. It's gotta stop."

"I'm sorry this is affecting you and Gem." He dug his fingers into thighs. "I'm doing my best to deal with everything."

"I'm worried about you."

"Who made you Dr. Phil?" Why did his best mate have to know him so well?

"Remember, I'm the deep, brooding, emotional musician?" Kyle said with a glint in his eye. "I observe things."

"You're a dick." Hunter's head slumped back and he glared at the overhead locker. "Stop with your psychoanalysis."

Kyle chuckled and shook his head. A huge grin spread across his face. "Never. Kara's a great girl. The minute she broke up with Conrad, you couldn't wait to get in her panties. She falls pregnant. You've had to face your worst nightmares. She's met your family. You've done everything to ensure she's safe and looked after. You left us on New Year's to see her. You call and text her. All you do is think about her."

"So? What's your point?"

"You're into her. Admit it."

"No," he snapped, clenching his hand into a fist. He liked her but wasn't into her. Why consider the possibility of something more when she wasn't into him? And even if she was, he couldn't go down a road that would only end in hurt. He couldn't do that to the mother of his child. "We're friends. That's it."

"All right." Kyle held up his palms. "I'm sorry. I'll back off. I get it. It's all about the baby. Not Kara."

Hunter's jaw ached from straining his muscles. Kara *had* gotten to him. She'd weaved her way into his life. Forced him to reassess everything—his lifestyle, his plans, his behavior. His future wasn't just about him, Gem, and Kyle, and their music anymore. Somehow, he had to fit a baby into the mix. Become a responsible father. *Me? Responsible? Who would have thought?* But he'd do it. "That's right. It's all about Ryan."

The seatbelt sign came on and the girls took to their seats. Gemma came and gave Kyle a kiss before she sat in the bay of seats across the aisle with Bec. Juliette cruised through the cabin and closed the overhead lockers. The door was shut, and the plane taxied toward the runway.

"Kyle, you wanna know what's really been getting to me?" Hunter wiped his hands down his jeans and glimpsed at the airport buildings as the plane passed. "Take out Kara, and the lawyers, and all the drama—this has been the hardest thing to comprehend since the scan. And it's been growing every day." It was the one thing that set a spark through his veins and had him counting down the days until the end of tour. "Last night, it blew into epic proportions."

"What is it?" Kyle asked.

The plane pointed down the runway to take off. The jets roared as the plane thundered down the tarmac and launched into the air.

Hunter put his stresses aside and smiled a beaming smile. "I can't believe I'm about to say this." He sucked in a deep breath, and warmth filled his heart. "But . . . I'm excited. I still don't know how the hell Kara and I are going to make it work, but I'm actually looking forward to having a baby. I'm going to be a daddy. A *fucking* daddy. I'm going to have a son."

Chapter 16

Kara held onto her baby bump as her driver navigated through the crazed streets and avenues of Midtown, dodging potholes and clattering over subway grates, taking her back to work after her lunchtime obstetrician appointment. With every yard they covered, more worry rippled through her mind, and tension tugged at the base of her neck. Her twenty-four-week scan showed that Ryan was on the small side, and her blood pressure was too high. She had to be careful, lower her stress levels, and get more rest. Was that possible with her current job demands? Would Conrad let her reduce her workload, maybe even her hours? Her health and Ryan were all that mattered.

First thing: she grabbed her cell phone and texted Hunter with the latest Ryan update.

Went to doctor. 24 weeks today.

A huge grin spread across her face when her phone tinkled, and she saw Hunter's reply.

Send me a picture.

Did he ever sleep?

During the past month, Hunter had texted her more often.

She loved the messages and the random phone calls they now shared. Most of them were baby-oriented, with him insisting she send him a picture of her growing belly every week. Some days it was hard to not let the protective shield around her heart falter.

He'd changed. His attitude toward the baby had done a complete turnaround since the first scan. But she had to remember he cared about Ryan—not her.

A new resilience had taken hold of her in the past few weeks. She was stronger. Grateful that she and Hunter had become friends.

Sitting up straight on the car seat, her belly popped out, round like a melon beneath her maternity top. She took a snap of her tummy and sent it to Hunter. Giles, sitting next to her, shook his head and turned to look out the window. At first, doing the photos had been weird, but now she loved taking the images. They gave her a record of her pregnancy, and the beautiful baby growing inside her. Treasured memories she could keepsake.

She attached the image to her message.

Here you go. Doc says baby small. Must eat more.

Seconds later, her phone buzzed.

Look after yourself. You're eating for two. H.

She also sent him a photo of the baby outfits she'd bought at the store across the street from her doctor's. Two onesies, white, and covered in music notes. How could she resist?

Cool. XOXO.

Hugs and kisses? They were for Ryan, but still, a warm glow washed over her and she hugged her cell phone to her chest. In eight weeks, he'd be home from tour. How would things change then?

Did he want to come to her neonatal classes? Did he want to help prep the nursery she hadn't got to yet? How often should they catch up before the baby? And what about after Ryan was born? Would she be doing the late nights and dealing with a screaming baby all alone? Nothing had been set in concrete.

Ergh! She couldn't worry about that now. She had too much to do. Orders had been flooding into Conrad's since fashion week, and she was already working with her team on next season's line.

When she arrived at the office, Giles ushered her into the building. No one on the street gave her a sideways glance.

"Thanks, Giles. See you tonight. Six o'clock, unless you hear from me."

"Yes, ma'am. Have a good day." He waved goodbye, slipped back out to the car, and the driver took off.

Why Hunter insisted she still have security baffled her. Life was somewhat normal.

She stepped out of the elevators onto her floor, hoping to have an easy afternoon at work, but Melissa, the receptionist, pulled her up straight away.

"Conrad wants to see you." Melissa yanked off her headset and jumped up, sending her chair spinning backward. "In his office. I don't know what it's about, but I warn you, he's been flying off at everyone for the past two hours. I think you could be the next."

"Great. What have I done now?" Kara adjusted her purse strap on her shoulder while juggling her shopping bag in her hand. The baby kicked violently. *Ow!* Kara grunted and clutched at the ache in her belly.

"You okay?" Melissa stepped forward, holding out her hand.

"Yeah. I'm fine. Baby's not happy about having to meet with Conrad either."

Walking through the design room, Kara weaved past workstations where colleagues huddled together going over design sketches and fabric swatches. Pattern-cutting tables were covered in scraps of material and paper. Sewing machines hummed and whirred. Seamstresses focused on their stitches. Half-dressed mannequins stood about the floor showing dresses due next week for the Tribeca Film Festival.

"Morning, gang." Kara dumped her bags underneath her desk, turned on her laptop, and smiled at her two team members. "Did we get those combed cotton samples in from Italy?" she asked Jon, the textile technician.

"Yes, we did." He swept his hand through his fire-truck red hair. "They're gorgeous. The weave is divine."

"Excellent." She straightened her shirt. "Conrad wants to see me and then we'll go through them. Tim, can you make sure we have all the briefs from Conrad?"

"All ready to go." He patted his pile of color-coded folders—red for pants, green for tops, and blue for dresses.

"Awesome. I won't be long."

"KARA!" Conrad boomed from his office doorway on the other side of the work floor. "My office. Now."

Kara drew in a steady breath. They'd had their strategy meetings and planning sessions earlier in the week. Her team's designs were on schedule, orders had been met, and production was happening. What could he want with her?

Holding her chin high, she entered his elaborate office and shut the door behind her. Bright, natural light beamed in through the huge windows that overlooked Bryant Park. Even with its bare trees and frosted brown grass, the park had a greater variety of colors than Conrad's office. Almost every item in it was black—the leather sofa, the desk, the chairs—or orange—the cushions, the wall art, the stationery. Kara would kill to add different colored cushions and a vibrant flower arrangement.

Jasmine wasn't in sight. *Good.*

"You needed to see me, Conrad?" Kara said with a lackluster

tone.

Conrad stepped aside from the mannequin he'd been blocking from view. Kara's heart lurched against her ribs. It was their dress—the one she'd designed with him before they broke up. A dark green Dutch silk gown, with abstract cutout cup-sleeves and hemline. They'd spent nights curled next to each other on his sofa in his loft apartment, drawing and sketching it. Discussing fabrics, the width of the box-pleats and the finishing details of the gown. He'd wanted royal elegance; Kara had wanted to jazz it up by adding some sexy flare with the delicate cut-outs.

Then he'd dumped her.

"You made it." She dashed forward and examined the creation. "It's beautiful."

"Elise saw the mock-up when she was in here a few weeks ago and loved it. Ordered it then and there."

Kara ran her hands over the bodice, the boning corseting the fine seamlines. But when she glanced at Conrad, the muscles in her neck stiffened. Black circles framed his eyes, his cheekbones had sunk, and his normal neatly combed hair was in desperate need of a cut. It seemed the stress of fashion week had taken its toll on everyone—especially him.

"This dress needs to go to Elise in three days, and it's not finished," he said. "I need your help. Please?"

"I don't work on couture anymore. Get Jasmine to help you." It was impossible to hide the coldness in her voice. While she didn't want Jasmine's hands on her design, she didn't want to work in close confines with Conrad. He'd become more erratic and demanding. Made every day at work unpleasant. She didn't know if it was because she was stressed, or hormonal, or whether Conrad had made it his mission to upset her. She had enough to worry about without adding him to her list.

"No. I need you." Pleading and begging flashed in his eyes,

but Kara ignored it. He ran his hand across the hipline of the skirt. "These box pleats are all wrong. Jasmine thinks they should be narrower and higher on the waistline. What do you think?"

How did this man achieve such success if he couldn't see his own vision in the gown? He was the head of the fashion house. Not her. Not Jasmine. Since when did Conrad practice self-doubt?

Kara's blood pressure spiked. She didn't have time for this nonsense. "No. If you do that then it will stick out like a balloon. Elise will not want to look like a church bell."

"Jasmine also suggested it might need something to enhance the cut-outs. Beads or rhinestones or something in bronze to work in with our urban-industrial look."

"Conrad, Elise isn't into bling. You should know that. She's more conservative than a nun's habit." What had Jasmine done to Conrad? He was a genius when it came to classic, elegant designs.

Desperation and fear filled his voice. "Please help me, Kar?"

She groaned and snatched the pincushion off his desk. "There's nothing wrong with the dress. My only suggestion would be to make the hemline shorter. Don't have so much length below the abstract cutouts. It's supposed to sit on the knee, not below." She slid her hand over the skirt and turned the edge over. With her growing belly, she struggled to lower herself to her knees and pinned the skirt to her desired length. Luckily, she'd worn dress pants today; she hadn't anticipated crawling around the floor.

Conrad squatted beside her. "You're right. I couldn't see it. I was worried about embellishments and not the simple elegance of the dress. Thank you. We're such a good team."

"Were," Kara mumbled under her breath.

Conrad sat back on his heels, his eyes on her belly. "How's

everything going with the baby?"

"Okay. I had my check-up this morning."

He stood and put out his hand to help her up. "Come and sit. There's something I want to talk to you about."

"What else do you need?" She took his offered hand. Maybe now would be a good time to ask about reducing her workload.

As she labored to her feet, a dull ache rippled across her lower abdomen. What had she eaten for lunch? A chicken salad with dressing. The indigestion was a bitch. She needed to go for a walk, not sit and chat.

"Kara, please?"

The concern on his face tugged at her heart. She did care for him—just not the way she used to. She lowered herself onto the sofa. "I'm listening."

He sat beside her. His hands shook as he wiped his palms on his trousers. "Has anything developed between you and Hunter?"

"Developed?" A breathy laugh burst from her lips. "Yes, Conrad, something *has* developed between us. We're now *civil* to each other. I give him updates on the baby. He lets me know where in the world he is."

"I need you to be honest with me." The severity in his tone caught her off guard.

"Why?"

"Because I want you back."

Pain shot through her chest, it was as if he'd rammed his pincushion, sharp ends first, into her heart. "You what?"

"I mean it. I haven't stopped thinking about you for weeks. On New Year's, you were right. I always run away when things get tough. I don't want to do that anymore. We were good together. I left because I failed you. We couldn't get pregnant after we tried for so long. I wasn't prepared to face months of IVF or surrogacy."

"Stop." She closed her eyes and shuddered. Nausea flooded her aching gut. How could he want her when he was with Jasmine? "You have a girlfriend."

"Don't worry about Jazzy. My work is suffering without you. You're my muse."

"No." Her head spun faster than a cotton bobbin being wound with thread.

He inched closer and took her hand in his. "Come back to me, Kar. Move in with me. Marry me. Let's be the family you always wanted."

The ringing in her ears was deafening. She struggled to draw breath. "Are you for real? It's not your baby. It's not your responsibility."

"But it's *your* baby. I've thought about it. I will love your baby as my own. You know I will."

Holy. Shit.

Conrad was offering her everything she'd ever dreamed of. Marriage. Family. All her dreams could come true. She could picture herself walking down the aisle in the beautiful white dress she'd designed for herself years ago and see him waiting for her at the altar with their friends and family gathered in the pews.

But she stopped at the seat near the front of the church. Hunter was there. Staring at her. She couldn't take the next step toward Conrad.

Hunter wanted nothing to do with her romantically, but he had changed her life forever. He'd changed her view of the world, the course of her dreams, and her future direction.

She had to move forward for her baby. There was no going back. Everything was clear. There were too many wrong elements in Conrad's equation. It wasn't about love or mistakes or regret. It was about him. He needed her for work, for inspiration. Nothing else.

"You can't say things like that. Not ever." Tears stung her eyes. "You're involved with another woman." Kara's hand shot over her mouth. "Oh . . . you haven't even broken up with her, have you? You were waiting to see my reaction before you told her. You *bastard.* If I say no, she would have been none the wiser. You self-centered *prick.*"

"Kar, it's not like that." He squeezed her hand, but she pulled free.

"Yes, it is. I know I'm better off without you. I was blinded by how much I loved you. You were my world. But you drowned me. It was all work and no play. I forgot who I was. I stopped going out, stopped playing sport, stopped hanging out with my friends. I stopped having fun. I won't let that happen again."

"You can't do those things now. You're having a child. It needs a father. I'm here for you."

Fire scorched through her veins. "Ryan has a father. *Hunter.* We all have to live with the choices we've made, and you made yours when you left. So if there is nothing else, I have work to do." She rubbed at the ache in her tummy. The pain was getting worse.

"Take some time to think about it."

"I don't need time. My answer is no. I don't love you anymore."

Hunter filled her mind. The way he protected his family, his caring nature, the fun they'd had together, his good heart— they were what she needed for Ryan.

Conrad gaped. "You will. I know you can."

"No." What had he expected? Her to fall into his arms and cry with happiness? Maybe a few months ago, she would have been that girl. But not anymore. Her belly grumbled and ached. "I needed to talk to you about reducing my hours because my doctor has concerns with my health. Can I schedule a meeting with you for tomorrow? I'm not feeling well." Kara's brow broke out in a clammy sweat. "I'm going to work from home for the rest of the day."

"Okay. Sure. No worries. I've put too much pressure on you. I'm sorry." He wrung his hands together. "My offer is still valid. Just say the word."

She stood and circled her hands over her tummy. "The answer will always be no." With her head held high, she strode out of the room.

"Kar, what's wrong?" Jon rushed to her side with Tim.

Fighting back the tears, she clutched onto Jon's shoulder for support. "I need to go home."

She never wanted to repeat what had happened to anyone in the office. But she felt sorry for Jasmine. Hopefully it wouldn't take her as long as it had taken Kara to realize that Conrad was a jerk.

"Is there anything we can do?" Jon picked up her shopping and her purse and handed it to her.

"Thanks, guys. But no. We'll meet tomorrow about the sampling, okay?" She plucked a couple of tissues from the box, called Giles, and headed home.

In her apartment, she dropped her gear on the floor and collapsed on the sofa. The floodgates opened once again. Maybe she should've taken Conrad back. It would have made things easier. He would've stuck around for a while. But it wouldn't have been for long. He would have rushed back to Jasmine or the next intern who walked through his door.

Her cell phone buzzed, and her heart skipped a beat. Hunter. A message from London. Through teary eyes, she gazed at the picture. It was of him, Gemma, and Kyle hugging each other in front of London's Tower Bridge and making funny faces. The caption read,

> *We're working hard today. You? UK done.*
> *Off to Japan tomorrow. H.*

She giggled and wiped her tear-streaked cheeks. He certainly brightened her mood. She circled her hand over the gentle kick fluttering in her belly and smiled. Life had sent her down one rocky road. She'd lost a lover in Conrad but gained a good friend in Hunter—something she'd never expected.

She turned to look at the pile of baby wares she'd ordered lying in the corner. The flat-packed cot and dressing table, the clothes, mobile, and rocker had all arrived. She didn't feel like doing work for Conrad; she'd rather clean her spare bedroom for the nursery.

Ryan was her future. It was time to prepare.

She sat up.

Arrrgggh!

She screamed. Violent cramps charged through her abdomen. She keeled over and clutched her tummy. Her eyes widened, and she struggled to breathe.

She fell to her knees on the floor and cried.

Owwww!

Her stomach contracted again. A warm dampness flooded between her legs. Horror swept across her skin. Scrambling to her feet, she dashed into the bathroom. She stripped her dress pants off and checked her panties.

Her hands trembled. Tears streamed down her cheeks.

There was blood.

Everywhere.

Chapter 17

"Kara's in hospital," Lexi blurted. "She's just gone in to surgery."

"What?" Hunter leapt from his hotel bed and glanced at the clock. Two a.m. His heart jarred like a jackhammer. "What's . . . what's happened?"

"It's the baby. Kara started bleeding and cramping. Her mom didn't have your number, so I called you." Lexi's voice quivered as she spoke at breakneck speed. "Hunt, I'm so scared. Kara has to have an emergency cesarean."

"Oh shit. Is she okay? What about the baby?" Tears burned his eyes. Horror clawed at his brain. It was too early for Ryan to be born. "Lex, I'm coming. I don't know how, but I'm coming home."

Storming out of his room, his mind swirled. He crossed the suite's living room, and bashed on Kyle and Gemma's bedroom door.

"Go away," Kyle bellowed.

Taking no notice, Hunter flung the door open.

"It's Kara." His whole body trembled. "She's in hospital. I have to go."

Gemma swiped her shirt off the floor, and ripped it on. "What's happened?"

"Emergency. Cesarean. I have to go. *Now.*" Fear gripped his throat and squeezed.

"All right. All right." Kyle swung out of bed and grabbed his boxer shorts. "Calm the fuck down. We'll sort it out."

Ten minutes later, a bleary-eyed Kate, Bec, Sophie, and their tour manager, Olsen, were in their suite sorting out the details. Hunter paced the length of the window that looked over the glittering London skyline. His mind on Kara and Ryan. They had to be okay. Had to be. Bec was booking flights for him to New York. Kate, Sophie, and their tour manager were going over the schedule and writing urgent press releases to cancel their scheduled concerts in Tokyo. The cursing and yelling were nothing but white noise in his ears.

"We'll come with you." Gemma handed him a cup of steaming hot coffee. "Kyle and I want to be there."

Hunter's hands shook as he took the cup and nodded.

"I talked to Lexi. There's no update yet. Kara's still in surgery." Gemma placed her hand on his shoulder. "They'll be okay."

Her words of comfort had no impact. He had to get to Kara.

"Right," Bec said, throwing her cell phone onto the coffee table. She looked up from her laptop. "The quickest way I can get you all there is on a commercial flight that leaves in a few hours. You'll get to New York around lunchtime. Drivers and security are on their way."

Sophie came over and rubbed his arm. "We'll deal with everything else. Don't worry. You get to Kara and your baby. Let us know what's happening as soon as you get there."

"I hate canceling shows," Olsen grumbled, stabbing his pen on the tabletop. "I know it's an emergency, but sorting out logistics is a nightmare."

"Fuck you." Hunter charged past Sophie toward Olsen, but Kyle stopped him.

"Hey, bud. It's okay. Go pack your shit, and let's get going." Kyle slapped him on the shoulder. "Focus on Kara and Ryan. They need you."

Ryan. I'm coming.

His pulse drummed in his ears as he stuffed his belongings into his suitcase. During the long eight-hour flight home, he chewed at his fingernails. He'd tried to call Kara several times since he landed, but she hadn't answered. His legs didn't stop jiggling for the entire traffic-jammed car ride to the hospital.

Please let them be okay.

Mid-afternoon, security ushered him, Gemma, and Kyle into the maternity ward at Lenox Hill Hospital. Hunter's feet couldn't carry him fast enough. Checking in at the nurse's station, every nerve stood on edge. He hooked his overnight duffel bag on his shoulder and dashed down the hallway. Kyle and Gemma following close behind.

Hunter hesitated outside of Kara's room. His heart hammered hard against his ribcage.

"We'll wait here." Gemma stepped forward and squeezed his arm.

Kyle gave him a hug. "Let us know if you need anything."

Hunter rolled his shoulders and stretched his neck. "I've got this . . . I think." Taking a shaky step forward, he swung the door open and entered the darkened room.

His heart ached at the sight of Kara lying on the bed with an IV in her arm. He met her gaze and she burst into tears. Dropping his bag on the floor, he rushed into her open arms, sat beside her and hugged her tight. He buried his face into her neck and absorbed her in. "I came as fast as I could. Is Ryan okay? Please tell me he's okay. Where is he?"

She wiped her cheek with her palm. "He's in neonatal

intensive care." She sniffled and clutched his hands on his lap. "He's so tiny, Hunt. They have him in a humidicrib, covered in tubes and monitors. But he's alive."

"What happened?" His throat was so dry it was hard to talk. "Are you okay?"

She shook her head, and tears glassed her cheeks. "My uterus gave up. The doctors couldn't stop the hemorrhaging. I had to have a hysterectomy. It's all gone. There's nothing left of me."

"Shh." He stroked her hair and brushed her tears with his thumb. "That's not true. We've got our son. We've got our baby boy. That's all that matters. I'm so sorry I wasn't here."

"Lexi and Hayden were here. Mom, Dad and Naomi came after my surgery."

But he hadn't been around. And he hated that. "I tried to call, but you didn't answer." He still trembled all over as he held her hands.

"Once my catheter was removed after lunch, I turned my phone on silent so I could get some rest. Lexi told me you were coming. I didn't think you'd get here so soon. I can't believe you've left tour."

"I had to come for Ryan. There was never any question I wouldn't. Kyle and Gem came too. They're outside waiting." He stroked her hair. "Are you allowed out of bed? Can we go and see Ryan?"

She nodded. "Yeah. I'd like that."

He carefully helped Kara into her wheelchair, clipped her IV pole into place, and pushed her out of the room. Kyle and Gemma greeted her with hugs and followed him as he wheeled Kara along the corridor and weaved around the odd person walking by. Trying to control his racing heart, he gripped the handles tighter and tighter. *I'm going to meet my son.*

"Shit." Kara swore and tousled her hand through her hair.

"Why are they still here?"

"Who?" Hunter eased his pace and looked around for a familiar face.

"My parents." Kara cast her chin toward a couple who stepped out of the elevator and strode toward them.

Hunter's skin prickled, and he slowed to a halt in front of Kara's father. He was a tall man with peppered hair. His stride was as stiff as his shirt collar. Her mom oozed with Upper Westside class—designer suit, jewelry and heels.

"I told you to go home," Kara said to them, adjusting the throw rug across her lap.

"We had a quick bite to eat in the cafeteria and were coming to check on you once more before we headed off. But this is a surprise." Her mother stood two inches taller. "Kara, darling. Aren't you going to introduce us?"

Kara flicked her hand toward them. "Hunt, these are my parents, Walter and Carol. Mom, Dad, this is Hunter. And you know Kyle and Gemma."

Hunter stepped around Kara's wheelchair and held out his hand for Walter. "I wish we were meeting under better circumstances, but nice to finally meet you."

Walter looked down his nose at Hunter's hand as if he'd dipped it in the sewers. *What the hell?*

Hunter withdrew his hand. He didn't have time for people with no manners. He turned to Kara's mom. "Hey, Mrs. Knight."

She extended her hand toward him. "Please, call me Carol."

Her long skinny fingers felt cold as ice, bony, and she lacked any form of grip when he shook her hand. She reminded him of his fragile grandmother.

Carol was quick to pull away and turned to give Gemma a hug. "Nice to see you again, Gemma dear. Hello Kyle."

Walter ignored Kyle and Gemma and stared straight at Hunter. Hate flared in his eyes. "You shouldn't have come.

You've done enough damage to my daughter to last a lifetime."

"Dad?" Kara slouched. "He has more right to be here than you."

Hunter had dealt with people like Walter before. They were quick to judge, quick to belittle, and yeah, formed an opinion of him based on his public reputation. But Walter's thoughts of him were the least of his worries. Didn't even cause a blip on his care factor radar. "Mr. Knight, I understand you may have your reservations about me. I'm more than happy to talk to you later. But I've just flown halfway around the world to be here. So please, excuse me. I want to see my son."

Hunter grabbed the handles of Kara's wheelchair and went to push past her parents when Walter caught him on the arm. His firm grip caught Hunter off guard. "A quick word before you go."

"Fine." Hunter nodded.

Walter led Hunter a few steps away from the others and lowered his gravelly voice. "I know this is a difficult time for you both, but when it is over, I swear, I will do everything within my power to keep my daughter and my grandson away from you. Do you hear me? I will never forgive you for what you've done to her. I don't care who you are. Your lifestyle is not for my daughter and my grandson."

Hunter's ears rang, and his fists clenched at his sides. Under Walter's threatening glare, a shudder ripped through him. This prick didn't know him. Hunter's past and issues with Kara didn't leave much room for a positive impression, but Hunter had changed. He'd had to. For Ryan.

"Screw you." Hunter reefed his arm from Walter's hold and realigned his jacket. "Who do you think *you* are? No one will keep me from my son. Not you. Not Kara. Not anyone. My son is my priority. Got that?"

He stormed back toward Kara, Kyle, and Gemma, who had

worry etched across their faces. He held onto the handles of Kara's wheelchair so tightly he thought he would snap them off.

"Your father's delightful," Hunter said to Kara, a bitter taste in his mouth.

"Why? What did he say?"

"Said he wants to keep me away from Ryan. From you."

"What?" Her voice pitched high. She pointed at her father who had stepped in front of her wheelchair. "You have no right to say that. Hunter is Ryan's father. Accept it, or you'll be the one cut off from seeing your grandchild. Do you hear me? I don't need this. Please . . . go home. Hunt's here, and he's all I need right now."

Hunter placed his hand on Kara's shoulder and gave her a gentle squeeze.

Walter's nostrils flared; his jaw clamped. His eyes blazed with get-your-hands-off-my-daughter rage, so Hunter threw him a nope-I'm-good kind of smile. Walter puffed out his chest and straightened his tie. "He will never be what you need, Kara. I know what's best for you."

"Calm down, Walter. Let them be." Carol gave Hunter a sympathetic smile and kissed Kara on the cheek goodbye. "We have to head back to the office. We have a dinner tonight, so we'll come and see you tomorrow after work." She waved farewell to Kyle and Gemma, grabbed Walter on the arm and guided him into an elevator.

Hunter leaned over the back of the wheelchair toward Kara. "Don't think your parents will invite me over for Sunday lunch anytime soon. Are you okay?"

"No. My dad's a jerk." She dabbed her eyes with her fingertips.

Hunter stepped around in front of her and squatted. His gut sank when he saw that the brightness in her blue eyes had faded. "Don't worry about your dad. I'm here for you and Ryan."

She cupped his cheek. "Thank you. Let's go and see him."

Hunter pushed Kara along the corridor toward NICU, Kyle and Gemma by his side.

Kyle slapped him on the back. "Hunt, not sure that charm of yours will win Walter over in a hurry."

"I wouldn't waste your time trying," Gemma said, taking two steps to Hunter's one. "He doesn't like me either."

Kara glanced up at him. "Promise me you'll never be an ass like my dad. Not to our son."

"Never," he replied. Her beautiful smile pushed Walter from his mind. "We're going to rock this parenting thing." Not that he had any clue what he had to do.

"Yes, we will." She pointed to turn around the corner. "This way. He's in Room Two."

Hunter's palms sweated as he stopped outside the entrance. He glanced at Kyle and Gemma, not sure if he had the strength to step through the door and deal with what he was about to face.

"We'll be over here in the waiting area." Gemma gave him a quick hug and drew Kyle over to the seats.

Kara gave Hunter a warm smile. "Ready?"

His heart pounded against his ribcage, and he drew air deep into his lungs. He gave her a short nod. "Yes. Let's do this. I want to meet my son."

Chapter 18

Hunter pushed Kara into the room. The rubber tires of her wheelchair squeaked on the linoleum floor. Five humidicribs, surrounded by monitors, machines, cords, and cables, filled the space. The subtle smell of newborn baby he recalled from holding infants in the past filled the air. His legs wobbled as he gawked at the cribs. Never in his wildest dreams did he think he'd have his own child. Now, he was only steps away from his new reality.

"He's at the end on the left." Kara pointed.

Hunter pushed Kara down the row. Nurses' and the other moms' eyes widened at him. Their mouths gaped, but no one said a word. With shaky hands, he helped Kara to stand. She gripped her IV pole in one hand, took his hand in the other, and drew him over to the crib.

Slipping her arm around his waist, she clutched onto his jacket. "I'd like you to meet our son."

What he saw took the breath from his lungs. A chill shuddered through his bones. Ryan was barely the size of Hunter's outstretched hand. "Oh shit, Kar. He's so small."

He placed one hand on top of the crib to steady himself, and a tear slipped from his eye.

An uncomfortable-looking respiratory ventilation mask and tubing covered Ryan's nose. Hunter's chest hurt watching Ryan's ribs rise and fall, thanks to the machines that blipped and whirred. Monitor pads stuck to Ryan's chest looked like they pulled on his skin. A drip and splint were bandaged to his petite arm. A miniature blue beanie covered his head. A doll-sized nappy was wrapped around his legs.

Hunter stroked his chin and wiped his damp cheek. He'd do anything for Ryan—give blood, his kidney, his lung. Absolutely anything. Was there something he could do? He'd never felt so helpless and useless in his life.

"Ryan's going to be okay." Kara clutched onto him harder. "He has to be."

Hunter drew her into his arms and hugged her. "Yeah, he will be." He rubbed her back. "You scared the shit out of me, Kar. Don't do that again."

When Hunter glanced back at Ryan, more worry embedded into each fiber in his body. How were they going to get through this? How could anything so small survive?

"Can I hold him?" he asked, desperate to connect with Ryan, to touch and cuddle him.

Her heart thudded against his. "No. Not yet. He's not stabilized. Hopefully in a few days. The only thing we can do is touch him through the window. Wash your hands first."

Hunter slipped from her hold, stepped over to the basin, and scrubbed his hands clean. "So . . . can you fill me in on everything? How is he doing?"

Kara's eyes glassed over and she stared at Ryan. "He can't breathe on his own. His lungs aren't fully developed. His eyes are still fused shut and they have to feed him through all that tubing." The lifeless, mechanical tone in Kara's voice ripped at

Hunter's soul.

"He's doing fine." A nurse stepped over and analyzed his monitors. "Hello, Mr. Collins. Nice to meet you. With Ryan extracted this early, he has a fifty to eighty percent chance of growing into a healthy young boy." Hunter felt the color drain from his face. Ryan was not out of the danger zone yet? The nurse wrote on her chart. "Every day, his chances improve. We'll do everything possible to ensure he makes it." She pointed to Ryan. "When you're ready, you can open the little door on that side of the crib."

Hunter's heart barreled up toward his throat. He flicked the latch open and reached inside. Holding his breath, he placed his trembling fingers on Ryan's arm. With gentle strokes, he touched his son. "Oh my God." His voice snagged in his throat. "He's so warm. And soft. And hairy."

Ryan almost didn't feel human.

"He's covered in down," the nurse explained. "That will disappear as he grows."

"Why is he so red?" Hunter took in every inch of Ryan's tiny, curled up body. Ten tiny fingers. Ten tiny toes.

"It's his blood close to the surface of his skin," the nurse said with a compassionate smile. "All his vitals are within the range of normal for his stage of development."

Hunter stroked Ryan's teeny hand. Ryan's fingers slowly curled around his index finger. So delicate. So fragile. So amazing. The air rushed from Hunter's lungs. "Kar, look. He's trying to grip on to me."

"He knows who his daddy is. I've been playing your music to him, so he'll know your voice."

"You did that?" He fought back the tears welling in his eyes.

"Yeah." She nodded. "I'd sit with my headphones on my belly and play your albums. He might know you, Kyle, and Gemma better than me."

"That's so cool." Kara had done that for Ryan? She left him speechless.

Her smile didn't reflect in her wet eyes. She touched his arms. "You stay here, and I'll go send Gem and Kyle in one at a time. I'll see you soon."

Holding onto her wheelchair, Kara shuffled out of the room.

Gemma came in. She snaked her arm around his waist and leaned over the crib. She covered her mouth with her hand. "Oh, Hunt. I'm so sorry."

He drew her close and kissed the top of her head. "I'm glad you're here. Wouldn't be able to face this without you. You're my rock."

Kyle and Gemma were his life-support. His strength. His grounding. He relied on them too much sometimes. But what were friends for?

"I can't believe you're a daddy." She rested her head against him.

"Me either."

"He's going to be a badass rock star like you. Looks like he's got the nurse swooning over him already."

The nurse smiled as she changed Ryan's IV bag.

"God help us." Hunter squeezed Gemma to his side.

"He'll be fine, right?" Hope swung in her voice, worry flooded her eyes.

"Only time will tell." He couldn't bear the thought of losing Ryan.

"Okay." Glancing at Ryan, she fidgeted with her necklace. She edged out of Hunter's hold. "After Kyle's been in, we'll go home. You and Kar need to spend time together. I'll go get him for you."

"Thanks, Gem."

She slipped outside, and Kyle came in. The moment Kyle stepped in beside him and put his arm around his shoulders,

Hunter's breath jolted in his lungs, and he lost it. Tears slipped from his stinging eyes—he didn't have the strength to hold himself together anymore. Kyle drew him into an embrace and hugged him.

"Hey, bud." Kyle patted his back. "How're you doing?"

"I stuffed up bad, didn't I?" From getting Kara pregnant, to causing her grief about wanting to keep the baby, to this . . . Ryan born premature. Had he put too much pressure and stress on her? Was this his fault somehow? Hunter stepped back and wiped his face on his jacket sleeve.

"This is a game changer." Kyle stuffed his hands into the pockets of his jeans and glanced at Ryan. "I'm no good with this shit, Hunt. Babies, that is. I don't know what to say. On one hand, I should say congratulations . . . I think. But look at him." Kyle peered into the crib. "He's a runt, like you were until you were sixteen."

"So there's hope for him." Hunter looked down at his son's fragile body nestled between the folds of a white baby blanket. It was hard to imagine that he was now responsible for this little human being. Nothing could be more surreal.

"Maybe. Who knows?" Kyle shrugged. "You want me to get you anything before Gem and I head off?"

"Nah. Thanks."

"We'll come and see you tomorrow." Kyle gave him a reassuring squeeze on the shoulder, then left.

Kara returned to his side. Her eyelashes were wet. Her cheeks were red, and her whole body stooped. He brushed her hair back and drew her into a hug. It was so good to see her after being away for two and a half months, but he wished it was under better circumstances. He wanted the Kara who glowed back.

He turned his head toward the baby. Ryan's little hands and legs flinch and kick. Was Ryan dreaming? He wondered what about. Hunter would do his best to make all his son's dreams come true. "He's amazing, Kar."

"I know. But I'm scared." She rested her head against his shoulder. "I don't want to leave him, but I'm tired. I need to lie down."

"Okay. I'll help you back to the room, but then, if it's all right, I want to come and see him again. Can I do that?"

"Of course it is. He's your son, too. I'll call an orderly to come and get me. You stay here with Ryan." She squeezed his hand. "I'll be okay."

Once Kara left, Hunter pulled up a chair by the crib and placed his hand inside next to Ryan. He stroked his baby's tiny limbs, his feet, and his chest. The nurse shuffled around him when she made her observations, reassuring him he wasn't in the way.

Hunter watched the steady blips on the heart monitor. Running his finger over Ryan's soft skin, uncertainty quivered in Hunter's chest. While he was thankful his son was safe, alive and getting all the care he needed, what was he supposed to do now that Ryan had arrived early? The thought of leaving Kara by herself to deal with the long and tough road ahead was unfathomable. Touring and schedules and travel had suddenly been thrown into turmoil. Rubbing his tired eyes, he didn't want to think about those things right now.

"Can I sing to him?" Hunter asked the nurse. "I need to do something."

"Sure. But please keep it quiet so you don't disturb the other nurses or moms in here. I think Ryan would like to hear your voice."

Hunter lost track of time. He sang. He touched. He savored every moment spent by his son's side. Ryan was a true miracle. But after traveling across the globe, Hunter's energy was at an all-time low. His eyelids grew heavy and weary.

He jumped when the nurse on duty touched his arm. "Hunter, it's midnight. Why don't you go and get some rest? We'll call you if there are any changes? We'll look after him."

"You sick of my singing?" He yawned, covering his mouth with his hand.

"Not at all. It's wonderful."

"I could do with some sleep. It's been a while." Hunter stood and stretched.

"The window bench seat in Kara's room is also a cot bed," the nurse said. "Ask the nurses in the ward to get you a pillow and blanket."

"Thanks. I'll do that." He pushed his chair out of the way.

He dragged his feet back to Kara's ward. He eased the door to her room open and found her sound asleep. Her long hair fell in a tangled mess on the pillow. The blankets were pulled up over her shoulders, and she cuddled the bedding underneath her chin. Soft little snuffles came from her mouth. Was she snoring? He grinned and slid inside.

At the sight of the cushioned bench seat, his body slouched. The seat looked just long enough for him to lie down. He could sleep anywhere—one skill gained from touring. He stretched out, tugged a cushion underneath his head, and closed his eyes. If Kara didn't want him there when she woke up, he'd leave. But for now, he needed to rest.

He folded one arm over his eyes and listened to the sound of nurses chattering out in the hallway, trolley carts wheeling up and down the corridors, and babies crying in other rooms within the ward. How long would it be until Ryan could cry? How long until they'd be able to hold him? Or feed him? Or take him home?

He turned on his side and glanced at Kara. She looked . . . beautiful. Her features were smooth, not etched with stress and worry. He'd caused too much of that over the past few months, but not anymore. He'd do whatever was necessary to ensure that she and Ryan got home soon. Happily. Healthily. Safely.

Fatigue took hold. He closed his eyes and drifted off to sleep.

***

When the door opened and hit the wall with a thud, Hunter woke with a start. The sun had not fully risen, but light filtered in through the sides of the window blinds. He blinked and rubbed his eyes. The digital clock on the wall blazed 6:37 a.m. He'd been asleep for close to six hours. Unbelievable.

Dr. Blakley and two other male doctors in white coats came into the room.

Kara stretched and sat up in her bed. She glanced at the doctors, then at him. Her eyes shone bright, and she smiled. "Hey Hunt, I didn't know you stayed. Thank you." Then she turned to the doctors. "Isn't it too early for rounds?"

Hunter sat up and the air turned to ice. The steely hardness on each of the doctors' faces made the hairs on the back of his neck stand on end. He leapt to his feet and stepped toward Kara's bed. "What's going on?"

"Kara. Hunter." Dr. Blakley hugged her clipboard to her chest. Her eyes were void of emotion. "There were some complications with Ryan."

Hunter clutched Kara's hand.

Dr. Blakley lifted her chin, stood up straighter. "We did everything we could . . . but I'm sorry. He wasn't strong enough. He passed away during our efforts to stabilize him."

"NOOOOO!" Kara screamed. Tears burst from her eyes.

"What?" Hunter's knees buckled. His whole body shook. He braced himself against the edge of the bed to stop collapsing to the floor.

"I don't believe you," Kara bawled, throwing her blankets

off her legs. "Take me to my baby?"

Hunter lunged for her, pulled her into his embrace, and held her tight. Her whole body trembled as she beat him with her fists. "Not Ryan. Please don't let them take Ryan from me. He's all I have. Not Ryan. Please. Not Ryan."

His heart was on fire. Tears burned his eyes as he held Kara closer.

"Our team did everything possible." The coldness in the doctor's voice was like a thousand steely daggers driven into Hunter's chest. "I'm sorry. He was too weak. His organs failed."

"He was fine last night when I left him." Shock, anger, fury, and disbelief hissed through Hunter's teeth. "How could this happen?"

"I'm truly sorry for your loss." Dr. Blakley stepped closer to the bed. "I know this is hard. We'll give you some time alone. When you're ready, I will arrange for him to be brought here for you to say your goodbyes."

"Nooooo. *No*," Kara cried, clutching onto his arm like he was a lifebuoy. "Bring him here now. Please. Please bring me Ryan."

"We'll arrange it as soon as it is possible." The short, stumpy doctor with thick black glasses said.

"Would you like a photographer as well?" the other doctor asked. *Pediatrician: Jonathan Forbes* was printed boldly on his ID badge. "There's also paperwork and arrangements we need to go through."

Hunter couldn't believe what he was hearing. The doctors just wanted to go through procedures and documentation?

"Get out," Hunter snarled and pointed at the door. "Get out now."

"We will. Take all the time you need." Dr. Blakley nodded. "We'll arrange for Ryan to be brought in to you within the next fifteen minutes. If you need anything else, please let me know. Once again, I'm sorry for your loss."

When the door closed behind them, Kara wailed. She clutched onto his shirt. Her tears soaked through to his skin. He wanted to scream, yell, and curse the world, but he needed to be strong for Kara, even though his own insides had been ripped apart.

He rested his head against hers and inhaled the floral scent of her hair, hoping it would somehow miraculously stop the pain that speared his spleen. But it didn't. His heart hurt and shuddered with every breath. He wanted it all to stop. Wanted it all to go away.

"Kar, I'm so sorry. I should have stayed with him last night," he whispered, and kissed the top of her head.

"We lost our baby." She convulsed and cried. "We lost our Ryan."

"Shh." He closed his eyes to stop them stinging. But it didn't work.

Kara didn't let go of him. The tears didn't stop flowing.

They intensified the moment the nurse wheeled Ryan into the room inside a crib.

Hunter's chest heaved when he looked down at his son. Swaddled in a pale blue baby blanket, Ryan looked like he was sleeping. The tubes were gone, and his red skin was not as flushed, but his tiny eyes were still clamped shut.

The nurse ran through some protocol. Security. Outside the door. Something about it being necessary to ensure babies weren't stolen. It was nothing but a muffled ringing in his ears before she backed out of the room and left them alone.

"Hunt, give him to me." Kara grabbed the triangle bar above her head, winced and heaved herself up straight. She rubbed her swollen abdomen, then held out her arms to Ryan.

"What?" Hunter's stomach flipped. Ryan was dead. He was torn, in two frames of mind, afraid to touch him, but desperate to do so as well.

"Hunter, please." The plea in her voice sliced his heart. "This will be the only chance I get to hold my baby. Please, give him to me."

Making his way over to the crib, his knees wobbled. Each footstep seemed to take one thousand years. His feet seemed to weigh one thousand tons. Gently, he slid his hands underneath Ryan and lifted him. His son's miniature body fit into the length of his hand. So light, fragile, and petite. A sob escaped Hunter's lips. He leaned down and kissed Ryan's forehead, warm and soft. His boy still smelled just like a newborn. He closed his eyes, begging for his son to wake up and this to all be a nightmare. But Ryan's body lay lifeless and still.

He turned to Kara and handed her their baby. She cradled him close to her chest and stroked his tiny face and head. "He's so perfect."

Hunter sat next to her, his arm around her shoulders. "Yeah, he is. With those long fingers of his, he would've been a great piano player."

"And with his handsome face, he's just like you." She drew her fingertips across Ryan's brow.

"Nah, he looks more like you. Picture perfect in every way."

Kara nudged her elbow into his side. "You're only saying that to make me feel better."

"I mean it, Kar. With his little ears, round face, and cute chin, he definitely takes after you." He rested his head against hers. As he stared down at his son, each breath was like a spear through his lungs. "I can't believe he's gone."

"Can I ask a favor?"

"Anything."

"Can we get the photos with him? Is that wrong?"

"No. Not at all."

Hunter made the arrangements with the hospital staff. After photos and selfies, Kara kissed Ryan on the head. "I love you, little man. May the angels watch over you in heaven." Carefully, she handed him to Hunter. "Here, take him. Otherwise I'll never be able to let him go."

Hunter snuggled Ryan, staring down at him. Memorizing every little feature and detail of his son's precious face. He didn't want to let him go. Couldn't let him go.

"Hunt? It's time," Kara whispered, tears glistening in her eyes.

He sniffled, pressed his lips to Ryan's cheek, and placed him back in the crib. He wiped the dampness from his eyes, but his heart was broken. *How the hell am I supposed to go on after this?*

He staggered and collapsed on the end of the bed.

Kara curled her arms around herself. "I don't want to say goodbye to him."

"Neither do I." Hunter's vision blurred. "Don't think I can."

When he saw how pale and drained of energy Kara was, he dug deep to draw on any remnant of strength he had remaining. He had to keep it together for her. Push all this emotion aside. Suppress it. Kill it. Avoid it. Like he'd always done. It was the only way to move on.

Sucking in jagged breaths, he seized a fine thread of composure. "You want me to make some calls? Your parents? Your sister? Shit . . . I better call my mom and dad. Kyle and Gem too."

Kara closed her eyes and forced a nod. But then she fell back against the pillow, curled on her side, and bawled.

Pain and heartache splintered his bones. He grabbed his cell phone from his jacket. Every breath he took pummeled against his heart. These calls would be the hardest he'd ever have to make.

Chapter 19

Propped up on the sofa in Hunter's apartment, Kara ignored the people who had come after the funeral service. She'd slipped into darkness. Her mind had shut down. Saying goodbye to Ryan had been too hard. The past four days had been a haze. She'd gone along with whatever Hunter had said. He'd brought her home from the hospital, dealt with the media lurking outside their apartment buildings, and organized today. He'd done everything for her, but she didn't care. Ryan was dead. Her sanctuary was numbness. Her heart was nothing but a black hole.

Kara drew the woolen blanket over her legs, too weary and weak to stand. The Cutifilm waterproof dressing covering her cesarean scar tweaked and pulled her skin. Her boobs hurt every time she thought of Ryan. Her floppy belly, a constant reminder he was gone.

She wanted everyone to leave. Being surrounded by friends and family did nothing to raise her spirits. All their pity and sorrow draped over her like a shroud. She couldn't breathe. Couldn't think. Couldn't escape.

"Kar, want one of these?" Gemma slipped in beside her, resting her butt on the arm of the sofa, and waved a plate of mini quiches in front of her. "They are freaking delicious."

The smell of egg and bacon curdled Kara's stomach. "No, thanks."

"You have to eat." Gemma took a bite of one and chewed. "I love Lillian's cooking. She's the best. Are you sure you don't want one?"

Hunter's family had flown in from Chicago two days ago. Lillian had insisted on preparing all the food for the gathering today. Kara hadn't objected. She didn't even want a wake to happen.

Kara grabbed another tissue from the box beside her and dabbed her watery eyes. "I'm fine, Gem. Really."

"Oh, sweetie. Don't cry again. Let me go get rid of this food, and I'll be back to give you an extra big hug." Gemma slid off the sofa and rushed toward the kitchen.

Kara felt him even before she glanced in his direction. That magnetic tug drew her. Dressed in a sharp black suit, shirt, and tie, Hunter stood, leaning against the grand piano. His eyes were glassed over by a sadness that reflected her own. He held her gaze, peering over the crystal rim of his JD on ice. Hayden and Lexi were talking to him, but it didn't look like he was listening.

Without excusing himself, he made his way toward her. Sitting down beside her, he hooked his arm around her shoulder, and rested his head against hers. She closed her eyes and breathed him in, absorbed his citrusy cologne into every cell in her body. It helped her keep herself together.

"This sucks," he whispered.

A heaviness swelled in her chest. Her vision blurred through watery eyes. "I miss Ryan. So much. Every time I breathe it hurts."

He downed his drink and placed the glass on the coffee

table. He took her hand in his. Usually she got tingles and warmth from his touch. Now she got nothing. Her body was dead. It had died with Ryan.

Hunter glanced vacantly across the crowd—her parents and Naomi hovered by the windows with her cousin, Jenny rushed around with platters of food, and their friends clustered in small groups, talking in hushed voices. He turned back to her, his eyes searching her face. "Do you want to do something crazy?"

A puff of air shot through her nose. "Being crazy is how we ended up here."

Hurt flickered in his eyes as he circled his thumb over the back of her hand.

"I'm sorry." She squeezed his hand. "What do you want to do?"

"Do you wanna get out of here? Get out of town for a few days?"

Her chest tightened. "What? Where? How?" What was he thinking? She needed to rest after her operation. She tried to clear her head, but grief kept fogging her thoughts.

"Hold on." He jumped up from the sofa, weaved around a few of her friends from work, and dragged Kyle and Gemma back with him. They sat on the end of the chaise and Hunter returned to sit beside her. "Kyle, are you using the beach house over the next few days?"

"No." Kyle said with an are-you-kidding-me tone. "It's the end of March, dude. It'll be freezing out there."

"Can I use it?" Hunter asked. "Kara and I need some timeout."

Why did he know exactly what she needed?

"You want us to come with you?" Gemma gaze jumped from Kara to Hunter and back again.

"No." Hunter shook his head. "We'll be fine."

Gemma clutched Kyle's hand, gave him a reassuring nod

before she turned to Hunter. "Do you want us to cancel the rest of tour?"

Kara's heart sank to the floor at the sight of the furrows etched into Hunter's brow. She rubbed his arm and rested her head back against the sofa. Everhide had canceled another three weeks of shows, erasing all their Asian tour dates, but the last four weeks in South America hadn't been ruled out.

"I can't think about that right now, Gem." Hunter threaded his fingers into his hair and ripped them through the loose strands. "I just need a few days to sort stuff out."

"The beach house is yours." Kyle stretched out his legs and crossed his ankles. "When do you want to go?"

"Now."

Kara's eyes widened, and she wiped her runny nose with a tissue. "Now? We can't leave now. All these people are here. Your family has to fly back to Chicago tomorrow morning."

"They'll understand." Hunter stretched and cracked his neck, one side then the other. "Are you in?"

Gemma slid her arm around Kyle's waist. "Kar. Go. We'll look after everyone. Go and get over the craze of the past few days."

"Gem, I don't know if that's possible." Kara couldn't think straight. All she wanted to do was cry. And be alone. She didn't care where.

"A few days away might do you some good." Gemma came over, sat beside her and gave her a warm hug.

"I love you, Gem." She squeezed Gemma tight, then turned to Hunter. Every time she looked at him, it hurt. He reminded her of Ryan. He was the only connection left to their son. And she never wanted to let that go. Ever. "Are you sure about this?"

"No. But I want to go."

Anywhere was better than sitting at home with a constant stream of visitors reminding her of her loss and making her feel worse. She slumped her shoulders and whispered, "Me too."

"Give me ten minutes and we'll be out of here." His tone took on a sense of urgency. "We'll do a quick stop via your place to grab your things and head off."

Her pulse showed the first signs of life in days. She didn't know if being alone with him in the outreaches of Long Island would help, but he was the only one who knew how she felt. She wanted to grieve, cry, scream, and shout with no one looking on her with pity. He'd come up with the perfect plan. Just what she needed. With Hunter, she could escape.

***

Kara couldn't remember dozing off on the drive out to Long Island. The constant revs of Hunter's GT Ford supercar must have lulled her to sleep. She stirred in the plush leather seat when the tires crunched on the gravel driveway leading up to Kyle's beach house.

It was nearly dark. Low clouds hovered with the threat of rain. Wind swept along the beach, rustling the dune grass in rippling waves. The ocean, unsettled and menacing, thrashed against the shore.

Hunter killed the engine, but Kara didn't move. She sat staring at the house. Its weathered shingles had seen better days. The hand-railing on the stairs leading into the house needed repair. The landscaping and overgrown hedges were in need of maintenance. This quaint house, hidden away from neighbors and the nearby town, would be her private getaway for the next few days. Somehow, she had to find her way back toward the light. But she couldn't see the path.

Half the nation would know she was here with Hunter by now. The paparazzi had been loitering outside their apartments for days, desperate to get the all-essential shot of them at their worst. It was hard enough having to deal with grief, but having her haggard face stuck all over the news made her want to dig a hole and hide.

Hunter jumped out of the car, rushed around to her side, and opened the door. The hydraulic lift whooshed, and frigid ocean air hit her face. She took his hand, but when she stood, her knees wobbled, and her head spun.

"Kar? You got your feet or not?"

"I think so." She took one step and staggered. "Just sore and stiff after the drive."

"I know you're supposed to walk, but we're about to be drenched. Let's speed this up. Can I carry you?" Before she finished her nod, he scooped her up in his arms. With her hands looped around his neck, he carried her up the stairs. She curled in close to him, nuzzled her face against his neck. She didn't want him to let her go. The scent of his cologne was the only thing that calmed her fragile mind. The warmth from his body was a protective shield against the weather.

He placed her gently onto her feet on the landing and opened the door. Holding her steady, he helped her cross to the faded floral sofa.

"Comfortable?" he asked, grabbing her every cushion in sight.

"Yeah, thanks." She shuffled around, and he tucked a fleecy throw blanket over her legs.

"I'll go grab our stuff before that rain hits." He dashed outside at lightning speed.

The musty smell from the house wrinkled her nose, and the cold air seeped into her bones. Isolation hit her. There was no city hustle and bustle around her to occupy her mind. No sirens. No alarms. No crowds. She grabbed a cushion and crushed it to her chest. The numbness that had been in place warped, twisted, and erupted in a flash of pain. She squeezed her eyes shut. Her chin trembled, and she curled into the back of the sofa. With a loud sob burning her throat, she cried.

I want Ryan. I want my baby back.

Over her tears, she heard Hunter curse as he struggled up the stairs with all their gear—bags, his guitar, coats, and other belongings. With a thud, he dropped everything by the staircase and rushed to her side.

He perched himself on the edge of the sofa next to her hip. He brushed the hair back from her face. "Hey. We're here now. Everything will be okay. Can I get you a cup of tea?"

"Thank you, but no."

"Do you want to talk? Eat? Drink? Crying is good too, if that's what you want to do. Whatever you need, I'm here."

Her heart spasmed at the sight of his wet eyes. He'd done so much for her already. How would she ever be able to thank him? "I'm tired. I want to go to bed." After days of minimal sleep, she hoped exhaustion would take over and she'd finally get some rest.

"I'll turn the heat on first. It's freezing in here." He jumped up, rubbed his hands together, and turned the thermostat on. "I've no idea how long it'll take to warm up the house. I've never been here in the cold to know if this thing even works."

Kara swung her legs off the sofa and clutched at her aching belly. The soreness and stitches meant every movement had to be slow and calculated.

"Kar, let me help you." He caught her arm to help her stand. But once she found her feet, he didn't let go. Instead, he drew her into his arms. She rested her chin on his shoulder, and he gently stroked her hair. She melted against him, and they stood in silence while the wind battered against the windowpanes and the ocean waves crashed rhythmically against the shore.

"Thank you, Hunt." She smoothed her hands over his back, the wool of his cable-knit sweater soft beneath her fingertips. "For everything. But I need to go to bed."

He scooped her up in his arms again and took her upstairs to the main bedroom. "Are you okay to sleep in Kyle's room? It's bigger than the other one, and it has the master bathroom."

"It'll be fine," she said.

He placed her on her feet and held her arms, making sure she had her balance. Red rimmed his eyes, and turmoil swirled in the pit of her stomach. She wanted him to go. Leave her alone. But then . . . she desperately wanted him to stay. No matter how much she wished that things between them were different, he was not hers to ask for anything more.

The heat kicked in and blasted through the vents in the ceiling. "At least we'll be toasty now." She smiled half-heartedly.

"Excellent." He wiped his hands on the back pockets of his jeans. "I'll go grab your bags."

She sat on the queen-sized bed and looked around the room. Faded navy blue curtains were drawn over wide windows. An old photo of Kyle's deceased family sat on top of the dresser. Wood-paneled walls looked aged against the renovated, modern bathroom. She hadn't been here since Gemma's party two years ago. So much had happened in that timeframe. Her head and heart ache.

Hunter's footsteps trudged up the staircase. "Here you go." He placed her luggage inside the doorway.

She wanted to see his effervescent smile again. See him do crazy fun things again. If he was himself, it might help her heal. But he was hurting too. And she didn't know how to help him, because she didn't know how to help herself.

"Night, Kar. Hope you get some sleep. See you in the morning."

He spun on his Nikes and disappeared down the stairs. Maybe something that would help him would come to mind tomorrow.

Finally, she was alone. Fatigue swept through her bones.

Every aching muscle in her body collapsed. Not even bothering to change, she curled up under the blankets, said a prayer to Ryan, and let her tears soak into the pillow.

Chapter 20

Hunter loped down the steps and left Kara to rest. She needed it. And so did he. But he was so wired after the long day, he needed to unwind first. The JD called to him.

He opened the sliding door onto the back deck. Ice-cold wind blasted his face. Shivering, he grabbed the alcohol and groceries that had been delivered. He stored the milk, coffee, tea, cheese, fruit, pasta, and some pre-made meals away in the kitchen with little to no care. There was more than enough food to last a week. Good. He wouldn't have to think. He'd been running on autopilot for the past few days. Now, he just wanted to stop.

Standing at the kitchen counter, he rubbed his hands over his face. Every time he closed his eyes he saw Ryan. The lifeless body wrapped in a satin sheet in the casket would forever haunt him. Having to lay him to rest had been unbearable. How was he supposed to move on?

Grabbing one bottle of JD and a glass of ice, he made his way over to the sofa and poured himself a drink. The first gulp burned his throat. It was like a shot of morphine injected straight to his bloodstream. The whiskey raced through his body scalding everything in its path. He rested his head back and stared at the wooden beam on the ceiling. The constant sound of the waves outside should have had a calming effect on him. But it didn't.

Everything seemed to press and tighten around him—the air, the sounds, his clothes. It was too much. He'd mastered controlling and hiding his emotions for years, let nothing touch his heart. But Ryan had changed everything. And now he was gone.

Hunter's breath seesawed in his lungs. He clutched at his chest, lurched forward, and leaned on his thighs. The back of his eyes stung like acid. With a trembling hand, he wiped the pooling tears from them with the pads of his fingers.

He wasn't coping.

Not at all.

He'd being composed for days—for Kara, for his family, for everyone. With no fight left, he couldn't keep up the façade any longer. He needed the one person in the world he could turn to for anything.

Reaching inside his jacket pocket, he grabbed his cell phone and swiped the screen. His thumb trembled as he hit number-one on speed dial.

"Hey, bud?" Kyle's voice was so low and soft he could hardly hear. "What's up?"

Hunter closed his eyes. His heart constricted so much he thought it would disintegrate. How could he put the pain, the loss, into words? How could he describe how a piece of him felt like it was missing? Fighting back his tears, his body shuddered.

"Hunt? . . . You there? . . . Everything okay?"

Hunter sniffled and wiped his nose. "How did you do it? How did you survive after your parents' accident?"

"I didn't." Kyle's voice wavered. "Not for a long time. There were days I couldn't even get out of bed."

Hunter recalled Kyle's depression. The darkness. The anger. The drinking. *Shit.* Did he have to go through all that? He stroked the stubble on his chin. "This is so fucked."

"Yep. I'm here for you. And so is Gem. And Kara, too. She's going through the same thing."

"She's a mess." He glanced up the staircase toward the bedroom, hoping she'd be able to sleep. "I don't know how to fix this."

"Time."

"I don't want time." His jaw cramped, causing his head to ache. "I want the pain to stop."

"It never goes away." Kyle's voice jolted through his heart. "You just learn to deal with it. My only advice is to talk. Talk to Kara. Tell her how you're feeling. You've been bottling all this shit up for days. It's eating you alive. I know, because I did the same. But once I opened up to you and Gem, it got better."

Hunter rubbed at the tension in his temples. He had to do something. Drinking was the most viable option at present.

"You going to be all right?" Kyle asked. "Want me to come out there?"

"No. Just needed to know you've got my back."

"Always."

"Thanks, bud."

The hollowness where his heart used to be ached. He ended the call and threw his cell phone onto the table. With a quick swipe, he grabbed his glass and downed his JD. Then another shot. And another. Flames flared in his gut, igniting an anger he didn't know he possessed. He clenched his hands and stared at the bulging veins protruding on the back of his wrist. All the burning questions he'd suppressed erupted in his mind.

Why?

Why did Ryan have to die?

Why didn't he make it?

With all the medical advancements and technology, why couldn't they have saved his son?

Was there some lesson in this madness? Was this a test of his spirit?

If it was, it had broken him. He'd give anything . . . *anything* . . . to have Ryan back.

He snatched the bottle of JD off the table, stormed outside, and headed onto the beach. The freezing wind whipped at his sweater and bit into his skin. The salt air sprayed against his cheeks and stung his eyes. With his hair lashing at his face, he turned to the heavens. Then, with all his might, he screamed. "Aaaarrggghhh! You motherfucker! Why did you take Ryan?" His voice rasped and ripped deep in his throat. His lips quivered, and he swayed on his feet. "Why? Why did you take our boy? Why? Please . . . tell me why?"

He fell to his knees on the sand, placed the bottle beside him, and buried his face in his hands. Ruined. Broken. Destroyed. He'd sworn that he wouldn't let anyone get close to him again. He'd tried to keep his distance from Kara and the baby, but they'd slipped through the cracks. This grief that consumed him was so much worse than any heartbreak he'd ever experienced.

He needed to do something—something he could pour all this anguish, frustration, and hurt into. Something that could help repair his shattered soul.

Sitting back on his haunches, he seized the JD, and drank. He wiped the back of his hand across his mouth and shivered. His breath misted. The first drops of rain splattered against his face. Reefing his shoulders back, he sucked in the saline air. Then, it hit him. He knew what he had to do. He had to play. He needed music.

Staggering to his feet, he stumbled over the dunes and headed for the house. He had to get inside before he froze to death.

After sliding the door shut behind him, he placed the bottle on top of the old piano in the far corner of the room. It hadn't been used in years. Kyle had wanted to get rid of it once his parents died, but Gemma wouldn't hear of it.

Rummaging through his bag by the steps, Hunter grabbed his journal and a pen. He took a seat at the piano, placed his book open on top and downed a few more mouthfuls of JD. The alcohol filled him with a fuzzy numbness. Perfect.

Opening the fallboard, its loud creak filled the room. Hunter winced. He didn't want to disturb Kara, just sit here and play quietly. Splaying his fingers over the faded ivory keys, he played a low, left-hand chord. The piano was a little out of tune, but it would have to do. The gentle thrum flowed through his fingers, up his arm and settled into the base of his neck. Music was his therapy. Let him feel everything. Writing "Better" had helped him get Amie out of his system. "Sorry" had been his message to Gemma, apologizing for hurting her. Creating "Treasure" with Kyle and Gemma had summed up the unfaltering bond he had with his two best friends. Maybe coming up with something for Ryan would help. It had to.

The notes on the piano didn't seem to go low enough or reflect how hollow he felt. He took another sip from his bottle and played again. Something came over him. All his anguish, his hurt, and his emptiness flooded from his veins into his fingertips. This time, the notes mirrored his broken heart. A tune formed in his mind.

Staring at his hands gliding over the keys, he pictured the moment he touched Ryan's soft skin. The moment Ryan's tiny hand had wrapped around his finger. Then, the moment he'd held his son's lifeless body in his hands. And that moment . . . that gut-wrenching moment . . . when he said goodbye.

Swallowing hard over the lump in his throat, he hummed.

Hmm hmm hmm hmmmm. Hmm hmm hmmmm.
Just one more day, one more day,
With you.
What I would give to have,
One more day, one more day,
With you.

Hunter dived for his journal and frantically wrote the lyrics before he returned to tinkering on the keys. His pulse throbbed in his ears like staccato notes. Words jumbled around inside his head until they appeared crystal clear.

I sit alone here in the dark,
Keep on wondering where you are.
Did the angels send you from heaven?
Only to realize they were mistaken?

You were the one to steal my heart,
Then so easily broke it apart.
I would give up everything to see you smile,
Just to hold your hand once again in mine.

Don't you know I'd give up everything,
Everything,
Just to have one more day, one more day,
With you.

His hands trembled as he struck the keys. Each time, he got louder. Angrier. More bitter. Singing through clenched teeth, hurt battered his ribs. His eyes burned in their sockets.

Don't you know I'd give up everything,
Everything,
Just to have one more day,
One more day,
With you.

He heard footsteps on the staircase and he jerked his hands off the piano. *Shit.* He'd been too loud.

Clutching the rail, Kara struggled down the steps. He brushed the tears from his eyes, leaped off the stool, and rushed to her side. "I'm sorry. I didn't mean to wake you."

"I wasn't asleep." She took one slow step at a time, holding her hand across her lower belly. "I don't rate having a cesarean." She sat halfway down the stairs and drew the fleecy throw around her shoulders. Hunter took a seat beside her. She turned to him, her eyes tired and dark. "I was listening to you sing. Was that song for Ryan?"

He nodded.

"It was beautiful."

"I didn't mean to get so vocal toward the end there, but—"

"I miss him so much, Hunt." She curled her hands around his arm, her touch gentle and warm. "Would you play that song for me again?"

"It's nothing serious. I was mucking around."

"I don't care. Please play it."

After a moment's hesitation, he patted her hand. "Sure."

He gently hooked his arm around hers and helped her down the stairs. She sat on the piano stool and he placed the throw across her back. He slid beside her, and his hands fell onto the keys. He played. This time he sang softer, without anger surging through him, but every note, every lyric, still stabbed his heart.

"I can't believe you just wrote that." She wiped her tear-streaked cheeks.

He took a steady breath to stop the raw ache inside his chest. "Playing is therapeutic. Not sure it's helping yet."

"I know, but I loved it. I love Ryan's song."

He stared at the lyrics before him. "I'd never be able to sing that live."

"Then don't." She rested her head against his shoulder. "It'll be your song for him."

"I can't believe he's gone, Kar."

He turned to her and tears threatened to fall. He wrapped his arms around her waist and drew her into a hug. Resting his head against hers, he stroked his fingers through the silky strands of her hair; it smelled like cherry blossoms.

She swiveled on the stool and edged closer. Slipping her arms around his shoulders she clutched onto him, tight. It felt so good to hold her. She made it possible to breathe.

He hadn't been this close to anyone in a long time. Didn't think he'd make it through losing Ryan without her. The warmth of her body seeped into his exhausted muscles and eased the tension coursing through him. Rubbing his hands over her back, he wished he could erase their sorrow. Make everything right. But nothing was ever that easy.

Kara sobbed, and his stomach sank. She pulled back and brushed her fingertips over his stubble. He closed his eyes. Her touch was so light and soothing. She leaned in and pressed her lips to his cheek. His heart jumped and skipped a beat. He didn't trust himself to move, for fear of doing something stupid. He just needed to hold her, to share the burden of their loss.

With the softest of touches, she pressed another kiss an inch closer to his mouth. Then another. He closed his eyes tighter. His equilibrium swayed. Her hand caressed the side of his face, skimming along the line of his jaw. With all his might, he willed his pulse to stay steady. Edging back, he met her gaze. The blue depths and darkness in her irises swam with sadness that mirrored his and wrenched at his soul. She looked so lost. Broken. Just how he felt.

He slid his hand up her back, and her body shivered. Threading his fingers under her hair, he curled them around the nape of her neck. "We'll get through this, Kar. Together."

She nodded. Her rosy pink lips quivered a few inches from his. Her warm breath teased his face, sweet and intoxicating. A single tear fell from her eye and caught on her lip. It glistened in the dim lighting, hovering like a lone jewel. Hypnotized by it, the whiskey he'd drunk fuzzed his logic. Because he wanted to kiss the droplet away. Kiss away her pain. Kiss her.

Within a single heartbeat, the distance between them vanished. Her mouth planted against his and the air rushed from his lungs. He wasn't sure who had moved first. Him. Her. Both together. It didn't matter. Fire charged across his skin and set a spark to every nerve. Cupping the side of her face, he parted his lips and kissed her. Slowly. Tenderly. Desperately. Absorbing her into every cell of his body. She sucked in a sharp breath and shuddered in his arms.

Shit. He had to stop. Had to pull away.

For one more second, he wanted to try and ease her hurt—not create more. He wanted to make everything right—not wrong. He wanted to make things better—not more complicated.

She grabbed the back of his neck, flicked her tongue against his, and deepened the kiss, urgent and needy. She obliterated every one of his thoughts. Snaking her hands over his shoulders and clutching at his sweater, she kissed his upper lip. His lower lip. He groaned against her mouth and drew her closer. Her touch had made him feel alive for the first time in days.

She whimpered and her whole body quaked. She jerked back, closed her eyes, and shook her head. "I'm so sorry." The agony in her voice speared his heart. "I didn't mean to kiss you. It was wrong of me."

She'd kissed him?

"No. No. It's my fault." He was an idiot for not thinking straight. He pressed his forehead to hers, and his heart raced. The sweet taste of her lingering on his lips tempted him to kiss her again. He squeezed his eyes shut and buried the want. "We're hurting. I shouldn't have done that." He'd had too much to drink. He didn't need further problems. "It won't happen again. I promise. Just got caught in the moment."

That was all it had been. A mad moment.

Kara straightened and wiped her eyes. "Better not write any more songs like that again then."

"That I can't promise." Music was something he could never go without. "Just don't sit next to me when I do."

"Okay."

Willing the blood rush to his head to settle, he glanced at the clock on the wall. It was almost two in the morning. "We better try and get some sleep."

She sniffled, drew the throw blanket back onto her shoulders, and wrapped her arms around herself. "Can I ask a favor? You can say no. I'll understand. I know it crosses all kinds of boundaries, but I don't care about anything anymore."

He rubbed her low on the back. "Ask away."

"Can you come and hold me? Lie next to me until I fall asleep?"

His heart thudded with an erratic beat. This blurred the lines they'd set. Was sleeping next to her, as a friend, wise?

Probably not.

To hell with rules for now. She needed him, and he needed her. For comfort. For strength. For support.

For Ryan.

"I can do that." He swept her up in his arms and carried her upstairs.

After brushing his teeth, changing, and drinking a ton of water to avoid a headache in the morning, he slid into bed next to her. Drawing the thick quilt over them, he spooned her from behind. Sharing a bed with someone . . . just holding . . . was something he hadn't done in a long time. There were no expectations, other than friendship.

He curled his arm over her and she snuggled it against her breast. After a few uncertain breaths, he relaxed. With her back flush against his chest, her butt tucked against his groin, her legs stretched out by his, she aligned perfectly against him. Just right.

"Night," she whispered.

He nuzzled into her hair and inhaled. The scent of her filled his head. So delicious, intoxicating. Her kiss was still imprinted on his mouth. "Night."

The warmth from her body enveloped him, and no matter how hard he tried, Kara seeped further into his soul. It scared the hell out of him, because he was on a path he wanted to avoid and one that would only cause more hurt. The emptiness in his chest flared. Soon he'd have to find the strength to rebuild that protective wall around his heart, push Kara away. But today was not the day.

Chapter 21

Rain splattered the back deck, turning the faded gray wood to dull, damp brown. Droplets of water zigzagged in silver streaks down the window panes. Kara curled up on the sofa at the beach house and watched the downpour, her mind swarming with images from the night before. Hearing Hunter sing. Holding him close. Kissing him.

He hadn't stopped her. Instead, he'd kissed her back. The feel of his lips against hers burned into her brain. The kiss had been so raw, so deep, so consuming. She hated herself for kissing him when they were both vulnerable and not in a sane mind. Hated that for the briefest of moments, when his lips were on hers, she hadn't thought about Ryan.

She had to move on but didn't want to complicate the situation by giving into her simmering feelings for Hunter. They were a brewing storm that needed to fizzle out. She needed his friendship and support, not added heartache. It was best to forget the kiss occurred. Act as if nothing had happened.

Hunter certainly was. He'd made her breakfast, got her cups of tea, helped her walk, fetched whatever she'd needed.

While she lay on the sofa reveling in her grief, he never sat still. He worked on his laptop, played his guitar, watched TV. Maybe it was his way of dealing with loss?

Day two away from the city brought a reprieve in the weather. Before it rained again, and in desperate need of some fresh air, Kara opted to walk down to the beach with him. With her arm hooked around his, she shuffled along the sand.

Sunshine that held no warmth kissed her face. She closed her eyes and inhaled the salty, fresh air. Dead seaweed crunched underfoot, and the crashing waves filled her ears. The elements did their best to distract her, but the loss of Ryan was always at the forefront of her mind.

It had been one week since he died. Her heart and soul were as crushed as they had been on that first day. How would she ever get past this?

After lunch, she sat out in the glass-enclosed patio overlooking the beach with a woolen blanket tucked around her. Staring at the book she was reading, she couldn't get lost in the latest action–suspense romance. The tension and turmoil on the pages only added to her already high blood pressure. Normally, she could sit for hours reading, or with her sketchpad and pencils in hand, drawing, designing, and dreaming up new creations. But since Ryan had gone, so had her inspiration.

She snapped the book shut and tossed it aside. Wrapping her arms around herself, she glanced across at Hunter who sat on the lounge chair beside her, playing his guitar. His fingers slipped and slid effortlessly over the strings, plucking and strumming low notes and chords. A constant low hum rumbled in his throat. Every now and then, he'd shoot forward and write in the journal that lay on the end of the seat.

"What are you writing?" she asked, straightening her scarf.

"Lyrics, notes, ideas, thoughts . . . feelings." His eyes mirrored the stormy, dark gray color of the unsettled ocean.

She dipped her head, wondering if there was anything in his notes about her. Would that book of his give her insight into what made the man before her tick? Other than Ryan, what occupied his mind? What were his dreams, and what held him back? What worried him, and what made him happy?

"Anything you want to share?" she asked.

He propped his guitar into position and played Ryan's song. Slower than the first time. Lower. He pinched his brows together. "I can't get this out of my head. I'm stuck. There's this voice telling me to pick myself up and move forward, but I can't. I feel sick to the stomach . . . with guilt."

"Why guilt?"

Putting his guitar down, he turned to face her and rested his elbows on his knees. "Kar, when I found out you were pregnant, all I did was pray for it to go away. I wanted no part in having a child. I'm not a religious man, but I keep wondering if my prayers were answered. Did someone take Ryan away from us because of me?"

Her gut twisted, remembering how much they'd fought over Ryan at the beginning. How much he'd wanted her to terminate. Well . . . his wish had been granted. Hadn't it? "You never wanted him in the first place."

He lowered his chin, his hair curtaining his face. "I know. But I changed. I wanted him so bad."

"You must be so relieved." Her tone was pure poison. "You're free. You can go back to your life, your tour, your girls, as if nothing happened. *We* never happened."

His head shot up. The pain in his eyes snipped like scissors through her heart, but all her anger and hurt spilled out like a stream of toxic acid she couldn't control. "You can forget me. Ryan. Everything."

"Kar. Don't say that."

Burning tears spilled down her cheeks. Her heart cried. "He

was *my* baby. MINE."

Rage flared in his eyes. "I lost him, too. He was *my* baby, too. Don't you dare say he wasn't. This affects me as much as it does you."

"How could it? It's my fault we lost him. It was *my* body that failed."

He lunged forward and sat beside her outstretched legs. He grabbed her hands, cupping them between his. "I don't believe that for a second. You did everything right."

His words did nothing to ease the torment in her heart. Was there something more that she should have done? More doctor visits? More rest? Less work? "It wasn't enough. I'm the guilty one. Not you. What did I do wrong?"

He drew her into his arms, and she shuddered. She clenched at handfuls of his jacket and cried.

"Nothing." He rubbed her back. His warmth seeped through to her flesh, but it offered no reprieve. "This will get easier. I promise."

"How?" Her eyes watered, stinging in the chilly air. "Because every time I look at you, I see him. I see Ryan."

He squeezed her tight. "I see him in you too. We just need more time."

She pressed her cheek against Hunter's shoulder, her tears soaking into his clothes. He tortured himself over Ryan's death like she did, blamed himself like she did, wondered if he'd done something wrong like she did. For some crazy reason, knowing he suffered and felt the same way gave her hope. She wasn't alone, and they needed each other's strength to move on. She'd been blinded by her loss, too self-absorbed. He'd been there for her; now she needed to do the same for him.

But when night fell, the darkness fogged her thoughts. The emptiness in her grew heavier.

Another storm hit the coastline. The shingled roof drummed

with a steady beat as the rain pounded against it. Her nerves jumped every time the lights flickered as if the power would go out. The whole house shuddered with each angry gust of wind, Kara thought they'd be blown away.

The fragrant smell of their Thai chicken dinner filled the small living room. As they watched a movie, Kara lay stretched out on the sofa, her head propped on a cushion that rested on Hunter's lap. His fingers combed through her hair. His touch, so soft and gentle, made it hard for her to keep her eyes open. Each stroke against her scalp eased her troubled mind. Thoughts of Ryan were not so painful. Thoughts of Hunter were not a pandemonium. But she kept the laces around her heart tied in a tight double knot. She wouldn't fall into a false sense of security, because she knew this time with him was temporary.

At the end of the movie she trudged upstairs and crawled into bed. Tugging the pillow underneath her head, she could make out the sound of Hunter playing his guitar over the noise of the storm. The mournful tune sawed at her heart. She brushed her hand over the side of the mattress where he lay on the first night, missing the warmth of his body. Without question, he'd comforted her. And he'd done the same again last night when she crept into his room and curled in beside him, not wanting to be alone.

The red numbers on the old digital clock blazed 11:37 p.m. when she heard Hunter come up stairs. Her pulse quickened when he shuffled into her room and crawled in beside her. He didn't say a word—only sniffled softly. He pressed his cheek against her shoulder and wetness dampened her shirt. Her heart plummeted knowing he was crying. When it came to coping with the death of their son, they were both going to have good days and bad. This one had been a mix. She drew his arm across her chest, squeezed it tight, and let her own teardrops soak into the sheets.

Her connection with Hunter could never be broken. But it would fade in time—and time was ticking. While she had three months off work for medical and bereavement leave, Hunter hadn't said anything about his plans. Was he going back on tour?

The next morning was quiet, she sat on the sofa reading while Hunter slept the hours away. It wasn't until lunchtime when she heard him talking on the phone upstairs but couldn't make out what he was saying. After twenty minutes, his loud footsteps clambered down the staircase. She looked up when he headed straight into the kitchen, but he didn't make coffee. Didn't grab the JD. Didn't grab food. Instead he just leaned against the counter and stared out the window.

"Hunt? Who was on the phone? Is everything okay?" She threw her book down. She'd been staring at the same page for the last five minutes.

He came over and sat on the rickety coffee table in front of her. "That was Kyle and Gem. We need to make a decision about tour." He wiped the corners of his mouth. "I don't know what to do. On the one hand, I want to get back onstage. But on the other, I don't think I can get up there and act as if nothing has happened. I'm not sure I'm ready."

Kara wriggled her slipper-covered toes, twisting and tensing them against the fluffy wool lining. She didn't want to go back to the city either. She wasn't ready to deal with all the pity, and sorrowful looks on everyone's faces. Staying hidden sounded ideal.

"When do they need to know by?"

"Sophie and Olsen want to know within the next two days so they can make the cancellations if needed."

"What do Gem and Kyle want to do?"

"They've left the decision up to me." He cupped his hands and blew a breath into his palms. He jiggled his leg and the coffee table protested with creaks.

"Hunt, you live for touring." She reached out and placed her hand on his bouncing knee to still it. "You shine onstage. It's who you are."

"But I can't leave you after everything that's happened. I . . . need to make sure you're okay."

"We knew this day would come. I'll go and stay with my parents until I'm healed. It's only for a few more weeks. Then . . . I'll see how I am. I know I have leave, but rather than sitting around feeling sorry for myself, I might go back to work early. I'm not looking forward to working with Conrad's mood swings, but it will be better than being at home alone."

At first, after Ryan died, all she'd wanted to do was be alone; now, the thought terrified her. She had to start from scratch. Find new goals, new dreams, and find herself. But she didn't have the strength yet. Staying in this protected bubble, locked away from the world, with Hunter, was what she needed.

"Why stay at Conrad's if you're unhappy?" he asked.

"My job is all I've got."

"No, it's not. You can do anything you want." He lowered his gaze and took her hand in his. With gentle strokes, he circled his thumb over the back of her wrist. The tiny tingles she got from his touch returned and interrupted her concentration.

She tugged her hand free from his and placed it on her lap. "I don't know what I want anymore, Hunt." She wanted to be with him, but not *with* him. "I need to find my feet again. Maybe it's time for us to take small steps forward." Heaviness weighed down her bones. Their time together was coming to an end. "Go back on tour. Doing what you love might help you move on."

"Kar, I don't think I can. Don't go to your parents. Stay with me? Come on tour with me?" A desperate pleading darkened his eyes.

"What?" She jerked her head back so fast, dizziness swirled

through her brain.

"I'll hire a doctor, a nurse, whatever you need."

"Don't be silly." Her heartbeat quickened. Was he serious? "I have doctor appointments and checkups already scheduled."

"I mean it." He shuffled forward on the table. "I'll have someone at your beck and call. We only have six cities in South America to visit. There's not a lot of travel. Come with me so I won't worry about you sitting at home alone and depressed."

Her chest seized. "I. Lost. Our. Son." Her volume soared. "I'm entitled to be depressed."

"You are. So am I. And I'm allowed to be concerned about you." He clenched his hands. "We can't stay locked away here forever. I thought being around each other might make it easier to face each day."

"How so? I'm not your girlfriend. Sex is not an option. So why do you want me on tour with you?"

"Do you think I give a shit about sex right now?" Hurt rippled through his eyes and made her feel small as an ant. "Why do you think that is all I ever want?"

Kara cocked her head. "Isn't it?"

"No. I want you to come with me because if I have to step out in public"—he flicked his hand toward the door—"and pretend life is great for all the fans, the media, and the bullshit that goes on, I want to be able to go back to my hotel room at night and be me. Be with someone who understands the crap I'm going through when I fall into a heap."

"You have Kyle and Gemma for that."

"And they're your friends too." He sighed, slouching his shoulders as if he was defeated. "It was only an idea. Stay with your folks if you want. I thought you coming might be good for both of us. Help us ease back into life."

"Tour is not my life. What would I do all day? Sit around in the hotel while you're at soundchecks, doing promo, and performing each night? Is that it? How would that be helping me?" Her tone was too sharp for her liking.

"You'd get the rest you needed. You could hang out with us, read, draw, sketch, design, go to a day spa—I don't know." The concern in his eyes caused her heart to crack. "Knowing you're there where I can see how you're doing every day would make me feel better. So I'm not worrying about you."

"You worry about me?"

"All the time." His voice softened. "You're my friend. I care."

The knot between her shoulder blades slackened. "And you can just click your fingers and make all this happen."

"Yeah. I can make shit happen." A smile played at the corner of his mouth.

But even though she was warming to the idea, one thing worried her more than anything: his expectations beyond these four walls. "And what about the sleeping arrangements?"

He lowered his gaze and rubbed his hand down his thigh. "I'll get Bec to book you your own room . . . or you can stay with me . . . I mean, us. Kyle, Gem, and I often share rooms, or suites. Whatever you're comfortable with."

"Hunt, we can't keep sleeping together." Her heart could not handle that. "What we've been doing here has been wonderful. It's what we've both needed. But anything more could lead us down a path we don't want."

He paused. His eyes drilled into hers, dark and intense. Her heart hammered in her chest. Unable to draw breath, her skin tingled. Did he feel that? Their connection? Was there something real between them?

"And what path is that, Kar?"

She closed her eyes and drew in a steady breath. This was a path she thought she'd never face. It was one that was too outrageous to contemplate.

After everything they'd been through during the past few

months, she'd grown to like him. She couldn't deny it. But their lives would never meld as one. Fashion and music only crossed for gala events. The risk, to see if what she felt for him was something special, was too high. She couldn't lose him— not after losing Ryan. She couldn't face another broken heart. "Hunt, don't let what we've been through with Ryan muddle your thoughts. We're just friends."

Somehow, she had to push her feelings for him aside. They were only side effects from carrying his baby.

She met his gaze. Something flashed in the depths of his eyes that snagged her heart. Was it doubt? Conflict? What-if scenarios?

Too late, it was gone.

Maybe it had been her wishful thinking.

"Yes . . . you're right. I understand if you don't want to come," he said, scratching his scruffy three-day growth. "The decision is yours. But I'd like you there with me. As my friend."

Losing Ryan was still raw. But each day, the scar on her heart healed a fraction. There were moments when grief consumed her, but Hunter was there. In some crazy mixed up way, she needed him. He was helping her to mend, and vice versa. And for that reason alone, she wanted to stay close to him for a little while longer. Even if it was only a few more weeks. Then they'd be back in New York and have to get on with their lives. They'd have to accept that Ryan was gone.

"Hunt, I'm warming to the idea. I haven't had a vacation in two years." Not that it would be much of a holiday. "But the ground rules have to be set. It's as friends. In separate rooms."

He swallowed, took a breath and nodded. "If that's what you want, I can accept that."

Yes. I can. I must. I do. Please don't make me regret this.

"Okay. If you're ready to go back on tour, I'll come with you."

Chapter 22

Hunter stepped off the private plane in the early morning Buenos Aires sunshine. With Kyle, Gemma and Kara by his side, sleek black cars whisked them from the tarmac and security led them through a discreet door into the terminal and up into the VIP Lounge. There, with the Everhide staff and their backup band, they waited for customs clearance.

Gemma and Kyle couldn't keep still, weaving around, hugging and catching up with Bec, Sophie, and the band after four weeks of tour being canceled. Unable to get swept up in their energy, Hunter stood by the bar with Kara. While he was physically present, his heart and mind were elsewhere. Was he an idiot for coming back on tour? Had he thought of everything to ensure Kara remained safe? That she would be an inconspicuous part of their team? Would she be able to rest and recover?

"How are you feeling?" He scanned Kara up and down. Neither had slept on the plane. Even with dark circles under her eyes, she looked kinda cute and sexy. She'd braided her hair, glossed her lips, and in her oversized "Everhide crew" shirt and loose-fitting pants she looked . . . hot. God, he was glad she was there. Dealing with the loss of Ryan was getting better, easier, and in the moments when he got overwhelmed, she'd become his safety net.

"It's good to stretch my legs. And my scar's not aching too much." Kara rubbed her abdomen.

It had been one month since her operation, and to make sure she was okay he had medical staff coming to the hotel to check on her later in the day.

She scratched her thigh and pinched at her pants. "These awful compression stockings are itchy and hot though. I can't wait to get them off."

Visions of pulling them off with his teeth shot through his mind.

Wrong. Wrong. Wrong. Wrong. WRONG!

"We'll be at the hotel soon. Do you want me to organize a wheelchair? It's a long walk through the terminal."

"No. I'll be okay. I just can't go fast."

"Once we get outside, it will be crazy. Promise me you'll stay with Giles and Bec." He hated having to leave her, but the paparazzi would be waiting for him, Kyle, and Gemma.

"I've been around you long enough to know the deal."

"Down here is different to home. It's not the fans you have to worry about—it's the press. The paparazzi have no rules. They'll hunt us like prey."

Sam, their head of security, had briefed them on the plane about getting everyone safely into the city. With all the cars, police escort and additional security, anyone would think the president was coming to town.

Hunter didn't know whether to be excited or terrified. "When we get to the hotel, Kyle, Gemma, and I have to go straight into a press conference. Would you mind checking into your room, and I'll catch up with you later?"

She placed her hand on his arm, and little sparks ran across his skin. *What was that?* Surely it was from being on edge about her wellbeing. "Hunt, stop worrying. I'll be fine."

The VIP airport customs officer walked from the counter over to Sophie and handed her the pile of passports. "Ms. Carter. You are clear to go. Security will escort you and your group to the cars that await you."

Hunter squeezed Kara on the arm. "I have to go with Kyle and Gem. Are you going to be all right?"

"Yes. Go." She smiled and shoved him on his way.

He nodded to Giles. "Don't let Kara out of your sight. I'll see you at the hotel."

Walking down the private corridor, Hunter's palms sweated. Drawing in a deep breath, he stepped through the doors, out onto the sidewalk with Kyle and Gemma, and straight into a wall of paparazzi. Flashes, shouts, and jostling people surrounded him. Lenses, cameras, and cell phones were shoved in his face. His heart thundered as hard as a jet plane taking off. Security made a pathway for them to their waiting convoy.

He slipped into his car and glanced over his shoulder to see how the team were doing. Over the heads of the paparazzi shoving cameras against the windows, he saw Kara slip into the end car with Bec and Giles. No one bothered them. Turning back around, he let out the breath he'd been holding.

Gemma touched his knee. "She'll be okay, Hunt."

"I know. It's cool." His voice may have been full of confidence, but his gut twisted and turned. "I'll feel better when we're at the hotel."

Led by two police motorbikes with flashing blue lights, their four-car convoy took off, a police cruiser following behind. When they turned onto the freeway into the city, Hunter gripped onto the handle above the window.

Kyle shook his head and pointed to the motorcycles trying

to keep pace with them. "Look at these crazy dickheads."

A man doubled on the back of one and propped a camera lens in their direction.

"We're not worth killing yourself over." Gemma gazed out the window. "That's bullshit."

Normally Hunter would wind down the window and give the photographer a great shot, but he wasn't in the mood. He peered over his shoulder once more to make sure the other cars were following. He grabbed his cell phone and texted Kara.

All okay?

She replied.

Yes. XO

He went to swipe his cell phone off but stared at his screen saver. A photo of him and Kara on the sofa at the beach house. He'd taken it to prove to her that his eyes were redder than hers. She'd won. He loved the photo of her smile.

How was he going to reset everything back to normal after tour?

Everhide's convoy exited the highway and the motorcyclist disappeared in the traffic. The car's tires thudded over the bumps in the road as they headed along wide streets and avenues full of gardens and parklands, past the dominating Obelisco de Buenos that was surrounded by tourists taking photos, Plaza de Mayo with the Argentinean flag flying in the breeze, and onto their hotel overlooking the river.

When Hunter stepped out of the car, the heat and stench hit him—car fumes, weird spicy foods, and cigarette smoke. Traffic rumbled by, but that didn't compare to the ear-splitting screeches coming from the fans, held back by street barriers and a line of police standing at the edge of the hotel's driveway.

Hunter peered over his shoulder. Kara's car waited in line at the hotel's entrance. She was here. All was good.

Seeing the fans usually sent a charge through his veins,

but today he didn't even get a hum. Drawing on a smile and mustering up a small element of zing, he headed over to the crowd with Kyle and Gemma, and security. As he played it up for photos and signed autographs, he kept glancing over his shoulder to make sure Kara slipped into the hotel with the team. Once she was through the doors, he breathed easier. By the time Kate came out to get them ten minutes later, he felt better. Now Kara was inside, he had nothing to worry about.

Kate circled her finger through the air. "Time to go. The press conference is ready. Let's get it over with so we can all crash."

Hell yeah.

Security escorted them through the elaborate lobby with its massive glass atrium and arched ceiling up to the fifth floor. After a quick recap of the meeting's agenda, Kate led them into a large room overflowing with journalists, TV presenters, radio hosts, and photographers. Just another typical press conference. But needles prickled the back of Hunter's neck, and his palms turned clammy. What was wrong with him? Was he on edge because this was his first interview since losing his son?

He stopped in the center of the stage with Kyle and Gemma to pose for photographs. He linked his arm around Gemma's waist, with Kyle on her opposite side, and camera flashes blinded him from every angle. Peering over the crowd, no faces looked familiar. Then he spotted Kara standing toward the back on the far side of the room next to Bec and Giles.

What the hell?

He'd told her not to come. Even though Kara had her baseball cap on and a plain T-shirt, she stood out like a spotlight. If the media got light of the fact she was here, they'd devour her.

He tugged on Gemma's shirt and leaned down to whisper in her ear, "Kara's here."

She gave a subtle nod and squeezed her arm around his

waist.

"All righty," Kate spoke into the mic at the lectern, "let's get underway."

While the guests settled, Hunter, Kyle, and Gemma took seats at the panel table behind them. Gemma whispered something into Kyle's ear, and he threw Hunter a worried look.

"Welcome." Kate took control of the room. "Everhide are excited to reach your beautiful country."

As Kate ran through her introductions, Hunter's leg jiggled. His gut didn't feel right. The air pressed into him from all sides. He'd done thousands of interviews; this one shouldn't be any different. He let out a slow and steady breath. Time to focus.

"What can fans expect from your two concerts here in Buenos Aires?" the first reporter asked, a timid lady whose voice was quiet and hard to hear.

Hunter slipped into performance mode, concentrating on their well-rehearsed responses. "The best show ever," he said in a would-you-expect-anything-less tone. "We'll cover songs from our new album, and some of our past hits, and guarantee a lot of fun on the night."

The next reporter, a lady wearing a bright yellow dress covered in polka dots, waved her pen at them as she spoke. "All your shows have been sell-outs. How does that make you feel, performing in front of thousands of fans every night?"

Hunter chuckled under his breath. He'd lost track of how many times he'd answered this question over the years. "It's freaking awesome," he hollered into the mic.

"Are you releasing another single off your album?" A man with ART-RADIO logoed on his shirt asked next.

"Yes. It will be 'Traveled,'" Gemma said. "We've been filming bits and pieces for the video clip while we've been touring. It will be out in a couple months."

Hunter's chest warmed as he gazed in Kara's direction.

Visions of her on set with them in LA filled his mind. Her dressing him. Being close to her in the trailer. Teasing and taunting each other. How life had changed since finding out she was pregnant.

"'Traveled' is my favorite track." Kyle grinned sheepishly. "It's about searching for love only to find it right at home on your doorstep." He leaned over and kissed Gemma on the cheek. She blushed as red as Kyle's scarlet T-shirt.

A wave of a*wwws* rippled across the audience.

Questions continued to fly back and forth for twenty-or-so minutes. Hunter lost track of time, and didn't look at the next man who stood and introduced himself. "Hello, I'm Gerard Rivers from *Entertainment On-Show*."

Hunter's heart stopped. His head whiplashed in Gerard's direction. Gemma and Kyle stiffened beside him.

Gerard's grin smeared across his face like cream cheese on a bagel. "While I'm sure everyone is glad to see you return to tour"—Gerard waved his hand across the crowd, his cocky tone cold—"Hunter, after what has happened, are you sure you're ready to return to the stage? How are you and Ms. Knight coping after the loss of your child?"

Gerard's question was like a punch to the guts. Hunter glared at Gerard, but out of the corner of his eye he saw Bec and Giles edge closer to Kara. He wished Kara wasn't in the room. She didn't need to listen to this asshole.

His heart struggled to beat, and his mind went blank, unable to remember what to say. With a trembling hand he circled his thumb over the inside of his right forearm. Over his new tattoo. *03/24.18:07—03/26.05:17*. Ryan's time of birth and the time of his death. His mind filled with images of his son's lifeless body. How was he coping? Not well.

Gerard, you son of a bitch. Why are you here?

Each breath was like razors slicing into his chest. With all his strength, Hunter hung onto composure by a thin thread. When Gemma placed her hand on his back, he nearly lost it. He took a sip of water and cleared his throat. *Focus, damn it.* "We're taking one day at a time. Thank you." Somehow, the words came out. He turned his head and scanned the room for the next reporter and their question.

But Gerard continued. "What is the status of your relationship with Ms. Knight? Has this incident brought the two of you together?"

Hunter's heart crashed against his ribs. He closed his eyes and clenched his fist beneath the table. "My personal life is none of your business, and not open for discussion."

"But the fans want to know." Gerard's pompous tone grated his nerves. "I heard she's here with you?"

The muscles in Hunter's neck pinched, and his mouth ran dry. He tried to resist looking in Kara's direction by staring at the back wall, but it was useless. He took a quick glance to make sure she was okay.

Gerard spun around, following his line of sight. He stopped when he spotted her. "It looks like I have my answer." He nudged the photographer sitting next to him and pointed his finger straight at Kara.

The blood drained from Hunter's face. The room erupted into commotion. Frantic voices buzzed in his ears. *"There she is." "Get her." "Now." "Hurry!"* Cameras swung in Kara's direction, and flashes went off in blinding spasms.

"Giles. Bec. Get her out of here," Hunter boomed into the mic. He shot from his chair, knocking it over and rushed across the stage to get to Kara. His legs couldn't carry him fast enough. At the bottom of the steps, blocked by the sea of photographers and reporters, his heart pummeled somewhere up near his throat.

The reporters kept up with their harrowing cries.

"Ms. Knight, Ms. Knight, why are you here with Everhide?"

"Are you in a relationship with Hunter?"

"How are you feeling after losing your baby?"

Every muscle in Hunter's body seized. He couldn't get to Kara. There were too many people jostling through the narrow doorway. Mick, his bodyguard, grabbed him by the shirt and pulled him back. Hunter fought against him, tried to free himself, tried to get to Kara. With Chester's help, Mick hauled him out of the room through another side door.

"What the fuck?" Hunter ripped free of their hold once he was in the hallway. "Where is she?"

Mick uttered into his security headset, then pointed his chin down the hallway. "Boardroom."

Farther down the corridor, the clamor from the reporters echoed off the tiled floor. With Hunter jammed between Mick and Chester, they charged through the throng of people like they were knocking pins out of the way in a bowling alley and made their way to the boardroom.

Hunter slid into the room, dashed past Giles and Bec and dropped to his knees in front of Kara who sat on a chair by the boardroom table. "Are you hurt?" His hand trembled as he brushed her hair back from the side of her face.

"No." She shook her head. Her whole body shuddered beneath his touch.

What was she thinking? "I asked you to stay in your room. I knew something like this would happen."

Her eyes glassed over, and she cried. He wrapped his arms around her and squeezed her tight, burying his face into her hair. "Bloody Gerard! Why does he have to be in our faces all the time?"

The voices and noise from the reporters rattled the closed door behind him. In crazed moments like this, Hunter was thankful for their bodyguards. Mick and Chester had stayed outside on guard with the hotel's security team. Giles stood like a statue inside the room. Sam had stayed back with Gemma and Kyle.

"Well. That was fun." Bec reached for the jug of water on the table and poured them a glass. Her voice was calm, as if no feather of hers had been ruffled. "The wolves are thick and furious today. Wasn't expecting excitement like this."

Hunter glared at Bec and snapped, "Excitement? Kara could've been hurt."

"Nah." Bec swished her hand at him. "We had everything under control."

Hunter wasn't so sure. Did she have everything in hand? Did security? Maybe he'd overreacted to what he, Gemma, and Kyle put up with most days on tour?

The door burst open. A blaze of flashing lights filled the room. Kyle, Gemma, Sophie, and Kate burst through the security guarded gap and slammed the door shut behind them.

"Kate." Hunter leaned back on his haunches, clutching onto Kara's hand in her lap. "We banned Gerard from our press conferences. How did he get here? How the hell did he find out Kara was with us?"

"I don't know. He's not on our registered guest list." She scrolled through her tablet. "He must have used a fake ID. Bribed someone. Who knows?"

Gemma and Kyle came to Kara's side.

Kyle sighed and crossed his arms. "Welcome to the world of crazy, Kar."

"More like insane," Kara voice still shook.

Gemma rubbed Kara's shoulder, her eyes flooded with concern. "The press can be such assholes. Gerard tops our list. I'm just glad you're all right, Kar."

"Thanks Gem." Kara patted Gemma's hand.

"We need to get you out of here." Hunter said to Kara. Her

lashes were wet with tears. "Back to your room. I need to make sure you're safe."

"Hunt, I'm fine." She touched his cheek. "It was only a fright. This is on par with when the press found out I was . . . pregnant." That last word seemed to snag in her throat. Hunter raised back to his knees, cupped her neck, and pressed his forehead to hers. She wrapped her arms around him and sobbed. "Why did they have to ask about Ryan?"

His whole body ached with loss. She was the only thing that made it bearable. "Shh. It's over."

Being confronted about Ryan hurt too much. It was as if the wound in his heart had torn open.

He'd thought he had his shit together. Thought he had enough experience with the media to handle any curveball questions. That obviously wasn't the case. This was why he wanted Kara here. She gave him a different kind of strength compared to Kyle and Gemma. "Thank you for being here," he whispered to her. "Makes this shit easier to deal with."

She clung to him tight, like she never wanted to let go. His heart lurched. Because soon, she would have to. Once tour was over and they got back to New York, they had to move on. Their work would consume them, and their separate social circles would ensure they wouldn't see each other often. He'd miss having her around, but he had to remember they could only ever be friends. Their differences and interests were too great. Like heavy metal and opera, they'd never tune together.

Sitting back on his heels, he glanced up at Kyle and Gemma. Kyle draped his arm around Gemma's shoulders. Their eyes ping-ponged between him and Kara. Little smirks curled their lips.

"What?" he asked.

Kyle's gaze shot to the ceiling. "Nothing."

But he wasn't giving off a "nothing" type of vibe.

"Not a thing going on here," Gemma said, with an oh-my-gosh look on her face.

Hunter went to question her, but her expression erased to blank.

Kara wiped her eyes on the tissue Sophie handed her from the sideboard. "Guys, go and finish your press conference. I'll wait here until it's over."

"No need," Kate cut in, looking up from her cell phone. "Conference is over. They had us for thirty minutes instead of an hour. It's no big deal. These reporters know the lines of conduct. It's assholes like Gerard who ruin it for everyone. But the whole city will know you're here now, Kara, so you'll be followed."

Kara hugged her arms around herself and shuddered. Even with all the plans and security in place, Hunter had failed her. He hadn't been able to protect her.

"Let's get everyone out of here," Sophie said. "I'll get security to clear the reporters. We'll have lunch in my suite, then rest and have an early dinner." She snapped her fingers. "Time to move, people. Because tomorrow is show day."

Hunter got to his feet and helped Kara to stand. Clutching onto his arms, she swayed.

Gemma stepped forward and placed her hand on Kara's back. "You got this, Kar?"

"Yeah." She nodded. "I didn't mean to ruin your press meet. Or get upset. But Ryan moments are tough."

Ryan moments.

Warmth spread throughout Hunter's system. That was the perfect way to summarize what had happened. The times when he broke, when she broke—he'd always call them *Ryan moments.*

One crisis was over. There would be more, but after everything they'd been through in the last few months, he thought no other drama would come close.

Hunter was burned out. He was tired of being upset over Ryan, worrying about Kara, and being stressed. It was time to put all those emotions to bed. As he clutched onto Kara's hand, his pulse eased. Thank God, she was all right.

He'd panicked when he saw the reporters go after Kara. Bec had assured him it was unnecessary. Had the long flight, the lack of sleep, and his security concerns messed with his head? Caused him to not think straight? *Most likely.* A good night's rest would put an end to his worries. Clear his foggy head. He had twelve shows and several promotional shoots to get through. Easy as a blues backbeat. Maybe he'd overreacted, but he cared for Kara. Maybe too much. He had to draw new lines. From now on, he wouldn't let anything rattle him. Surely nothing could.

Not even Kara.

Chapter 23

The colorful cramped city of Rio De Janeiro, surrounded by towering mountains and beautiful beaches, begged Kara to venture outside. She buckled up her sandals and glanced out the full-length window over the long stretch of private golden beach. Crystal blue waters rolled onto the shore and crashed against a few large rocks that stood in the water. The doctor had just given her the six-week all-clear after her in-room checkup, and she craved fresh air. While her friends were at a photoshoot with one of their tour sponsors, she jumped at the opportunity to take a walk along the secluded stretch of sand. With no paparazzi in sight, she had the whole day to herself and her first chance to clear her mind.

It had been one week since that fateful press conference in Buenos Aires. The unrelenting harassment from the media had frightened her, and left her paranoid and unnerved. She jumped at every knock on her hotel room door, glanced over her shoulder every time she walked through the lobby, and panicked every time she saw a large camera. The only thing that made her feel safe and secure was Hunter being by her side.

Hunter was tougher, stronger, not as emotional. He'd taken on a new resilience. It was hard for her to comprehend. He seemed to be coping. Better than she was. He didn't tear up when she needed to cry on his shoulder, when losing Ryan consumed her. With the weight in her chest not so tight and her mind not so bleak, maybe she, too, was coming to terms with their loss. Just not as fast.

What troubled her now was how close she and Hunter had become. It was all the little things that had her asking questions. Had they become more than friends? When they ate together, his leg would rest against hers. His smile seemed genuine when he looked at her. The warm kiss he left on her cheek before he headed onstage seemed to linger.

What was happening? Did she want a relationship with him? She saw through his ego, and was touched by his heart of gold and protective nature. He was ambitious, passionate, and cared for her. These were more important to her than any prestigious family background. She wondered if being with him was possible. Could extreme opposites be together? Did he feel the same way? Or was she heading for more heartache and trouble? Hunter continually messed with her head.

She picked up her cell phone to call Giles, but it vibrated in her hand before she could hit his number.

She swiped the screen. "Hey, Gem. What's up?"

"Need a favor. Can you come to my room?"

"Um . . . I was about to head out. But sure."

Grabbing her tote, big floppy hat, and sunglasses, she headed down the hall to Gemma's suite. She knocked and Bec opened the door. Kara hesitated at the sight of the stress drawn on Bec's pale face. She hurried past her into a room of gloomy faces.

Kara scanned everyone present. "What's up?"

Gemma sat at the desk getting her hair and makeup done by Carla. The boys sat on the sofa strumming on their guitars. *Da-da-da-da-da-da da da dada da.* Sophie and Kate hovered by the table near the kitchenette, working tablets, cell phones, and laptops.

"Margo's sick." Gemma grimaced as Carla pulled and curled Gemma's hair with a flatiron. "She's had to go to the hospital again. The doctors don't know what's wrong with her."

Kara dumped her tote and hat on the coffee table. "That's not good. I hope she's okay."

Hunter strummed loud chords on his guitar. "So do we."

Wearing blue jeans and a white shirt, with black Ray-Bans perched on top of his head, he looked every inch the hot rock star with the bad boy attitude. She'd love to straddle his lap and do bad girl things to him. Everything about him that used to turn her off, now turned her on. *Damn!* She was in trouble.

Gemma flicked a curl off her face. "We're in a jam again. I was . . . or, we were wondering if you'd be up to helping out in wardrobe for the shoot today? No pressure."

Kara's pulse spiked remembering the video shoot in LA. The exhilaration of calling Adrian and sourcing clothes, dressing her friends in the trailer, and being on set watching the filming. Then she glanced at Hunter and her heart took on an erratic beat. Looking at him was like staring at a pinboard of memories. The shoot. His teasing. His flirtation. His body. His muscles. Him half-naked.

Could she do another shoot? With her changing feelings for Hunter, would she be able to remain professional? Keep her feelings under wraps?

Of course she could.

She ran her hand over her belly and brushed across her cesarean section scar. With her Cutifilm covering and stitches gone, her tummy was no longer sore or as swollen as it had been. She was stronger and more mobile. Sitting around all day while Everhide were off doing their rock star thing was getting boring. She needed something to do. Going to the beach would be nice, but she could do that tomorrow.

Another shoot sounded perfect. "If I take it easy, I'll be fine. As long as I don't have to lift anything heavy and can sit down when needed."

"Excellent. You're hired." Kyle swung his hand around in a circle and pointed to Bec. "Bec has all the details."

"You three wouldn't survive without me." Bec grabbed her tablet. She skimmed through several screens before reading out loud. "Bierveza are bringing the clothing. I've been trying to get in touch with their rep, but she's not returning my calls. We're supposed to meet them downstairs in the Martini Ice Bar for the shoot at eleven o'clock."

"That's in . . . ten minutes." Kara's mind ticked as fast as her watch. She had to change. Dressed in a tank top and shorts, she was ready to head to the beach, not work. She needed to do her hair. Makeup. She couldn't go to a shoot as their stylist looking like they'd dragged her off the street.

"You can do a lot in ten minutes, Kar." Hunter's wink sent warmth to her cheeks. "Want me to come and help you change?"

"If you helped, I'd need half an hour."

The smile that charged across his face made her breath hitch.

"You only need *one* outfit change, not *three.*" Hunter ran his thumb across his lower lip. He eyed her up and down with a look in his eyes that hinted at mischief. At this rate, she'd have to change her panties too. But what had her heart aching was that she knew he was joking. She didn't want to joke anymore. If she was to survive this trip, she needed him to stop with the flirtations. Because every moment she spent with him, she was falling deeper and deeper.

Bec handed Kara her tablet. "Here. This is the briefing for the shoot."

Reining in her thoughts, Kara skimmed the document. She covered her mouth to stifle her laugh. "This is a photoshoot for a *beer* company?" Her gaze jumped from Gemma to Kyle before settling back on Hunter. "Won't you upset Jack Daniels?"

"Nah. JD will always be number one. But we have to keep the sponsors happy," Hunter said, resting his arm across the back of the sofa.

Kara passed the tablet back to Bec. "If you don't want to be late for the shoot, I'll go change into something more respectable."

"Are you sure you don't need a hand?" Hunter asked again, humor shining in his eyes.

She sighed and picked up her tote. How was she going to make it through the day with him? Did he not realize that the comments he made without a second thought affected her? "I'm more than capable of dressing myself."

"Kar?" Gemma peeked around Carla who was applying Gemma's eye makeup. "Thanks for this. I owe you. You name it. Anything. It's yours."

Kara headed toward the door, a smile quivered across her lips. "I might hold you to that one day, Gem."

Opening the door, Kara glanced back over her shoulder toward Hunter who was goofing around on his guitar and talking to Kyle. Her heart sank to the pit of her stomach. She may need to call on Gemma's offer, to save herself from Hunter, and it may be sooner rather than later.

***

Twenty minutes later, stepping into the Martini Ice Bar with Everhide and their entourage, Kara's nose wrinkled at the foul stench of stale alcohol and cigarette smoke. Slick chrome lined the countertop and island in the center of the room. Large globes dangled on chains of alternate length from the ceiling. Mirrors lined the wall behind the serving counter, and glass shelves were stacked with rows and rows of neatly aligned liquor bottles. The trendy layout would rival that of any high-end bar in Manhattan.

Film crew scuttled around prepping lighting, mounting cameras, and angling reflectors. The hum of activity looked like semi-coordinated chaos. Kara wiped her hands on her dress pants, ready to help her friends. There was no way she'd let Hunter affect her like he had in LA.

Kate and Sophie rushed off to find the representative from the beer company while Kara stayed huddled with her friends and Bec off to one side of the bar. Kara's mouth gaped when she caught sight of the far side of the room. Sitting on stools, in front of temporary mirrors, were a dozen models in skimpy dresses and stiletto shoes, with glittery makeup adorning their faces.

Great. I'll never look that gorgeous. I'm too . . . average.

Hunter's eyes lit up at the sight of the girls, and he rubbed his hands together. "Some days, our job can be tough."

Kara's heart lurched. The grin covering Hunter's entire face didn't make her feel any better. While Kyle took a quick glimpse at the models and then turned away, Hunter remained fixed on the ladies. Kara didn't exist.

Gemma strained her neck, standing on her tippy-toes to see. "Hang on. If they're for you, where are my guys?"

"Over there." Kyle wrapped his arm around Gemma's shoulder and pointed toward the far wall where a few hot young men stood dressed in open button-down shirts and jeans.

Gemma pumped her fist. "All right."

None of the male models appealed to Kara. She had different tastes in men. She glanced sideways at Hunter. Yep . . . her tastes, list of qualities and requirements in a man had changed.

Sophie and Kate led a tall woman who was the spitting image of Penelope Cruz over to greet them. "You're here. Exzellent." Her accent was strong and sultry. "I'm Marlena, the marketing manager at Bierveza. We're nearly all zet. I'll run through the agenda and zen I'll show you to the clothez."

After introductions and running through the requirements for the photoshoot, Marlena led them around the corner of the room and over to a bright red modesty panel and a large rack of clothes.

"Margo emailed me everyone's sizes, zo I hope everything fits." Marlena flipped the coat hangers along the rack. "This section is for Gemma, this one for Kyle, and these are for Hunter. Choose whatever you like. Please get them changed and let me know when you're ready."

"Sure," Kara nodded and eyed the clothes.

Marlena dipped her head and dashed back toward the film crew.

Kara stretched her neck from side to side and jumped into work mode. She sifted through the guys' clothes first. Leather pants, torn jeans, classic-cut suits and stripy, paisley, silky, and sparkly shirts were all at her fingertips.

She glanced at Hunter standing a few feet away from her. The models still mesmerized him. Were they clothed how he liked his women to dress? Her head swirled. She shouldn't be feeling like this—jealous, envious, possessive. It was wrong, and she knew it.

She skimmed through Gemma's section of clothing. It was jam-packed with short skirts, skimpy tops, bralettes, mesh, sequins, and even smaller, tighter dresses than the ones the models were wearing. Kara could never wear anything like this. They were so different from the conservative fashions she wore and designed.

"Gem, you wouldn't want to wear something like this, would you?" Kara winced and held up an electric blue mini-dress that was no longer than a tank top.

Gemma stepped in beside her. "Ah . . . that would be a no. I know I'm small, but I don't think even I'd fit into that."

"It's stretchy though. Look at this." Kara stretched it like an elastic band and flicked it at Gemma.

"Ow!" Gemma gave her an I-can't-believe-you-just-did-that laugh. She jostled over to Kara, wrapped one arm around Kara's waist and hugged her. "Love having you here."

"Yeah. It's awesome."

Being on tour and hanging out, they had grown closer. Their friendship was something Kara cherished.

"Now . . . what are you going to dress me in?" Gemma pulled a pair of pink hot pants off the rack. "These are a definite no."

Kara analyzed what the models were wearing, the several pairs of shoes that lay on the floor underneath the rack, and then looked back to the clothing. She needed to make Gemma stand out against the girls. They were all in bright colors, so Gemma needed to be plain. She chose a black sequined miniskirt and backless mesh top and handed them to Gemma, who went to change without question.

Off Kyle's section of the rack she grabbed navy jeans and a red button-down shirt. He too went to change.

Then she moved to Hunter's clothes. Running her hand across the trousers, denim jeans, suits, and bright-colored shirts and tops, her fingers quivered. Hunter would look hot as hell in this gear. He looked good in anything, but when he wore a suit, a button-down shirt and his hair out, it really got her blood pumping. *Hmm* . . . she better dress him in something more causal.

He shimmied up beside her. "Doesn't this bring back memories?" Heat flushed her skin when he slid his hand around her lower back and leaned in close. "Wanna help me change?"

"Please don't start." She took a step sideways, hoping to lower her body temperature. "We're way past that."

"I'm only stirring." His eyes sparkled as blue as the clear ocean outside.

"I know. That's the thing." She had to look away, otherwise she would drown in his gaze. What was wrong with her? She wasn't pregnant. Her hormones should have settled. Why, whenever he was near, did her head and heart not cooperate? "Stop. Please?"

"Okay then, Ms. Knight." Hunter lowered his voice and drew down his brows. "What attire will I be wearing for my professional photographic shoot today?"

Kara smiled, shook her head, and fought the urge to flirt back. "You and serious don't go together. Here." She shoved a pair of white jeans and a linen button-down shirt at him. "Put these on."

Hunter clutched the clothes to his chest and backed away, giving her a salute with his free hand. "Yes, ma'am."

Her heart wanted to follow him, but she reeled it back into place.

Once Everhide came out from behind the modesty screen all dressed and ready, they had quick introductions to the models and crew, and got into position. Wanting to keep out of the way, Kara lingered at the back of the room with Bec, Sophie, and Kate.

"Here we go again. Another photoshoot." Taking a seat on one of the bar stools at a high table, Bec's tone lacked any form of enthusiasm.

"What's wrong?" Kara sat on the stool next to her. Her eyes darted around the room at the action and bustle. Orders were being barked, the rent-a-crowd shuffled into position for the shoot. "Is this one going to differ from the one in LA?"

"Oh yeah." Bec bobbed her head. "The LA shoot was tame compared to what's about to happen here. When it's only the three of them, it's easy. But when extras are involved, Gem, Kyle, and Hunter turn everything into a crazed party. It's not just them I'm worried about; the production team often push the professional boundaries."

Sophie sat and folded her arms. "Kara, I'm surprised in your line of business you haven't attended more shoots."

"I never get the chance." Kara fidgeted with a drink coaster on the table. "At Conrad's we have a marketing team that does our promotional work."

"Well, this will be an eye-opener for you." Kate flicked her chin toward the crowd. "Watch and learn."

Kara wanted to ask more questions, but the lights dimmed. Disco LEDs spun a rainbow of colors across the group and deafening music blared through the sound system. Lunchtime daylight was turned into a partying club at midnight.

Gorgeous female bar attendants dressed in low-cut midriff tops that barely covered their ample bosoms appeared from the room behind the bar. The Bierveza logo was blazed across the front of their tops and the backs of their shiny black hot pants that rode up their butt cheeks. Towering tall in their stilettos and with smiles painted in bright red lipstick, they handed out drinks to everyone.

Kara gawked at the crowd who partied, danced, and drank. Hunter's eyes feasted on each girl who walked past. Jealousy oozed through Kara's veins like thick, green, oozy slime.

Cameras swirled around the group of people. Flashes went off. There was a never-ending *click, click, click* from the photographer. The production manager kept ordering Hunter, Kyle, and Gemma to stand in different places, and realign the hold on their beer bottles for the cameras. He ordered the models to move in closer. The music and noise grew louder, ringing in Kara's ears. Her eyes transfixed on Hunter. The tension in her neck twisted and tightened.

With a beaming smile, Hunter gyrated against one model. He turned and did the same to another. The song changed to "Pony" by Ginuwine, and his seductive dancing jumped to a whole new level. He slipped one hand around the waist of the girl in front of him, flicked his hair back, and laughed. He downed his beer, and the girl slid her hands up over his chest and hooked them around his neck. After his mouthful of beer, he looked down at her, desire sparkling in his eyes, his smile curling with sexiness.

Kara didn't know if the heat she felt was from her raging jealousy or the chemistry onset. Her heart constricted so hard she thought her ribs cracked.

Why couldn't he look at her like that? Just her.

Glancing at Gemma and Kyle, they were dancing close to other people too, but they weren't smothered and surrounded by the models like Hunter.

She glanced to Bec, to Kate and Sophie. They didn't seem concerned about Hunter's behavior. Wasn't he pushing the professional boundaries?

Half a second later, another model moved in on Hunter. His eyes lit up and his grin broadened. He loved this. The attention. The girls clawing and vying for the opportunity to be with him.

Then the model kissed him.

Kara froze. Hunter ripped his head back. He grimaced and waggled his finger at the girl. He turned away and danced with someone else. It didn't matter. *That girl kissed him.*

Touching her throat, Kara's hand trembled. Seeing him all over the models shouldn't be upsetting her like this. This was his life: touring, girls, partying. This was a photoshoot. So why did it hurt so much? Whether it happened here or somewhere else, he'd always be with some girl. Want to sleep with someone new. He would never change. Not for her. Not for anyone. She'd been avoiding the truth about her feelings for him for too long.

Shit.

She was in love.

With a man she could never have.

A man she should never love.

There was only one thing to do.

Block him out of her heart.

Once and for all.

Pushing all her hurt and jealousy deep inside, a shudder shot down her spine. She had to get through the day.

Get your shit together. You can do this.

But with each passing hour, it got harder and harder. The photoshoot seemed never-ending. Cuts. Reshoots. New positions. At break she went into robot mode, coordinating outfit changes for her friends.

"This is awesome fun, isn't it?" Gemma danced around on the spot.

None of Gemma's vibrant energy touched Kara. She pulled her shoulders back. Every muscle on her face ached, fighting the urge to cry.

"How do you do it?" she asked Gemma and searched the rack for her next outfit. "How do you handle seeing girls throwing themselves at Kyle? Twerking against him? Kissing him? Doesn't it bother you?"

"Bah!" Gemma flicked her hand. "We've been doing this for years, don't forget. It's like acting. It's not real. And I'm the one who gets to take him home at the end of the day."

"How can you be so sure? How can you trust him?"

"We've been through so much." She glanced at Kyle talking to Bec at the back of the room. A smile as bright as the spotlights lit her face. Her eyes went doey and overflowed with love. "I guess I'm secure in our relationship. I love him, and he loves me. Nothing else matters."

"Lucky you." Kara blinked a tear from her eye.

"Kar, what's up?" Gemma placed her hand on Kara's arm. "Are you not feeling well? Do you need to sit down?"

Kara sucked in a deep breath, drew herself up tall, and wiped her watery eyes. But she couldn't help herself. She looked in Hunter's direction. He stood by the bar chatting up the models.

"My suspicions are right, aren't they?" Gemma had followed her gaze. "It's not about Ryan anymore, is it? You've fallen for him, haven't you?"

Kara's heart spasmed. Somehow she managed to nod. "I never meant to. I swore to myself over and over I wouldn't let him get to me. But he has. And there's nothing I can do about it. Look at this life you lead. I don't belong in this world."

"You seem to fit in fine."

"No, I'm not." This was their domain. She didn't belong, and it was time to get out. She fumbled with a pair of shorts. "Please don't say anything to Hunter. He doesn't need to worry about me. I'm a big girl. I'll get over him." She no longer possessed the strength to hold herself together. "I should've never come on tour. I never thought I'd call on that favor you offered earlier today. But I am. Gem, I need to go home."

"We've only got two and a half more weeks of tour and we're done."

"I know. But you don't need me." She watched Hunter laugh, his arm was wrapped around some girl's waist. The knife twisted in her heart. "And he certainly doesn't."

"Kar, please stay."

She shook her head. Her mind was made up. "I can't. I'll talk to Bec and get her to book me a flight."

"I think you're crazy. You and Hunter need to sort your shit out. You're still getting over losing Ryan. You need to be honest with each other." Gemma sucked in a sharp breath and grimaced. "I will admit, tour is not the place for it. We're all tired. Emotional. Worn out. But please, give him a chance."

"That's just it. He's had multiple chances, and every time he's turned me down. There's only so much rejection I can take. I can't handle it anymore. Not this time. It hurts too much. I need to go home."

She felt Hunter's eyes on her and met his gaze.

His face drew with concern and he mouthed, *"Are you okay?"*

Kara gave him a reassuring smile, and before she could blink, he turned back to talk to the models. Clenching her jaw, she closed her eyes, trying to erase the image of him burning her brain.

Gemma wrapped her arms around Kara and gave her a huge hug. "I knew you liked him, but not this bad. What kind of terrible friend am I? Please don't do anything rash. Let's finish this shoot, and then we'll talk."

Someone called out that the break would be over in five minutes.

Gemma stepped back and turned to the clothes rack. "Everything will work out. I promise. But for now, get me into a new outfit so I can go get those hunky men dripping all over me again."

Kara forced a smile and handed Gemma a pair of ripped denim shorts and sequined top.

But for Kara, the afternoon deteriorated. Watching Hunter with girls hanging off him pushed her over the edge. She walked across the room to Bec and had a quiet chat. Within ten minutes, Bec had organized a flight for Kara and Giles to go back to New York later that night.

"All booked." Bec placed her cell phone on the table. Bec's eyes were curious, but she didn't question her. Kara suspected she knew why: Hunter was the reason she was here, and now he was the reason for her leaving.

"Thanks for helping out today. You're a lifesaver. And . . . after all that's happened, I hope you're on the road to a full recovery."

"Thanks, Bec." Kara gave her a heartwarming smile. "You've been wonderful."

After the shoot and whispering a don't-you-say-a-word farewell to Gemma, Kara left her friends chatting and having photos with the rent-a-crowd. Hunter, surrounded by girls, didn't even notice when she slipped away and headed back to her room.

Tired and upset, Kara packed the last of her things into her suitcase, zipped it, and stood it by the entrance, ready to leave.

There was a loud knock at her door. Her heart seized. She knew that knock. *Shit.* She still had half an hour before she had to leave. Did Gemma say something to Hunter?

Her heart shuddered and ached. How was she going to say goodbye?

With trembling hands, she opened the door.

There he stood, sexy as always. Torn jeans and a black button-down shirt highlighting his azure eyes. "Hey. You ready to head out for an early dinner?" His gaze jumped past her. Concern flashed in his eyes when he caught sight of her suitcase. "Kar? . . . What's going on?"

She gripped onto the door to steady herself. "I'm going home." She held her chin high. "Tonight."

"What? No." He pushed past her and stepped inside her room. The door fell shut with a loud click. "You can't."

"I have to." She turned and followed him into the room. He stood by the bed. She hovered near the TV. "The past ten days have been great on one hand, and shit on the other. I can't do this anymore. I didn't know what to expect when I came away with you."

"What do you mean?"

"I was so numb after losing Ryan, anything sounded viable. I've loved spending time with you, and that's now become a problem." She fumbled with her hands. "Those nights next to you at the beach house, it was like I was the center of your world. But since we've been away, I know I'm not. One moment I think we're more than friends, then I see you at shoots like today, and I get jealous of the girls around you. I don't want to be like that. I don't want to miss you in my bed at night like I have been. I need to get my life back on track. Move on. Without you."

"Kar, you're not making any sense." He clutched at a handful of his hair. His eyes were wild and worried. "We're just friends. What have I done to make you think otherwise?"

Everything. Your smiles. Your touches. Your caring.

She puffed out a breath. "It's like what you said to me months ago, '*It's not you; it's me*'. Since our night together, I've always felt that there was something between us that was stronger than our connection over Ryan. I've fallen for you, and I shouldn't have. So to move on, I need to put distance between us. I'll be okay. But I need to go home."

She turned to pick up her purse but he rushed forward and caught her on the arm. "Kar. Wait. You can't leave. Please stay."

"Why?" Every muscle in her body ached, tired of suppressing her feelings for him. "Give me one good reason why."

His eyes burned into hers. A muscle in his tensed jaw ticked. He clenched his fists. But he said nothing.

She was stupid to think he might have felt the same way about her. She grabbed the handle of her suitcase. His hand shot on top of hers.

"Kara?"

"Yes, Hunter."

"Don't do this." His voice quivered as much as his fingers

did on top of hers. "Not now."

"I have to."

She turned to go, but he didn't release his grip. He stepped toward her. His warm hands charged up to cup her face, and he kissed her so hard her knees buckled. His mouth, hot and fiery against hers, sent shards of pain through her chest. Tears slipped from her eyes, and her body shuddered. Wrapping his arms around her, he crushed her against his chest. Her heart pounded like a drum against his. He kissed her top lip. Her lower lip. His teasing tongue sent goosebumps shooting down her arms.

Please stop. Please stop. Please stop.

But she couldn't. She melted against him. Her hands clutched at his shirt, tugging on it, pulling on it, grasping it. She wanted him to fix her wounded heart. Her broken soul. But he never would. He'd only make it worse.

With every thread of willpower, she pushed hard against his chest. She stepped back and wiped her lips with quivering fingers. Her eyes stung like acid. She shook her head and pointed her finger toward his chest. "No. Don't do this to me. Not now."

"What? Why?" The desperation in his voice crushed her soul.

"Unless you can stand there and say you want me, all of me, just me, you can't kiss me like that." Her knees weakened, unsure if she could stay upright. "If you don't want me, I have to go."

Fear flared in his eyes. His whole body stiffened. His mouth moved . . . but no words came out. Not even a sound.

"That's what I thought. I'm nothing to you. Nothing." Before her heart shattered onto the floor, she charged past him. "Goodbye, Hunter." She grabbed her luggage and headed out the door.

Taking weary steps down the corridor, she listened for him to call out, come running after her, stop her. But he never did. Dragging her suitcase and her heart down the hall, she headed for the elevator.

It was time to go home.

Time to move on.

Time for no more Hunter.

Chapter 24

Sitting on the terrace at the New York Country Club, Kara already regretted agreeing to meet her parents for brunch. They were late. Still playing golf. But it was the pitiful glances and overzealous whispers from the people sitting at nearby tables that provided her with the painful reminder that losing Ryan and her involvement with Hunter were still hot topics.

"I thought she went on tour with him."

"Why is she back?"

"She looks terrible."

Would she ever escape being the talk of the town?

Crawling out of the confines of her apartment a week after arriving home, Kara had thought the summer sunshine would improve her mood, but it didn't. While the sun touched and warmed her skin, it could not penetrate her heart. It was dead. Broken. And all because of her own stupidity.

She stared at the bubbles rising in her champagne glass, watching them pop and disappear into nothingness. She let out a sharp puff of air, not missing the irony. She'd overcome hurdle after hurdle. She'd fought for her dreams; struggled to overcome her grief; and just when things were looking better . . . hopeful . . . optimistic . . . *pop* . . . everything was gone.

All thanks to Hunter *Fucking* Collins. All thanks to one night with him.

What a fool she'd been to think he was into her. Hunter had no heart—not when it came to getting close to someone. He lived in a protective sphere with Kyle and Gemma that no one would ever penetrate. He'd closed himself off to the prospect of love. It was her own stupid fault for thinking it would be different with her.

Picking up her flute, she took a dainty sip when she really wanted to knock back the whole thing in one gulp. Alcohol numbed the pain. Falling pregnant with Ryan was the worst thing that had ever happened. The rare moments of bliss, of feeling him growing inside her, the scan, having Hunter wanting to be involved in Ryan's life, and the growth in their friendship, were now smothered by regret, loss, and hate.

She regretted sleeping with Hunter.

She would never get over losing Ryan

She hated herself for falling in love with a rock star.

A rock star who was never her boyfriend.

And would never be.

How could she be so in love with someone who'd never been hers to begin with?

She blinked her stinging eyes, and every muscle in her jaw ached. Hunter's kiss still burned in her brain. The one he'd planted so hard against her mouth before she left Rio. The taste of him was branded onto her lips. For one moment, she thought he'd beg her to stay. That he'd tell her he loved her. She'd wanted him to run down that hotel hallway after her, stop her leaving the lobby or, even more gallantly, stop the plane from leaving the airport gate like in some Hollywood movie. But her life was no fairytale.

Since leaving Rio, he'd sent one text.

Hope you got home okay.

She didn't bother to reply. She needed to cut him off.

Hunter was right to not come after her. She wasn't girlfriend material. Why would anyone want to be with her? The ultimate goal of finding a partner was to get married and have a family. And that was the one thing she could no longer give. Her operation had left her barren. Her broken heart had left her cynical.

Her only logical conclusion . . . love sucked.

She knocked back her glass of champagne and refilled it with the bottle from the ice bucket. Impatient, she scrolled through her cell phone messages. She froze at the Google alert for Conrad's Fashion House.

Conrad Hesterfield announces engagement to Jasmine Milne.

What? Her heart hit the ground. With a shaky tap of her fingernail, she opened the link.

After a short, scandalous, and steamy courtship, one of New York's most eligible bachelors, thirty-five-year-old Conrad Hesterfield, heir and head designer at the elite Conrad Fashion House, is to wed Jasmine Milne, a young innovative designer, aged nineteen, in the fall. Jasmine will debut her first line of couture at New York Fashion Week in September alongside Conrad's own collection.

Kara swiped the screen closed and threw her cell phone onto the table. *Well that's great!* In less than twelve months, Jasmine had won Conrad over, got her own line, and got a ring on her finger.

Everyone was moving on with their lives while hers had been stripped bare and dealt another blow. She didn't care that Conrad was marrying Jasmine. She cared about her job. With Jasmine progressing with her own line, were Kara's prospects of advancement in the company in jeopardy? The possibility of heading up one of the design teams looked further out of reach. She loved working in product development for the ready-to-wear collections, but turning out T-shirts, tops, jeans, and jackets hadn't grabbed hold of her passion like haute couture had. Even her desire for that had fizzled out.

Out of the corner of her eye, she caught sight of her mother and father walking toward her. With fake smiles plastered on their faces, they waved like royals, saying hellos to the people they passed. Kara wasn't sure she could stomach brunch with them, but it was an excuse to stop staring at the four walls of her apartment.

Her mother patted Kara on the shoulder. "Sit up straight, dear." She glided around to the opposite side of the table and sat next to Kara's father. "Sit like a lady, not a beast."

Kara edged back on her seat, but her shoulders felt too heavy to straighten. "Good game?" she asked out of politeness rather than interest.

Before her mom could speak, her dad cut in. "Scored three over par. Excellent round. Your mother, on the other hand, not so good. Lost three balls into the water."

"At least we beat Bart and Florence." Her mother shrugged one shoulder, her smile simmered with satisfaction. Then she glanced at Kara. Her expression changed to one of disapproval. "Why aren't you wearing the dress I had sent to you from Saks yesterday? You look like you're ready for the beach, not brunch. I'm amazed the club let you in."

Kara ran her hands over her blue and red maxi dress. "What I'm wearing is fine. The dress you bought me is too small. My figure has changed after being pregnant." At the base of her belly she had a little protruding bulge, and her hips were a fraction wider. If anything, the aftermath of carrying Ryan finally gave her some curves. She was no longer as straight as Park Avenue.

"Shh. Keep your voice down." Her father's gaze darted around the tables nearby.

"What, Daddy?" Kara tilted her head. "Still ashamed I got knocked up by Hunter?" Just mentioning Hunter's name churned her stomach more than the stench of the salmon, the pancakes, and the eggs coming from the next table. "God … you must be so relieved that I lost Ryan."

Her father's eyes burned into hers. She'd hit the mark. He hadn't invited her out to the country club since he'd found out she was pregnant. What used to be a monthly occurrence was erased from her calendar. Her having a baby outside of marriage wasn't something he wanted to rave to his friends about. Didn't put her on her father's I'm-so-proud-of-you list. Not that she ever made it. Well . . . he could be happy now. Ryan was gone. And so was Hunter.

"Don't say things like that." Hurt flickered through his eyes, but Kara ignored him and sipped her champagne. She didn't care. Nothing could affect her anymore. Her dad leaned in. "I'm devastated you lost your child. Our grandchild. But I'm pleased to see you have come to your senses."

They were interrupted by the waiter who poured her parents' coffee, refilled her champagne flute and took their food orders, but her father's eyes never left hers.

Once the waiter left, he lowered his voice. "Going away with that band was only going to lead to more trouble. From now on, I want you to stay away from that crowd."

Her knuckles turned white around the stem of her glass. "That *crowd* are my friends."

Blotches of red broke out on her father's neck. "Well, it's

time to find new ones. You're a good girl. You shouldn't be hanging around people like that. That kind of crazy, messed up, unstable lifestyle is not for my little girl."

Every word dripping out of her father's mouth bristled her spine. Stung the back of her eyes. Her friends did live a mad life, but they treasured and respected every moment of it. It was tough being in the limelight and after knowing them for years, she'd grown close to them. She loved being part of the inner circle of people they trusted. That was why she enjoyed hanging out with them. They were grounded, worked hard, and took nothing for granted. Not like here at the club where everything was fake—from the smiles to the cosmetic enhancements.

Her dad stroked his short beard, one side, then the other. "I'm sorry, but Hunter was nothing but a bad influence on you. He never cared for you. That type of person has no morals or values. After everything that's happened, I'll do my best to make sure he doesn't come near you ever again."

Staring into the depths of her glass, her vision blurred. Hunter did care. His passion, his loyalty, and his caring soul were greater than that of most other people she'd ever met. He did like her . . . he just didn't love her. Her stupid heart had led her astray.

She sniffled and brushed a tear from her cheek. "You're wrong about him. Wrong about my friends." She hated that her father was so quick to judge. God, she'd been like that too. But Hunter had changed her. She'd learned to look beyond first impressions, the arrogance, the shields and the masks people wore. She'd been the one who was arrogant and naïve. Not anymore. "But you're right. I do need to move on."

How? She didn't know.

"That's my girl." Her dad took a mouthful of coffee. "Your mother and I have talked. We've put up with your . . . how shall I put it . . . rebellious ways for long enough."

Scolding heat crept into Kara's cheeks. She went to object, but her father silenced her with a wave of his hand.

"It's time to put the past behind you. You're a young lady now. You need a good career and a solid foundation for your future. We want you to come and work in the family business. We'll pay for your studies, get you licensed to trade, give you on-the-job training. Naomi will help you. Put this fickle fashion dream of yours to rest."

Kara gritted her teeth. "I don't want to work on Wall Street."

Her dad's eyes narrowed into slits as thin as a poker machine's. "Yes. It's time."

Nausea pooled in her stomach. This was her dad's dream. Not hers. And it never would be.

The waiter placed their smoked salmon omelets in front of them and rushed off to serve another table. She picked up her fork and pushed a piece of the eggy dish around the plate. Her appetite disappeared as did her listening while her father rattled on. "We can fast track your studies . . . "

She zoned out and gazed at a golfer teeing off in front of the terrace. He swung. The metal tink of the ball struck her chest. As the ball sliced through the air, sailed off into the distance, it was as if the last thread that was holding her life together snapped. Disappeared. Vanished into nothingness. Gone.

She had nothing left.

Her career was at a dead end. She had no baby . . . no boyfriend.

Her cell phone vibrated on the table.

Her father's eyes flashed red.

"It's Nae." Kara read the Caller ID. Her sister only rang when it was urgent, or she wanted something.

Her mother hovered her coffee a few inches from her mouth. "Oh, she has some exciting news."

"Please, take the call." Her dad flicked his hand at Kara.

"Maybe she can talk some sense into you."

Kara walked over to the edge of the terrace. "Hi Nae, what's up?"

"Are you at the club with Mom and Dad? Have they told you the news?" There was a nervous shake to Naomi's voice.

"News? No. What news?" *God, please don't be pregnant. Don't rub it in my face.*

"Dad made me vice president. He says I'm ready."

Kara closed her eyes. *Daddy's angel reaches new heights.* "That's . . . wonderful news. Congratulations." But she couldn't muster up any excitement. "It's earlier than expected, but that's awesome, right?"

"Yes and no." Naomi's voice flatlined. "I've worked my ass off for this role. Born and bred for it. I'll be one of the youngest vice presidents on Wall Street. I love my job, but . . . I had no other option. I'm so envious of you. You can do whatever you want, whereas I'll be tied to this company forever."

"What?" Naomi? Envious? Since when? "If you don't like it, leave."

"God no. Work is my life. It's in my blood." Naomi's voice softened. "But Anthony and I are bordering on divorce because we never see each other. My daughter is two years' old, and Daddy reads her stock market reports. He's prepping her for the business already. I don't want that. She will always be able to make her own career choices and never be obligated to work for the family." She paused. "Same goes for you, Kar. Don't come and work here if you don't want to. I've always admired you for following your dreams and your heart. You're so strong. Don't let Daddy get to you."

Kara's head spun. Naomi? Admired her? She'd gone mad. "I won't."

"Kar, I'm terrified to take on this role. Being responsible for hundreds of employees, profitability and growth. I don't think

I'm good enough."

Naomi was queen of confidence; how could she doubt herself? "Nae, you're brilliant at what you do. I'm proud of you. Knock 'em dead. Just don't become an ass like our father. Everyone loves you. Like I do."

"Thanks, Kar. You're the best. Dad wants to send out a press release, but I wanted to let you know before he gloats across Manhattan."

Kara humphed. She knew her father. This chest-pounding boast would go global.

Naomi sighed. "Promise me one thing, Kar. Stay true to yourself. It's what I love about you most."

"Um . . . thanks."

"Let's catch up for a drink soon, okay?"

"Sure."

Kara ended the call. *Wow!* For so long Kara had been envious of Naomi—her marriage, her daughter, her home, their father's favoritism, but she never knew Naomi felt like she had no choice. That she suffered from self-doubt. Like she did. Someone who she thought had the perfect life hid behind a skyscraper of masks. Was nothing real anymore? Was no one ever honest about their feelings? Their life? Their problems?

Kara had done that for too long. With Conrad. With her feelings for Hunter. She'd wouldn't let her mistakes hold her back. Not anymore.

She strolled back to her parents.

"Naomi tell you the news?" Her dad's voice boomed with pride.

Kara nodded, still in shock.

Her dad continued. "With Naomi stepping up to vice, it's perfect timing for you to come into the organization. I want my two girls to present a strong and united front."

Kara glanced around the clubhouse terrace with all its

finery—the white walls, steep roof, and manicured gardens, the diners eating their Sunday brunch. She could imagine the people's conversations, the ladies talking about their latest shopping expeditions, new cosmetic enhancements, the trending gossip, and bragging about their children. The men wouldn't be much better, talking about politics, investments, stocks, clients, business deals, and their love of all things sport.

A pretentious world. Superficial and shallow. This was not her life anymore. She didn't know where she belonged. Maybe it was time to look for a new job in another fashion house, but until she ignited her love of design again, now wasn't the best time. She knew only one thing for sure: she wouldn't, under any circumstance, work in her family's business. She'd sooner prick herself with a million pins than sit behind a desk, trading stocks, bonds, futures, and options. While she wasn't jumping for joy at returning to work at Conrad's, anything, anything, *anything* would be better than working for her father.

"Dad, stop." She pushed her untouched plate of food away. "Wall Street is not an option."

She ignored the disappointment clouding her parents' eyes. There were some things she'd never compromise: her love of fashion being one. It was in her blood and it would never die. Her fire for it just needed to be washed, wrung out, and reworked into something new.

Until it became clear in her mind what she wanted to do, she'd go back to Conrad's. Do her job. Work until her fingers bled if she had to. Drown herself in office tasks so she wouldn't have to think about anything or anyone else. Not Ryan. Not her parents. And least of all . . . Hunter.

After Conrad broke up with her, she'd been adamant she would get through her operation and find a new man. Now, after Hunter, she wanted no one. Her life was in total upheaval.

When everything was gone, what was left? *Drink?* Hard

liquor sounded good.

"I'm not hungry. I'll be at the bar." Before they could object, she stood and headed inside. Taking a seat on one of the black metal stools, she placed her purse beside her.

"Hey Kar, haven't seen you in months. How're you doing?" Felix, the bartender, asked as he polished a wine glass with a linen cloth. "What can I get you?"

"Jack Daniels. On ice. Make it a double."

Whiskey would give her courage a kick and her confidence a boost. Help her stop mulling over everything she'd lost. Stop her thinking about Hunter, wondering where he was, who he was with, and how much she missed him. At the sight of the JD bottle, the amber liquid being splashed into the glass and the seductive aroma filling her head, he blazed to life in her mind.

Okay. Maybe JD wasn't the best choice.

One of Everhide's older singles "Miss You" wafted through the sound system, and Kara let out a you've-got-to-be-kidding-me laugh. Hunter taunted her everwhere she went.

Kyle's, Gemma's, and Hunter's voices trickled through the speakers.

My friends keep telling me,
That you're doing better.
But for me walking the streets alone,
It's nothing but cloudy weather.
All I do is think about you,
Wondering where did I go wrong?
Was there something I didn't say?
Because I loved you all along.

She pictured Hunter closing his eyes as he sang. Mic in hand. Perfect lips pressed against the metal. Veins in his neck straining as he hit the notes.

Didn't I love you the right way?

Didn't I tell you that enough?
Wasn't I the one for you?
I thought that we were in love.

When I close my eyes at night,
I can feel you in my arms.
I miss the taste of your kisses,
And the beating of your heart.
Knowing that once I could call you all mine,
Now I can't believe that you're gone.
Tell me, tell me, tell me,
Where did I go wrong?

When I see you out at night,
It breaks my heart apart.
Every day I miss you, babe,
No, nothing at all feels right.
Tell me how I'm supposed to get over this?
How am I to move on?
When all I do is miss you,
Miss you more and more.

Kara shot back the whiskey and slammed the glass onto the counter.

To hell with you, Hunter.

There was no going backward. She clutched the crystal tumbler of whiskey until her knuckles ached. No more analyzing and critiquing every touch, every look, and every moment she'd spent with Hunter. She meant nothing to him. It was time for him to mean nothing to her. A steely resilience took hold of her. She'd outgrown being told what to do by her parents. Survived trauma and heartbreak. It was time to rebuild herself. She'd go back to her foundations. At Conrad's she'd find her strength and her passion again. At work, she could forget about Hunter, her love for him, and move on.

With a wave of her hand, she ordered another double shot.

Taking a mouthful of whiskey, she swirled it around in her mouth. She closed her eyes and imagined her heart slowing down. Growing colder. Growing harder. Stronger. With one ripping, burning, blazing gulp, she swallowed. And drowned Hunter out of her system.

Once and for all.

He was gone.

A new Kara was born.

Chapter 25

Dusk blanketed Lower Manhattan in a soft golden light that filtered through Hunter's apartment windows, hit his glass of JD, and refracted a kaleidoscope of color onto the shiny black piano surface. The rainbow effect was unable to filter through to his clouded mind. He sat at his piano. This was what he needed—a break. No stress. Just him, music, and a bottle of JD. Brushing his fingers over the keys, he played a low, slow tune.

Da-da. Dum. Dum. Dum. Da-da. Dum. Dum. Dum

Nothing meaningful. Nothing new.

While the One World Trade Center dominated the view south, it was the small cobblestone street half a mile farther down the avenue that held his focus. The street that led to Kara's place.

He'd been home from tour for two days. He hadn't called her, texted her, or seen her. Ever since she left him in Rio two weeks ago, after one text he'd sent, there had been total radio silence. Every night, thoughts of her kept him awake, and when he caught some sleep, she invaded his dreams. He looked for her face in the crowd at every concert, hoping she'd miraculously returned. But she never did.

He couldn't blame her. He'd been an insensitive prick at the shoot, hanging out with the models. And that stupid girl who'd kissed him during the session still boiled his blood. *Bitch.* He'd been so close to calling *cut* and having her thrown out. That was what he should've done. He didn't want girls all over him anymore. He wanted . . . Kara. She'd been there for him, and he'd left her alone. He'd screwed up. Again.

He'd been foolish to kiss her, thinking it would be enough to make her stay. When she'd asked him if he wanted to be with her, it took every ounce of his being to hold his tongue. Because she deserved someone so much better than him. How could he ask her to settle for a man who wasn't good enough? When he saw her heart break, it tore him apart. He'd never wanted to hurt her. But what else could he do? He had to let her go. They lived two streets away from each other, but they were worlds' apart.

He closed his eyes. His fingers glided over the ivory keys. The sound resonated throughout his living room and seeped into the marrow of his bones.

Grabbing his glass, he sipped his whiskey and opened the journal resting on top of the piano. He flipped through the pages and stopped at the lyrics and notes he'd written for Ryan's song. His fingers fell to the keys.

Dum. Dum. Dum.

Nope. Better not. Still too raw. Even after two months.

The elevator in the hallway dinged. Gemma's soft footsteps scuffed on the hardwood floors.

"Evening." She tossed her access card onto the coffee table and sat beside him on the piano stool. She looked over her shoulder toward the kitchen. "What happened in here?"

His backpack lay on the dining table, untouched since he came home. Dirty coffee cups and glasses sat on the counter by the sink. Five new bottles of whiskey stood front and center on the dining room table next to leftover containers from last night's dinner. The sixth bottle of JD sat open in front of him. She flicked her ponytail over her shoulder. "Want some help to clean up?"

"Nah. Leave it." He'd get to it. Maybe tomorrow.

She yawned and covered her mouth. "It feels like forever since I've been here."

"Yeah," His voice was deadpan. "It's been too long."

With only a brief few days over Christmas and New Year's, and the void of three weeks when Ryan died, he hadn't been home for nine months. Where had the time gone?

Gemma rubbed her bleary eyes. "I don't think I've ever slept so good in my life. I've barely risen for two days. I missed my bed and my shower. And I love not living out of a suitcase. Let's not tour again for ages. I'm drained. So looking forward to a break."

He tinkered on the keys. "It will be nice to stay home for a while. No planes. No shows. Just chill."

"Absolutely." She slapped his thigh. "For the next two weeks anyway."

Promotions, events, and appearances were lined up for summer. Tour was over, but the work was never done.

Hunter glanced toward the hallway. "Where's Kyle?"

"He was waiting for dinner to be delivered. He'll be here soon."

"Good. I'm starving." He hadn't eaten since reheating last night's leftover pasta in the microwave for breakfast this morning. Then he'd slept most of the day away. JD was his staple.

"Whatcha working on?" She glanced at his journal.

He quickly flipped the pages over to his latest work-in-progress. Not even Kyle and Gemma would hear Ryan's song. It was too private. Too painful.

He wiped his hands on his jeans and scanned the scribble on the new page. He'd written this a few days after Kara left Rio. Before Ryan, he wrote songs about partying, picking up girls, Amie screwing him over or his unbreakable bond with Kyle and Gemma. Now Kara was inside his head, and his lyrics came out full of anguish, turmoil, and heartache. While he wrote a lot of his thoughts down, many would never be made into songs. But this one was good. It summed up how he felt. "I've been working on this for just over a week. Working title is 'Torture.' I've got this real mellow melody for it in mind."

Gemma clapped her hands and shuffled closer to him on the seat. "Awesome. Let's hear what you've got."

Her enthusiasm was like a jump-start to his heart. Yep . . . with Gemma and Kyle, he'd be fine. His two best friends and music were all he needed. He had to remember that.

The first time of playing songs for each other were usually awkward, rough, and unrefined. But this one was clear. He took another swig of JD and let the burn slide down his throat, loosening his vocal cords. He put his glass down, cracked his knuckles, placed his fingers on the smooth ivory, and played. "Okay. 'Torture.' Here we go."

He licked his lips and sang, deep and slow.

> *Loving you is like t-t-t-torture, you'll be the death of me,*
> *You stole my heart and threw away the key.*
> *You tied me down when I looked away,*
> *Injected me with something I can't explain.*
> *Electric shocks surge through to my brain,*
> *You're like a drug surging through my veins.*
>
> *I wish I, I wish I could walk away,*
> *Because baby,*
> *Loving you is like t-t-t-torture.*
> *Torture.*

And all I know, and all I know,
Is I want it more and more,
More and more.

Loving you is like t-t-t-torture, feel like you're drowning
me,
Can't come up for air, yeah, I'm struggling, cannot
breathe.
You hold me down and smother me,
Your kisses are so hard they keep on blinding me.

Loving you is like t-t-t-torture, a mixture of pleasure and
pain,
You can dominate me, in every possible way.
My hands are bound, my tongue is tied,
Loving you sure is one wild ride.

Gemma sat still, staring at the keys. "Wow. You're really fucked up, aren't you? The song is awesome. But totally twisted."

"Is it too much?" Doubt washed over him.

"No. I think it's brilliant. I love it. I'd like to see it as a psycho, fun, crazy-in-love song, not an I-want-to-slash-my-wrists one." She placed her hands and mimicked the keys he'd played perfectly, taking it up an octave, then down an octave. Then she stopped. "It's about Kara, isn't it?"

His stomach dropped, hovering somewhere around the piano's lowest note. "What makes you say that? I wrote a fucking song. That's all."

She groaned and dropped her head back. "When are you going to stop with all this bullshit and admit that you're into her? Why are you fighting it?"

"It's not meant to be, Gem." He shot down a mouthful of JD and refilled his glass.

"Have you gone to see her since we've been home?"

The whiskey churned in his gut. "No. I can't."

"Why not?"

His heart screamed as loud as the fire-truck sirens wailing past his building. "It hurts."

"Because you're not being honest with yourself." She grabbed his glass, knocked back the JD, and slammed the empty glass down. The whiskey fumes on her breath wafted through the air and she slowly shook her head. "You two have grown so close. I never would have believed it if I hadn't seen it for myself. On tour, your eyes were on her every time she was in the room. You rushed to her side when you thought she was hurt. You always sat close to her. You were always touching her. You were never that affectionate with Amie . . . or me. You're into her, so what's your problem? What are you so afraid of?"

He rubbed at his chest, wishing he could erase the pain. "Hurting her."

"You already have." Gemma splayed her hands on the keys and pressed them hard. The strum echoed through the room. "She left Rio because of you."

"I know." He slumped on the stool as visions of Kara's eyes, full of tears, flickered through his mind.

Gemma looked up at him from underneath her long lashes. "I thought I knew you. Nothing Kyle and I say or do is getting through to you. We've given you time and space, but enough is enough." She clutched his hand on top of his thigh and squeezed it tight. "You can't keep lying to yourself. You said you'd never lie to me. So I'm gonna ask you again: why the fuck are you doing this to yourself? To her?"

Tugging free of her hold, he dragged his fingers down his face. She was too perceptive. His head ached, tired of everyone's concern and worry.

Like a high-tension steel cable breaking, something inside him snapped. He clamped his fist and slapped his palms down on top of the piano. "Because I don't want to hurt anymore."

Every muscle in his jaw ached. "I don't want to hurt anyone. Or be hurt again. Isn't that enough?"

"No. It's not." Gemma's tone, clipped and sharp, stung.

He closed his eyes, hating how she stressed about him. She was one of the reasons why he was like this. She may have forgiven him, but he could never forget. "I remember how much I hurt you, and it killed me. You're my best friend. What kind of person does that make me? Other than a complete shithead? Then Amie screwed me over. I thought nothing could hurt me ever again. But then I lost Ryan. I lost my son. I can't take any more heartache. I've got nothing left."

Gemma curled her arm around his and rested her head against his shoulder. "I was heartbroken and shattered after Ben—afraid to open up to anyone. But then there was you. After being friends for so many years, you were suddenly my light. Yeah, you broke my heart, and it sucked. It was one of the worst days of my life. But look at me now. Kyle and I. In a crazy twist of fate, we're together and happy. He's my one. You've had an unlucky run with love. Don't block yourself off from ever experiencing it again."

"Kara's not the one." Even saying her name hurt his throat.

"How do you know?"

"We're too different. I'm a rock star; she's a princess. She wants marriage . . . and wanted kids." His voice snagged like splintered wood. Had her desire for children changed now she couldn't carry her own? "You, me, and Kyle are never around. We're always traveling, touring, and living our crazy lives. I'm not the guy for someone who wants a homebody."

"Being with someone is about compromise. You should know that." Gemma jabbed him in the side, but he didn't flinch. "After everything the two of you went through, it's changed you too. You were so excited to become a father. Maybe what you want in life is now different. Maybe the thought of being with one girl isn't scary anymore."

It wasn't. But his past haunted him. "I don't trust myself." The hardest of truths quivered his voice. "Look what I did to you."

Pain swirled in Gemma's vivid green eyes. "Is this about being faithful?"

Hunter hung his head. He'd cheated on her. Because Amie, someone he'd thought was better, had come along. God, he was pathetic. He hated himself so much.

Gemma stroked his hair and tucked it behind his ear. "Being faithful and committed is easy when you give your heart to someone."

The last remnant of daylight disappeared, and the city lights took over the sky.

He puffed air through his nose. "I don't think I have any heart left to give. I'm the tin man."

"You have too much heart. That's your problem. But you're not letting it beat. Give it a chance. Think how awesome it would be if it worked out. If not, I'll be there for Kara. And Kyle and I will always be here for you. We're not going anywhere."

He grabbed her hand, placed it on her leg, and squeezed it. "We've got each other's back. Haven't we?" He brushed his thumb over the tattoo on the inside of her left wrist, the *GKH*— initials of their names. "I love you."

She clutched his hand. "I know you do. And I love you. After everything the three of us have been through, we deserve some happiness. I found mine with Kyle. I've been lucky to find my forever guy in one of my best friends. That blows my mind every time I think about it. Now, why don't you stop this nonsense, let go of those chains, and take a leap of faith?"

His throat ran dry and he struggled to swallow. "Because I'm terrified of how I feel for her."

"I know you are. But love can also be exhilarating." She

nudged his arm. "Do me a favor. Do yourself a favor. Go and see her."

He tilted his head and stared at the downlight. Visions of Kara filled his mind. In LA on the shoot. The snow fight in Chicago. Ryan's scan. Being with her on tour. No one riled him up, pissed him off, excited him, or fucked up his head like she did. He hated not being around her. Was that enough to go on? Like a Zippo struggling to light, his heart tried to kick to life. His past relationships had sprouted from friendship first. Maybe this would be a case of third time lucky.

Gemma was right. He was crazy not to do something about it.

The elevator pinged, and Kyle walked in. "What's up?"

Hunter swung around one way on the stool, Gemma the other. He hooked his arm around her neck and tickled her in the ribs. "You need to control your fiancée."

Kyle laughed, placing the takeaway on the coffee table. "Control Gem? Are you kidding me? Why? What's going on?"

"Hunt has to go out." Gemma punched him in the arm.

He bit on his lip and nodded. *Yeah. He did.* He turned to grab the bottle of JD, but Gemma stopped him.

"You don't need that. Let the feels in."

"I hate you."

Smile lines creased the corner of her eyes. "Hate you, too."

She was the best. But hopefully he was about to find something better. He stood and kissed her on the head. "Thank you."

"You're welcome." Gemma leapt from the stool and dashed over to Kyle. She flung her arms around his neck, jumped up, hooked her legs around his waist, and kissed him.

"Okay." Kyle clutched her ass and mumbled over her kisses. "What's going on?"

Hunter smiled, chuckling at them. Gemma was right. Seeing

how happy they were gave him a spark of hope it might happen to him one day.

"Hunt needed a kick in the butt." Gemma pressed her cheek against Kyle's and gave Hunter a wink. "He's going to see Kara."

Kyle lay Gemma down on the chaise, hovering over her, and nestled between her legs. He nuzzled into her neck. He didn't even bother to look up. "About time, Hunt. Good luck."

"I just need to do something. In the office. I'll be out of here in a few minutes."

Five minutes later, Hunter stuffed the printed-out piece of paper into his jeans pocket and walked out of the office. He grabbed his wallet and cell phone. He rolled his eyes at Kyle and Gemma making out of the sofa. "Please don't have sex on my sofa while I'm gone."

"Why not?" Gemma giggled like a schoolgirl. "We have before. Many times."

"Whatever. I'm out of here." With his heart hammering, he headed for the elevator.

***

It took Hunter seven minutes to walk to Kara's. Pacing the pavement in front of her building, his stomach flipped, and he wiped his sweaty palms on his jeans. God, he hoped he was doing the right thing.

With a shaky hand, he entered his access code into the panel by the foyer door. He held his breath, hoping Kara hadn't canceled his details from the system. The door latch clicked open. The air rushed from his lungs and he dashed inside. Not bothering to wait for the slow elevator, he darted up the stairs, two steps at a time.

At her door, he hesitated. Music played softly on the other side. *Shit.* This was it. Did he look okay? He smoothed his hands through his hair. Smelled his shirt. It was fine, freshly laundered. His breath reeked of whiskey, but that was a given. It'd have to do.

He closed his eyes. With a tremble in his hand, he knocked.

Something fell onto the floor. Sounded like books. She swore. The music was turned off. Then nothing. She swore again, much closer this time. Maybe she'd peered through the spy hole. The safety lock clicked, and she opened the door.

The sight of her stole his breath. His heart raced. There she stood in a gorgeous short red wrap dress. Makeup on. Hair pulled into a messy chignon. Barefoot and beautiful.

"Hey." She folded her arms and leaned against her door. "I heard you were home. What are you doing here?"

He stuffed his hands into the back pockets of his jeans to stop them shaking. "Ca . . . can I come in?"

"Um." She glanced at her watch. "I'm going out soon. Catching up with some girls for dinner and drinks."

Shit. Bad timing. "Can I have ten minutes? We need to talk."

"I have nothing to say to you." She checked her watch again.

"I do. Please?"

"Fine." She rolled her eyes and waved him inside.

He followed her toward the kitchen, past her sofas and the coffee table covered in an array of fashion magazines and sketch pads. Were they what fell onto the floor? The four-seat dining table by the window looked never used, and a half-eaten pizza lay in its open box on the kitchen counter. His belly grumbled at the site of the pepperoni pizza, but no, he had to talk to her first.

Grabbing onto the back of the nearest kitchen stool, he turned to face her.

She ambled toward him with her arms crossed and stopped at the edge of the counter. "So, what do you want?"

He leaned awkwardly against the stool. It was too low to rest his hips against. It spun when he placed his hand on it, and he nearly toppled over.

He gave up and just stood. "You look good."

No, she looked hot. Any guy would notice her.

Ow. He didn't like the thought of other guys trying to hook up with her. "Where are you going tonight?"

"Not that it's any of your business, but to a new wine bar in the West Village." She lifted her chin. "Time's ticking. What did you want to say?"

His mind hazed. Where was her banter, her quick retorts? This would be harder than he'd thought. He just had to be honest. "I want to apologize. For Rio. For not calling. For everything. I screwed up, Kar. Can I do anything to make it up to you?"

"Yes." Defiance hardened her gaze. "Leave."

He stepped toward her. "I can't do that."

She slid back a foot. "Why not?"

"Because I can't stop thinking about you."

"You have to." The chill in her voice stabbed him through the center of his chest. "Hunter, let's be serious. We've been through some real shitty months, and we'll be bound by that forever. But it's time to put whatever was or was not between us to an end."

"End? No." He wouldn't accept that.

She shook her head. "I miss Ryan every day. He was the greatest gift. I got to be pregnant. I got to carry him. I got to be a mommy for a day and a half. I've come to terms with the fact he's gone . . . I'm moving on. On my own. And I'm okay with that. I'm going to focus on me for a change."

He wanted to be there for her, support her. *She* was all he could focus on.

He stepped forward, caressed the back of her neck, and kissed her. Her beautiful soft lips. Warm, sweet, and mozzarella cheesy.

She pushed hard against his chest and arched her back. Her

eyes searched his face. "What the hell was that?"

"You talk too much." He kissed her again. He wanted to taste her, feel her tongue against his, but she pursed her lips tight.

She broke from his kiss once again. "Stop." Her voice quivered with breathlessness.

His mind was a tornado of want and worry. He stroked her hair and cupped the side of her face. "You said in Rio I wasn't allowed to kiss you unless I could stand before you and tell you that I wanted you. So here I am. I should have told you then, but I was a fool." His heartbeat battered against his ribs. It was as if he stood on the very edge of the stage, turned his back to the crowd, closed his eyes and fell. Hoping to be caught. By her. "Because I do want you, Kar. All of you. In every possible way."

She swayed. Closed her eyes. Shook her head in short, sharp movements. "It's too late. I'm done." When she met his gaze, the coldness in her stare chilled his blood.

Fuck. Had he missed his chance? What could he do? What could he say? This was why he avoided getting involved with anyone. All this emotional bullshit was too much. But he had to dig deep, for her. "I'm not. I've fought the way I feel for you for too long. I don't want to do that anymore."

"Please stop." She placed her fingers over his lips and took two steps back. "It doesn't matter how you feel for me or how I feel for you."

"Yes, it does." He ripped his fingers through his hair, a glimmer of hope rising in his chest. "How do you feel about me?"

"I'm trying not to feel anything," she said through clasped teeth. Her eyes swam with unrest. "I was doing just fine until you walked through my door."

He placed his hands over his heart. "Kar, please. My guard is down. I'm yours if you want me. I'm willing to give you my all. Give me . . . us a chance."

"You're crazy." Her lips trembled. Tears pooled in her eyes.

"I've been called a lot worse. Maybe I am crazy, because I want to give us a shot. You made me realize how shut off I was from letting anyone get close."

She folded her arms and looked straight through him. Every muscle in his chest ached so much he didn't want to breathe. He glanced around the room, at her wall art, her kitchen light, her clock. This conversation wasn't going to plan. He needed a moment to think, to come up with a new approach. He stepped past her and paced the floor. Scenarios of what to say swirled through his head. Nothing seemed to hit the mark. He'd have to wing it. He took a few deep breaths and stopped a few feet from her. "After everything we've been through, don't we deserve to see if what we have is something special?"

"How can we?" A tear slipped from one eye and her jaw tensed. She stabbed her finger at him. "You're so wrong for me."

"Do you think I don't know that? Which is why I've tried to just be friends." He took one step forward and splayed his hands out in front. For months she'd made him question every element of his life. Everything had altered course the moment he'd found out she was pregnant.

"So many times, I've asked myself how could someone like me be worthy of someone like you? You're all class, Kar, and I'm a whore. I've lived up to every sordid word ever said about me. But *you're* the one I want to change for. I wanted to be a father to our child. I wanted to be your strength when we lost him." He closed his eyes to gather his jumbled thoughts. "I want to mean something to you. I want to be more than a friend, more than a quick fuck, and more than a short-term fling. I want to be the right man for you."

She turned her head toward the windows. It was as if nothing he said was breaking through her walls. What did he have to do to prove to her that he was the one for her? That she was the one who had claimed his heart?

Her chin quivered. "You're not around enough."

He took slow steps toward her, standing by the counter, and softened his voice. "Gem, Kyle, and I have more control over what we do with our careers now. We pull the strings. We don't have to travel as much. We can break up tours so we get days off, so you and I can be with each other. I'll ensure I'm not away for long periods of time." He stopped a foot away from her and brushed the tear from her cheek.

Shards of silver flickered in the depths of her deep blue eyes. "We're too different."

"No, we're too alike. We're stubborn, determined, and drive each other crazy. You're beautiful and sexy and hot as hell. You woke me up. I've been selfish for too long. I want to be all that you deserve."

"I'm too scared," she whispered and rounded her shoulders. "How could you want me when I'm not whole anymore? I can't have children. You can have anyone on the planet. Why me?"

"You're perfect." He stroked her brow and ran his fingers through the silken strands of her hair. "You're one of the most amazing women I've ever met. Inside and out. You're the one I want."

"Hunt, please don't say that." She grabbed his hands and drew them away from her face.

"Why not? It's true. I want to be with you. So much it hurts."

She closed her eyes and lowered her chin; her hair curtained her face.

"Kar?" His throat tightened like a vise. Should he give her time to think? Hug her? Kiss her? This was unchartered territory. He rubbed her arms. His mind spun. "Babe?"

She whimpered as if crying. And then he saw it. The shake of her head.

She didn't say a word. Nothing. Not a thing.

But she didn't have to.

Kara didn't want him.

Shit!

His heart exploded like a supernova, destroyed. Gritting his teeth, he fought against the sting in his eyes. He shouldn't have come. He should never have listened to Gemma and her crap.

Fuck this bullshit.

He reefed the piece of paper from his jeans pocket and slapped it down on the kitchen counter beside her. "Here. Have this." His voice, full of anger and self-hate, choked in his throat. "It's season tickets to the ballet. I wanted to go to the fucking ballet with you because I know you love it. I wanted to take you out on dates. Do anything to be with you. But now, you can do what you like with them. Burn them for all I care."

She stared at the printout, sniffled, and folded her arms around her waist. She still couldn't meet his gaze. His heart couldn't take any more.

He walked backward toward the door. He held his hands out wide, defeated. "Fools. That's what we are, Kar. A couple of fools for not being *fucking* honest with each other. I'm sorry I didn't tell you how I felt sooner. I wanted to protect you from someone like me. But it doesn't matter now. You don't want me. Fine. I'm so done. Bye, Kar."

He turned for the door.

His hand froze two inches from the handle. A sharp breath speared his lungs.

To stop his knees from buckling, he caught hold of the doorjamb. He clenched his jaw, hard. He slapped his hand hard against the door. It stung like hell. *But no.* This wasn't happening. He wouldn't give up on her that easily.

He rushed back to where she still stood by the kitchen counter. "I've had to say goodbye to you too many times over the past few months. I don't want to do that anymore." He cupped the side of her face and kissed her. Kissed her as if he was taking his last breath. "Please. Give us a chance," he begged between kisses. Her eyes glistened with tears. He wanted to see an end to them and focus on putting a smile back onto her face.

"I don't want to hurt anymore, Hunt."

"Neither do I. All I know is that I want you. Nothing else matters. Be mine."

She closed her eyes. "Say that again."

"Be mine." He brushed his fingers down her cheek. "*You* are the one I want."

She placed one hand onto his chest and clutched a handful of his T-shirt. "I like the sound of that. I want you too. Denying how I feel about you has been torture."

Unable to suppress his grin, he dipped his chin. "Would you believe I wrote a song about torture . . . about you?"

"I'm not sure I like being the inspiration behind any of your songs." She wrinkled her nose. "That's kind of weird."

"I'm all kinds of weird. Comes with the territory." Snaking his hand around the back of her neck, he drew her closer. His voice was barely above a whisper. "No more fighting. No more denying. All I want to do right now is kiss you. Really kiss you. Can I do that?"

"Yeah." Her cheeks flushed, and she hooked her arms around his waist. "I'd like that very much."

His gaze fell to her lips. She licked them, leaving a glistening sheen. His pulse quickened. Leaning in, he hovered an inch away from her mouth. Warmth skittered across his skin. She was so beautiful. Not wanting to hold back for another second, he pressed his lips to hers.

Breath shot from his lungs. Wanting to taste her, he parted his lips and licked into her warm, wet mouth. Her tongue met his and fire ignited his soul, unleashed after being caged up for too long. Desire, hunger, and want for her surged through his body. God, he'd been a fool for not admitting how he felt.

Her hands slid up his back, sending shivers down his spine. She clutched onto his shoulders and arched her chest against his. *Heaven.* Sensing her need for more, he dipped his head and deepened their kiss. Hot and heavy. Her tongue dancing with his sent a fevered rush of blood to his groin.

Before his willpower failed, he rested his forehead against hers, and snaked his hands around her waist. "I've wanted to kiss you like that for months. Without being drunk like I was on New Year's Eve, or being upset like we were at the beach house, or out of desperation like I was in Rio. I've wanted to kiss you again like I did on our night together."

She glided her fingers down his jaw. "I've wanted more than your kisses. I've wanted more from you ever since I found out I was pregnant. I want more, now."

His cock ached. He slid his hand up her waistline and stroked his thumb over the side of her breast. If her want matched his, control would be hard. Having her body press against his tested his restraint. But he'd do anything for her. "Kar, I know you've gotta go out tonight. So we better stop. I'd love to take you to bed. More than anything. But I can wait. Until you're ready. Until you're able."

Her eyes darkened, sexy and seductive. "I am able. And healed." She stepped over to the hall table, picked up her phone and texted, her thumbs flying over the screen. "I canceled my plans." She slid back to him and weaved her hands around his neck. "No more wasted moments." She pressed her lips to his, grabbed him by the hand, and led him toward her bedroom.

His heart beat like a bass drum. It had taken too long to get here. Too much trauma. Too much tragedy. One thing he'd learned was that time was precious, and he wouldn't squander another second.

He'd come up with a plan. He'd make being in a relationship

with her tie in with her job and his ever-changing schedule. But for now, he was here. And he had all night to make up for their mistakes, missed opportunities and make some smoldering-hot new memories.

Chapter 26

Kara drew Hunter into her bedroom and stopped by the end of her bed. Blue evening light filtered through her sheer curtains. Soft shadows danced across his face. She placed her trembling hand onto his chest, and his heart pounded in rhythm with hers. After months of anguish, pain, and hiding her feelings, having him here was like a surreal dream.

The moment he'd said he wanted her, her resolve had shattered. How could she not take this chance? They had a connection. She could feel it. It was too powerful.

Raking her fingernails down his stomach, every ridge of his abs hardened beneath her fingertips. Just touching him without restraint ripped open the seams on her pent-up emotions. She wanted to rush, take it slow, rip his clothes off, seal every treasured moment to memory. When she craved him, how could she stay in control? She fumbled with the edge of his T-shirt and tugged it over his head, loving the way his hair fell in soft waves to his shoulders.

He traced the edge of her face with soft strokes and her eyes fluttered closed. *Just breathe.* Warm hands cupped her cheeks, and he pressed his mouth to hers. Hot and delicious, languid and slow. So much better than any time before. No nerves, no sadness, no desperation—just desire. With a tilt of his head, he deepened his kiss. Kissed her like he needed her more than oxygen.

Threading her fingers into his hair, fire charged through her veins. She drew him closer and her mouth molded against his. Urgent. Hungry. Demanding.

"Kar." He smiled over her kisses. His hands slipped down her arms and curled around her waist. "God, I want you so bad, but let's not rush. I want to savor every inch of you. Touch you. Taste you. Make you come as many times as you want."

She'd settle for one. Any more would be a bonus. She brushed her hands over his bare flesh, his skin cool beneath her fiery fingertips. This wasn't where she'd expected to end up this evening. After weeks of trying to block him from her heart, she'd been so close to pushing him away. Afraid of more hurt, her self-doubt and her insecurities. He'd fought for her. Maybe he was her knight in shining armor. No . . . no, he wasn't. He was her rock star!

He untied the sash of her wrap-dress and peeled it from her shoulders. His gaze fell to her chest, then back up to her face. A smile curled at the edge of his mouth. "You're so beautiful, Kar."

Hearing him say that weirded her out. Compliments regarding her looks never came her way, so the honesty in his tone made her blush. Made her heart skip faster.

"You're body's pretty rockin', too." She traced the V-line of muscle down to the top of his jeans.

His eyes shimmered in the soft light. "We really need to work on your dirty talk."

"You want me to dress up like a schoolgirl and you can play the teacher?" She brushed her hand over his groin and cupped his hardened cock. "Then you can teach me what you like."

He groaned. "You like role-playing? That's so hot."

"There's a lot you don't know about me." She unbuckled his belt and tugged it from the loops.

"I know. But I'm liking you more and more each minute." He cupped her breast and circled his thumb across her nipple, sending it into a hardened peak. "And right now, I want you. Just you."

He could say that to her a thousand times and she would never get sick of hearing it.

He guided her backward. Her knees hit the edge of the mattress and he lay her down on her unmade bed. Skimming his hands over her body, he ripped off her panties. "Hmm. Better." His eyes never left hers as he slipped off his shoes and discarded his jeans and boxer-briefs.

He crawled onto the bed and hovered over her. Nudging between her legs, he lowered his weight onto her. Skin on skin. Heart on heart. Breath against breath.

With featherlight strokes, she traced her fingertips across the arch of his eyebrows, down the edge of his sharp jawline, and across his soft lips. "Kiss me."

He propped his arms either side of her head, and pressed his lips against her forehead, her eyelids, her cheeks, and then her mouth. Inhaling his eau de whiskey breath and citrusy scent, she flicked her tongue against his. His lips were soft like velvet, smooth like satin, warm like sunshine, hot like fire. Each kiss, each touch, each connection sent tingles shooting across her skin.

He made her feel again. Made her heart beat.

Working his way down her body, he kissed a heated trail toward her chest, leaving goose bumps in his wake. He licked and circled one nipple then the other. *Oh yes.*

"I love your boobs." His gentle breath brushed over each one, hardened her aroused buds even more, making them ache with pleasure.

She arched into his touch, wanting more of his tender strokes. Closing her eyes, she sank deeper into the pillow.

With gentle nips and licks, he kissed his way further down her body. He hesitated at her cesarean scar, and her heart faltered. With his calloused fingertip, he slowly traced the length of the red mark. It was weird because his touch, although there, was numb against her skin. She winced. The back of her eyes stung. Would she ever get full sensation back? Probably not. The nerves had been destroyed.

He sucked in a deep breath and pressed tiny kisses along her scar, then rested his cheek against her belly. Her heart ached as she stroked his hair. He lay still, brushing his thumb over the place where her womb used to be. He wiped his eyes, glided his hands over her hip and hugged her tight.

She threaded her fingers into his hair and drew him back to her face. His eyes were as watery as hers. She cupped his cheek. "We're gonna be okay, Hunt."

"Yeah. We are."

Hunter lying naked on top of her made it easier for her to focus. With their tragic loss behind them, it was time to look forward. No more sadness. "It's time for new memories. Good ones." She pressed her lips to his.

"I like the sound of that." He entwined their fingers and pinned her hands beside her head. He rocked and pressed his hips against hers. "I want to do everything to you. Kiss you. Touch you. Make you come."

She slipped her hands from his and slid them around his waist. She wriggled beneath him, edging his erection toward her opening. "Is this a multiple-choice or can I have all of the above?"

A naughty smile curled across his lips. "You can have all, multiple times."

Heat crept into her cheeks and butterflies cartwheeled in her belly. "You better plan on staying—"

He shut her up with a steamy kiss that stole the air from her lungs. She felt like she was melting into the mattress.

He reached for his wallet on the nightstand, but she stopped him. She swallowed the lump in her throat. "Is there any chance you have STDs?"

"No. No chance." He sighed, squeezing his eyes shut as if annoyed at the interruption. "I haven't been with anyone . . . for months. My last medical before we went to South America was all clear. Why?"

She sucked her bottom lip between her teeth. Knowing he hadn't slept with anyone while they dealt with Ryan eased her mind. She met his concerned gaze. "Since there's no way I can fall pregnant, I want to know if I feel different. If things have changed after my hysterectomy. If my endo's gone." Butterflies swarmed in her belly. "Make love to me . . . without a condom."

He closed his eyes and rested his forehead against hers. "Kar, I've never had unprotected sex."

She rubbed her hand over his tattooed arm. "There will be something in this for both of us. Please?"

A crease formed between his brows. "Are you sure?"

She brushed his worry away with the stroke of her fingertip. "Yeah, I am."

He nodded, and his gaze softened. "Okay."

She pulled him on top of her and drew his lips to hers. His kisses, hungry and passionate, consumed her, tingling every hair on her body. With a nudge of his knee, he edged her legs wider. Teased the head of his penis against her arousal. "Still want me?"

Her muscles clenched, and she flexed her hips against his, eager to have him inside her. "Yes."

He gave a little nod. A little grin.

Was he anxious like she was? What if sex felt different? What if it wasn't the same? Her heart strained against her ribs and she said a silent prayer. *Please, let everything be okay.*

With a gentle drive of his hips, he eased inside her. Slowly. Steadily. Seductively. Hunter moaned, closed his eyes and penetrated deep. "You're so hot and wet and *mmm*. All in a very . . . good . . . way."

Kara clutched his back. Tightened her core around him. *Oh . . . God . . . yes. That's good.* "You mean that? It's not . . . different?"

"No. I mean, yes." His naked flesh pressed against hers and sent shivers up her spine. "No rubber is awesome. Hotter. Definitely hotter."

Kissing the base of his throat and working her way up to nibble his ear, she rocked her hips in time with his thrusts. Savored each penetration. "You feel incredible."

In fact . . . really incredible.

She screwed her eyes shut and bit down on her lip.

Oh . . . wow.

She wasn't expecting this. It to be this good.

There was no pain. *None.*

A tear slipped from her eye. For the first time in her life, there was no soreness or discomfort. No endometriosis to deal with.

She wrapped her arms around his shoulders, buried her face into his neck and trembled. Kissed his salty skin.

"Hey." Hunter stopped moving and brushed her temple with his thumb. "Babe, what's wrong? Is it hurting? You want to stop?"

She shook her head, rustling against her pillow. "No. That's just it. It's wonderful. There's no pain. At all."

His eyes glistened, warm and tender. "That's awesome. Because I like being inside you."

Kara arched her chest, pressing her breasts against him. The friction of her body against his teased her nipples. "Then don't stop."

"Good, because you're driving me wild."

Drawing her knee up beside him, he thrust into her deep and hard. *Oh wow. That . . . feels so good.* His gorgeous smile filled her heart with a new warmth, warmth that had been absent for too long. He drove into her, again and again. Her core begged for release, tightening around him. Wanting him to go harder. Harder. Harder.

"*Fuck.*" He hissed through his teeth.

He eased back an inch then penetrated her all the way.

Heat exploded from her core, and the most intense orgasm ripped through her. *Oh yes!* After months of pain, heartache and torture all her burning desire, frustration and rampant want for him burst from her body. Every nerve ending sparked and erupted.

Hunter rocked into her and stilled. He groaned and shuddered. Closed his eyes and tensed his jaw. With a thrust of his hips, he convulsed with his release.

Her heartbeat pounded against his. She wrapped her legs around him and held him close. Didn't want to let him go. Not yet. With his cock still throbbing inside her, he smiled at her. He stroked her hair and kissed her. Tender, delicious and deep. She'd never felt so connected to anyone before. Not like this.

He was too perfect. Perfect, even with all his faults.

"Thank you," she whispered. "For not walking away."

"I couldn't. Not this time." He withdrew and lay beside her. Drawing her into his arms, he kissed her forehead and chuckled, "So . . . that was round one. You wanted me to stay the night, right?"

"It depends." She stroked his smooth skin. "What does round two involve?"

"Anything and everything. But exhaustion from tour has caught up with me. I need a quick power-nap. Give me half an hour, then it's on. I promise."

Her belly flipped. "I'll hold you to that."

She went to leave, but he held her tighter. "Stay with me. I don't want to let you go."

"I won't. Let me clean up and I'll be back."

After a quick dash to the bathroom, she returned to his side. Snuggling against his chest, his body warmth enveloped her. She listened to his rhythmic heartbeat, and his breathing eased. His body relaxed. Within a few minutes, he was sound asleep.

She smiled and inhaled the scent of his skin. Her heart seesawed between deliriously happy, and dauntingly terrified. Had she made a mistake? How could they make being together work? How was she going to let go of her fears? That she wasn't attractive enough to hold his interest. That their lives were too different. That losing their son had left a permanent darkness inside her mind.

She flicked her apprehensive thoughts aside, filled her lungs and pressed her lips against his chest. *Stop worrying about the future. Live in the moment.* Hunter was here. Sleeping beside her. That was all that mattered. But could she let go of everything that had happened and give him her heart? Give him her all?

It was too late.

She already had.

She closed her eyes, steadied her breath, and whispered, "I love you, Hunt."

Chapter 27

Holding his breath, Hunter slipped out from underneath Kara's bedsheets as quietly as possible, and grabbed his clothes. He needed coffee. His heart pounded as he tiptoed across the floorboards. His head spun, still reeling from last night. Kara had said she loved him. He was half asleep, but he'd heard it. Just like that . . . she loved him. How was he supposed to react? He was crazy about her, ready to commit to her. But was this love? All he knew was that he'd never cared for anyone the way he cared for Kara.

Squeak. The floor protested.

Shit!

He winced, froze on the spot, and peered back over his shoulder.

Kara looked up at him through sleepy eyes. "Trying to sneak off without saying goodbye?"

"No. Definitely not." He stood naked in the middle of the room, holding his clothes in front of his groin. "I was going to make coffee."

"No, you weren't." She tugged the sheet under her chin.

Disappointment clouded her eyes. "You're running. Looking for a quick escape. I get it. It's what you do."

Hunter dropped his clothing to the floor and crawled back onto the bed. Hovering over her, he kissed her forehead. "You're wrong. I'm going to the kitchen. For coffee."

"Are you sure?" The lines of concern disappeared as a saucy smile curled across her lips. "Because I'd love you to stay a little longer."

Blood rushed to his groin knowing what lay underneath the sheet. "How long I stay depends on you. Do you have plans?"

"I was going to call work to see if I could go back early. I know I have another month off, but I think I'm ready."

He trailed his finger from the tip of her chin down her throat, over her sheet-covered chest. "Is there anything I could do to make you change your mind?" His hunger for her flared as he circled her nipple. He loved the way it hardened with one small tweak. His cock stood to attention, and he nudged it against her thigh.

"You might be able to persuade me." She snatched his hand away from her breast and kissed it. "But first, I want to know something. I want to know what happens now. With us?"

His balls retracted. Total mood-killer. But he knew they had to discuss how they would navigate their way forward.

He slumped beside her, his head resting on the pillow. She flicked the sheet across his waist. Catching a glimpse of her nakedness made it hard for him to concentrate. He edged closer to her and glided his hand over her hip. "What I'd like to happen is to stay here and fuck you all day. Like I did last night."

Scanning her curves, he remembered every detail of last night. After a forty-five-minute power nap, they'd hit the shower. He'd gone down on her. Nailed her on the bathroom countertop. Then they'd done it again back in bed.

With her sweetness filling his mind, he leaned in to kiss

her, but she placed her fingertips over his lips. "I'm serious. Last night was incredible. But now we've got the lust out of our system and emotions have settled, I need to know, before this goes any further, is this what you want?"

He curled a strand of her long silky hair around his finger. He'd never been good at deep-and-meaningful conversations. He'd only had them with Gemma and Kyle. But for the first time in a long time, he was serious about someone. He wouldn't run anymore. "I meant what I said last night. I want to be with you."

She lowered her gaze and twisted the edge of the sheet around her fingers. "So much has changed. I've changed. You've changed. I'm giving you the opportunity to back out."

"Why? I thought . . . this was what you wanted?" *Holy shit!* Was he now the one who wanted a relationship and she didn't? The world had gone insane.

Oh crap. What if he had misheard her? Maybe she didn't love him. *Ouch!*

Her eyes glassed over. "I've had to reevaluate everything in my life over the past few months. I've learned to fight for what I want, stand on my own two feet, and rely on no one else but me. Everything I ever dreamed of—marriage, babies, family—got taken away from me. I've had to start anew. For the first time, I don't have a picture in my head of what my future looks like. I want to focus on my career. If you don't want that or support that, I'm giving you the chance to walk away."

"Kar, I don't want to leave." He stroked the side of her face and tucked her hair behind her ear. "I think we've both learned that life can change in the blink of an eye. I've never been one to set goals or make plans. I've always had people around me to do that. I've always lived in the moment. But now, I do think of my future. Because I want you to be a part of it."

Her gaze softened. She grabbed his hand and entwined her fingers with his. "Yeah?"

"I'm not gonna lie here next to you and promise you the world, or marriage, or kids. I can't do that. But I can promise to be faithful, to be committed, and to do everything possible to make you happy."

He hesitated, surprised at his own words. It was as if a bolt of electric energy zapped his brain, and everything was clearer. He'd changed. Hell, he'd been prepared to become a father. Have kids. Want kids. What surprised him even more was that the thought of marriage didn't freak him out either. But he wanted to take it slow. Take it one step at a time.

She brushed her fingers down his cheek. "Put your mind at ease, Hunt. I don't want to get married or have kids. Not now. Not for a long time. I want to enjoy life—remember what it feels like to live again. Be crazy. Have fun. And you're perfect for that."

But a darkness swam in the depths of her eyes, and concern rippled beneath his skin. Was she being honest with him? Within a blink it was gone, and a smile drew across her face.

He kissed her forehead and curled his hand around her waist. "I'm far from perfect, but I'm a master at having fun. I am the life of the party."

"Yes. I know that. But can I scare you a little?" With her tone playful and light, she held her thumb and index finger an inch apart in front of his face. "If at some point in the future things get serious between us, remember I already have designed my wedding dress. And when I had my hysterectomy, they managed to save and freeze eight eggs from my damaged ovaries."

His heart jumped to his throat. *What?* His pulse rang in his ears and frazzled his brain. *Holy crap!* He wiped his hand down his face and his mouth gaped. "You mean . . . one day . . . a surrogate baby might be an option? Why didn't you tell me?"

While he was nowhere near prepared to go through that right now, the possibility of being able to have kids didn't have him rushing for the door. After everything they'd been through, there were so many other things graver than autism to face. They'd experienced the very worst. Maybe in the future, he could give her everything she wanted.

"We weren't together." She shrugged a shoulder. "It didn't matter. I won't ever be able to carry my own baby."

"I know. I'm still not going anywhere." Snaking his hand around the back of her neck, he pressed his forehead against hers. "We can't predict the future, but I want to face it with you. Don't go back to work yet. Kyle, Gem and I have two weeks off. We want to head to the beach house for vacation and enjoy the start of summer before our schedule gets crazy. Come with us."

"You're serious, aren't you?" She slid her hand down his chest and circled his nipple. Tingles shivered across his skin. "About me? About us? Last night wasn't just talk and crazy, hot sex?"

"No. I can be serious when I have to be. You should know that by now. But I like my fun. And I can promise we'll have plenty on vacation." He grazed his fingers down her leg and up the inside of her thigh. Color flushed her cheeks and he smiled. Stroking and tickling her skin, he worked his way closer to the apex of her thighs. He hovered his mouth an inch away from her lips. "So, what do you say?"

"Deal."

God, she turned him on.

He drew the sheet away and rolled on top of her. He nudged her legs wider with his knee and rubbed his hardened cock against her. "Excellent. Now . . . time for breakfast."

Her giggle was as intoxicating as JD. "I don't think I have any food here. I haven't been grocery shopping. We'll have to go out."

He shook his head and gave her his best mischievous grin. "Nah. I have what I want to eat right here."

He didn't want to leave her bed. Didn't want to ignore how he felt. Didn't want to run away from the prospect of a future with her. Maybe he was into her more than he'd initially thought, and he didn't want to screw this up. He needed to be sure that what he felt in his heart aligned with his head. And until then, he was adamant about having fun.

Savoring the lingering rosy scent of her shower gel lingering on her skin, he kissed down her neck, licked and sucked her nipples, and headed between her legs. He trailed his tongue up through her hot slit. Her arousal was slick and salty. She moaned and clutched at the bedding. Now this was something he could get used to. For him, breakfast was served.

Chapter 28

Life had changed. Hunter didn't think it could get much better. After two weeks' vacation, he'd come back to work with a renewed energy. He felt human again—like himself, only better. Because he had Kara.

But he was worried. After back-to-back meetings over the past couple of weeks, his work was about to get crazy and his travel plans would take him away from her—award shows, music festivals, and concert appearances, photoshoots, interviews, and guest performances. In the car on the way to a fitting at Conrad's, he rubbed at the worry aching his brow. Had he done enough to ensure their relationship would survive?

During his team discussions, rather than sitting and going along with what everyone scheduled into Everhide's calendar, he now spoke up. He made sure that there were breaks, days off, so he'd be able to fly home and see her. There'd be no more than a week or two apart. He wanted to assure her she could trust him, and committed. For him, it was as if someone had flicked a switch. He only had eyes for Kara.

With Kyle, Gemma and Emily, their new stylist, they neared

Bryant Park. The summer heat penetrated the windows, the car's air-conditioning struggled to keep everyone cool. Beside him, Emily fidgeted and fussed with her folders, her cell phone, her dress. His hand twitched and clenched. He just wanted her to sit still.

Margo had resigned after tour due to poor health—the doctors had discovered a problem with a valve in her heart, and she needed surgery. It didn't matter what Everhide offered her or how much they'd begged her to stay. She declined. Emily, her assistant, had stepped into the role.

Things wouldn't be the same without Margo. She'd worked for them since they signed their first record deal. Just when things were falling into place in his personal life, one of the wheels that kept Everhide moving fell off.

Emily had much to live up to. She hadn't impressed him to date. She'd mixed up times for appointments, brought wrong outfits to a photoshoot, and forgot to pack essential belts and shoes. Hunter's tolerance had worn thin.

But his mood lifted when the car turned onto 42nd Street.

Gemma, sitting opposite him, clapped, her face bright and cheerful. "I love dress-up day."

Kyle ran his hand down Gemma's thigh. "Ah, the fun of being measured, fitted, and toyed with like a ragdoll for hours. The only good thing about it is I get to see you in your underwear for the majority of the afternoon."

Hunter pushed his Ray-Bans farther onto the bridge of his nose. Watching Gemma and Kyle together made him miss Kara. She'd left for work this morning before he woke.

At the building's entrance, the four of them piled out of the car and took the elevator up to Conrad's studio. Hunter followed everyone into the large reception area decked out in Conrad's signature black and orange. While the black furniture and carpet were elegant, the orange chairs, and abstract art were as eccentric as Conrad himself.

Conrad burst through the double doors that led to the offices and workrooms. Hunter bit his cheek to stop himself from laughing. In his bright orange trousers and shirt, and with his peroxided unruly hair, Conrad looked like he was channeling his inner Andy Warhol. "Are you ready, my sweets? Come on through."

Entering the large private fitting room Hunter had hoped to see Kara. All he saw was Jasmine, her pale pink hair twisted into two knobs on top of her head, unzipping garment bags by the mirror-lined wall. Between her and Conrad, there was no lack of color.

Hunter skimmed over the tables full of purses, belts, ties, and shoes that lay by the large windows. Nothing cool caught his eye. But the white backdrop mounted on the far side of the room for photos brought a smirk to his face. What stupid poses could he come up with today? It was time for Emily to see what it was really like to work with Everhide.

The door on the opposite side of the room flung open, and Kara walked in. His pulse jumped. She placed her laptop on the work desk and smiled at him. His stride didn't falter. He scooted across the room and gave her a kiss on the cheek. She smelled of her J'Adore perfume. *Mmm.* "Missed you this morning."

She blushed and patted his forearm. "Some of us work during daylight hours."

He stole a quick kiss from her lips. "Hey . . . I was up early. My first meeting was at ten."

"That *is* early for you." A teasing smile rippled across her lips. How he'd love to kiss them more, but this was work time, not play.

Conrad stood at the end of the racks and clicked his fingers. ""Righto. Let's get started. Emily, can you help Kara with Gemma's dresses? Jazzie and I will do the guys' suits."

Hunter jerked his head in Conrad and Jasmine's direction and kept his voice low. "How are they today?"

Since Kara had come back to work, he'd been worried about her. Conrad had ordered her back into couture and VIP client design. She'd complained about how uncomfortable it was to work with Conrad and Jasmine every day, that he was rude and even more arrogant than before.

She glanced toward Conrad and Jasmine and grumbled, "If they can refrain from groping each other and he doesn't talk to me like I'm a peasant, I'll be fine."

Where was Conrad's regard? Hunter wished there was something he could do to make Kara feel better and love her job again. Seeing her upset formed an ache deep inside his chest. "You let me know if he pisses you off."

She fumbled to pick up her pen on the desk. "It's okay. You just behave."

Hunter felt Conrad's gaze on him. His spine stiffened, and he turned. Conrad glared down the bridge of his nose in their direction. *What is his problem?*

Hunter didn't have time for whatever was up Conrad's ass. He spun back to Kara. "Time to work, babe."

She nodded and slipped over to join Gemma and Emily. He rubbed his hands together and sashayed toward the rack of clothes. He loved fashion. It made him feel good. He eyed suit after suit, shirt after shirt. But he winced at some of the bold color choices and quirky fabric patterns. He hadn't picked any of those. *What the hell?*

Jasmine batted her eyelids and kissed Conrad, for longer than what Hunter deemed professional. *Ergh.*

Hunter cleared his throat, loud enough for all to hear. Jasmine peeled herself away from Conrad. A coy smile lit her face. She grabbed a suit off the rack and held it toward Hunter. The bright red fabric strained his eyeballs. He ignored Jasmine and gave Emily a questioning look. "Who ordered this?"

Emily pointed her chin toward Conrad as she zipped Gemma into a black cocktail dress. "Conrad suggested we try some bold new colors."

"Really?" Hunter slipped off his shoes and stripped down to his Calvins. "I don't mind red, but this is wrong." Hunter pulled on a silky white button-down shirt and the horrendous jacket and pants. He swung his arms about, and shook his legs, but everything was tight and itchy.

Conrad slid over to him after handing Kyle a white shirt. He brushed his hands over Hunter's shoulder line and examined the suit. "It was Jazzie's idea. The color is fun. Brings out your vibrant personality."

Hunter looked at his reflection in the mirror and screwed up his nose. "Yeah, but I'm not this vibrant." He rolled his shoulders and tugged on the sleeves. "You have all our measurements, Conrad. Why does this feel small?"

Had he put on weight?

Conrad straightened the lapels on Hunter's jacket. "Jazzie suggested streamlining the cut." He took a step back, pursed his lips together and looked Hunter up and down. "You look fabulous. The skinny-leg trouser is in."

"I don't care what's in." Hunter twisted the leg of the suit around his thigh, but it wouldn't sit right. "I don't like it."

Hunter turned to Kyle for his opinion. But when he saw that Kyle was dressed in the same style of suit only in bright blue, Hunter pointed and burst out laughing. "You look like a fucking Smurf. That's hideous."

"And you look like a freaking popsicle." Kyle held his belly and laughed. "Conrad, these suits are rancid. I'm not wearing this." Kyle ripped off his clothes and handed them in a bunched-up mess to Jasmine.

Jasmine's mouth gaped, and the color drained from her

face.

Gemma turned to Conrad and stretched the high neckline of her sequined outfit. "And why have you changed the style of this dress? What's with the puffy sleeves? I don't do puffy. This isn't what I wanted."

Jasmine's chin trembled. She burst into tears and rushed from the room.

"Now look what you've done." Conrad threw his hands in the air. "You didn't have to upset her like that. Jazzie worked really hard on these designs."

"Sorry. Not our problem." Hunter removed his jacket and held it out to Conrad on his hooked finger. "Next time, please ask us before you change the styles and colors. Don't waste our time." Hunter impressed himself. He'd kept his tone civil, his manners in check, and his real opinion of Conrad on mute.

When he first met Conrad six years ago, Hunter had been inspired. Conrad had been a young successful businessman and great designer. But since hooking up with Jasmine, he'd changed. For the worse. Hunter used to think Kara had been the one suffocating Conrad, but maybe it was the other way around. She'd been the driving force and the power behind the designs. The one who'd added the wow factor to Conrad's creations.

Conrad's loss was his gain.

Kara snatched the jacket off Hunter's finger and hung it up. "Conrad, I told you they wouldn't like the designs. I know the style they like. So do you."

Conrad ripped the coat hangers along the rack and grabbed another outfit for Kyle. "Your *boyfriend*, Kyle and Gemma are just being difficult."

"No, they're not." Kara fumed. "You made a poor call letting Jasmine make those suits and changing Gemma's dress without her approval."

"Umm." Emily's timid voice quivered. "I'm sorry. I authorized the changes to the dress, but not the suits."

Gemma's eyes widened, and her jaw clenched. A red rash crept up the side of her neck. "Don't ever change something I've ordered. Got it?"

Yet another mistake from Emily. She'd better learn fast and not mess with their clothes.

Emily lowered her head and nodded. "Yes. I'm sorry."

Kara flicked her ponytail over her shoulder. "Conrad, be grateful that we're friends with these guys, and we can talk about any issues. Other clients may not be so forgiving."

Hunter had never heard Kara talk to Conrad like this. Ever. Her newfound directness. Her no-nonsense attitude. He loved it. He loved her standing strong and defiant, and putting Conrad in his place.

Hunter whispered to her, "You. Feisty. Total turn-on."

"Behave," she mouthed.

By all means. He wanted this fitting over and done with.

Kara chose a new jacket for him and slipping it on felt better straight away. He turned to the mirror. "Oh yeah. This one's much nicer." Tugging on the cuffs of the shimmery black suit, highlighted with a fine silver thread through the fabric, he turned this way and that, studying his reflection in the mirror. It was perfect. Smoking. Sexy. Hot.

Kara straightened his collar and she beamed. "I helped with this one. This is from the range of fabrics you picked last time you were here." She slid her hands down his chest, across his hips, and over the pleats on the front of his trousers. Every touch made his pulse quicken. He willed his body to remain controlled. But blood flooded toward his groin. His temperature jumped a few degrees.

Shit.

He captured her hand. "You'll have to stop touching me like

that."

She glanced at his hardening crotch, then met his eyes. Her eyebrow arched into a perfect curve. "Does this happen at all your fittings?"

Heat touched his cheeks. "It's never happened before."

"Interesting." A satisfied smile flitted across her face.

"Kara? What are you doing?" Conrad waved his hand at her before sweeping around Kyle who had changed into a navy-checked ensemble. "Don't just stand there. Take the hemline up on Hunter's trousers. Check the seamlines. Make yourself useful."

Hunter's fists clenched. He didn't like the way Conrad talked to Kara. At all. He sucked in a loud breath. His nostrils flared and his mouth twitched into a sneer. Gemma, changing into a gold lacy number, glared at him and shook her head. A warning to keep calm.

Kara sighed and grabbed her pincushion cuff off the desk. She saluted Conrad, got down on her hands and knees, and ran her hands over Hunter's trouser bottoms. With pins caught between her lips, she mumbled, "This classic cut suits you much better."

Conrad adjusted Kyle's sleeves and shot death stares at Hunter, hard and fast.

Hunter's spine went ramrod straight. He'd had enough. "Conrad, what's your problem? Is it me, or Kara, or both of us?"

Conrad jammed his hand on his hip. "I have a problem that Kara's come back to work with a bad attitude. I assume I have you to thank for that. All she does is argue and criticize everything we do."

"Maybe she's got a point." Hunter shrugged. He loved Kara's blunt sarcasm and wit.

Conrad's eyebrows shot skyward. His mouth gaped.

Kara took the pins from her mouth and peered around

Hunter's legs. "Conrad, what is wrong with challenging you and making sure the designs are exactly what you want or . . . in this case . . . what the client wants? Or are you upset I'm not submissive and at your beck and call anymore?"

Hunter's balls jumped at the thought of Kara being submissive. Or maybe she could be the dominant. He'd be willing to try anything with her. His dick throbbed and ached. Definitely not good when she was crawling around the floor and jostling near his groin. *Oh God, please help.*

"Kara." Conrad's tone was clipped and cold. "It's not your place to criticize me. You should support the bold direction I'm taking with the designs."

"It would be easier if the designs had your usual classic elegance." Kara tugged hard on the bottom of Hunter's trousers "Not some quirky . . . Smurf-wear."

Hunter bit his inside cheek to stop himself from chuckling. Conrad's eyes narrowed into an evil glare, but he didn't utter another word.

When Kara finished pinning, Hunter helped her to stand. Her cheeks had flushed red. Her hand shook when she wiped her brow. She'd been giving as good as she got, but clearly, Conrad had hurt her. He hated seeing her flustered and upset by Conrad. Conrad used to respect and relish her input. Now he treated her like scum. She deserved better. Hunter lowered his voice. "Do you still like working for this asshole?"

She leaned in to whisper, "You know I don't. But he's my boss."

Hunter's mind rippled like a Mexican wave. Tension twisted in his temples. Then *snap*. Everything cleared. A solution formed. Was his thinking rational or was it because Kara was his girlfriend? Kyle and Gemma would pull him into line if he wasn't."

"Wait here," he said to Kara, and rushed over to Kyle and

Gemma. "Guys, we need to talk."

He led them over to the photography backdrop, far enough away so no one else could listen. They huddled in a tight circle.

"I know I'm putting you on the spot, but we don't make decisions without each other. Tell me if I'm way off the mark." He glanced over Gemma's shoulder and saw Conrad having heated words with Kara. "I know Emily hasn't been working for us long, but she's a freaking nightmare. She's stuffed up too many times, and we can't afford that. What if we cut our losses and ask Kara to come and work for us?"

Gemma's eyes lit up. "I'd love that. Kara would be brilliant. You won't get any objections from me. I'm over Emily's screw-ups."

"Are you sure about this?" Kyle, the logical one, always had to play devil's advocate. "Are you doing this because Kara's your girlfriend?"

"For me, the girlfriend thing is a bonus." He wouldn't deny that. "Like you and Gem, I'm more than happy to mix business with pleasure."

"It does have some positives." Kyle snuck a kiss from Gemma, then gave him an I-hope-you-know-what-you're-doing look. "Do you think she'd be good at the job?"

"Yeah. She's got industry experience. She can design. She can source. Work in with our suppliers. She knows what we like. Does she need any other qualifications?"

"Well . . .no." Kyle dipped his head side to side. "She did a great job in LA and Rio. Emily is making silly mistakes. So . . . I agree with you. I'm in."

"Hurry up, you lot." Conrad strummed his fingers on his folded arms. "We haven't got all day."

Hunter ignored Conrad, and his excitement got the better of him. "I'm going to ask Kara now. Okay?"

"Hell yeah. Go for it." Gemma slapped him on the back. "Kyle and I better go and keep Conrad happy. Make it quick. And remember, she could say no."

If Kara turned down the offer, they needed to find a new stylist. Emily's days were numbered.

"Kara," Hunter called, waving her over to join him. Gemma and Kyle gave him the thumbs up and scooted back to Conrad and Emily.

"What's going on?" Kara stopped in front of him.

Hunter's stomach flipped, and he fidgeted with a button on his shirt. "We've got an idea, something for you to think about. If you don't like it here at Conrad anymore . . . how would you like to come and work with us? Emily's not working out. The job's yours if you want it."

"What?" Kara's voice struck a high note. Her eyes darted in Conrad's direction, even though there was no way he could hear their conversation. "You can't offer me a job while I'm here at work."

"Yes, I can. I just did. Kyle and Gem agree." He kept his tone soft and sure. "Think about it. We can discuss the details later. Working with us would be fun. Unlike here with Conrad."

"But you'd be my boss?"

"I know." He half grinned. "Kind of cool, isn't it? Sleeping with the boss."

She pointed her thumb in Conrad's direction. "Been there. Done that. Didn't work out."

Ouch. That was a nail gun to the chest. "I can't imagine the two of you banging like we do."

She lowered her eyes, and her cheeks blushed. "We didn't. I've never had sex like you and I do."

"That's because I'm the best. And you know it." He blew on his fingers and polished them against his chest. Then he winced and adjusted the crotch of his trousers. "We need to stop talking about sex because my balls are aching."

"I'll relieve them later. I promise." Her eyes shimmered, looking at him through her long, thick eyelashes. "You're serious about this, aren't you? About offering me a job?"

"Yes. You always said you wanted to influence fashion. You can do that by using Gem, Kyle, and me. We have millions of followers on social media. Design and source whatever you want; we'll wear it. You could be the next Kate Young."

"You want me to use and abuse your celebrity status?"

"Sure. What are friends for? We won't mind. You're not some money-hungry corporate who thinks we're nothing but a product." He slid his arms around her waist. His thighs brushed against hers. Silver shards flicked in the depths of her blue eyes. *God, she's so beautiful.* "And you know what else would be great if you worked with us? We'd be together. All the time. And I'd like that. Very much."

"You'd like that?" She stroked her long fingernails down the side of his face, tickling his stubble. "Is there any other reason you want me around?"

He drew in a slow breath. When he was with her, the world seemed right. He hadn't known he was missing something in his life until she came along. His heart boomed like a beatbox in the Bronx. He leaned in and hovered his lips an inch from hers. "Yes. I want you with me . . . all the time . . . because I love you."

He pressed his lips against hers. Her mouth quivered beneath his. No, her whole body trembled beneath his touch. He eased back and held her arms.

"Get a room," Kyle called out.

Hunter's gaze never left Kara's, but he flipped Kyle the bird. Her eyes darted around his face but lacked any form of emotion. *Shit.*

Had something he'd said come out wrong? Panic gurgled up his throat. Time to backtrack. "If you love your job, stay here. You coming to work for us was just an idea," he rambled. "We'd love to have you. Take the job, don't take the job—I don't care. All I know is I want to be with you more and more each day."

She closed her eyes and swayed. "I'm sorry . . . what did you say after *I love you*? Because everything went fuzzy."

The hugest grin spread across his face. He wasn't sure if he could remember. "You want me to repeat everything? Or just the part where I said I love you?"

Tears pooled in her eyes, and she linked her fingers behind his neck. "That bit. If I have to work on my dirty talk, you need to work on being romantic. This is not the most ideal place for you to tell me you love me for the first time. But I'll take it."

"Would it make a difference if I whispered it in your ear like this?" He nuzzled into her ear, blew gently down her neck, nibbled on her earlobe, and whispered, "I love you."

She giggled and flinched. "Much better."

While he'd love to spend more time kissing her, he had work to do. He withdrew her hands from around his neck. "Come on. We'd better get back to these fittings. If we don't move now, I'll be walking around for the rest of the day with a permanent hard-on."

"Yes. We should be professional." She stepped back and smoothed her hands down the front of her shirt. "Let me think about the job, okay? And please, don't say anything to Conrad."

"I wouldn't dream of it." Although it would give him an endless amount of satisfaction to do so.

"Kara? Hunter?" Conrad hollered from across the room and snatched a dress off the rack for Gemma. Emily was with Kyle choosing items off the accessories table. "It's not time for personal hook-ups."

Hunter's fists twitched. God, he'd love to flatten Conrad to the ground.

Kara gave Conrad a smug smile. "We were discussing work."

"Didn't look like it." He said, pinning in the darts on Gemma's dress. "Just get on with the fittings, please?"

Knots twisted in the base of Hunter's neck, but he held his tongue. He peeled off his jacket and shirt and hung it on the rack. Kara selected his next outfit and he shrugged it on. For the next few ensembles, every time Hunter glanced at Kara, her talent struck him—her attention to detail, her eye for coordination, her flair. He loved that her passion for fashion was the same as his was for music.

He hoped she'd take the job.

After everything they'd been through together, didn't they deserve to be happy?

She held out the last suit and shirt for him to try on.

Conrad stormed over to them. ""No. No. *No*. Kara. That's the wrong shirt. Don't mix up the designs." Conrad reefed a slivery floral button-down off a hanger and thrust it at Hunter's chest. "This is the correct one."

"But the patterns and colors clash."

"No, they don't."

The hair's on Hunter's arms stood on end. Conrad and Kara stared at each other, cold, stubborn and fierce.

Should he step away? Say something? He didn't want to be in the middle of this, but he'd stay and support Kara. With every breath. Because she was right.

Kara jabbed her finger toward Conrad. "You've lost it, Conrad. Your pizazz and sophistication, your eye for detail has gone. You don't won't my input. And that's fine. It's your company, your creative directive. But I'll not put up with double standards, be belittled and treated like crap when I know I'm right. I want no part in your insecure, power-hungry games. Here . . . have your Goddamn shirt." She shoved the silk into Conrad's hands. "You dress Hunter."

"Kara." Conrad gaped.

"No. I'm done." She drew in a deep breath. Defiance flared

in her eyes. "I quit."

Holy shit!

Hunter's eyes widened. His heart filled with pride and warmth. Kara had put Conrad in his place. What an amazing, strong and incredible woman to fall in love with.

That's my *girl.*

My Kara.

Chapter 29

The limousine meandered toward the Dolby Theatre in Los Angeles for the Radio Disney Music Awards. Kara sat with Everhide, fidgeting with the beads and sequins on her clutch. Their car joined the snail-paced queue dropping off guests for the red carpet. Tonight was her first awards show. Her first major public appearance with Hunter as his girlfriend. As Everhide's new stylist.

She closed her eyes and fiddled with her diamond chandelier earring. She loved Hunter. Really loved him. And for the first time in months, she was happy. There was no way that this job could be a mistake. She loved the work, the freedom to create, and was relishing in the early praise and recognition she got from influential industry heavy-weights—the bloggers, the magazines, the fashion elite. She'd found something to own and thrive in, no longer worried about being second best to the likes of her sister or at Conrad's. She'd found an opportunity to shine, thanks to Hunter's belief in her.

Sitting opposite Kara, Gemma's eyes sparkled bright and she flicked her chin toward Hunter. "Kar, are you set to step out with this bozo?"

Kara's stomach fluttered, flipped, and flopped, but she was ready. "Yes." She smiled at Hunter, adoration seeping into every pore. He rocked his charcoal Armani suit.

"Good, because when the media sees you with him, they'll go crazy." Gemma's gleaming smile warped into a grimace. She bit her tongue between her teeth, squirmed and tugged at the top of her strapless gold Zuhair Murad pantsuit.

Kara slapped Gemma's knee. "Leave your top alone. It won't fall down." Kara had had that top tailored meticulously and had stuck Gemma into it with enough Hollywood tape to hold the San Andreas fault line together. It wasn't going anywhere.

"Think I'll have to have words with my stylist. No strapless tops in the future." Gemma's eyes, lined in silver glitter, shimmered and glistened.

Kara giggled. After quitting four weeks ago, Conrad had walked her out the door. She commenced work for Everhide the next day. In becoming their stylist she'd found her ultimate job. She'd become a procurement and logistics specialist— ordering, shipping, and fitting; sorting, coordinating, and dressing. On top of their contracted designers and suppliers, fashion houses randomly sent her clothing and accessories, begging her to have Gemma or the guys wear their brands. Kara's blog and Instagram accounts had skyrocketed from thousands of followers to millions. Influencing what people wore and creating fashion trends this way was beyond Kara's wildest dreams.

Kyle raised his chin and adjusted his tie and shirt collar as the car inched closer to the venue. "Ready for the cameras, Kar?"

She took a deep breath to keep her pulse as cool as Louis Vuitton's latest cruise-wear collection. She was getting used to the paparazzi hanging around. At least they kept their distance and didn't harass her like they did after losing Ryan. Nothing would ever be that bad.

She smiled at Hunter and squeezed his hand. "As long as I don't fall over and make a fool of myself, everything will be okay."

"You'll be fine." Hunter kissed the back of her hand. "You're gorgeous. Guaranteed to be the best on the red carpet."

The car jerked to a halt. Ushers opened the door, and Kyle and Gemma were the first out.

"Party time." Hunter slid out of the car, turned around, and offered Kara his hand.

She placed her hand in his and stepped out into the hot summer evening air. Her fingers trembled as she straightened the skirt of her knee-length Chanel dress. Screams from the crowd in the stands erupted and rang in her ears. Her heart pounded and she squinted at the blinding onslaught of camera flashes.

This is crazy.

"Ready?" Warmth simmered in Hunter's eyes and he kissed her on the cheek.

"I think I want to throw up." She held her clutch against her knotted belly not knowing where to look—at the stands, the cameras, or the reporters waving and yelling.

Hunter gave her a reassuring smile and entwined his fingers with hers. "Don't let go of me. I'll lead the way."

He drew her over to the barricaded stands where hundreds of overzealous fans scrambled for pictures and called out her friends' names. Kara released her hold on Hunter's hand so he could join Kyle and Gemma, but he gripped onto her tighter. "I'm not letting you go."

Her cheeks blushed, and his touch erased her nerves. With him by her side, each step would be easy.

Farther down the carpet in the main media section, each

guest was invited to have individual photos. The chants for Hunter grew to a level of insanity. *"Hunter. Hunter. Can we take your photo, please? Is that Ms. Knight? Are you two now an item? Please, Mr. Collins. A photo."*

Kara squeezed Hunter's hand to get his attention. "It's okay. Go and have your photo taken. I'll wait here."

Hunter hesitated for the briefest of moments before he released his hold and stepped in front of the promo wall. Kara giggled as he struck a pose, flashed his Hollywood smile, and was snapped from every angle by the feisty photographers.

Gemma shimmied over to her side. "I don't know what you've done to him, but I like it. He never, and I mean never, held my hand on a red carpet, or Amie's. He would run to play up to the crowds the second he was out of the car. You've certainly captured him, Kar. You're so good for each other."

"It feels surreal."

"I remember feeling like that when Kyle and I got together. It's awesome. And that buzz still hasn't gone away. We're two lucky girls. Our guys are freaking hot."

"You've got that right."

Movement caught Kara's eye. *Speak of the devil.* Amie weaved around the throng of publicists, celebrities, and security people crowding the red carpet. She wore a slinky lemon-colored cocktail dress, and towering stilettos, and had sapphires dangling around her neck.

Kara's chest seized. *Great. Why did she have to be here?*

"Kara." Amie's cold tone lacked any form of friendliness. "Never thought I'd see you on the red carpet."

Hunter's arms appeared around Kara's waist and he kissed her on the cheek. He turned and jerked his chin at Amie. "Evening."

Amie folded her arms. "So . . . you two are together? Thought you were smart, Kara? Don't fool yourself into thinking you can tame Hunter's wild ways for long. He loves the ladies too much."

Hunter snuggled against Kara and gave Amie a smug smirk. "Actually, Amie, Kara has tamed me. I'm all hers."

Kara's heart danced, and she tucked her arm around his back, underneath his jacket, and smiled. *Yes, I'm totally smitten.*

"For now." Amie leered at Hunter. "When it's over, you know where to find me."

"Never going to happen." Hunter shook his head. "I deleted your phone number and don't care where you live now. I've moved on. You should do the same."

He kissed Kara again, grabbed her hand, and they joined Gemma and Kyle for photos. Hunter's beaming smile never left his face as he held her close for the rest of the red-carpet walk.

But not once did he answer reporters' eager questions if they were together or not. Why was that? Maybe he wasn't ready to announce their relationship to the public? Had her assumptions been miscalculated?

She knew he loved her. Being together was a big step for them both. Maybe he needed more time. And that was fine; they'd only been together for a smidgen over two months.

Taking their seats in the VIP area in the auditorium, Kara's concerns evaporated, and her skin tingled with the electric vibe in the air. She sat transfixed by the cameras, the audio cues, the production crew, the performers, the screens, the crowd in the mosh pit going wild, and the presentations. The exhilarating energy in the room bubbled like effervescence through her veins.

Nominated for Best Song of the Year, Everhide were up against Shawn Mendes, Drake and Taylor Swift. They didn't think they'd win. As the time for their category grew closer, Kara's palms turned clammy. The back of her dress clung to her perspiring skin. How did her friends remain so calm?

Then came the moment they'd been waiting for. Kara held

her breath. Hunter entwined his fingers with hers and squeezed. His leg jiggled. Gemma and Kyle sat with their eyes glued to the screens onstage. The nominee videos flashed before them and the host, Carmel, announced each finalist.

"And the winner . . ." Carmel opened the envelope, " . . . for Best Song of the Year is . . . I love these guys. EVERHIDE."

Aaarrrgghhh!

Hunter, Kyle, and Gemma screamed, jumped to their feet, and threw their arms around each other. Kara's heart beat as loud as the crowd clapped, whistled and roared. Hunter bent down and kissed her lips, sending heat shivering across her skin. He winked and took off to the stage with Gemma and Kyle.

Kara placed her hand on her chest, her pulse still racing. Her friends had worked so hard; they deserved any and every accolade. Tears stung her eyes as Gemma accepted the golden statuette of the mouse wearing headphones. Gemma held it above her head and screamed into the mic. "YEAH! Thank you!" She shuffled to stand with Kyle to one side so Hunter could make their acceptance speech.

"This is freaking awesome. Thank you." A gleaming smile lit his face. "Kyle, Gem, you rock my world, and thank you for writing the most amazing song. To our management, production, and creative teams, thank you for your tireless, endless efforts to help us bring our music to the world. To the team at Sony who keep helping us reach new heights, cheers. And to you . . . the fans, thank you." Hunter paused, drew his shoulders back, and took a breath. "Thank you for your understanding and ongoing support through what has been a trying and difficult year.

"This song, 'Stay,' is about fighting for the one you love and wanting to be a better person." Hunter scanned the audience, his confidence unfaltering. "We all have the power to be better people. But the change starts with one person and one person only . . . and that's you. Time is precious; don't waste it by being a dick. I'd like to say a special thank you to the person who gave me my wake-up call. To my girlfriend, Kara."

Kara's breath caught in her lungs. She touched her fingertips to her lips. *What is he doing?* He waved and winked at her. This was not the acceptance speech he'd run through earlier in the day.

Hunter continued, "After a traumatic year, you have been my strength, and my downright pain in the ass." A ripple of laughter rolled through the crowd. "But after losing . . . our son . . ." He shuffled on his feet and blew out a slow breath. "You've made me reevaluate everything. You make me appreciate every day I wake up breathing and being able to do what I love, with these two people standing by my side. I'm hoping *you stay* around for a long time too." He placed his hand over his chest. "Thank you, from the bottom of my heart, for making me a better person. Love you, babe." He blew her a kiss, and it slammed into her chest.

Her heart thundered like one thousand drums. He'd just declared his love for her in front of the world. *Wow.* With trembling fingers, she wiped the tears from her eyes, careful not to scratch her eyeballs out with her long fingernails. That hot and handsome man was hers. All hers. She mouthed *"I love you too"* back to him.

He smiled and pumped his fist into the air. His voice boomed through the speakers. "Thank you, everyone. Everhide rocks. Be kind to one another. Cheers!"

In a daze, Kara floated to her feet. Everyone in the auditorium stood and applauded as Everhide walked toward the side of the stage. Her breathing was so hard she thought the bodice on her dress might rip. The second the TV production crew gave the cue that telecasting had cut for an ad break and set change, she charged from her seat. She had to find Hunter.

Flashing her VIP pass, she slipped backstage, rushed past

the camera crew, and into the interview area where Hunter stood talking to someone with Kyle and Gemma. The moment Hunter finished, he dashed over. He swooped her up in his arms and spun her around.

"You know you're crazy, right?" she gushed.

"Yes. We established that a long time ago." He placed her on her feet and grinned.

"Huge brownie points for the most romantic declaration ever. I don't think you can top that. What you said out there was beautiful. Thank you."

"I meant every word, Kar. I'm better because of you. You're mine. For keeps."

She tugged on the lapels of his jacket. The soft wool slipped beneath her fingertips. Drawing him close, she kissed him. Knowing he felt the same way about her as she did for him, she knew she'd made the right decision about her job, their relationship—about *him*. She was meant to be with Hunter. With his heart beating against hers, he was right about one thing—she wasn't going anywhere. Not now. Not ever. Life couldn't get much better.

Chapter 30

"No peeking." Hunter adjusted the blindfold over Kara's eyes, took her hands, and guided her into the building. His heart rate jumped a scale as he pushed the heavy revolving doors open with his butt. He led her across the foyer with its elaborate carpet, through the gilded gold doors and down the steps at the side of the auditorium. "You're not allowed to take the cover off your eyes until I say."

"Where are we?" Kara giggled, taking cautious steps in her silver stilettos. One hand was in his, the other outstretched, feeling her way through the air. "It smells *old*. Feels . . . *big*. Are we in a theater?"

His cheeks ached from smiling and he steered her to the front of the hall. They'd returned home yesterday after three weeks of travel. The promotion of Everhide's latest single was done. Tonight, he'd survived his first night at the ballet. Just. But date night wasn't over yet. He was getting more creative in his ways to surprise Kara, from filling hotel rooms with flowers, to fine dining, to gifts. He adored the way her face lit up, he loved making love to her, and he was crazy about the way she made him feel. *Move over, Cupid. Romance has a new king.*

Time to impress his girl. Ignoring his gut that jumped around like a rave party, he hoped tonight went to plan.

He led her halfway across the floor, folded the seat down, and helped her to sit, ensuring her skirt didn't get caught on the arms. "I've just spent the evening at the ballet with you. Now you have to do something for me."

"What are you doing?" She giggled.

He may not have been able to see her bright eyes, but he knew she was nervous. So was he. She touched her silky blindfold. "Can I take this off yet?"

"Nope. Stay." He hooked off his tie and threw it with his dinner jacket beside her. After spinning on his heels, he dashed across the floor and up the steps onto the stage, his shoes clopping on the floor. Picking up his acoustic guitar, he took a seat on the single cabaret chair at the front, and stared down at Kara. The tempo of his heartbeat jumped. He could play in front of thousands of fans without a care, but tonight it was an audience of one. Just Kara. He couldn't remember being this nervous.

"Okay." He fidgeted with his manbun, loosening the band. "You can take the blindfold off."

Kara untied the scarf and gaped. "We're at Radio City? How the hell—?"

He couldn't grin any wider. Her reaction was priceless. He wiped his sweaty palm on his trousers. "Sophie's girlfriend pulled some strings." It helped that Gayle, his manger's girlfriend, worked here. He owed her big time for organizing tonight. "There was no show on, so why not?"

Kara glanced over her shoulder at the tiered rows of empty seats, at the vacant stage behind him and all around.

"You done?" Hunter chuckled, tapping his fingers against the body of his guitar. "I wanna sing you a song. I wrote it for you."

"You wrote me a song?" Bewilderment widened her eyes.

"Yeah. Can I sing it?"

She eased back into her seat, straightened her skirt, and nodded.

Damn, this would be harder than he'd thought. Taking a deep breath, he strummed at his strings and sang.

> *The moment that I met you I knew that something changed.*
> *Couldn't breathe, couldn't think, my mind's a constant race.*
> *I've had a few lovers, yeah, there're a few names on my list,*
> *But my heart didn't start beating until the moment that we kissed.*
> *I've traveled the world to find you, babe, I've been everywhere,*
> *When you're not beside me all I wish is that you were here.*

Closing his eyes, he absorbed the acoustics in the hall. He loved performing here. Loved the way the auditorium amplified his voice, the sound of his guitar, and, right now, his crazy heartbeat. None of that compared to how he felt for Kara. *I can do this.*

> *So no matter where you run to, no matter where you hide,*
> *I'll travel the world over, to keep you by my side.*
> *Because we belong together—there's no doubt in my mind,*
> *You're my treasure, my love, the one I was meant to find.*
>
> *I know we haven't been together for very long,*
> *But the way my heart feels, I know this can't be wrong.*
> *Don't want to be lonely or miss you every night,*
> *Every day that I'm with you always feels right.*

Kara placed her hands over her heart. He gave her a wink and softened his voice.

> *No crazy promises, not offering you a ring,*
> *Not today, but who knows what the future will bring?*
> *But I want to ask you one question that is for sure,*
> *It's because each day I love you more and more.*
> *I'm wondering if you feel the same way about me,*
> *And Kara if you do, girl, please move in with me?*

Kara sat there. Frozen.

Maybe she hadn't heard him right. Maybe he was taking their relationship too fast. They'd only been together three months. *Shit.*

He put his guitar down and jumped off the stage. Walking toward her, he outstretched his hands. His chest pounded with his heartbeat. With his mind racing, he ad-libbed and sang another verse.

> *Did I stutter, or stumble, were my words not right?*
> *Wanted to ask you this for the past few days and nights.*

He grabbed her hands and helped her to stand. He stroked the side of her face. Staring into the depths of her beautiful blue eyes, he lowered his voice to sing just above a whisper.

> *I'm wondering if you feel the same way about me,*
> *And if you do, Kara . . . please move in with me?*

A tear slipped onto her cheek. He brushed it away with his thumb. "Will you please say something? You're killing me here."

Her eyes searched his face. "You want me to move in with you?"

"I know we haven't been together long. Only three months,

two days, and six hours. But if you're as crazy about me as I am for you, let's do it."

She clutched onto the front of his shirt and kissed him. Hard. He curled his arms around her and drew her close. He flicked his tongue against hers, savoring the taste of her on his lips. Kissing her was like music. It filled his soul. Made him feel alive.

Melting into his arms, she rested her forehead against his. "You did all this for me? Just to ask me to move in with you?"

"Yeah."

"You're so crazy." She weaved her hands around his neck. "Yes. Yes, I'll move in with you."

YES!

"But . . ." she winced, "could we move into my place, rather than yours?"

What? Panic gripped his throat. How could he downsize and move into her shoebox-sized place? It would be like going back to living in an apartment the same size as the one he lived in with Kyle and Gemma before they became successful. His current walk-in wardrobe and master bedroom was as big as Kara's entire apartment. He had his home studio, his piano, his office, spare bedrooms, space. *Shit.* He had to give all that up for her?

He'd do anything for Kara, but he had to make her see reason. "I could. But my place is five times bigger than yours, with much better facilities and views, and—"

She placed her fingertips over his mouth. Her eyes glistened in the soft light. "Hunt, stop panicking. I was joking."

Oh, thank God. His knees buckled. Stars appeared before his eyes as his blood pressure plummeted back to normal.

"I would love to move in with you. On one condition: I want you to come with me when we tell my father. I want to see the look on his face."

His chest tightened. His relationship with Walter had not improved since dating Kara. "Are you sure you're not just with me to piss your old man off?"

"No." Her tone dissolved his concerns. "I want him to see how happy I am. That I'm living my life my way. I'm away from his obnoxious world and a better person because of it. Because of you. And I love you with all my heart."

"What if he disowns you?"

She shrugged a shoulder. "He needs to respect my choices and my decisions. He doesn't have control over me anymore. I know who I am. You make me feel beautiful, loved, and make me believe anything is possible. I belong in your world, not his. I can be true to myself when I'm with you."

Fate had set one of its most difficult challenges when it plotted to bring Kara and him together. It had persevered and twisted their lives in cruel, traumatic, and bizarre ways. Somehow it had worked. Kara had become Hunter's world as much as music.

There was no turning back. Gone were his desires for loose girls, quick lays, and cheap encounters. There was no one else but her. For the first time in a long time, he meant something to someone. He was loved and valued. That was all he ever wanted.

He kissed her palm. "I like it when you're with me too."

"So when can I move in?"

"How's tomorrow?"

"Deal." She nodded. "Are there any other surprises tonight?"

"No. We have to get out of here. Gayle is lurking around somewhere, waiting for us to leave. Let's go home."

***

Pouring JD into two crystal tumblers, Hunter sat at Kara's dining table for a quick nightcap before bed. He'd done it. He'd asked Kara to move in. She'd said yes. Sipping on his whiskey, he couldn't wipe the grin from his face. He'd never lived with someone he loved like Kara. It would be exciting, terrifying, thrilling, scary, trying, and absolutely amazing.

He glanced at his watch. 12:13 a.m. Kara had ducked off to the bathroom a few minutes ago but seemed to be taking a long time. He hoped she was okay.

Better check.

He downed the last mouthful of his whiskey as she walked out of her room. The glass slipped in his fingertips. Thank God he was still sitting down. Kara sauntered toward him wearing nothing but black lacy lingerie and knee-high stiletto boots—those boots he loved. Those boots that screamed, 'come fuck me.' He swallowed hard. Blood engorged his dick. His pulse jumped two octaves.

"Wow!" He placed his glass on the table. His hunger for her crept toward a burning craving as he scanned every inch of her body. He wriggled his finger at her. "Come here."

Blushing, she straddled his waist. He glided his hands over her smooth thighs, cupped her ass, and tilted his hips against her. His cock, hard as steel, pressed against her crotch.

She flicked her hair over one shoulder, leaned in, kissed up the length of his throat, and made her way to his mouth. "I was wondering if there was anything else I could do to top off our night?"

Rocking her hips against his, she moaned.

Sweet Jesus.

"Mmm, let me think." He skimmed his hand up her side and molded his hand around her breast. Dragging his thumb over the lace, he felt her nipple harden beneath his touch. "I think there is. I'd like to make love to you while you wear nothing but those boots."

She caught her bottom lip with her teeth as she unbuttoned his shirt. Desire glinted in her gorgeous eyes. "I'd like that too."

He caressed the side of her face. She was so beautiful.

Twelve months ago, he never would've believed he would end up here. One amazing night with her had contorted into a living nightmare, a heartbreaking tragedy, and now into something beyond his wildest dreams. They'd clawed their way back from the darkness. Become stronger. Better. *One.* There was nowhere else he'd rather be.

Knotting his hands through her hair, he drew her lips to his. ""God, I love you, Kar. I'm going to like living with you. Very much."

He didn't think he had room in his life for anything but music, Kyle and Gemma. But Kara had blended in seamlessly. Provided him with balance.

She was the piece of music that had been missing from his soul. He thought he was damaged from too many broken hearts, ruined after losing Ryan, but Kara had put him back together. She was his future. Life flowed through his veins again because of her. She synced perfectly with his best friends and music. Every note, every bar and every beat Hunter now played was, and would always be, for Kara.

Thank you for reading. I hope you enjoyed RUINED - The Price of Play. Hunter's and Kara's journey continues in BOOK 5, REWIND - The Price of Fate. But for now, continue the series with Book 3:
RAPT - The Price of Love.

Details for the next book and information on my other titles are on the following pages.

P.S. If you loved RUINED - The Price of Play, would you kindly take a moment and leave a quick review.
They are music for an author's soul.
Visit this title on Amazon to leave a Customer Product Review.
Thank you.

NEXT IN SERIES

RAPT – The Price of Love

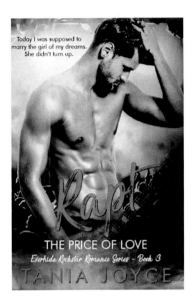

AVAILABLE ON AMAZON

NEWSLETTER

To stay informed about new releases, giveaway, special features and events, sign-up to Tania Joyce's monthly newsletter. Subscribe at: http://taniajoyce.com/newsletter/subscribe

FOLLOW TANIA JOYCE

You can follow and find Tania Joyce on the following social media platforms.

Amazon: https://amazon.com/author/taniajoyce
BookBub: https://www.bookbub.com/authors/tania-joyce
Facebook: https://www.facebook.com/taniajoycebooks
Goodreads: https://www.goodreads.com/taniajoyce
Instagram: https://www.instagram.com/taniajoycebooks/
Pinterest: https://www.pinterest.com/taniajoycebooks
TikTok: https://www.tiktok.com/@taniajoyce
Web: http://taniajoyce.com

BOOKS BY TANIA JOYCE

For eBooks visit Amazon.Com.
Paperbacks available online at most book retailers.

The Flintlocks Series

The Everhide Series

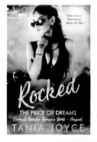   

  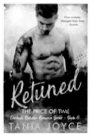

Billionaires and College Romance

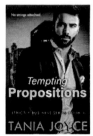  

Made in United States
North Haven, CT
25 January 2024

47883411R00207